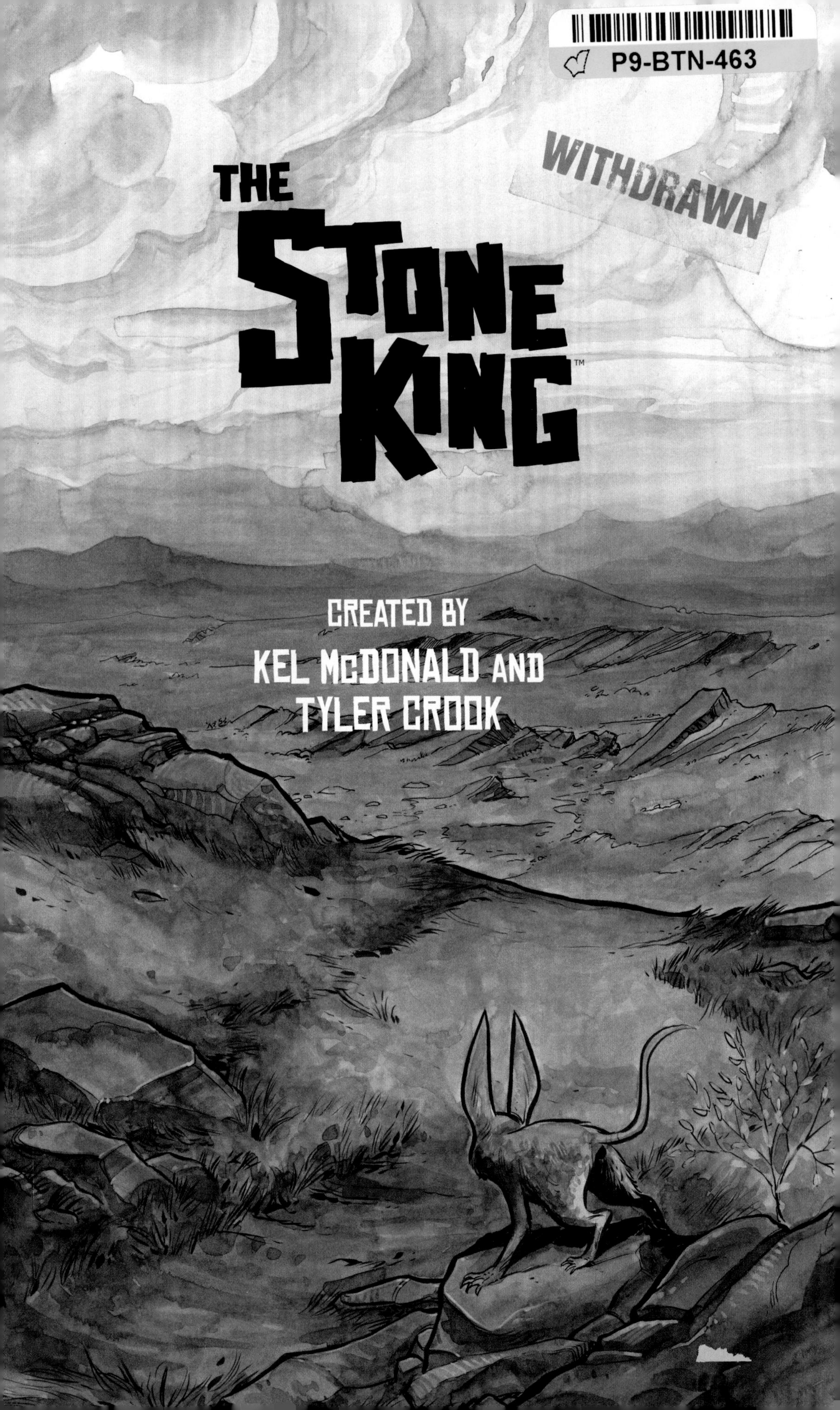
THE STONE KING™
CREATED BY
KEL McDONALD AND
TYLER CROOK

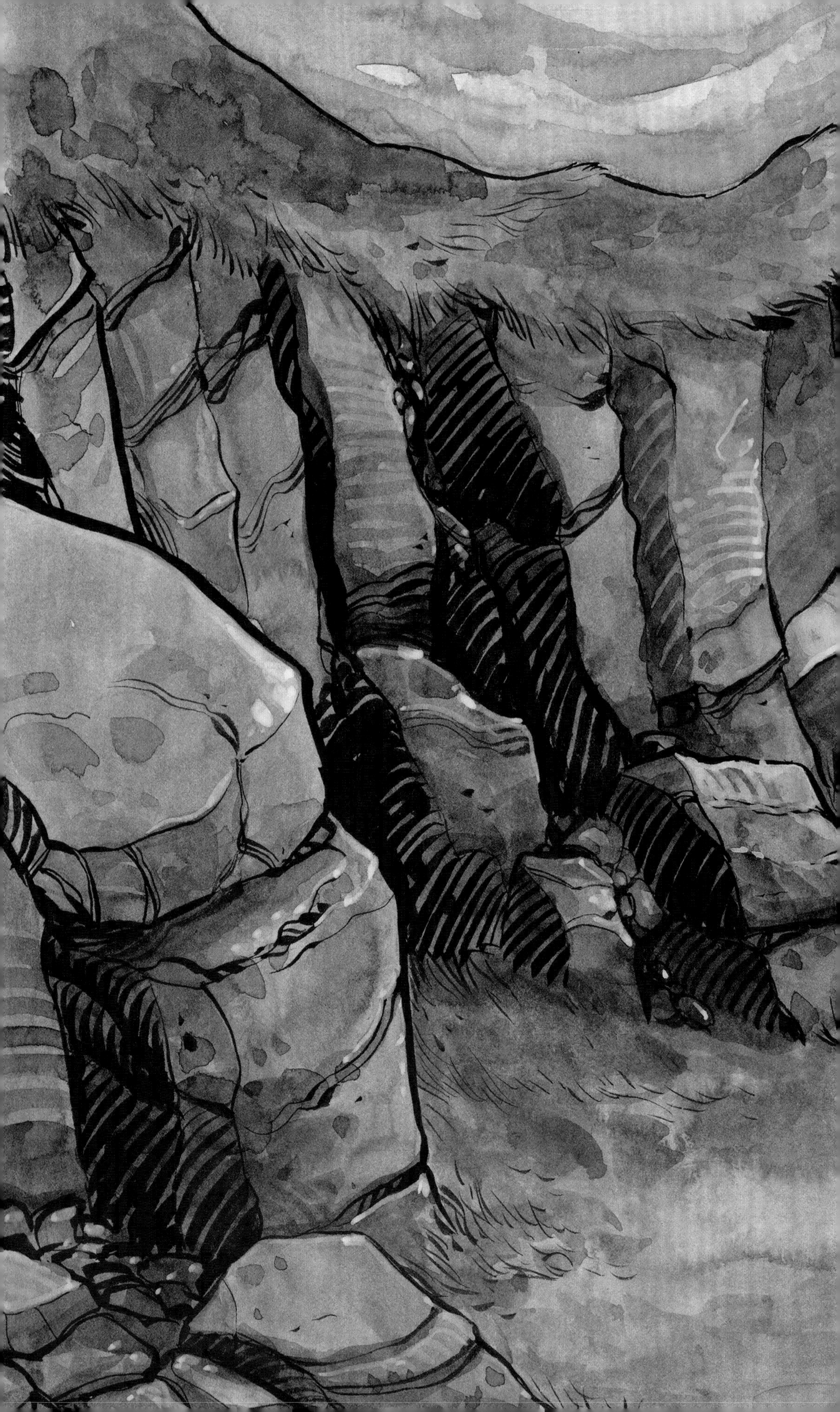

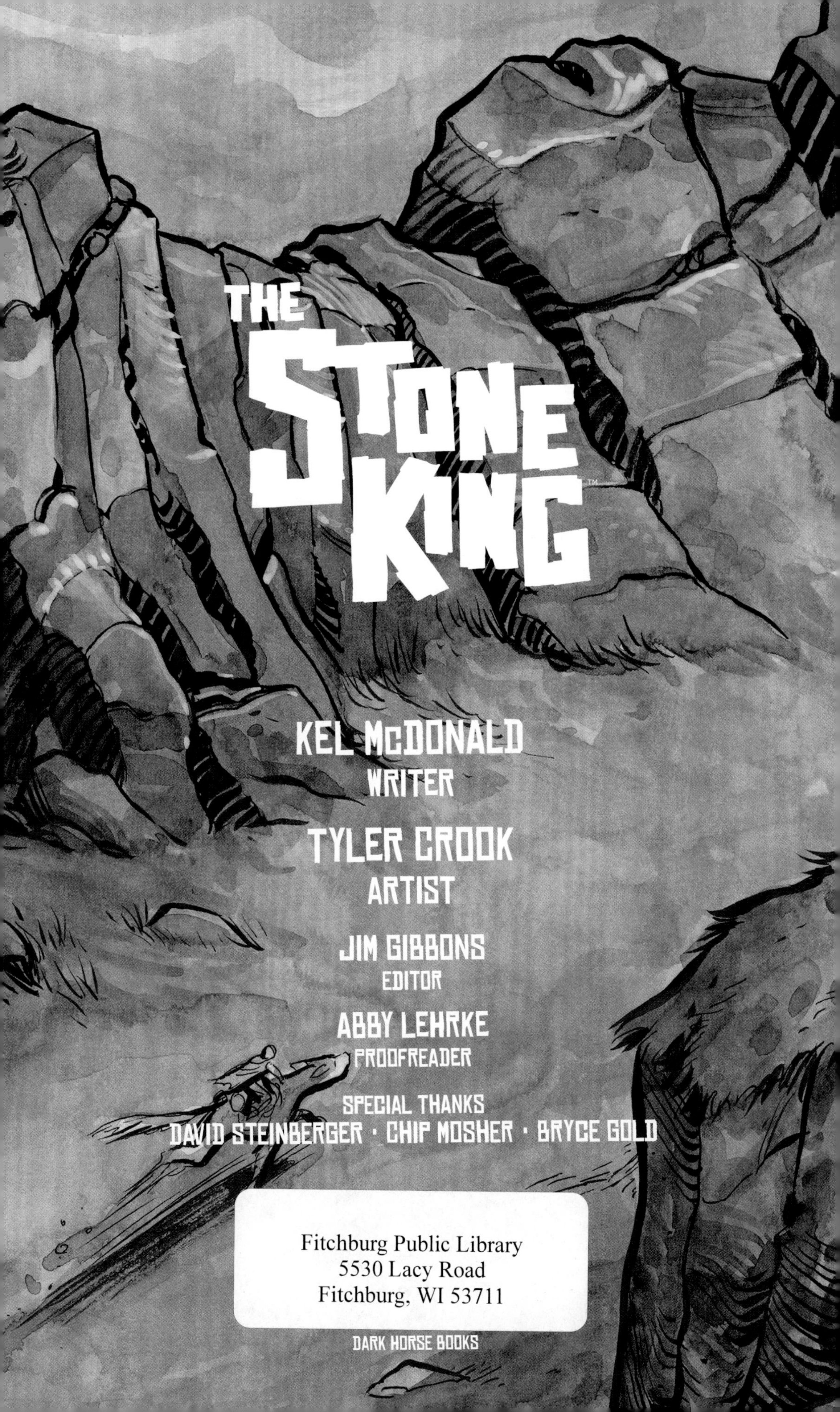

THE STONE KING™

KEL McDONALD
WRITER

TYLER CROOK
ARTIST

JIM GIBBONS
EDITOR

ABBY LEHRKE
PROOFREADER

SPECIAL THANKS
DAVID STEINBERGER · CHIP MOSHER · BRYCE GOLD

DARK HORSE BOOKS

DARK HORSE TEAM
PRESIDENT AND PUBLISHER MIKE RICHARDSON
EDITOR DANIEL CHABON
ASSISTANT EDITORS CHUCK HOWITT AND KONNER KNUDSEN
DESIGNER KATHLEEN BARNETT
DIGITAL ART TECHNICIAN JASON RICKERD

Neil Hankerson Executive Vice President • Tom Weddle Chief Financial Officer • Dale LaFountain Chief Information Officer • Tim Wiesch Vice President of Licensing • Matt Parkinson Vice President of Marketing • Vanessa Todd-Holmes Vice President of Production and Scheduling • Mark Bernardi Vice President of Book Trade and Digital Sales • Randy Lahrman Vice President of Product Development • Ken Lizzi General Counsel • Dave Marshall Editor in Chief • Davey Estrada Editorial Director • Chris Warner Senior Books Editor • Cary Grazzini Director of Specialty Projects • Lia Ribacchi Art Director • Matt Dryer Director of Digital Art and Prepress • Michael Gombos Senior Director of Licensed Publications • Kari Yadro Director of Custom Programs • Kari Torson Director of International Licensing

Published by Dark Horse Books
A division of Dark Horse Comics LLC
10956 SE Main Street, Milwaukie, OR 97222

First edition: May 2022 | Trade paperback ISBN: 978-1-50672-448-5

Printed in China | 10 9 8 7 6 5 4 3 2 1

Comic Shop Locator Service: comicshoplocator.com

Library of Congress Cataloging-in-Publication Data

Names: McDonald, Kel, writer. | Crook, Tyler, artist.
Title: The stone king / Kel McDonald, writer ; Tyler Crook, artist.
Description: First edition. | Milwaukie, OR : Dark Horse Books, 2022. |
  "This volume collects issue #1 through #4 of the Dark Horse comic book
  series The Stone King." | Summary: "Ave has decided to illegally harvest
  healing moss from the Stone King, a mighty giant who roams the lands.
  Her theft goes even better than she could have dreamed. But what she
  thought would buy her a ticket to adventure and a better life, brings
  disaster instead. Now her home is in danger and fixing her mistakes is
  the city's only hope"-- Provided by publisher.
Identifiers: LCCN 2021046447 | ISBN 9781506724485 (trade paperback)
Subjects: LCGFT: Comics (Graphic works)
Classification: LCC PN6728.S749 M33 2022 | DDC 741.5/973--dc23/eng/20211006
LC record available at https://lccn.loc.gov/2021046447

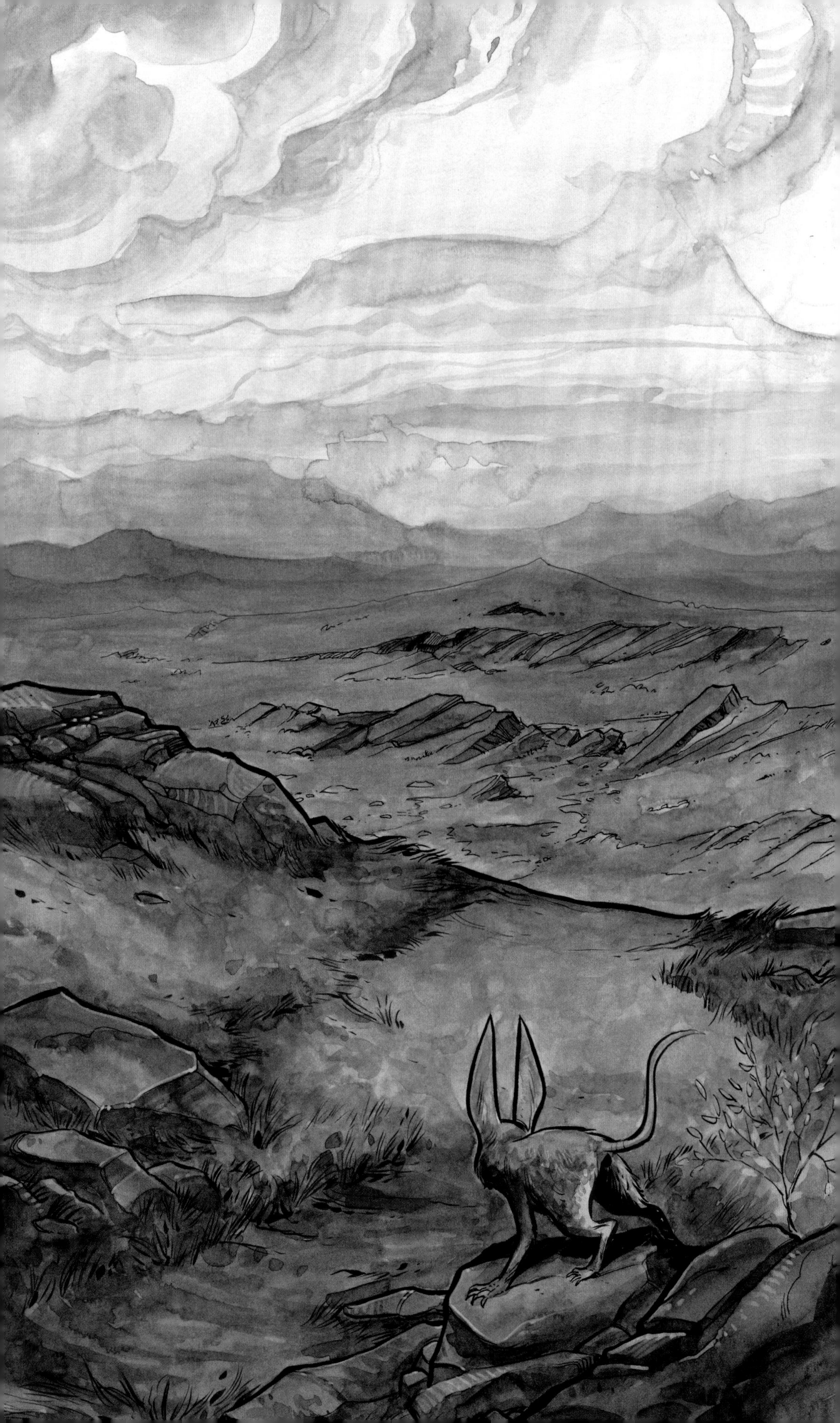

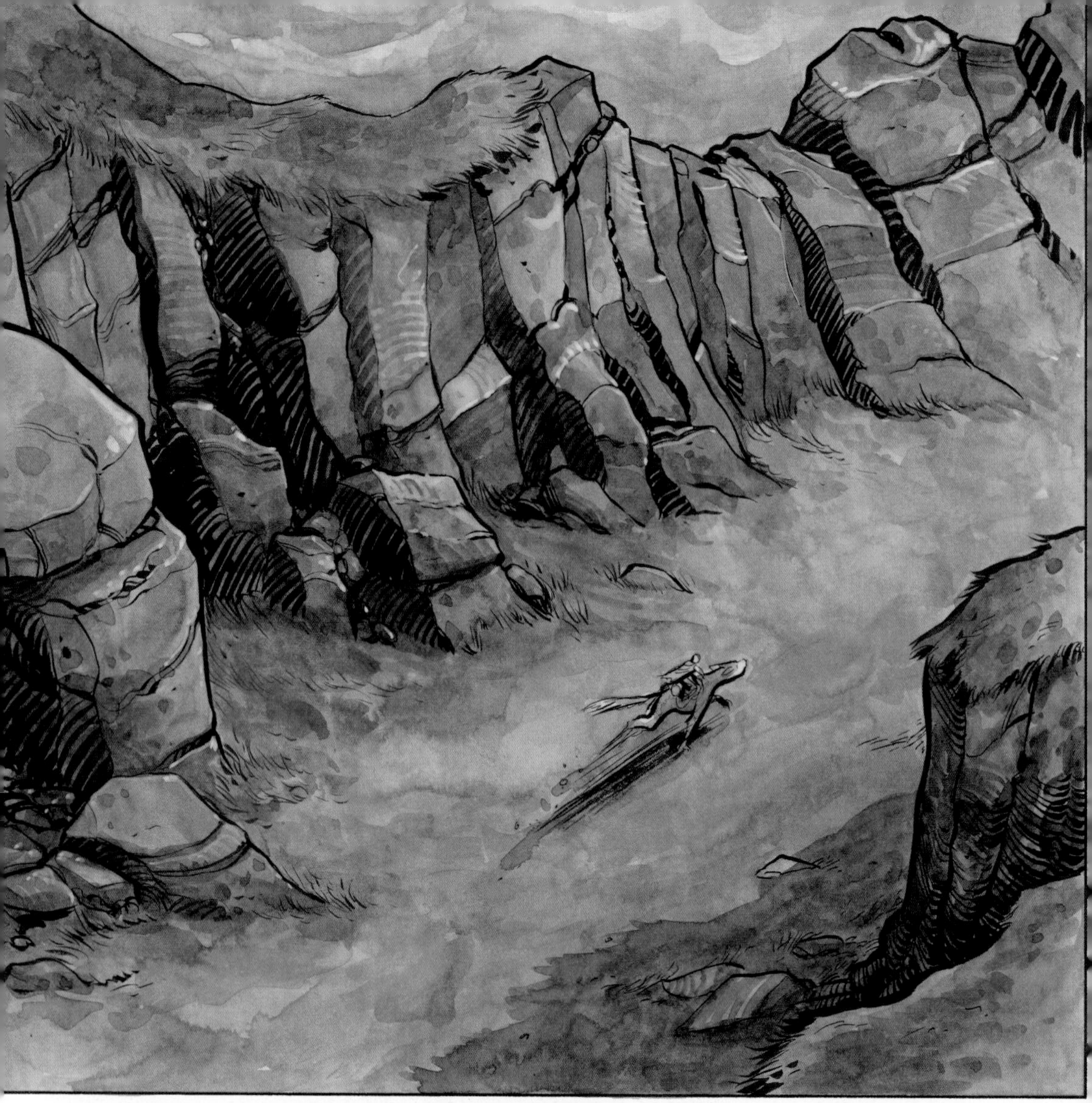

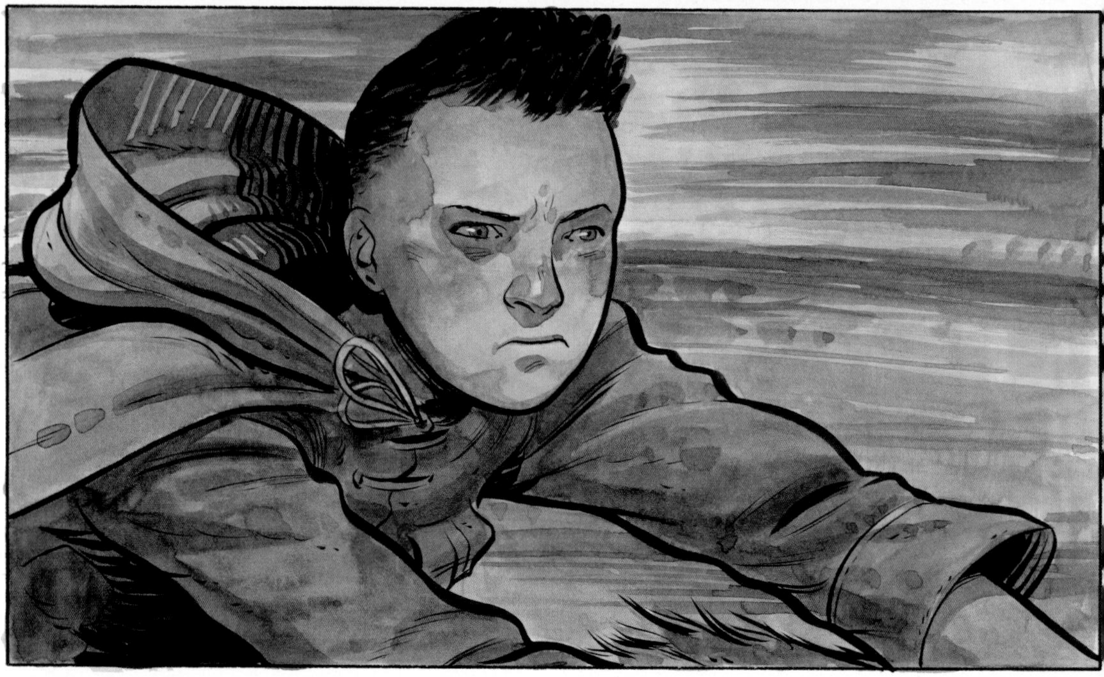

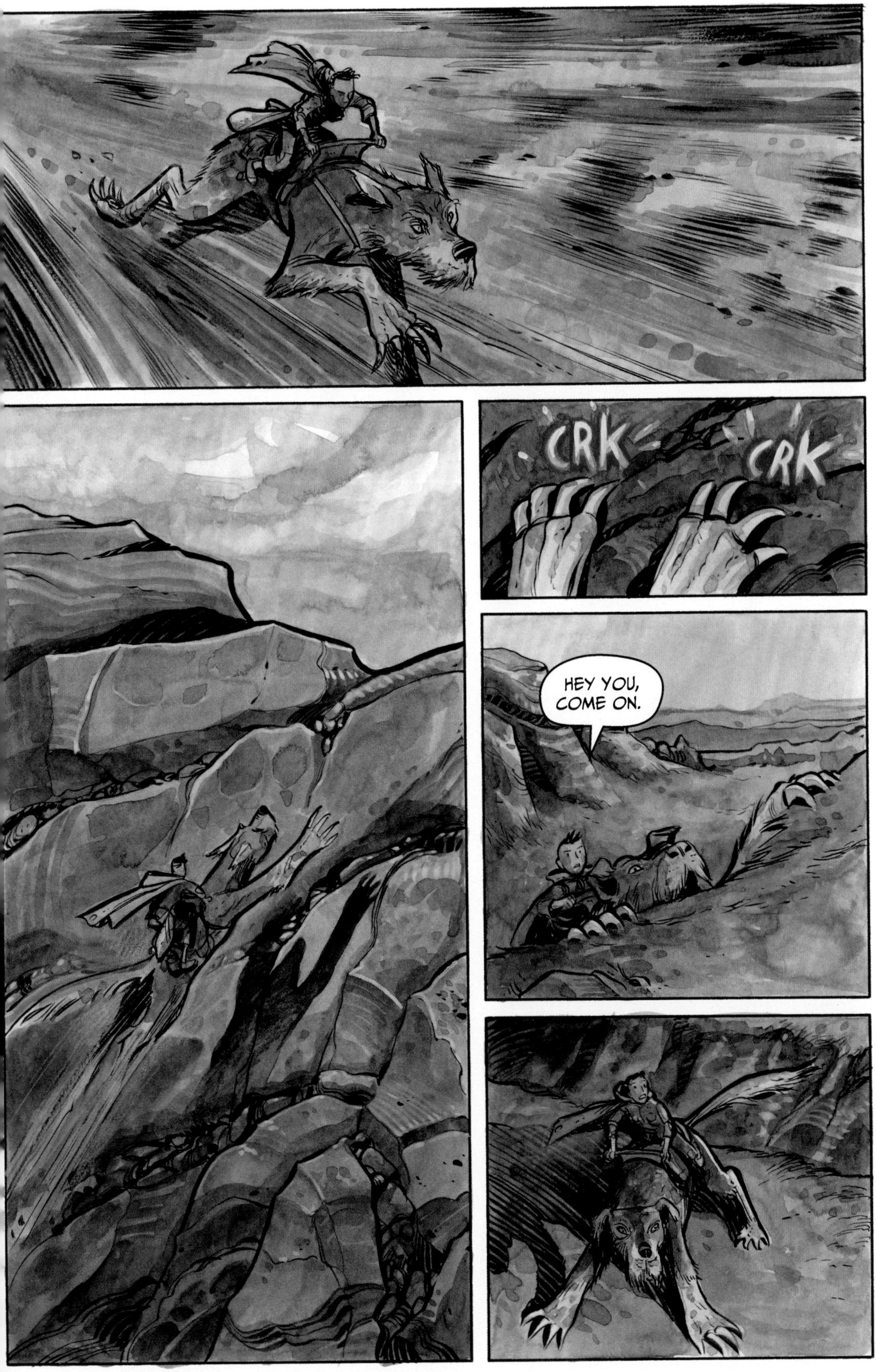
CRK
CRK
HEY YOU, COME ON.

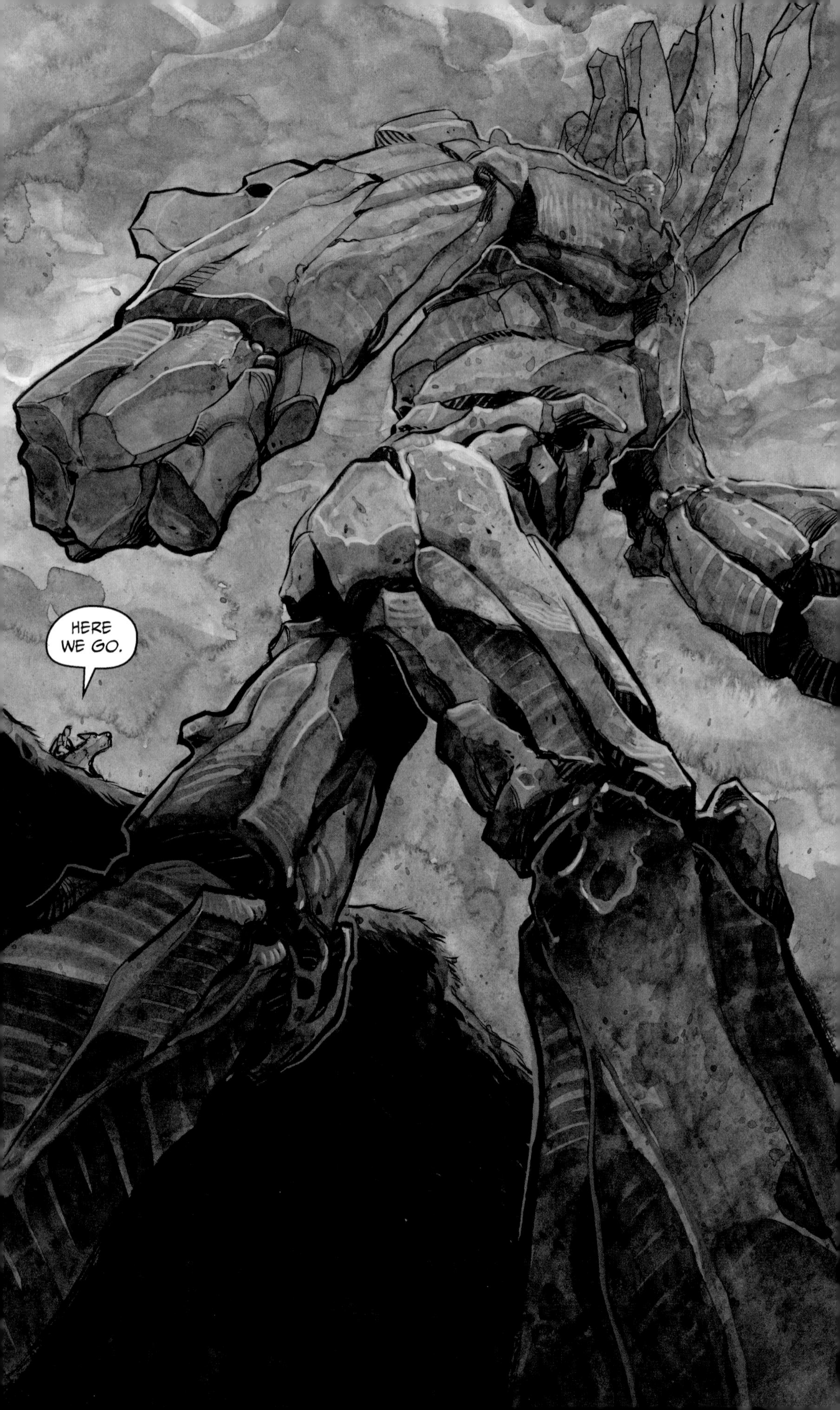
HERE WE GO.

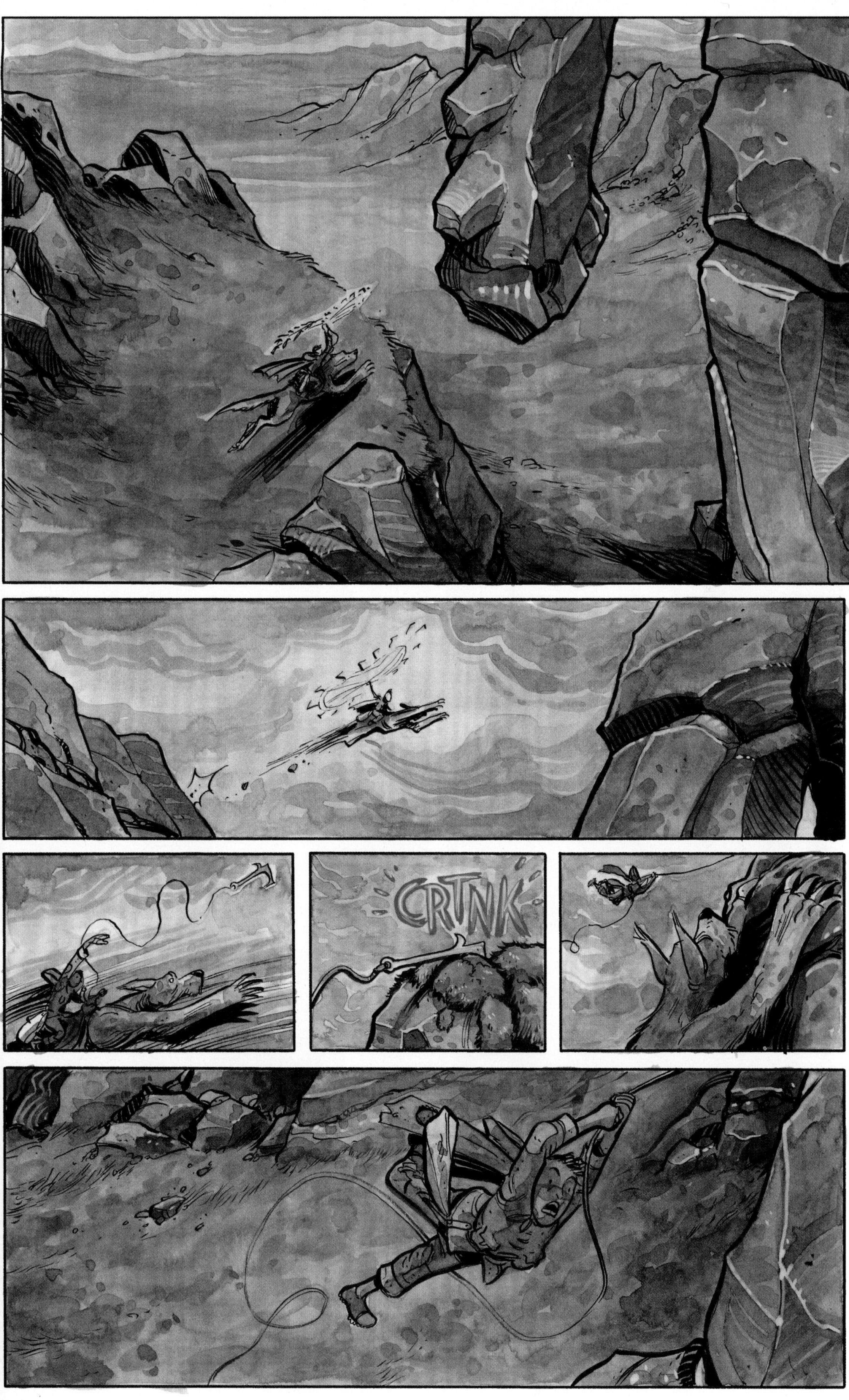
CRTNK

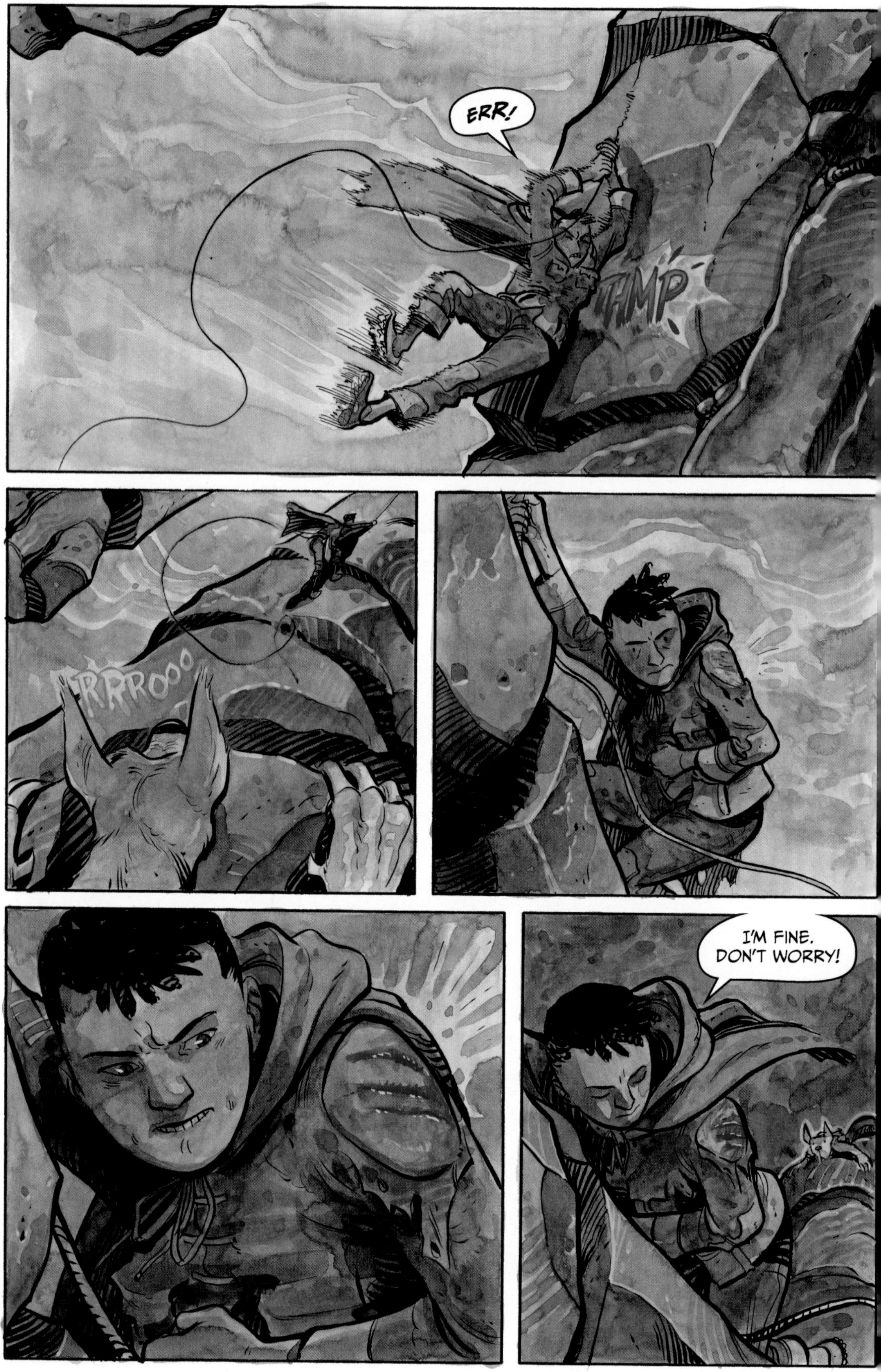
ERR!
THMP
RRROOO
I'M FINE. DON'T WORRY!

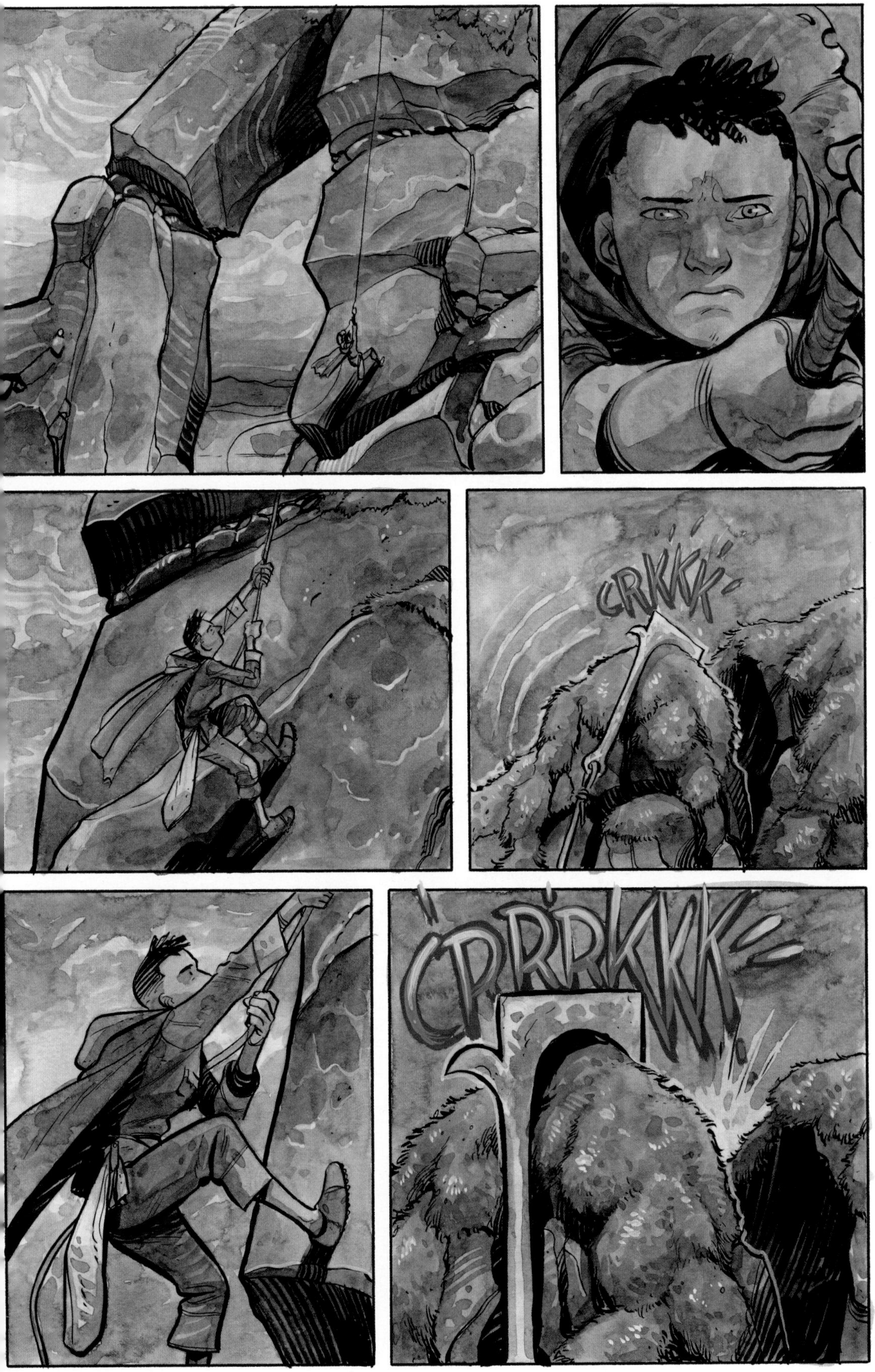
CRKKK
CRRRKKK

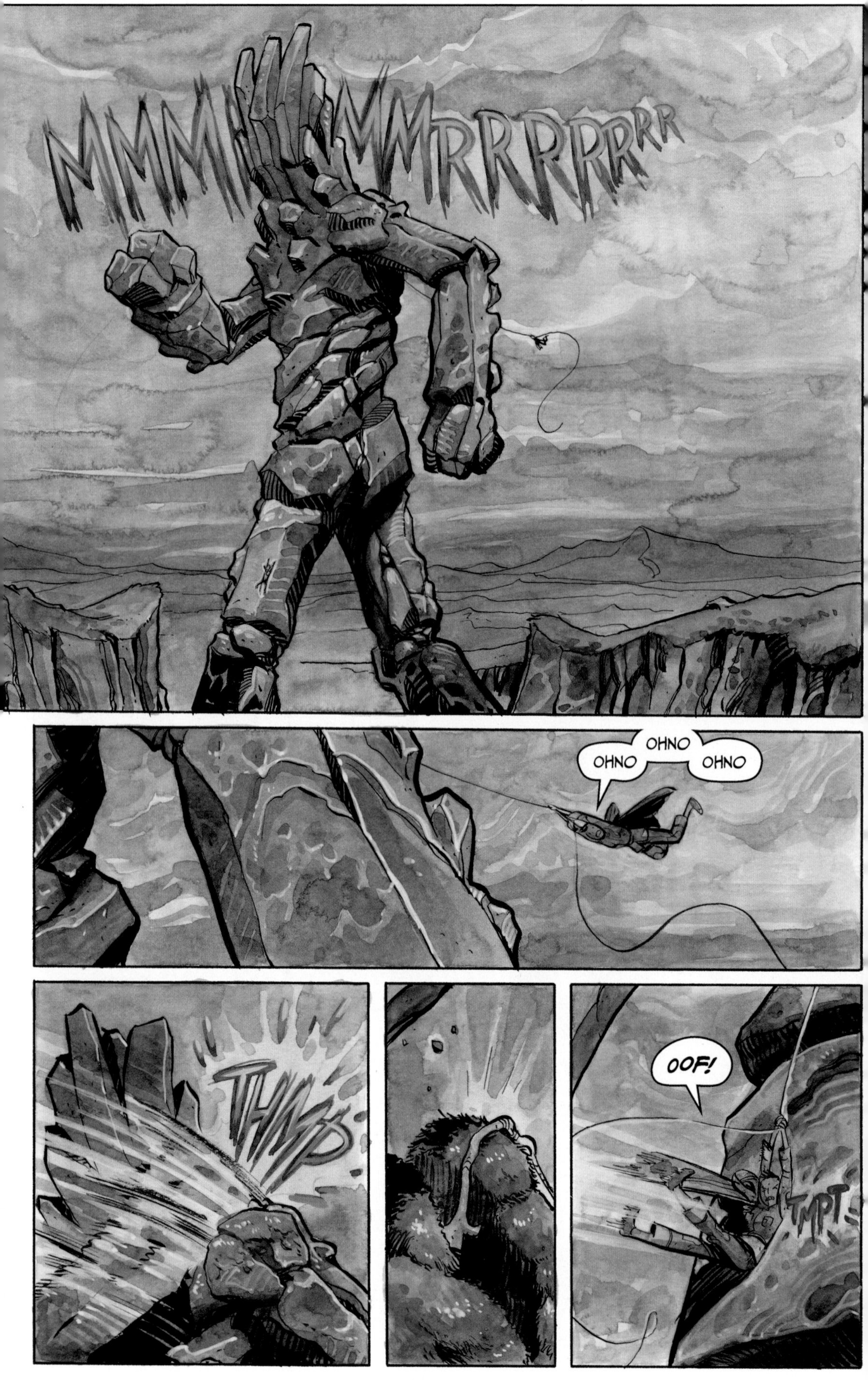

OHNO
OHNO
OHNO
OOF!
TMPT

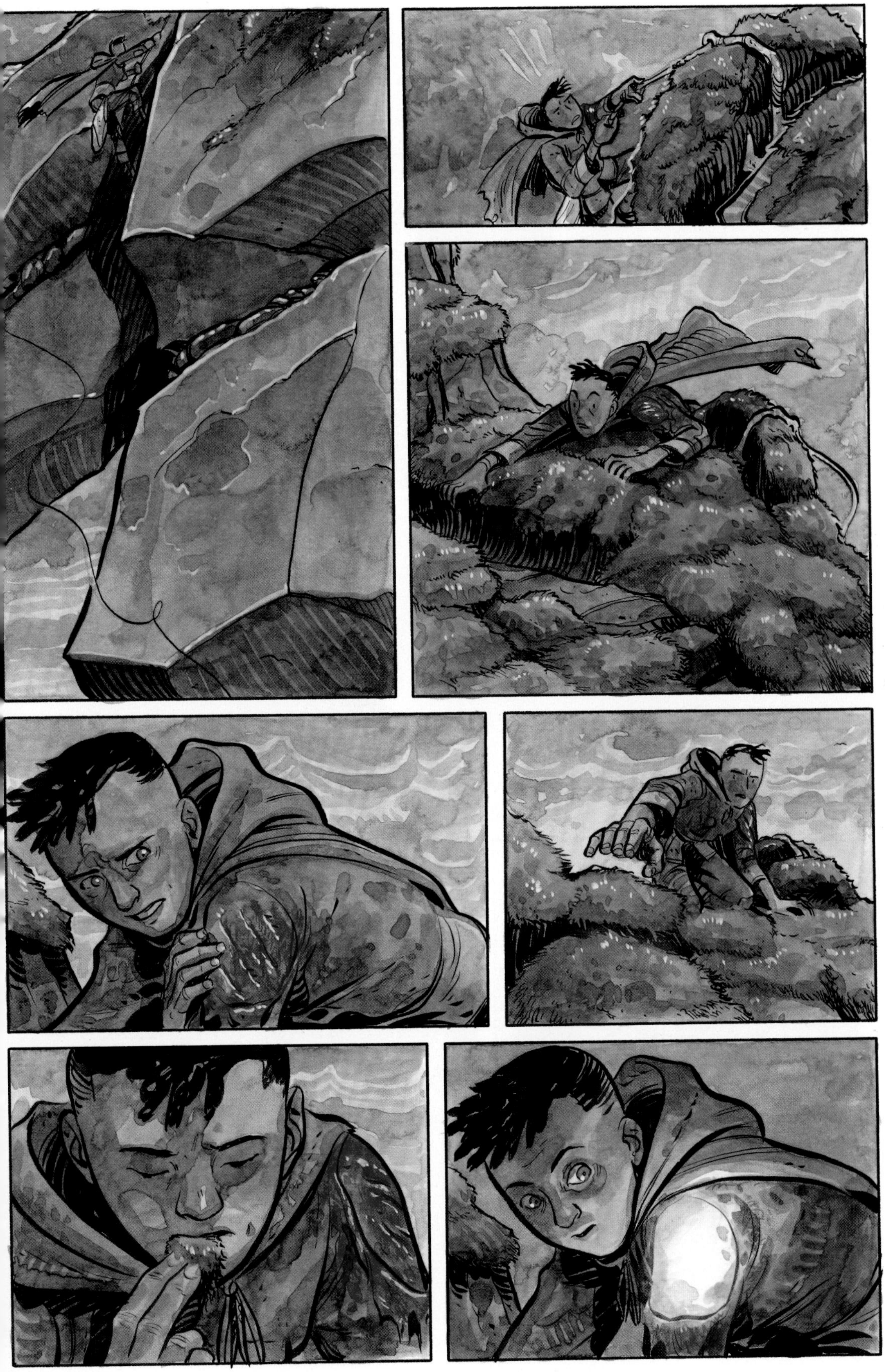

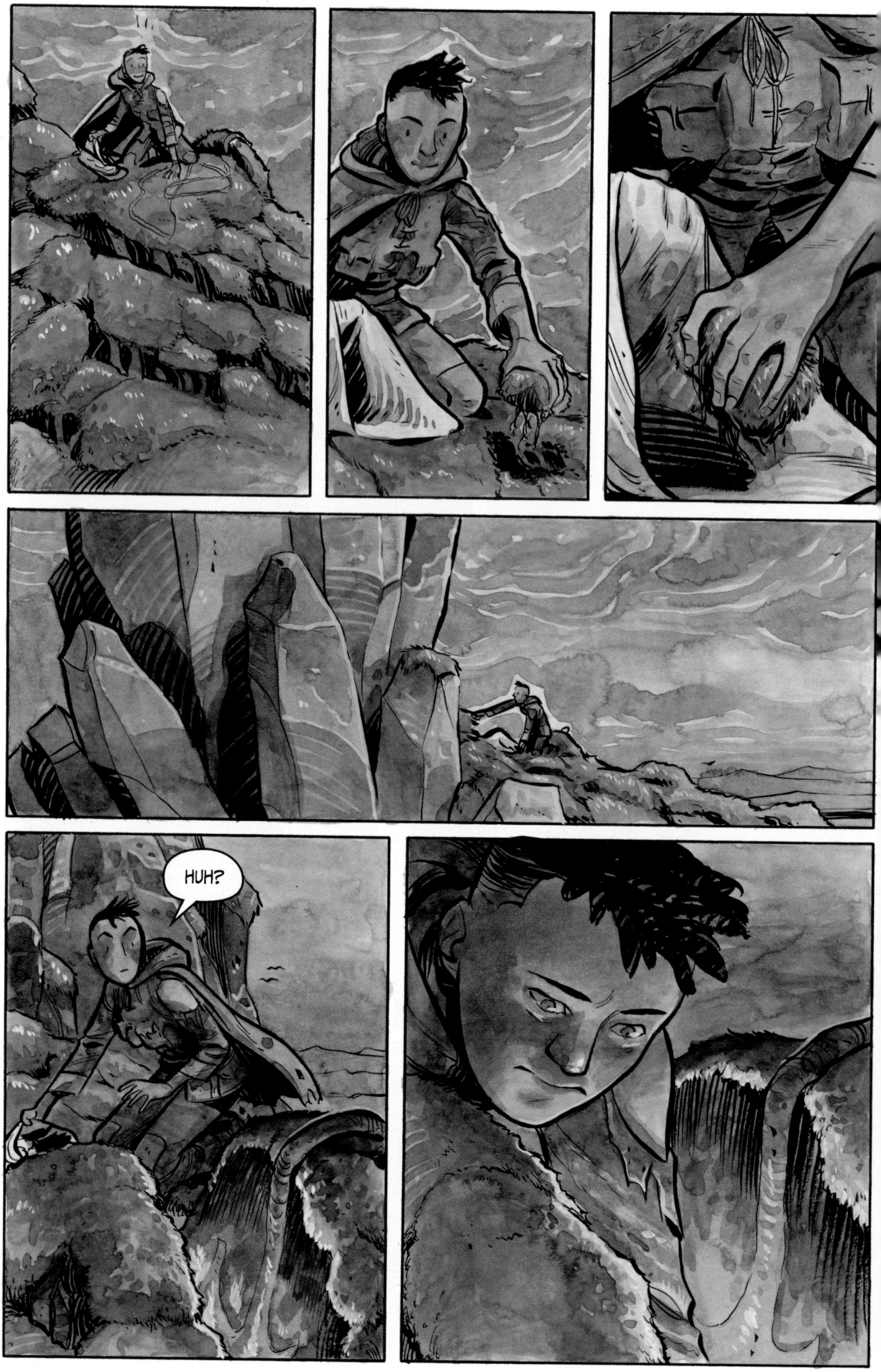
HUH?

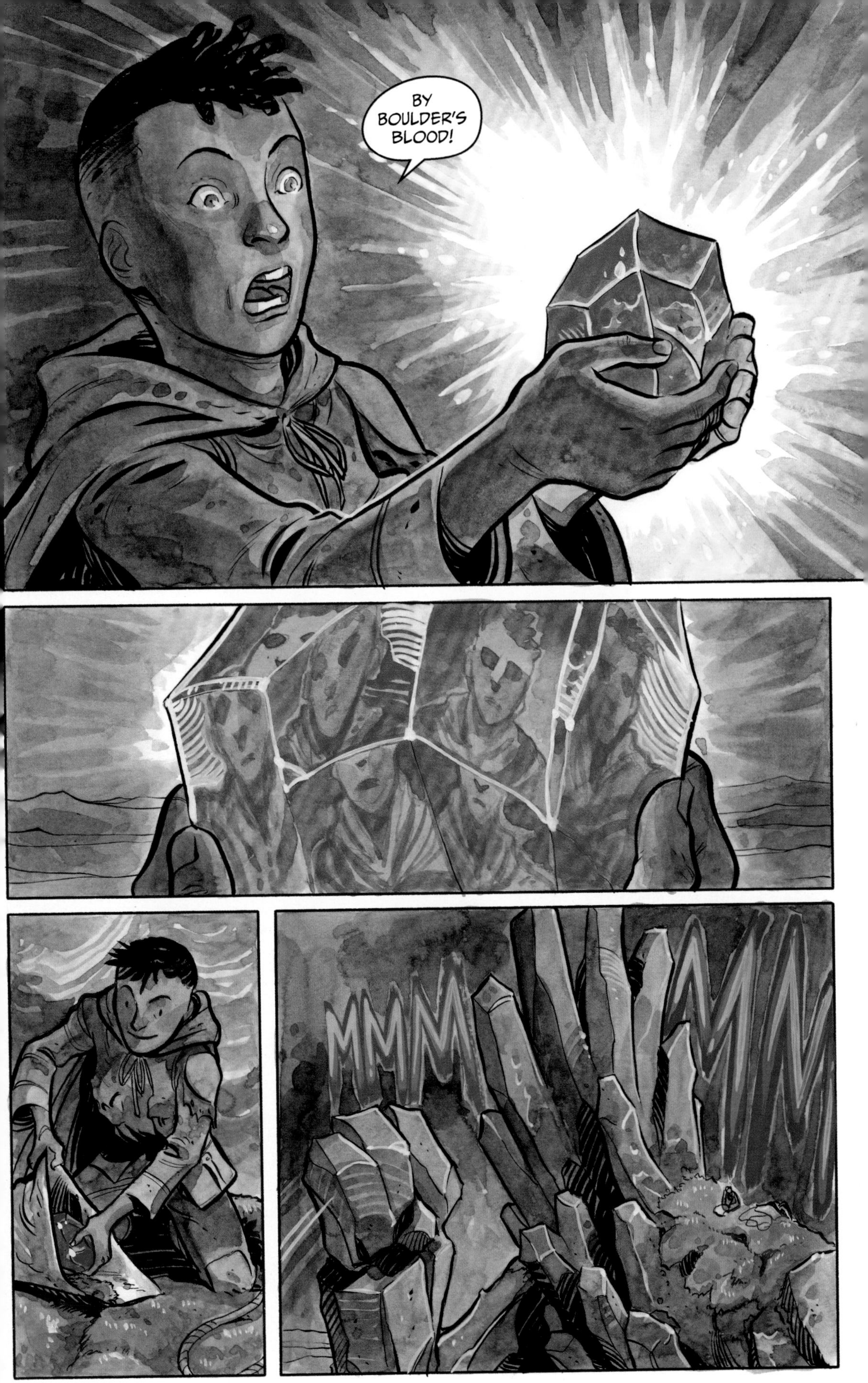
BY BOULDER'S BLOOD!
MMMM
MMM

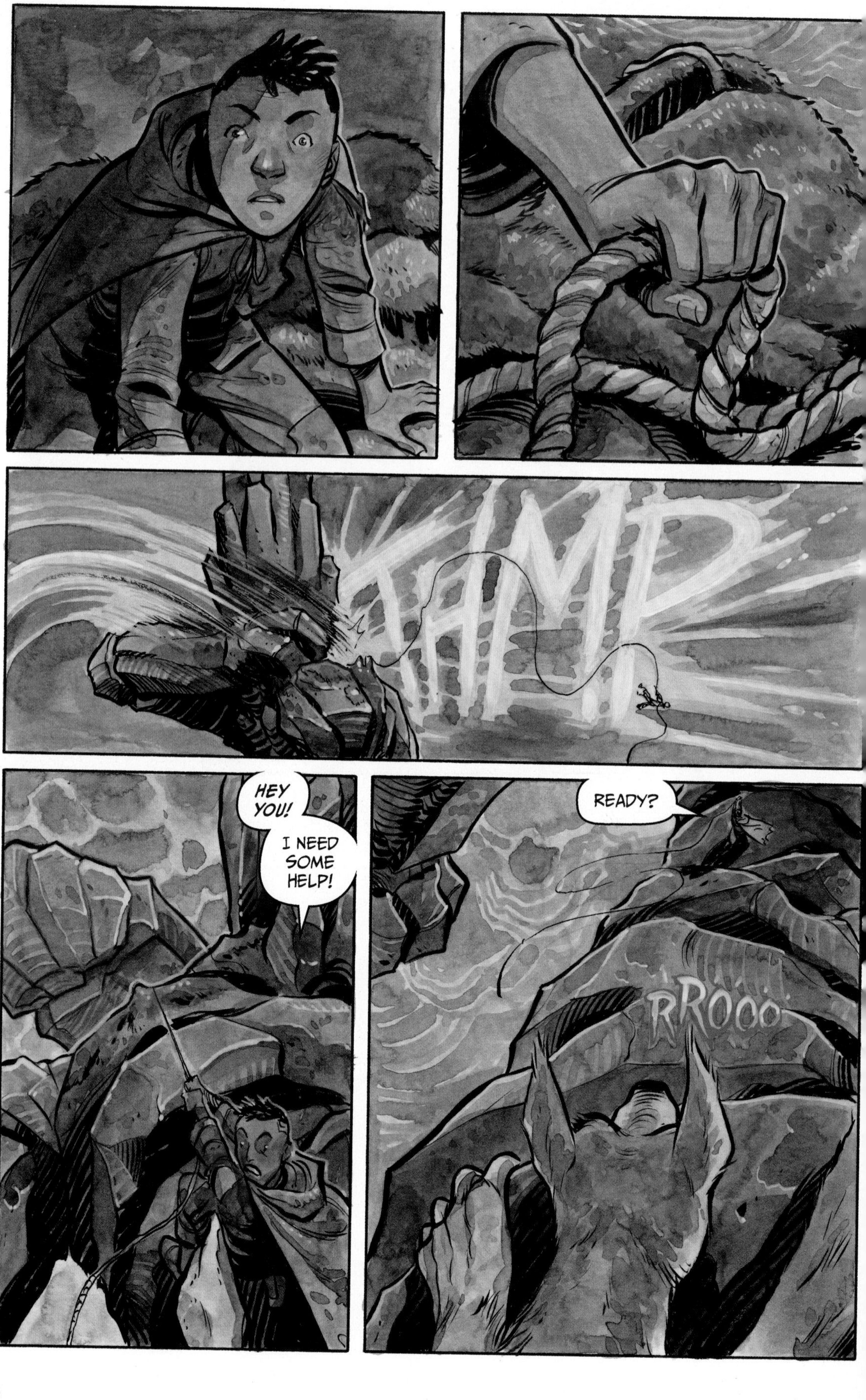
THMP
HEY YOU!
I NEED SOME HELP!
READY?
RROOO

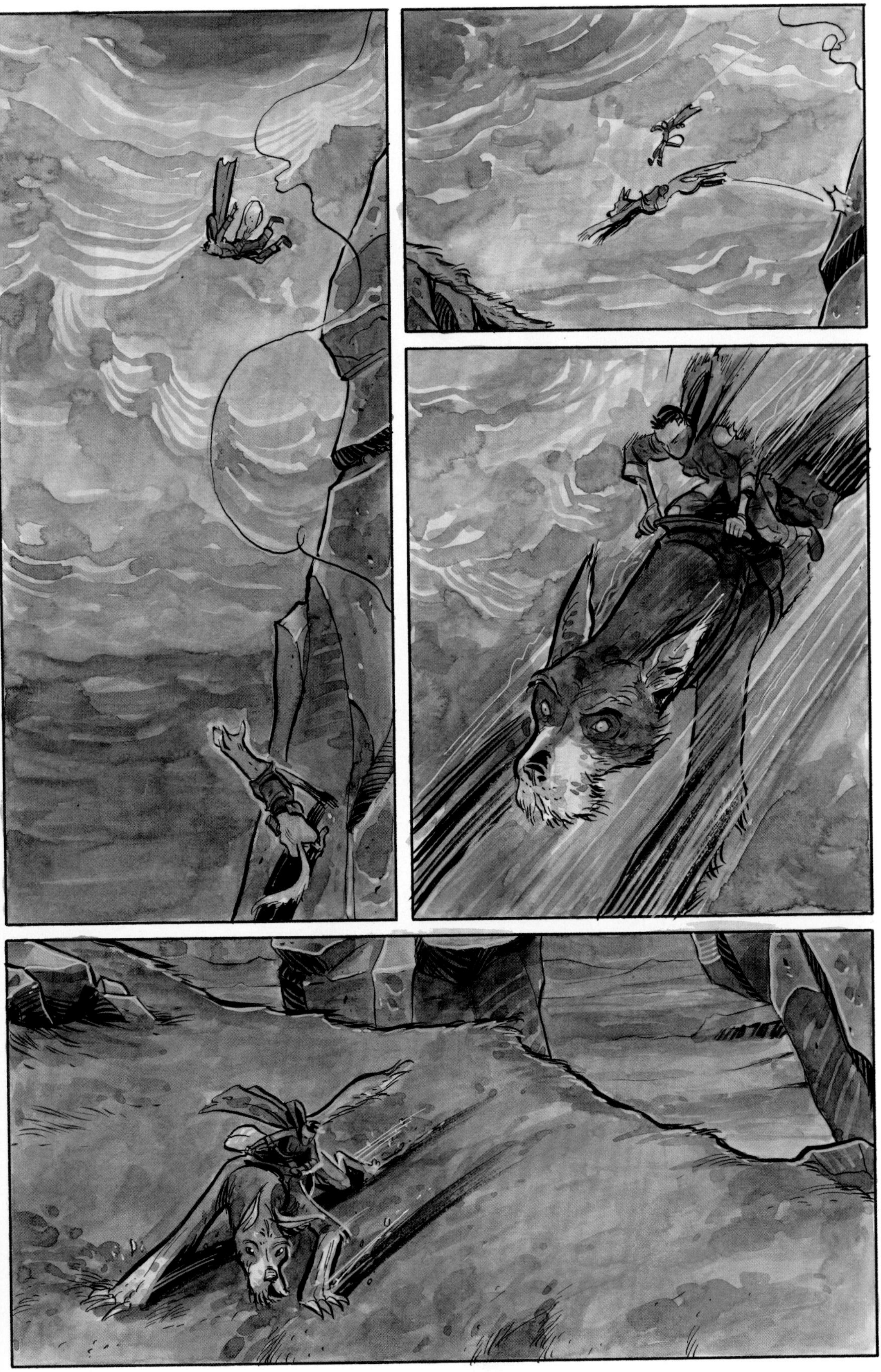

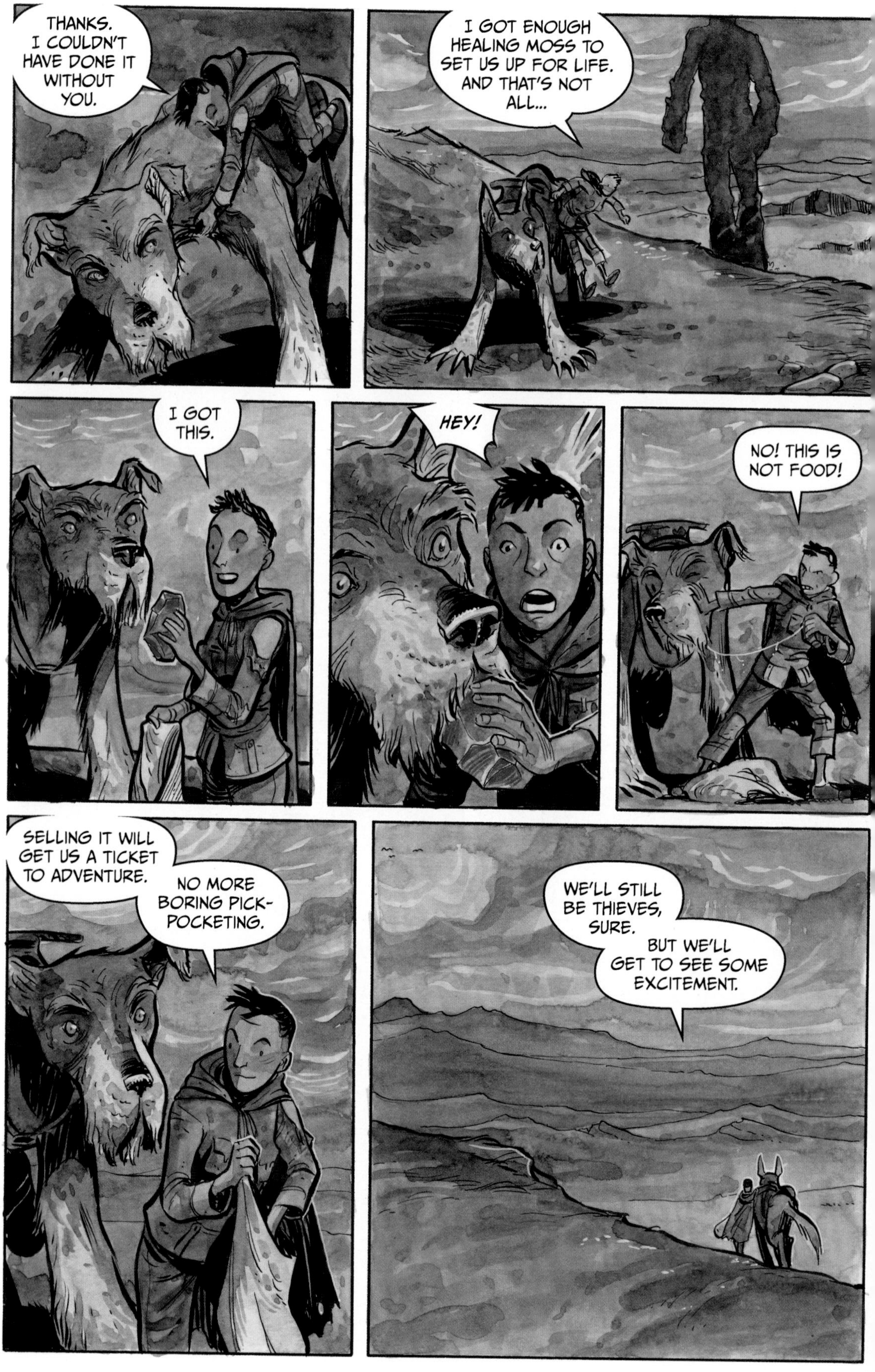
THANKS. I COULDN'T HAVE DONE IT WITHOUT YOU.
I GOT ENOUGH HEALING MOSS TO SET US UP FOR LIFE. AND THAT'S NOT ALL...
I GOT THIS.
HEY!
NO! THIS IS NOT FOOD!
SELLING IT WILL GET US A TICKET TO ADVENTURE.
NO MORE BORING PICK-POCKETING.
WE'LL STILL BE THIEVES, SURE.
BUT WE'LL GET TO SEE SOME EXCITEMENT.

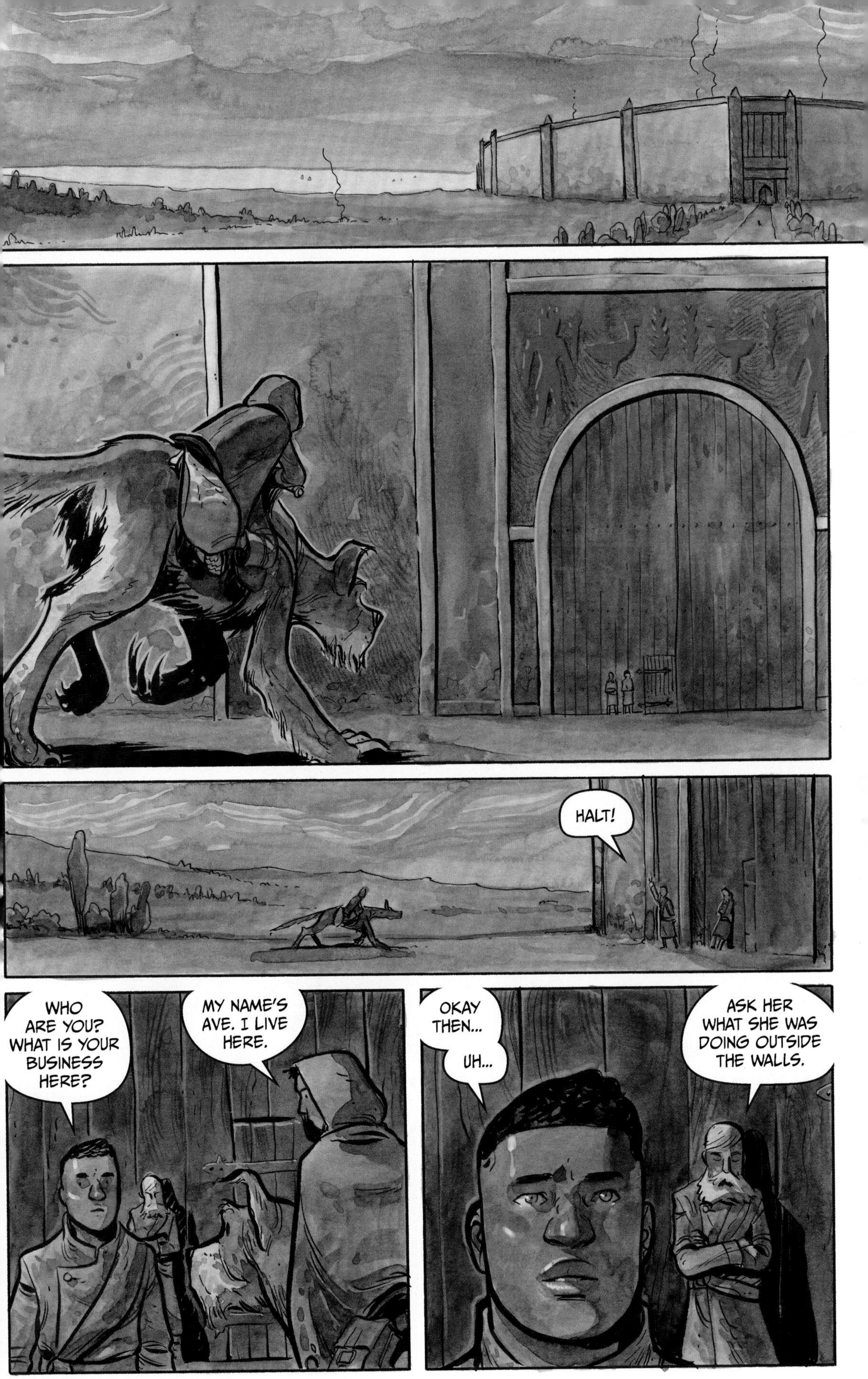

HALT!
WHO ARE YOU? WHAT IS YOUR BUSINESS HERE?
MY NAME'S AVE. I LIVE HERE.
OKAY THEN...
UH...
ASK HER WHAT SHE WAS DOING OUTSIDE THE WALLS.

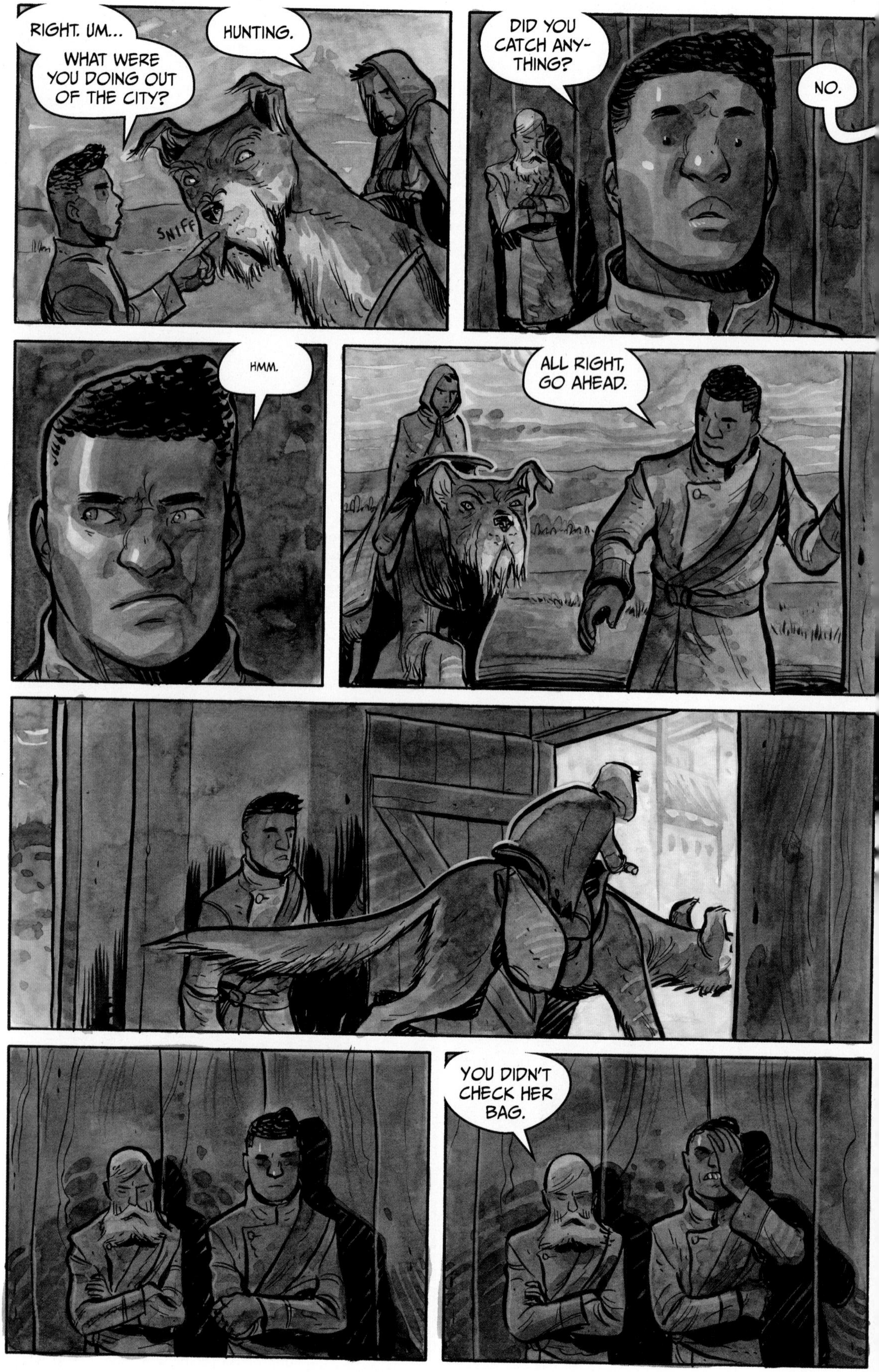
RIGHT. UM...
WHAT WERE YOU DOING OUT OF THE CITY?
HUNTING.
SNIFF
DID YOU CATCH ANY-THING?
NO.
HMM.
ALL RIGHT, GO AHEAD.
YOU DIDN'T CHECK HER BAG.

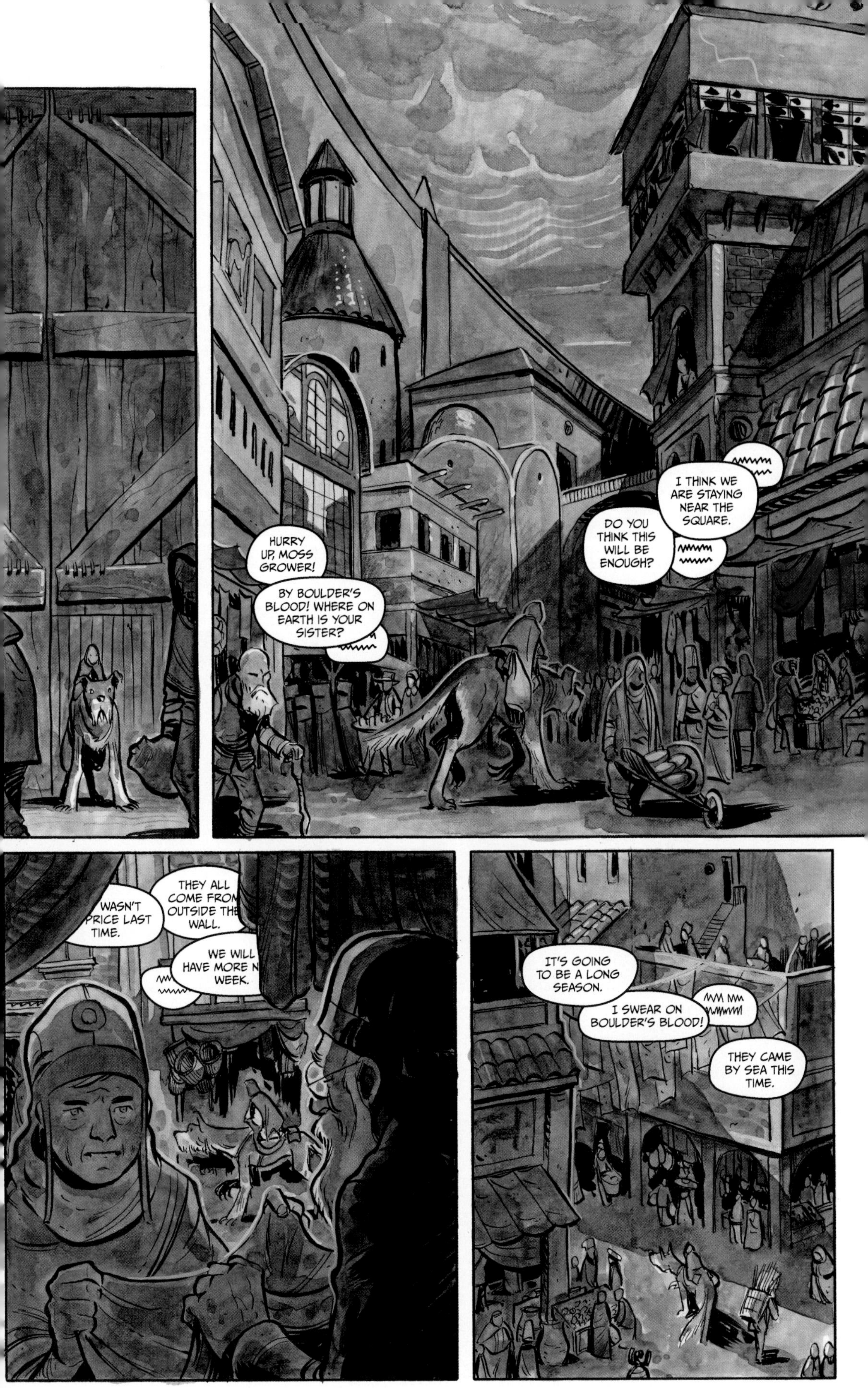
HURRY UP, MOSS GROWER!
BY BOULDER'S BLOOD! WHERE ON EARTH IS YOUR SISTER?
DO YOU THINK THIS WILL BE ENOUGH?
I THINK WE ARE STAYING NEAR THE SQUARE.
WASN'T PRICE LAST TIME.
THEY ALL COME FROM OUTSIDE THE WALL.
WE WILL HAVE MORE N WEEK.
IT'S GOING TO BE A LONG SEASON.
I SWEAR ON BOULDER'S BLOOD!
THEY CAME BY SEA THIS TIME.

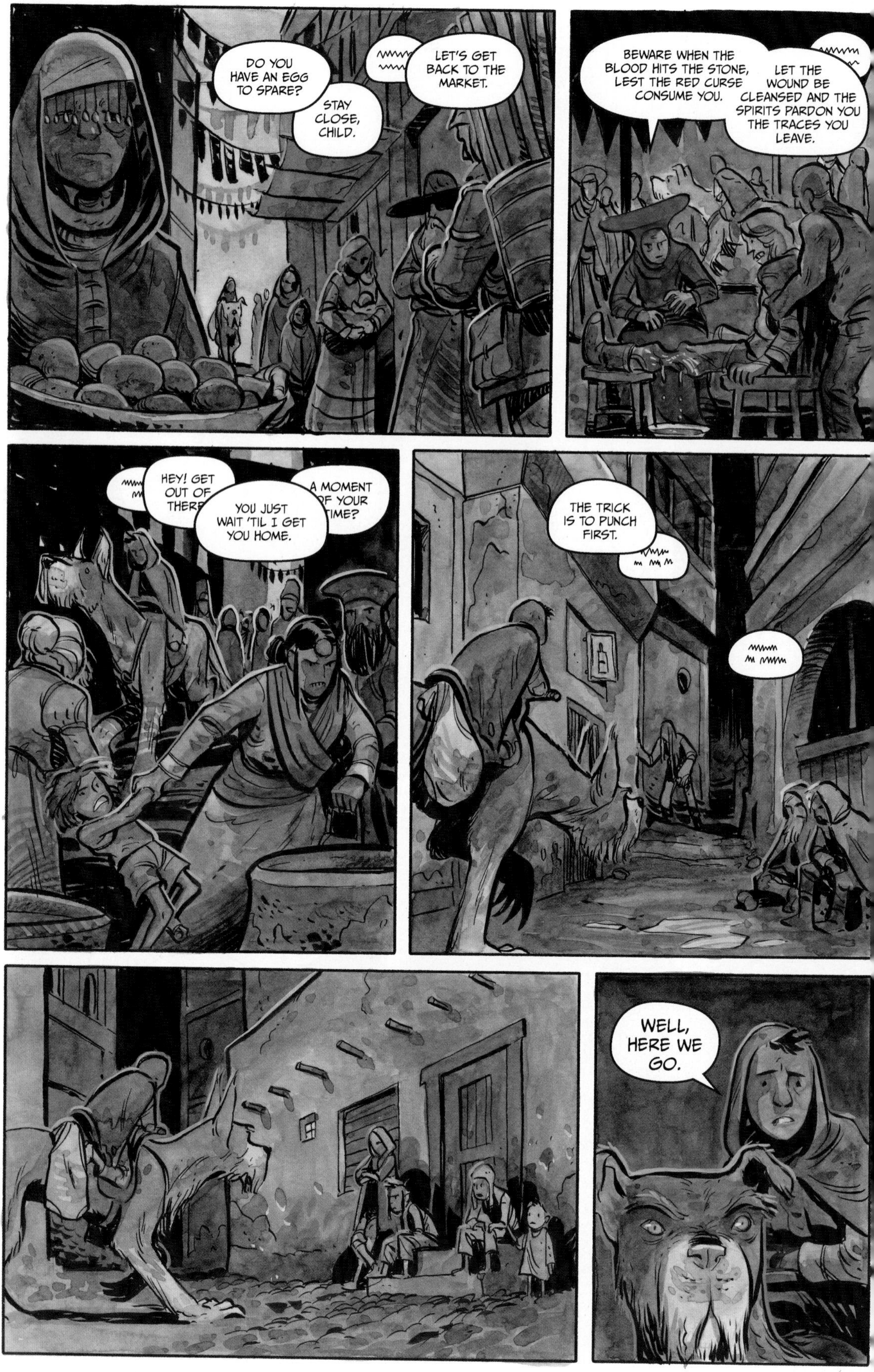
DO YOU HAVE AN EGG TO SPARE?
STAY CLOSE, CHILD.
LET'S GET BACK TO THE MARKET.
BEWARE WHEN THE BLOOD HITS THE STONE, LEST THE RED CURSE CONSUME YOU.
LET THE WOUND BE CLEANSED AND THE SPIRITS PARDON YOU THE TRACES YOU LEAVE.
HEY! GET OUT OF THER
YOU JUST WAIT 'TIL I GET YOU HOME.
A MOMENT OF YOUR TIME?
THE TRICK IS TO PUNCH FIRST.
WELL, HERE WE GO.

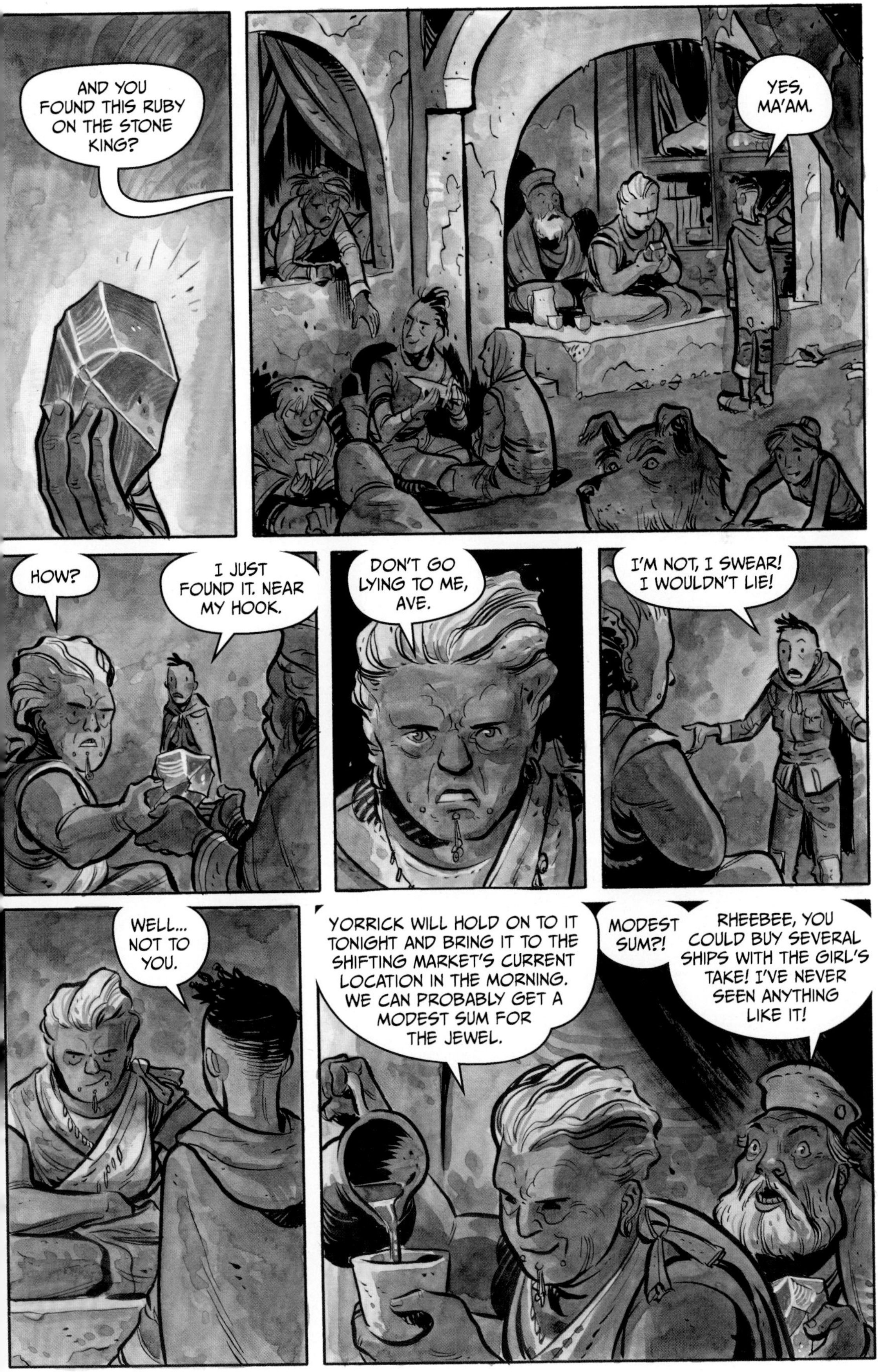
AND YOU FOUND THIS RUBY ON THE STONE KING?
YES, MA'AM.
HOW?
I JUST FOUND IT. NEAR MY HOOK.
DON'T GO LYING TO ME, AVE.
I'M NOT, I SWEAR! I WOULDN'T LIE!
WELL... NOT TO YOU.
YORRICK WILL HOLD ON TO IT TONIGHT AND BRING IT TO THE SHIFTING MARKET'S CURRENT LOCATION IN THE MORNING. WE CAN PROBABLY GET A MODEST SUM FOR THE JEWEL.
MODEST SUM?!
RHEEBEE, YOU COULD BUY SEVERAL SHIPS WITH THE GIRL'S TAKE! I'VE NEVER SEEN ANYTHING LIKE IT!

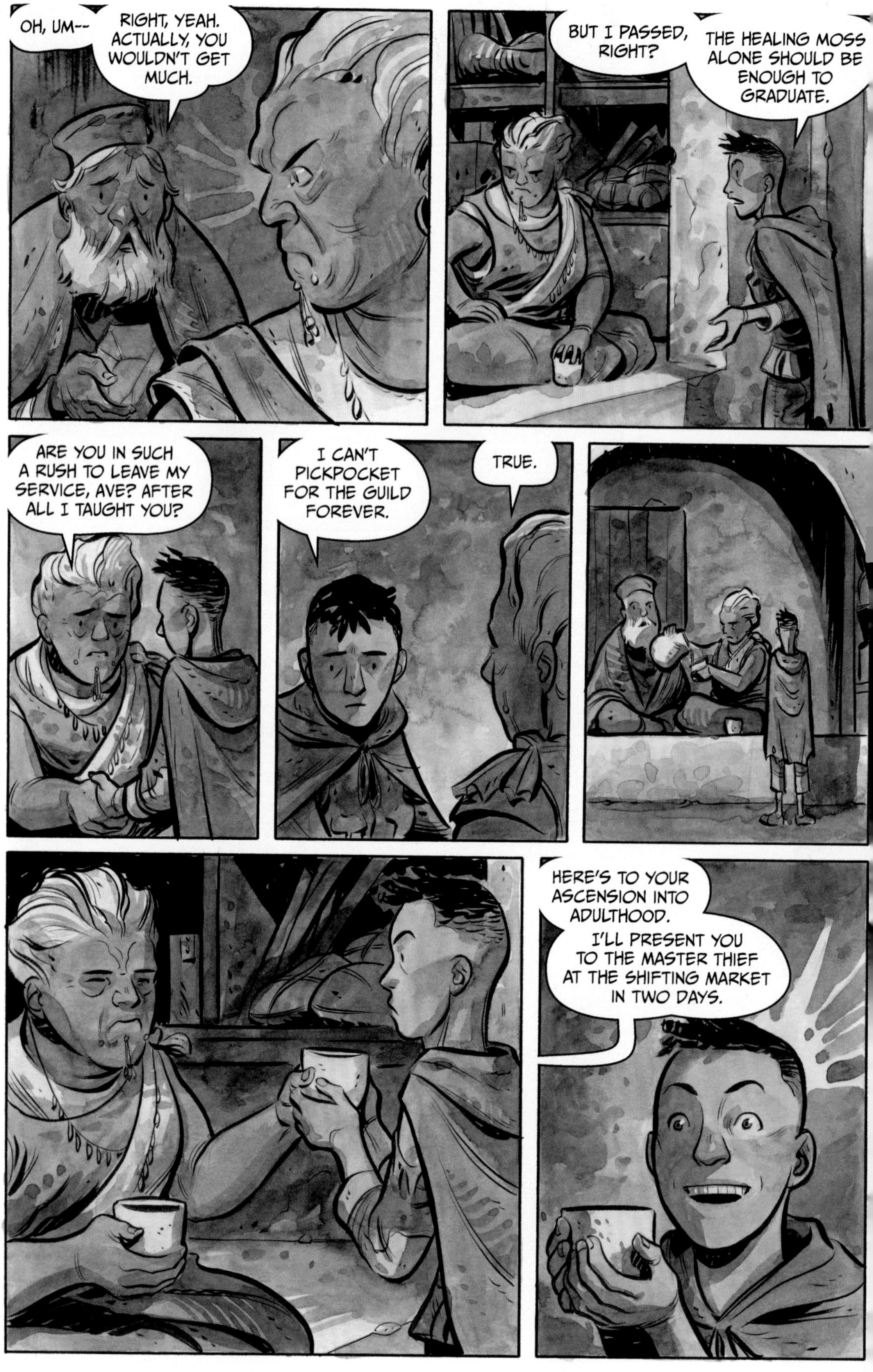
OH, UM--
RIGHT, YEAH. ACTUALLY, YOU WOULDN'T GET MUCH.
BUT I PASSED, RIGHT?
THE HEALING MOSS ALONE SHOULD BE ENOUGH TO GRADUATE.
ARE YOU IN SUCH A RUSH TO LEAVE MY SERVICE, AVE? AFTER ALL I TAUGHT YOU?
I CAN'T PICKPOCKET FOR THE GUILD FOREVER.
TRUE.
HERE'S TO YOUR ASCENSION INTO ADULTHOOD.
I'LL PRESENT YOU TO THE MASTER THIEF AT THE SHIFTING MARKET IN TWO DAYS.

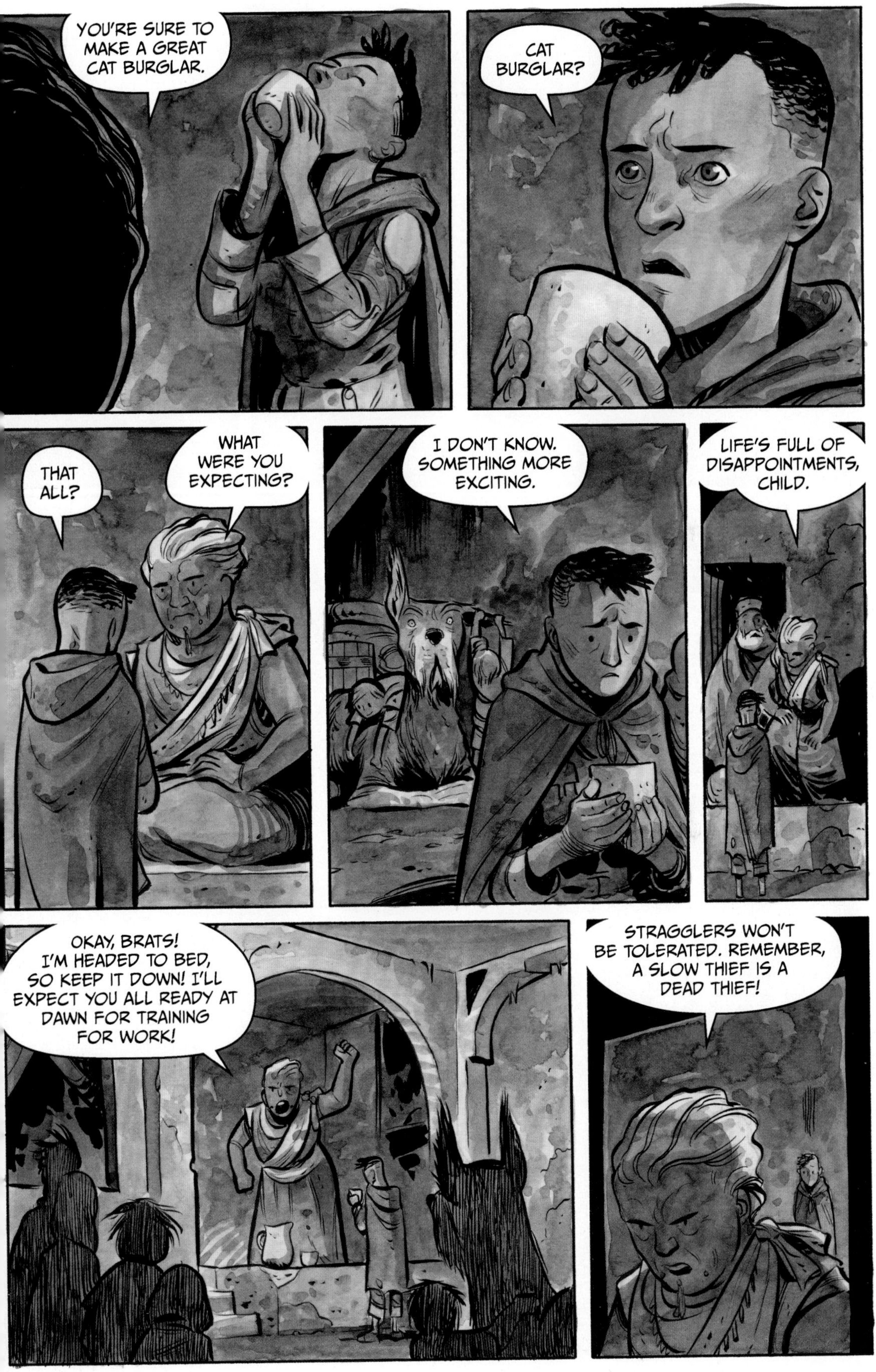

YOU'RE SURE TO MAKE A GREAT CAT BURGLAR.
CAT BURGLAR?
THAT ALL?
WHAT WERE YOU EXPECTING?
I DON'T KNOW. SOMETHING MORE EXCITING.
LIFE'S FULL OF DISAPPOINTMENTS, CHILD.
OKAY, BRATS! I'M HEADED TO BED, SO KEEP IT DOWN! I'LL EXPECT YOU ALL READY AT DAWN FOR TRAINING FOR WORK!
STRAGGLERS WON'T BE TOLERATED. REMEMBER, A SLOW THIEF IS A DEAD THIEF!

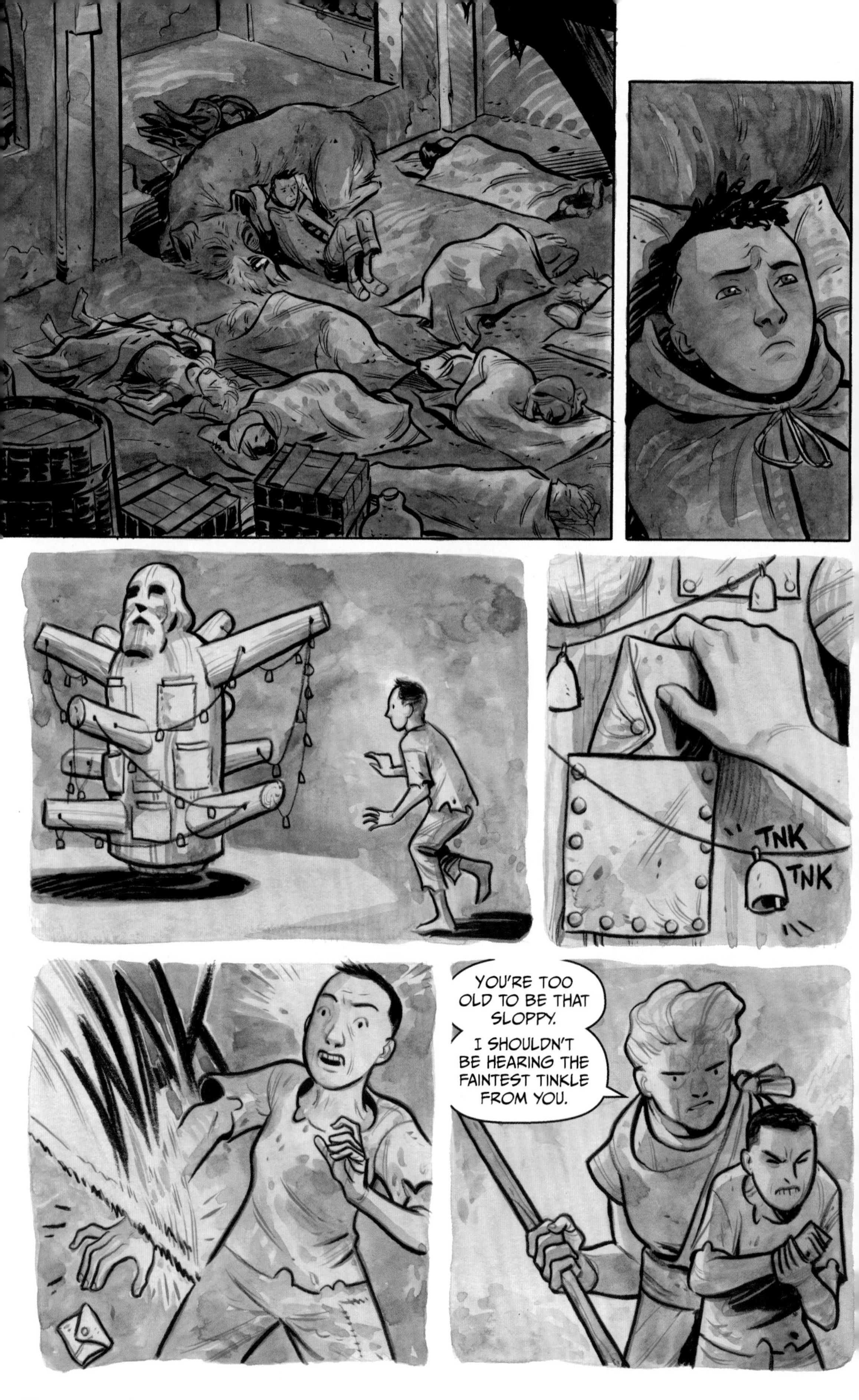
TNK
TNK
YOU'RE TOO OLD TO BE THAT SLOPPY.
I SHOULDN'T BE HEARING THE FAINTEST TINKLE FROM YOU.

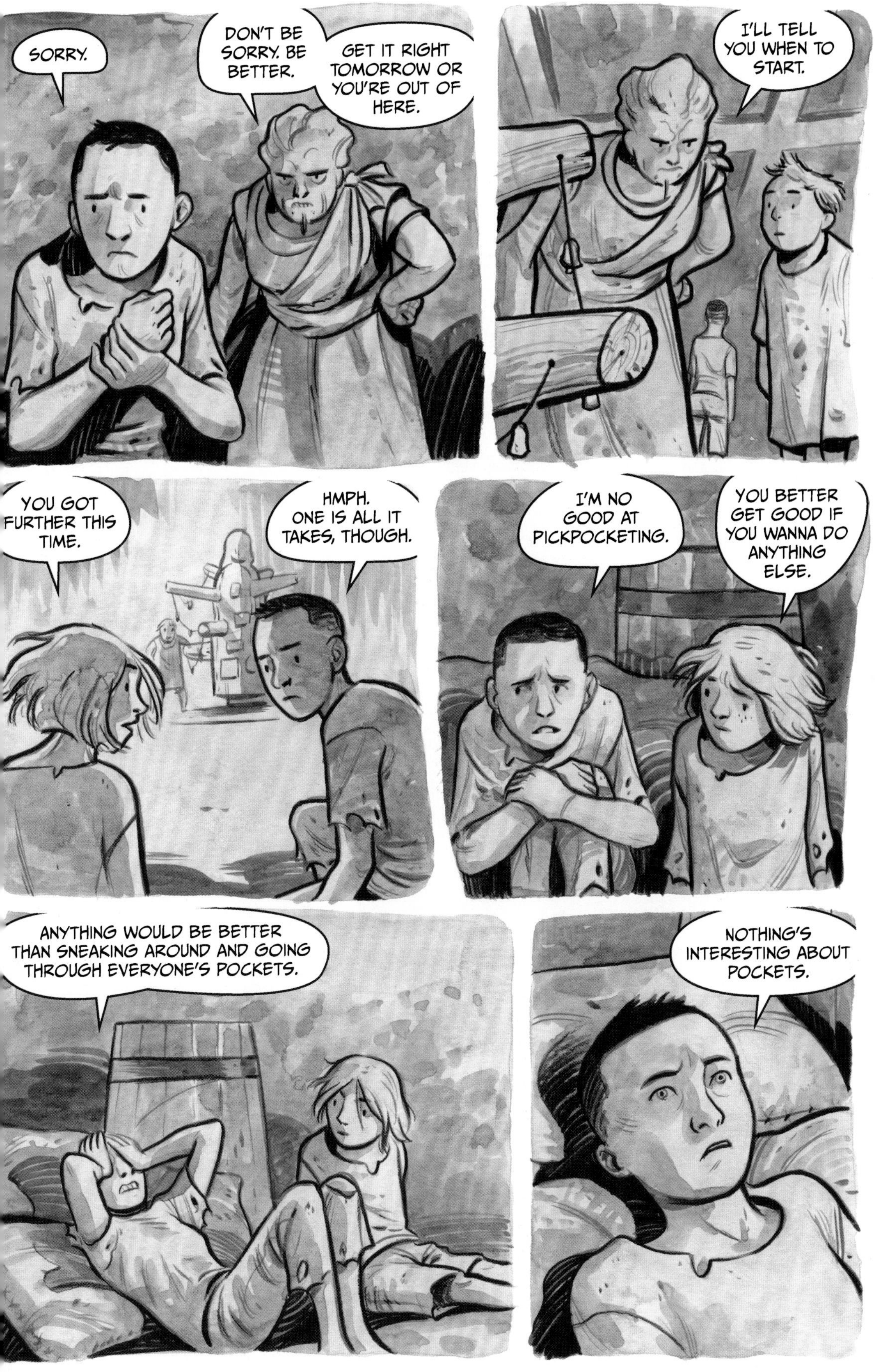
SORRY.
DON'T BE SORRY. BE BETTER.
GET IT RIGHT TOMORROW OR YOU'RE OUT OF HERE.
I'LL TELL YOU WHEN TO START.
YOU GOT FURTHER THIS TIME.
HMPH. ONE IS ALL IT TAKES, THOUGH.
I'M NO GOOD AT PICKPOCKETING.
YOU BETTER GET GOOD IF YOU WANNA DO ANYTHING ELSE.
ANYTHING WOULD BE BETTER THAN SNEAKING AROUND AND GOING THROUGH EVERYONE'S POCKETS.
NOTHING'S INTERESTING ABOUT POCKETS.

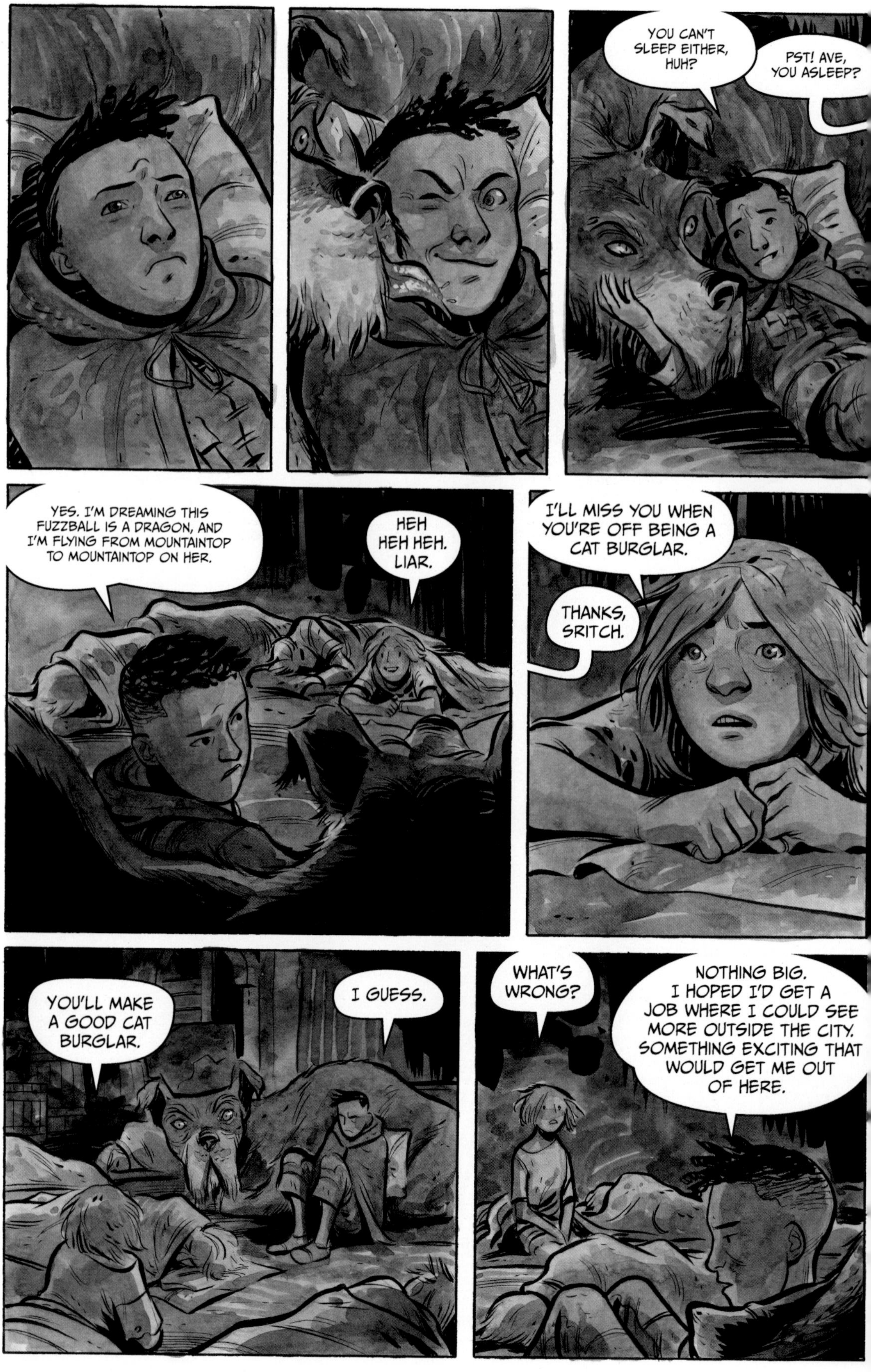
PST! AVE, YOU ASLEEP?
YOU CAN'T SLEEP EITHER, HUH?
YES. I'M DREAMING THIS FUZZBALL IS A DRAGON, AND I'M FLYING FROM MOUNTAINTOP TO MOUNTAINTOP ON HER.
HEH HEH HEH. LIAR.
I'LL MISS YOU WHEN YOU'RE OFF BEING A CAT BURGLAR.
THANKS, SRITCH.
YOU'LL MAKE A GOOD CAT BURGLAR.
I GUESS.
WHAT'S WRONG?
NOTHING BIG. I HOPED I'D GET A JOB WHERE I COULD SEE MORE OUTSIDE THE CITY. SOMETHING EXCITING THAT WOULD GET ME OUT OF HERE.

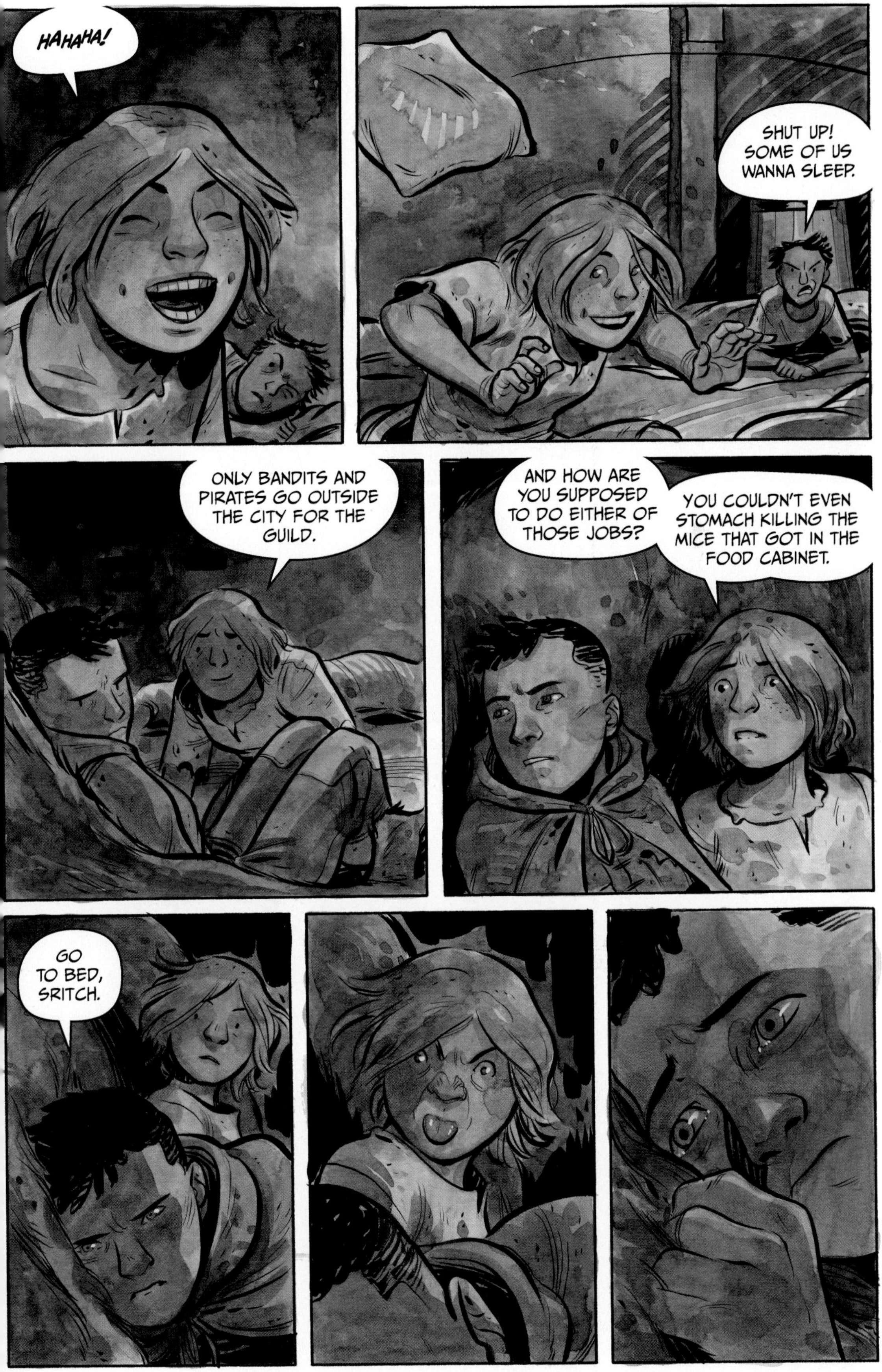
HAHAHA!
SHUT UP! SOME OF US WANNA SLEEP.
ONLY BANDITS AND PIRATES GO OUTSIDE THE CITY FOR THE GUILD.
AND HOW ARE YOU SUPPOSED TO DO EITHER OF THOSE JOBS?
YOU COULDN'T EVEN STOMACH KILLING THE MICE THAT GOT IN THE FOOD CABINET.
GO TO BED, SRITCH.

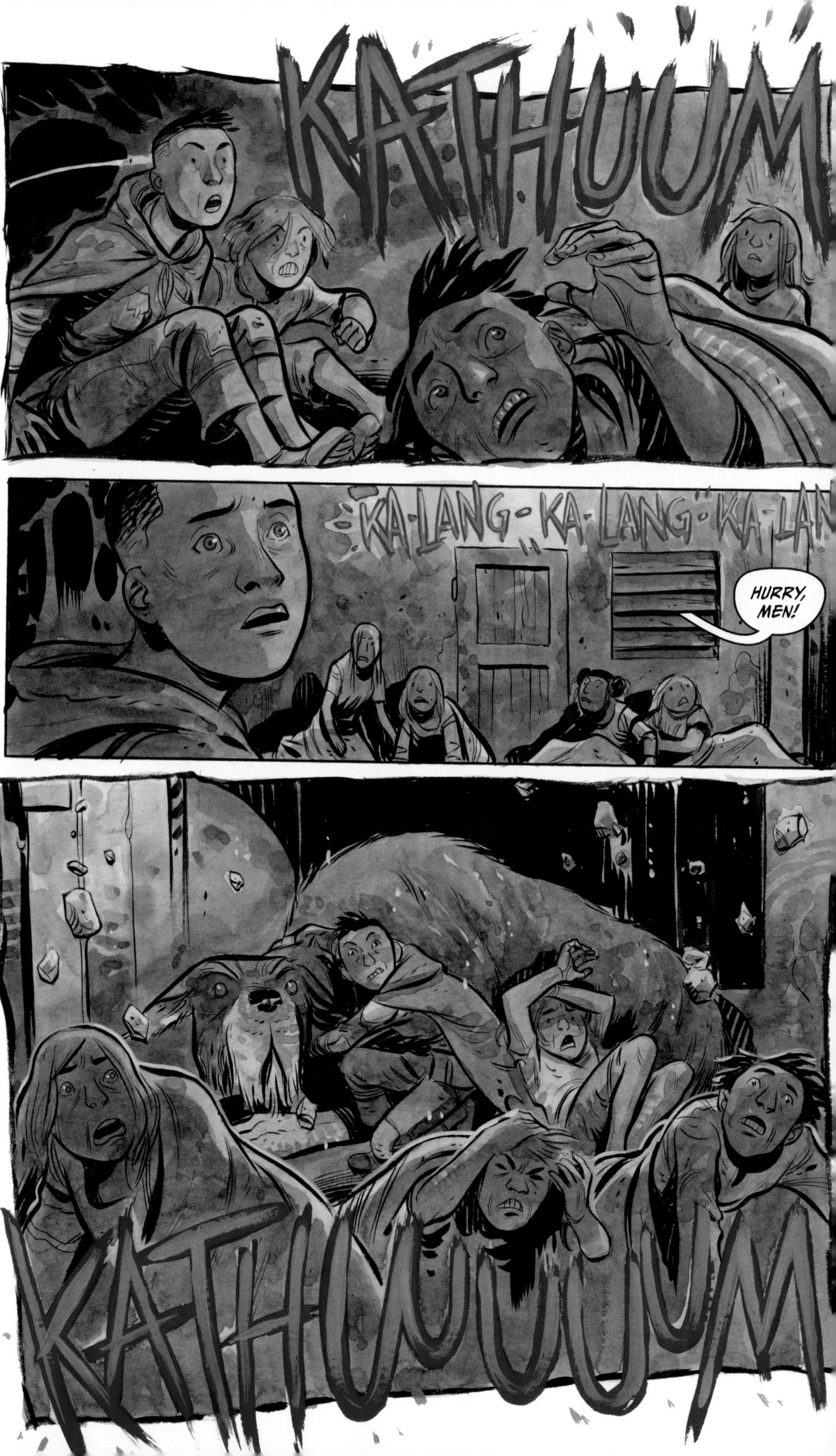
KATHUUM
KA-LANG-KA-LANG-KA-LAN
HURRY, MEN!
KATHUUUUUM

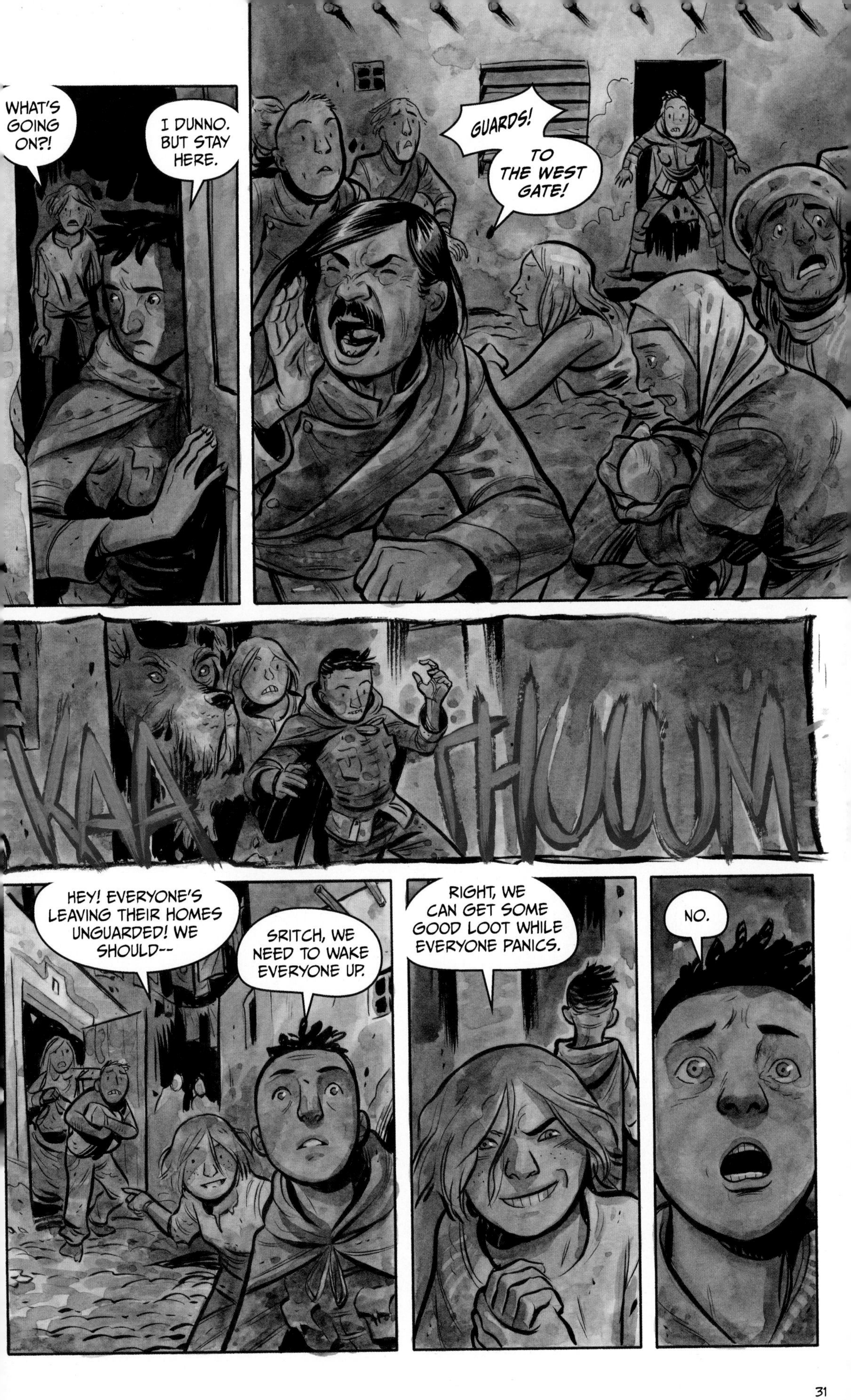
WHAT'S GOING ON?!
I DUNNO. BUT STAY HERE.
GUARDS!
TO THE WEST GATE!
KAA THUUUM
HEY! EVERYONE'S LEAVING THEIR HOMES UNGUARDED! WE SHOULD--
SRITCH, WE NEED TO WAKE EVERYONE UP.
RIGHT, WE CAN GET SOME GOOD LOOT WHILE EVERYONE PANICS.
NO.

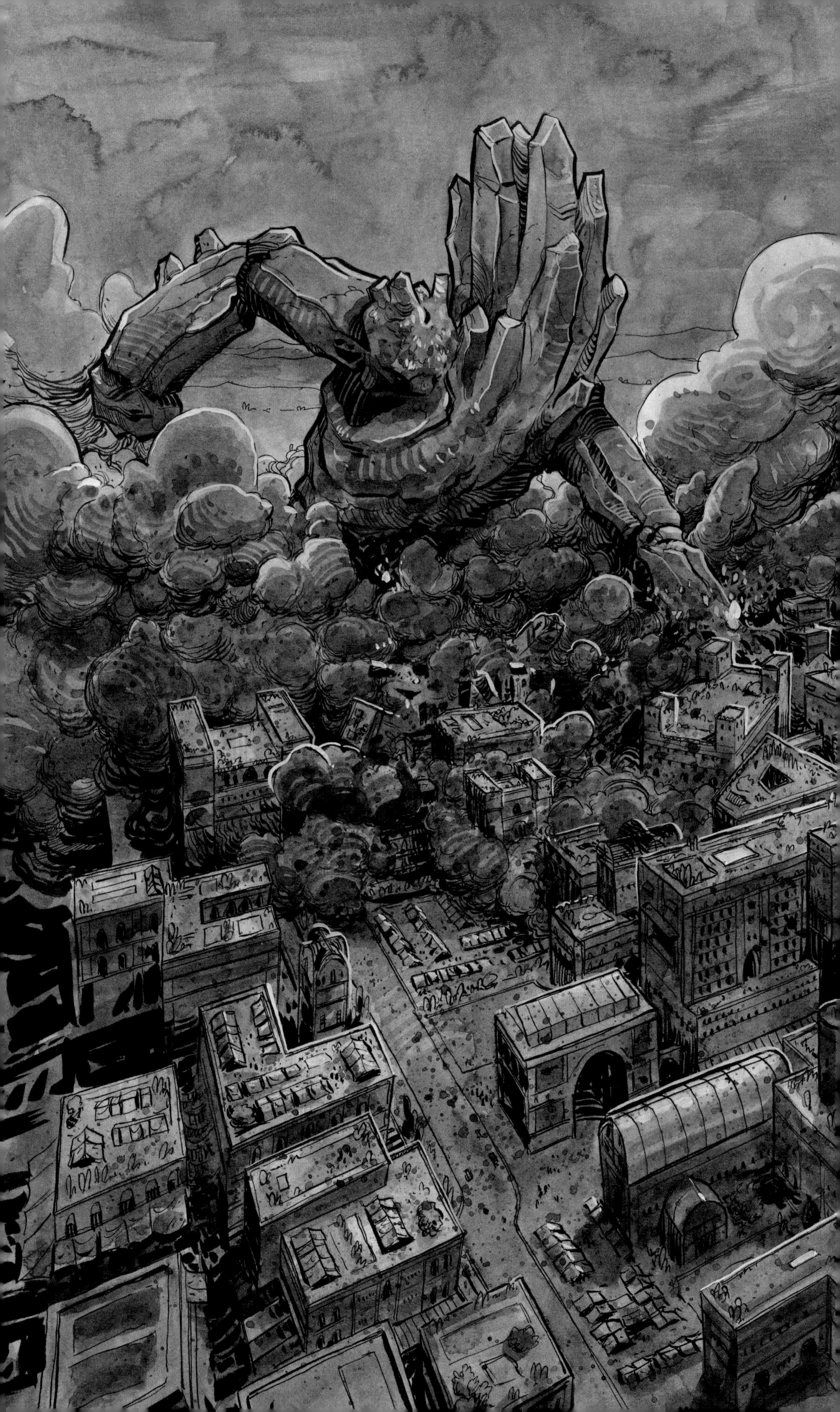

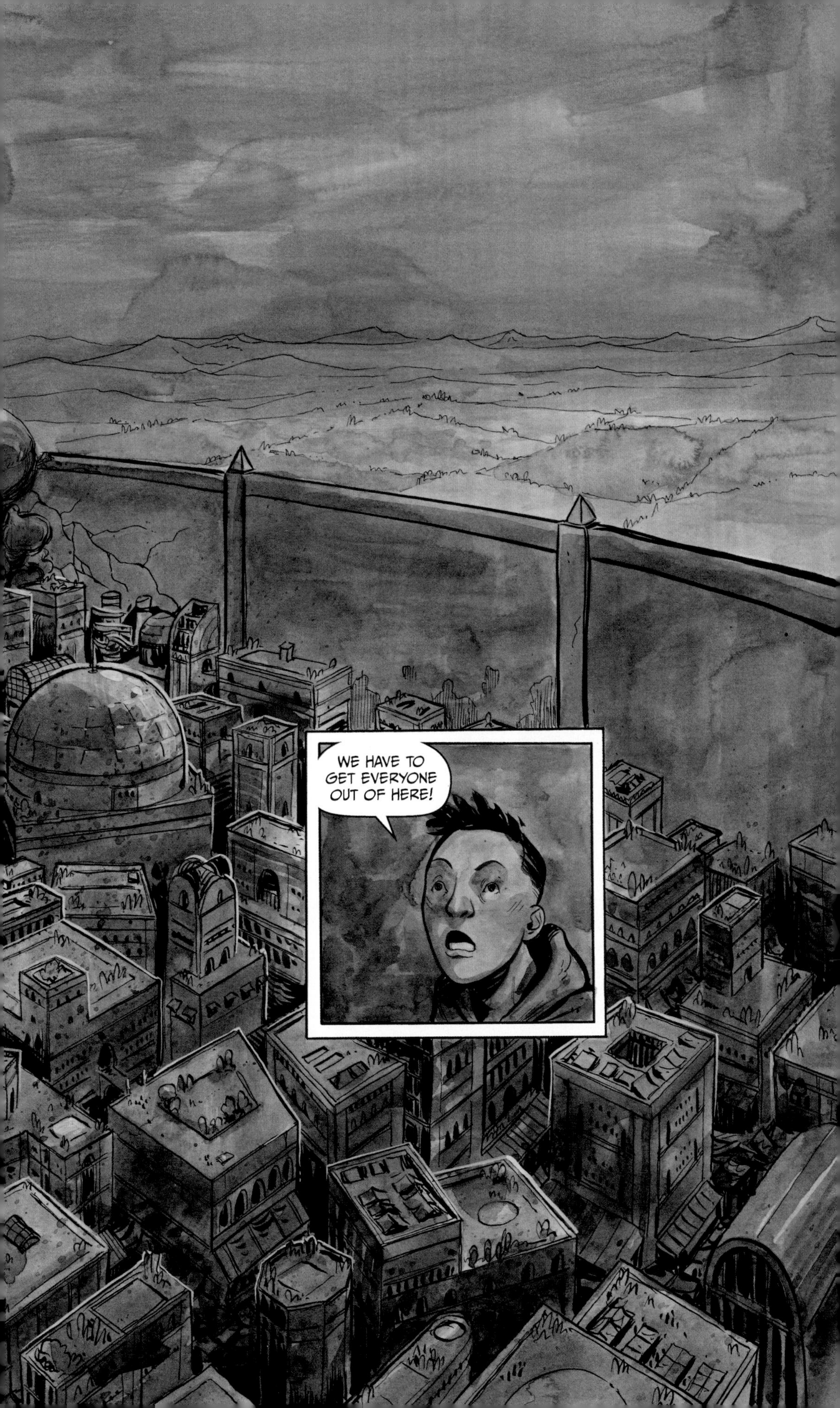
WE HAVE TO GET EVERYONE OUT OF HERE!

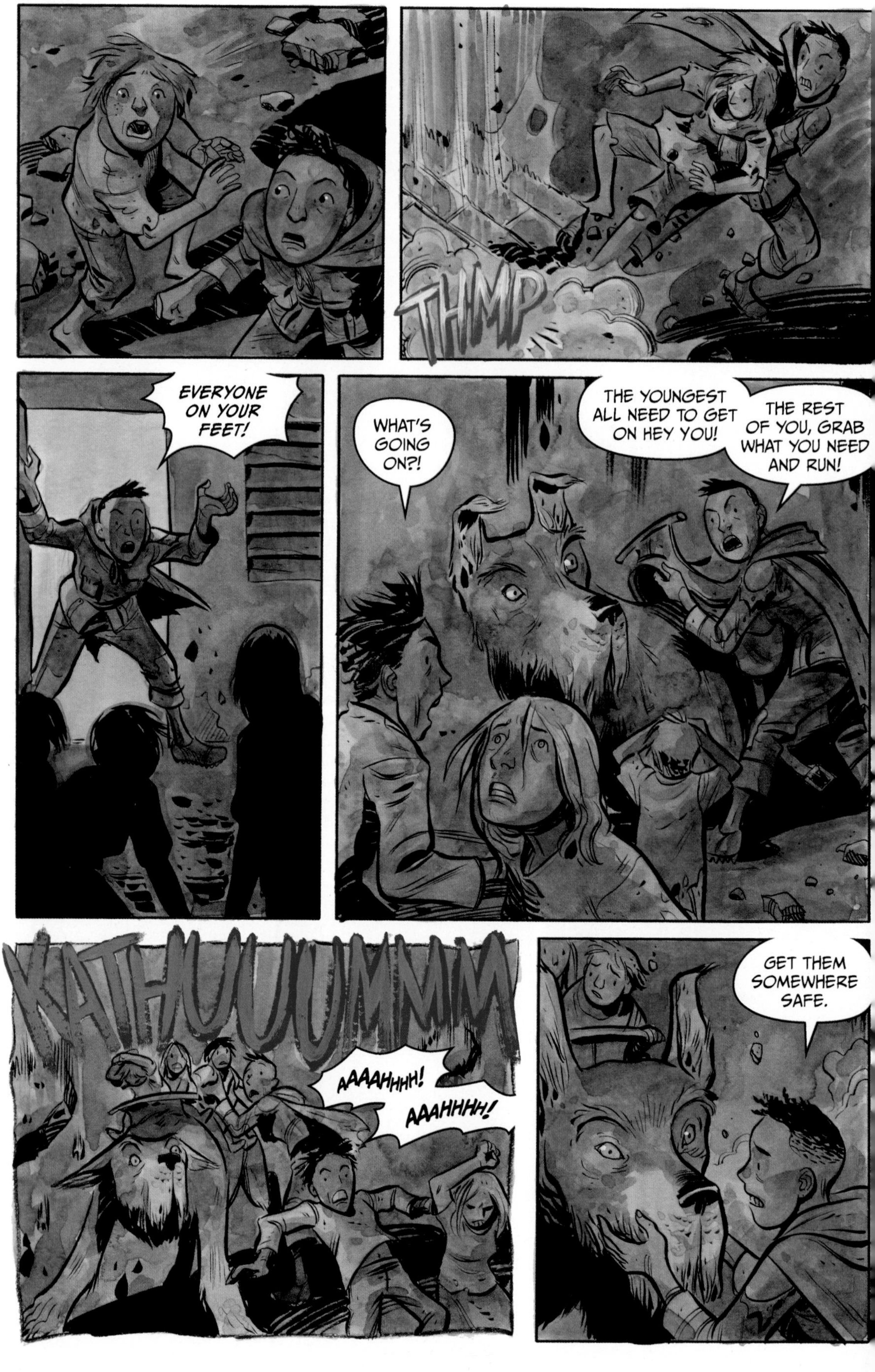
THMP
EVERYONE ON YOUR FEET!
WHAT'S GOING ON?!
THE YOUNGEST ALL NEED TO GET ON HEY YOU!
THE REST OF YOU, GRAB WHAT YOU NEED AND RUN!
KATHUUUMMM
AAAAHHHH!
AAAHHHH!
GET THEM SOMEWHERE SAFE.

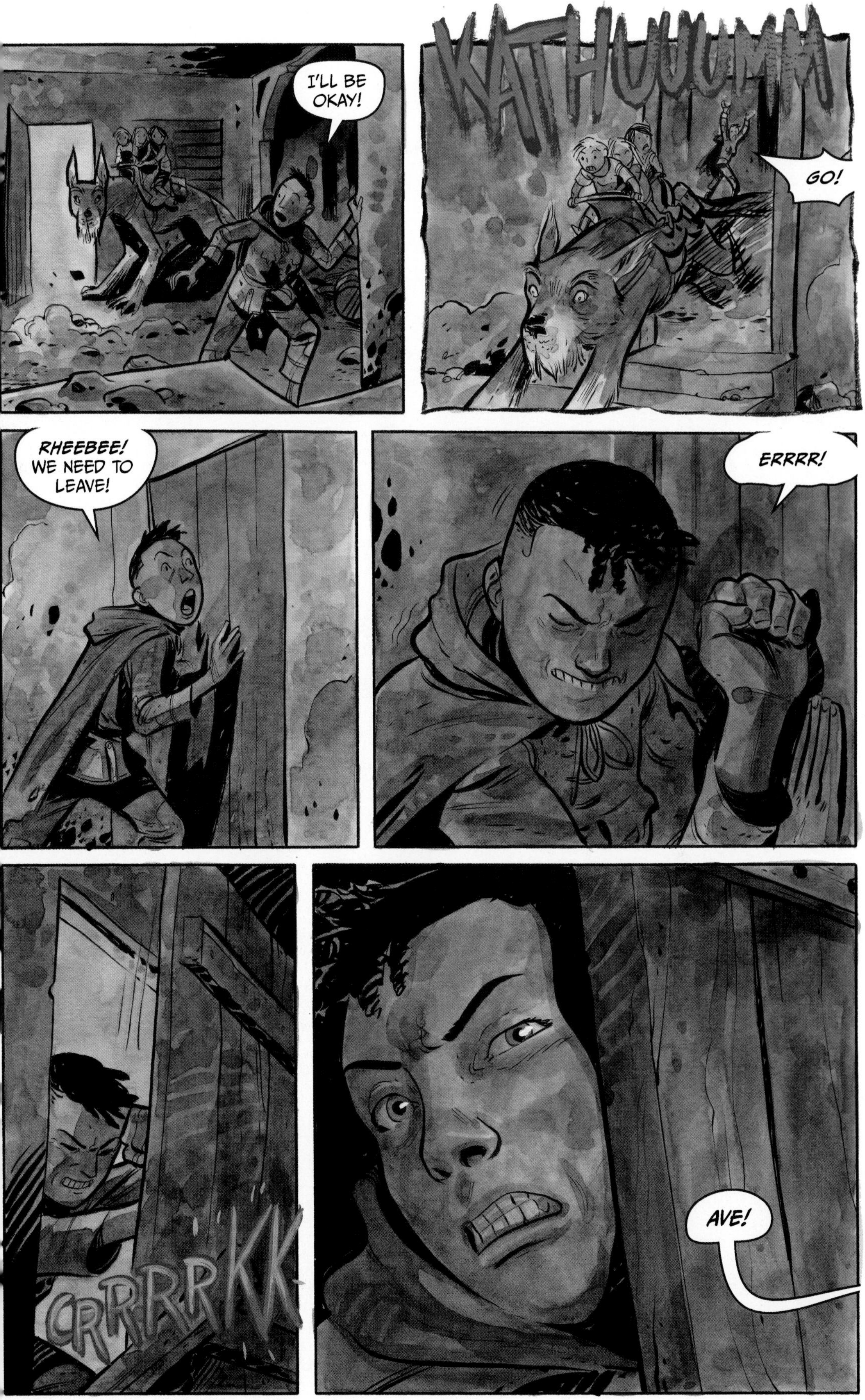
I'LL BE OKAY!
KATHUUUMM
GO!
RHEEBEE! WE NEED TO LEAVE!
ERRRR!
CRRRRKK
AVE!

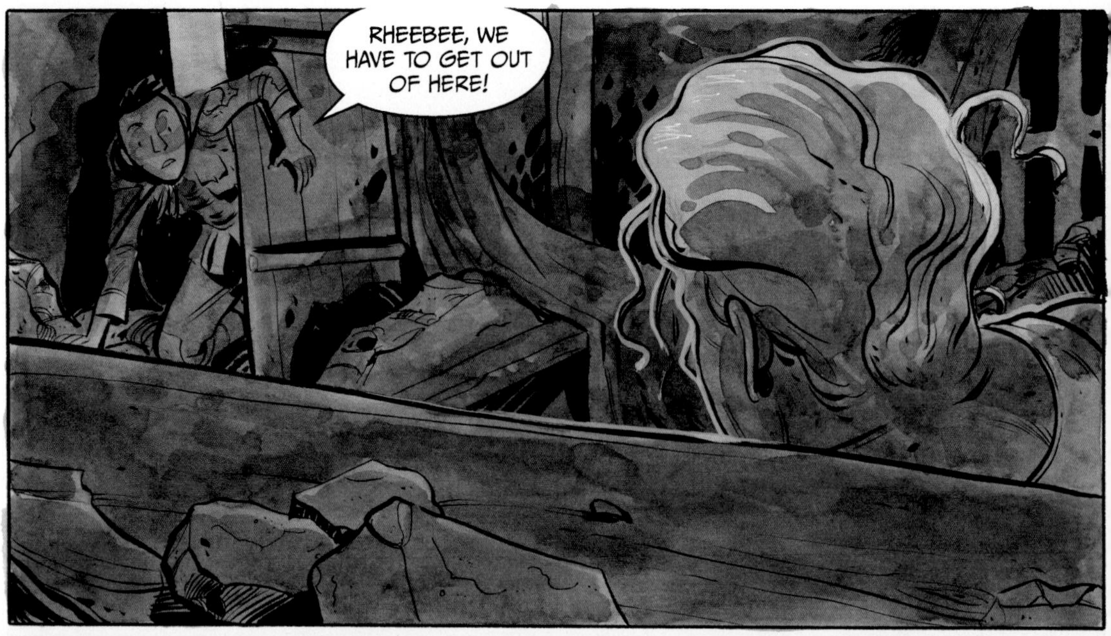
RHEEBEE, WE HAVE TO GET OUT OF HERE!

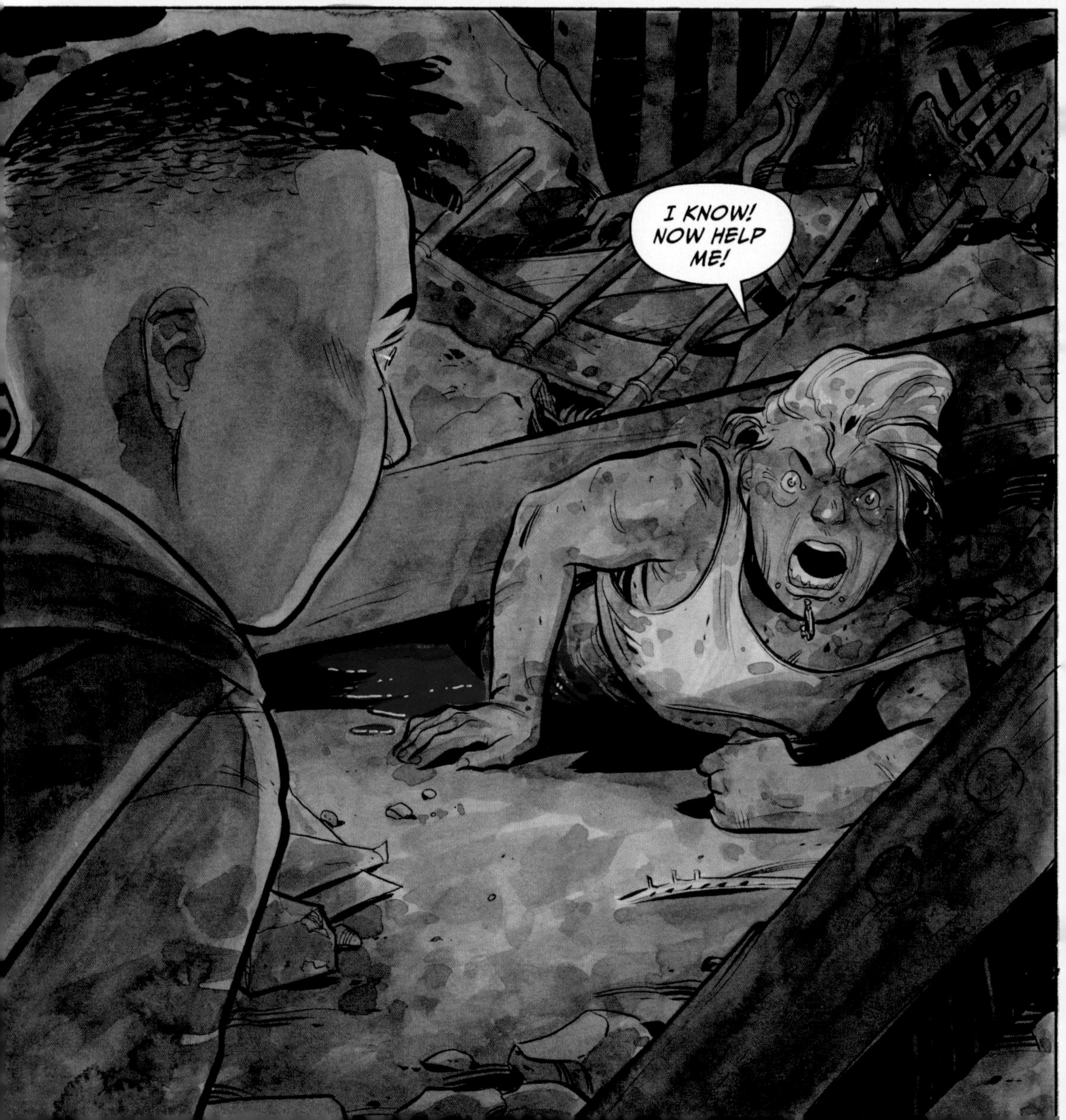
I KNOW! NOW HELP ME!

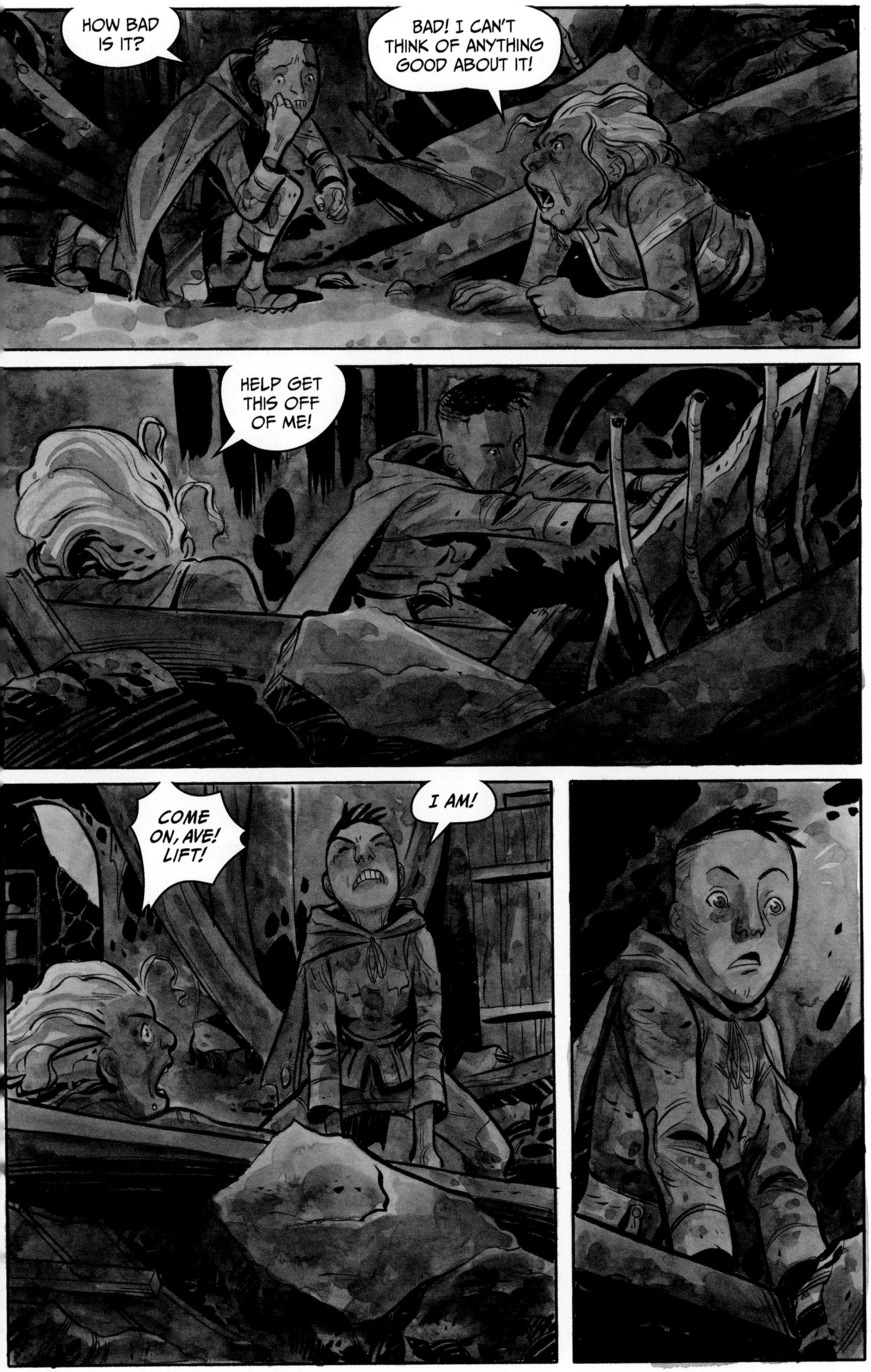
HOW BAD IS IT?
BAD! I CAN'T THINK OF ANYTHING GOOD ABOUT IT!
HELP GET THIS OFF OF ME!
COME ON, AVE! LIFT!
I AM!

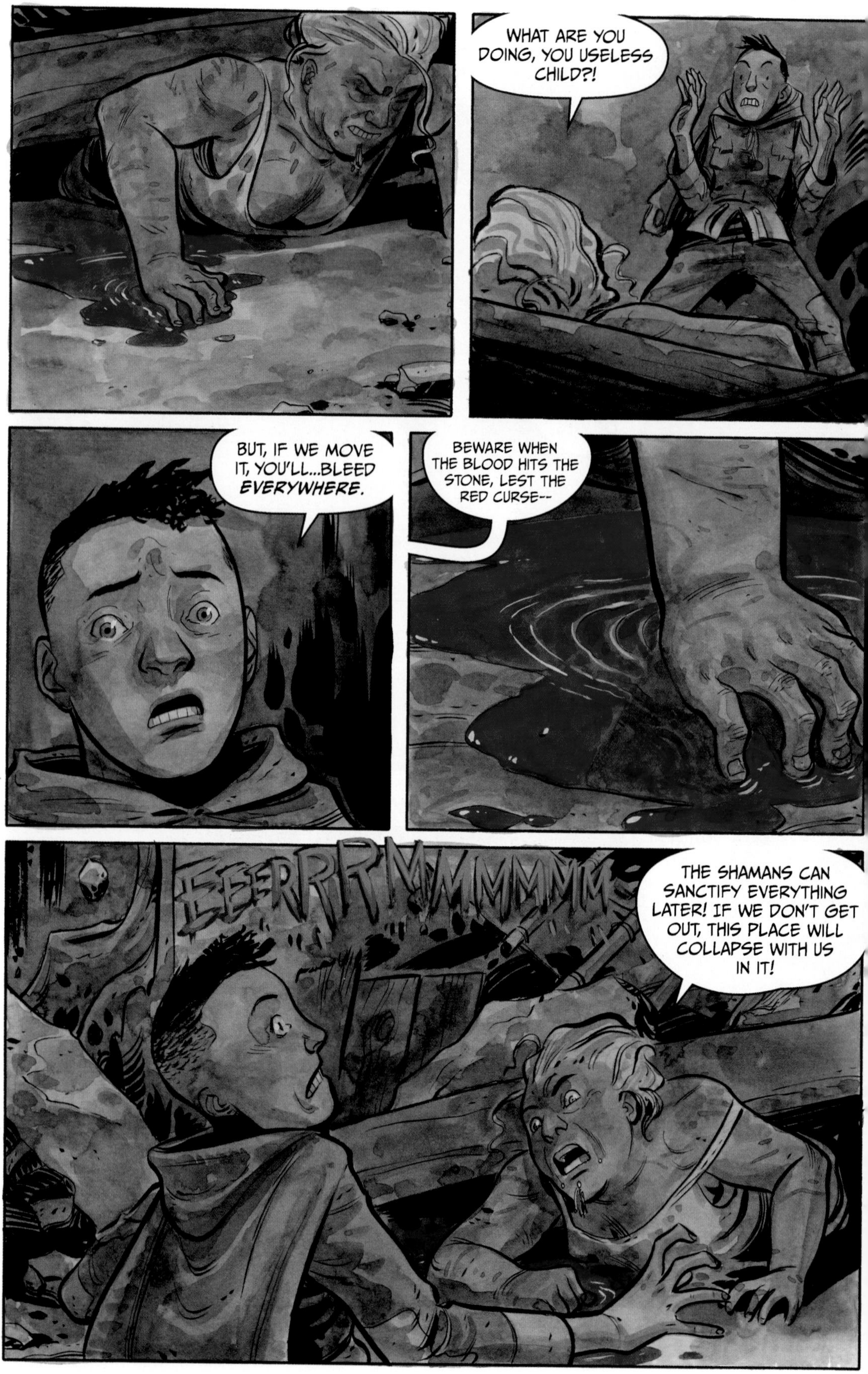
WHAT ARE YOU DOING, YOU USELESS CHILD?!
BUT, IF WE MOVE IT, YOU'LL...BLEED *EVERYWHERE.*
BEWARE WHEN THE BLOOD HITS THE STONE, LEST THE RED CURSE--
EEERRRRMMMMMMM
THE SHAMANS CAN SANCTIFY EVERYTHING LATER! IF WE DON'T GET OUT, THIS PLACE WILL COLLAPSE WITH US IN IT!

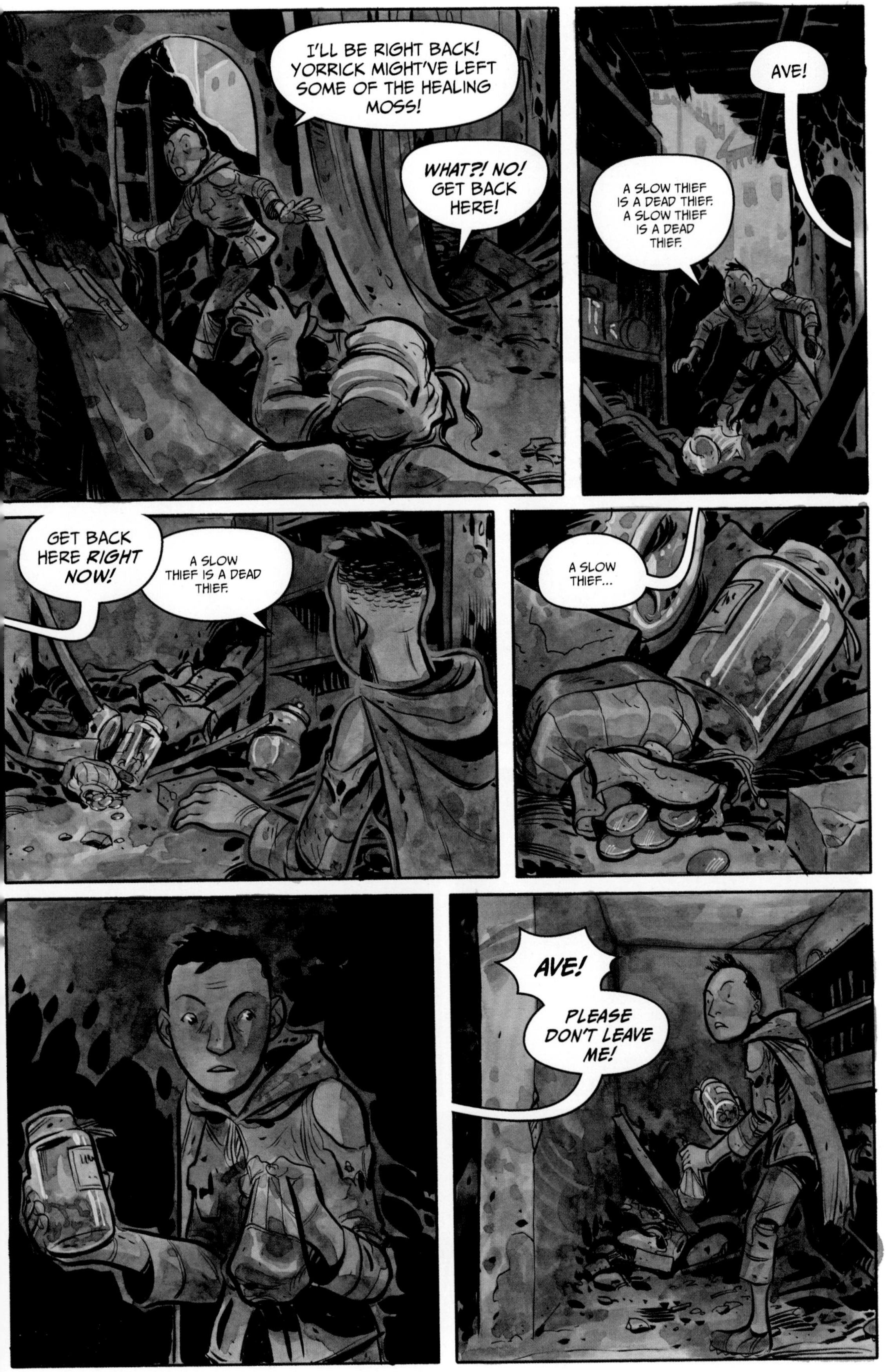
I'LL BE RIGHT BACK! YORRICK MIGHT'VE LEFT SOME OF THE HEALING MOSS!
WHAT?! NO! GET BACK HERE!
AVE!
A SLOW THIEF IS A DEAD THIEF. A SLOW THIEF IS A DEAD THIEF.
GET BACK HERE RIGHT NOW!
A SLOW THIEF IS A DEAD THIEF.
A SLOW THIEF...
AVE!
PLEASE DON'T LEAVE ME!

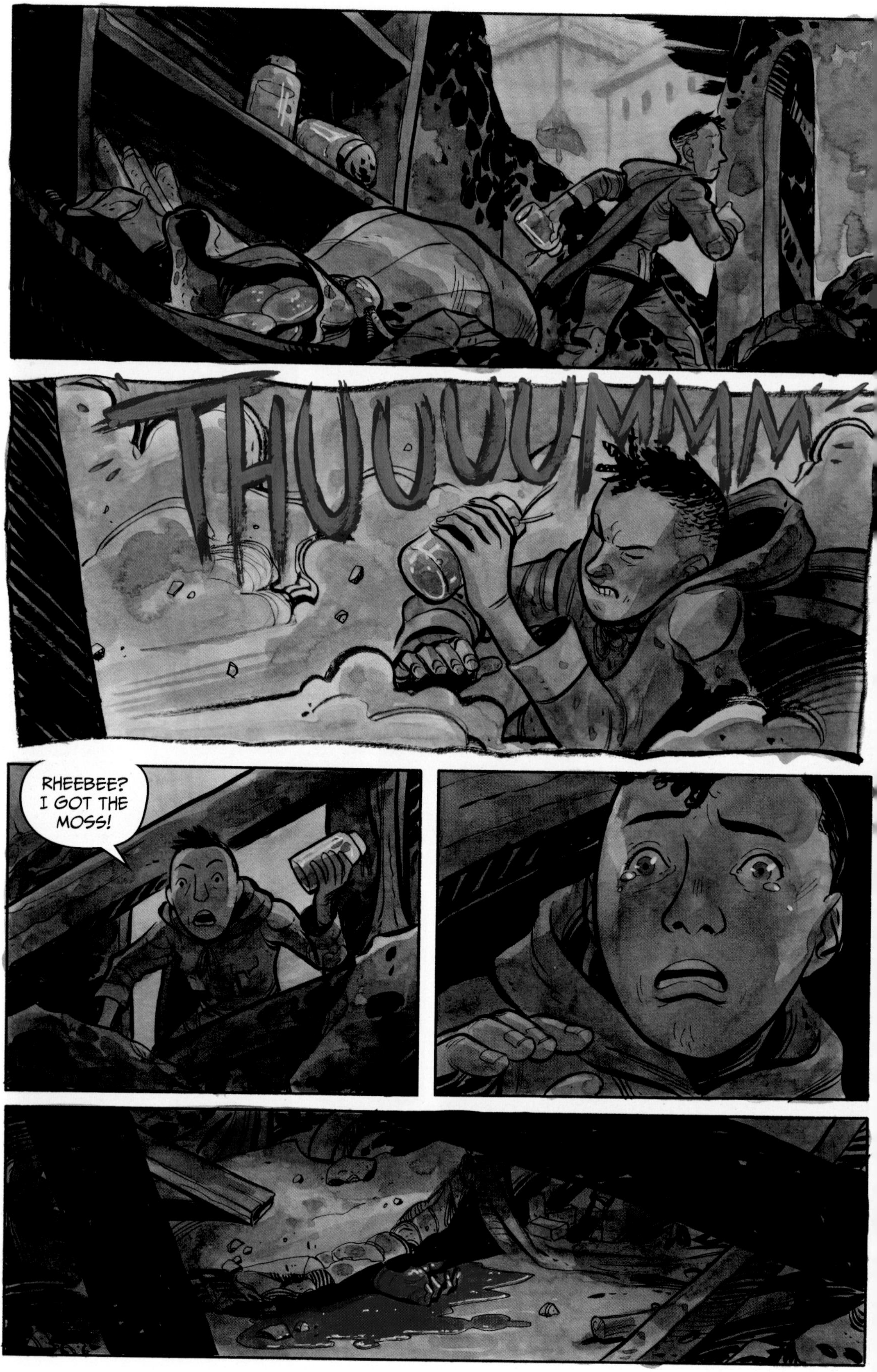
THUUUUMMM
RHEEBEE? I GOT THE MOSS!

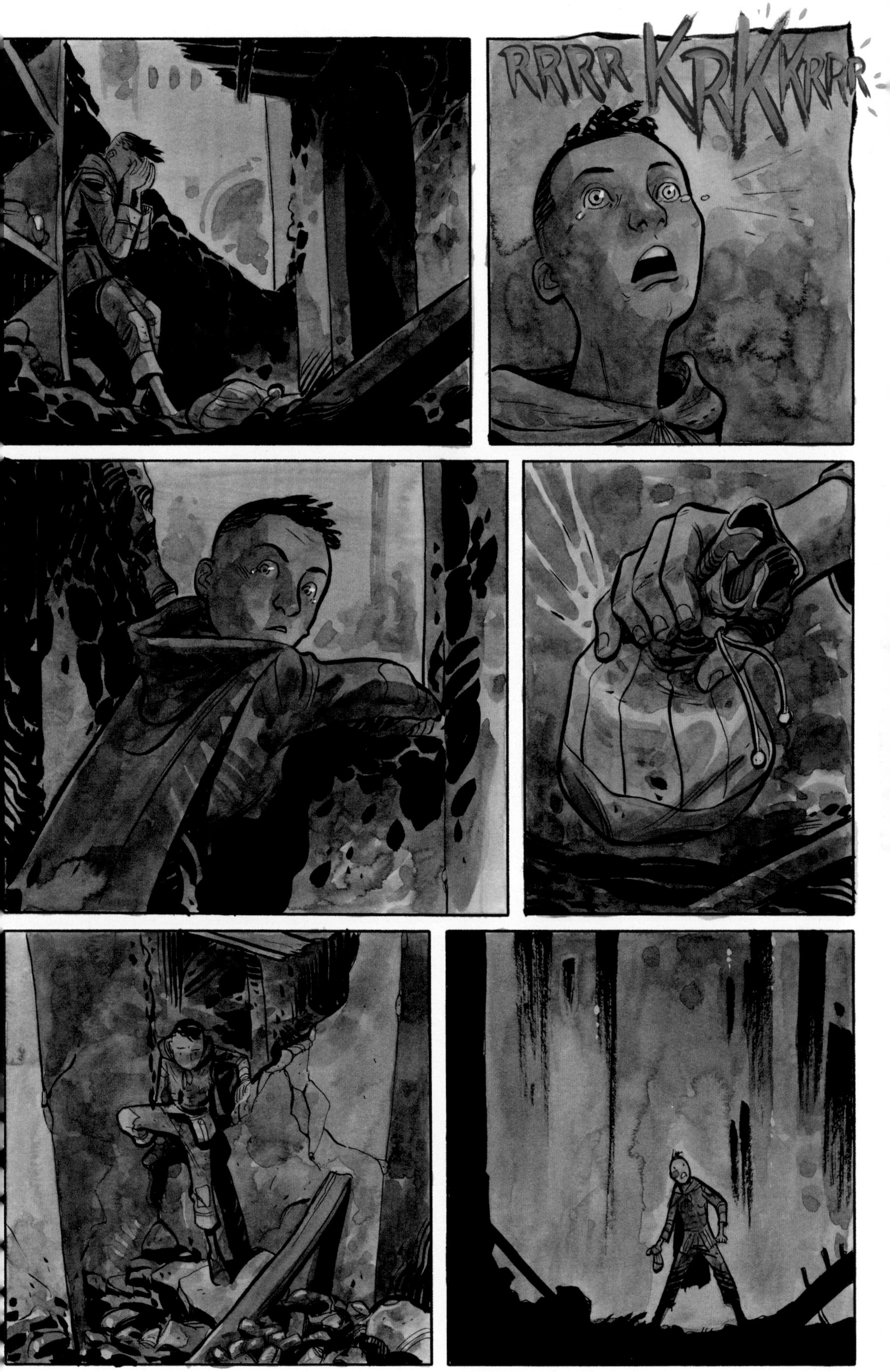
RRRRR KRKKRRR

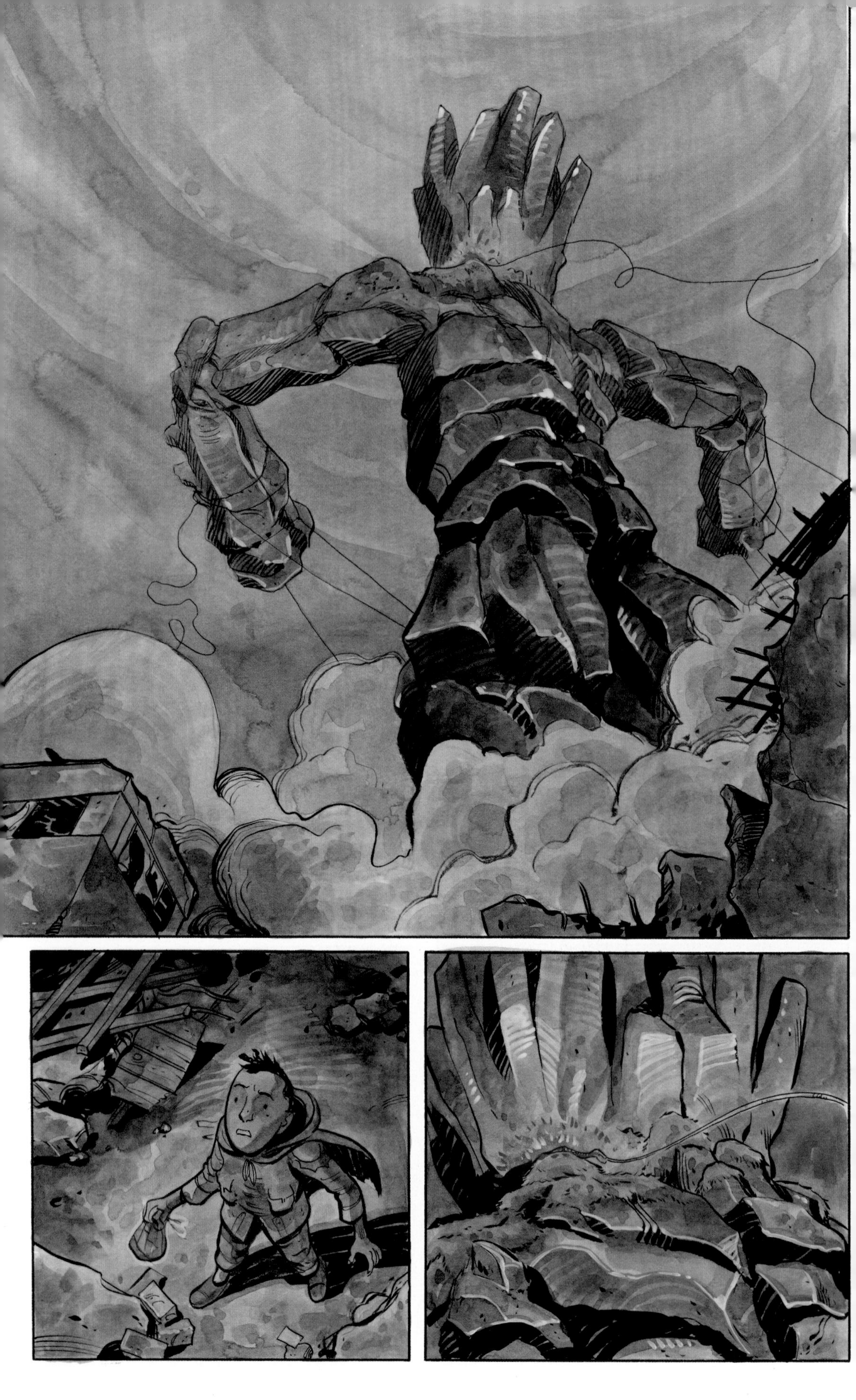

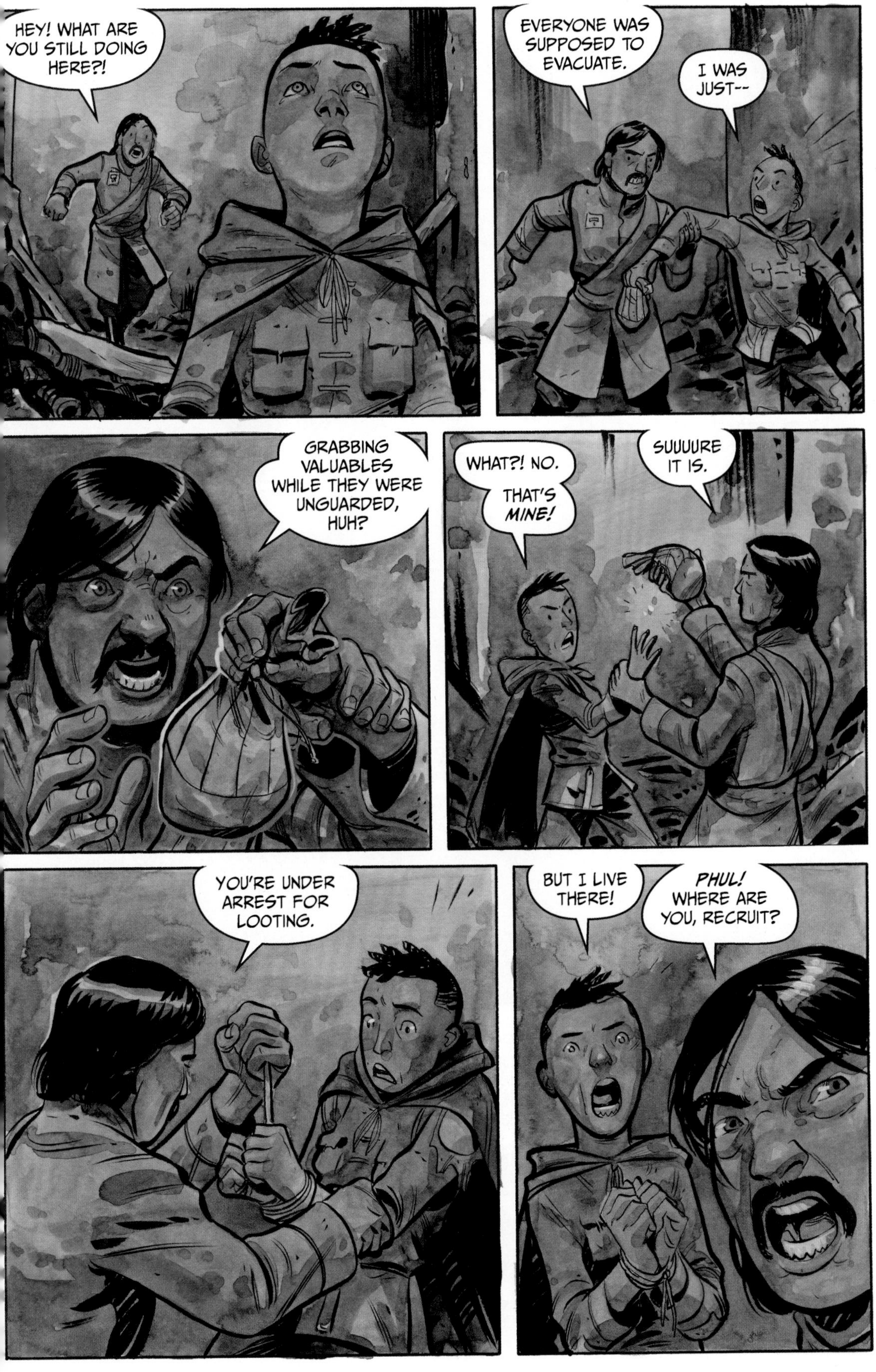
HEY! WHAT ARE YOU STILL DOING HERE?!
EVERYONE WAS SUPPOSED TO EVACUATE.
I WAS JUST--
GRABBING VALUABLES WHILE THEY WERE UNGUARDED, HUH?
WHAT?! NO.
THAT'S *MINE!*
SUUUURE IT IS.
YOU'RE UNDER ARREST FOR LOOTING.
BUT I LIVE THERE!
PHUL! WHERE ARE YOU, RECRUIT?

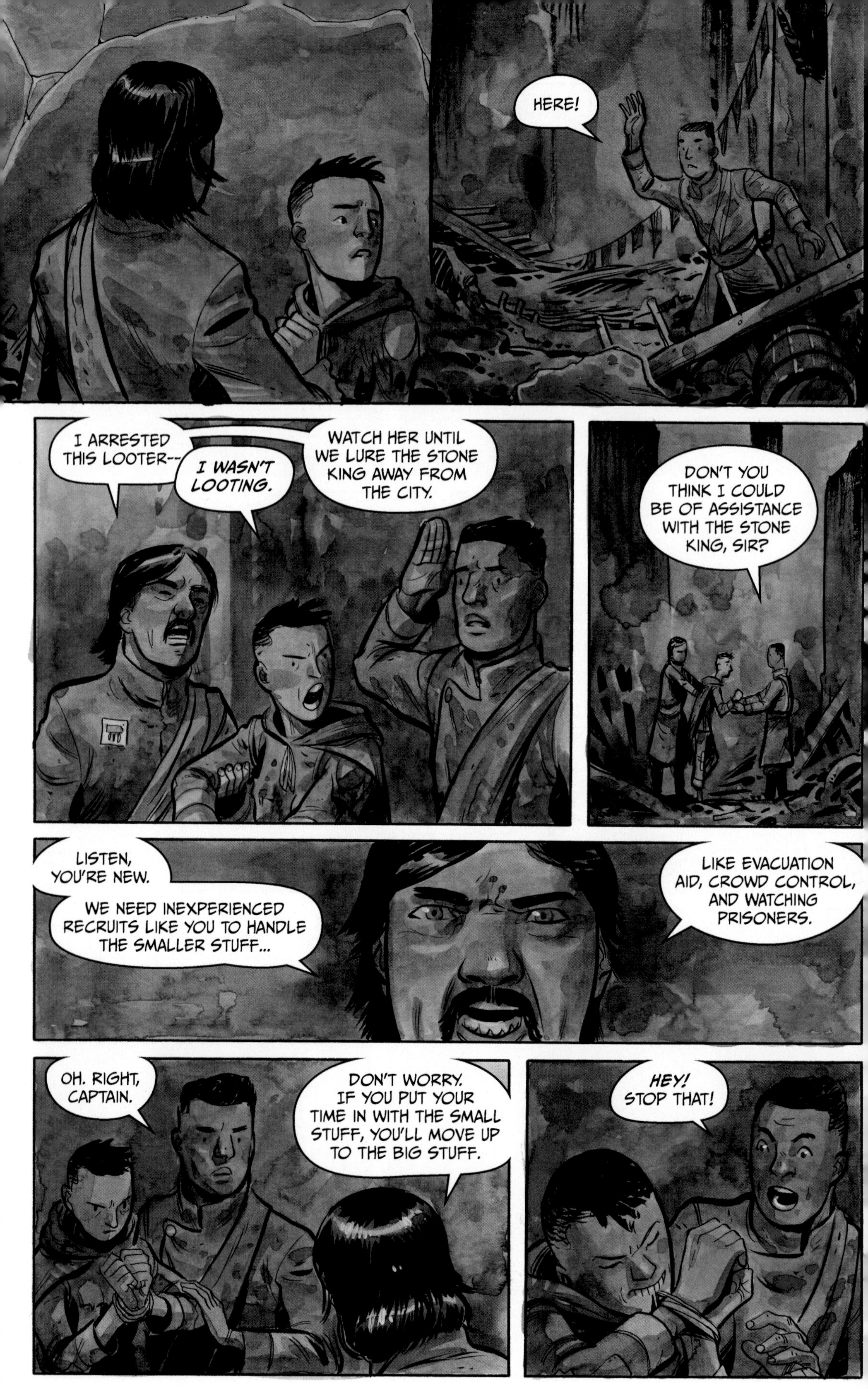
HERE!
I ARRESTED THIS LOOTER--
I WASN'T LOOTING.
WATCH HER UNTIL WE LURE THE STONE KING AWAY FROM THE CITY.
DON'T YOU THINK I COULD BE OF ASSISTANCE WITH THE STONE KING, SIR?
LISTEN, YOU'RE NEW.
WE NEED INEXPERIENCED RECRUITS LIKE YOU TO HANDLE THE SMALLER STUFF...
LIKE EVACUATION AID, CROWD CONTROL, AND WATCHING PRISONERS.
OH. RIGHT, CAPTAIN.
DON'T WORRY. IF YOU PUT YOUR TIME IN WITH THE SMALL STUFF, YOU'LL MOVE UP TO THE BIG STUFF.
HEY! STOP THAT!

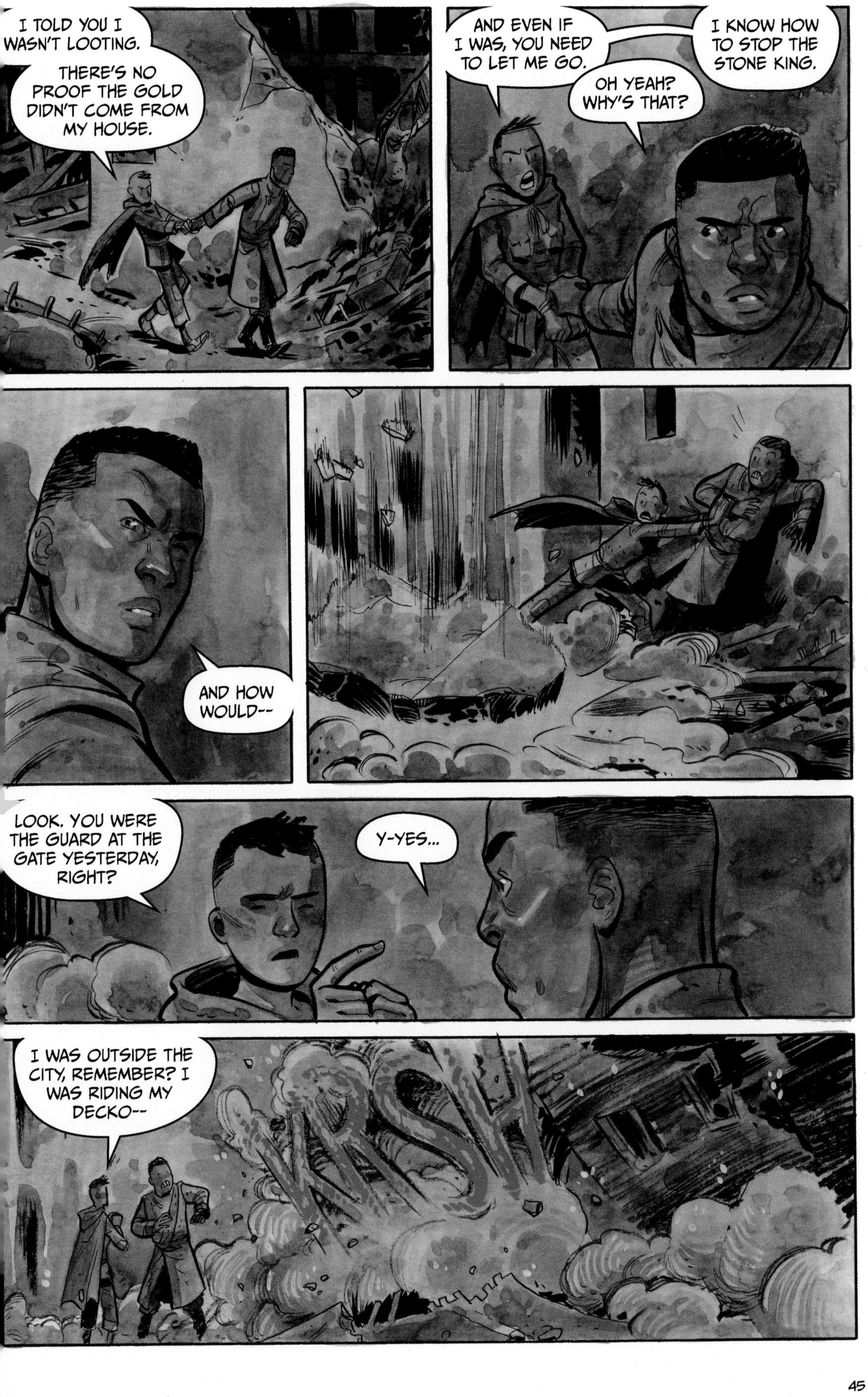
I TOLD YOU I WASN'T LOOTING.
THERE'S NO PROOF THE GOLD DIDN'T COME FROM MY HOUSE.
AND EVEN IF I WAS, YOU NEED TO LET ME GO.
OH YEAH? WHY'S THAT?
I KNOW HOW TO STOP THE STONE KING.
AND HOW WOULD--
LOOK. YOU WERE THE GUARD AT THE GATE YESTERDAY, RIGHT?
Y-YES...
I WAS OUTSIDE THE CITY, REMEMBER? I WAS RIDING MY DECKO--

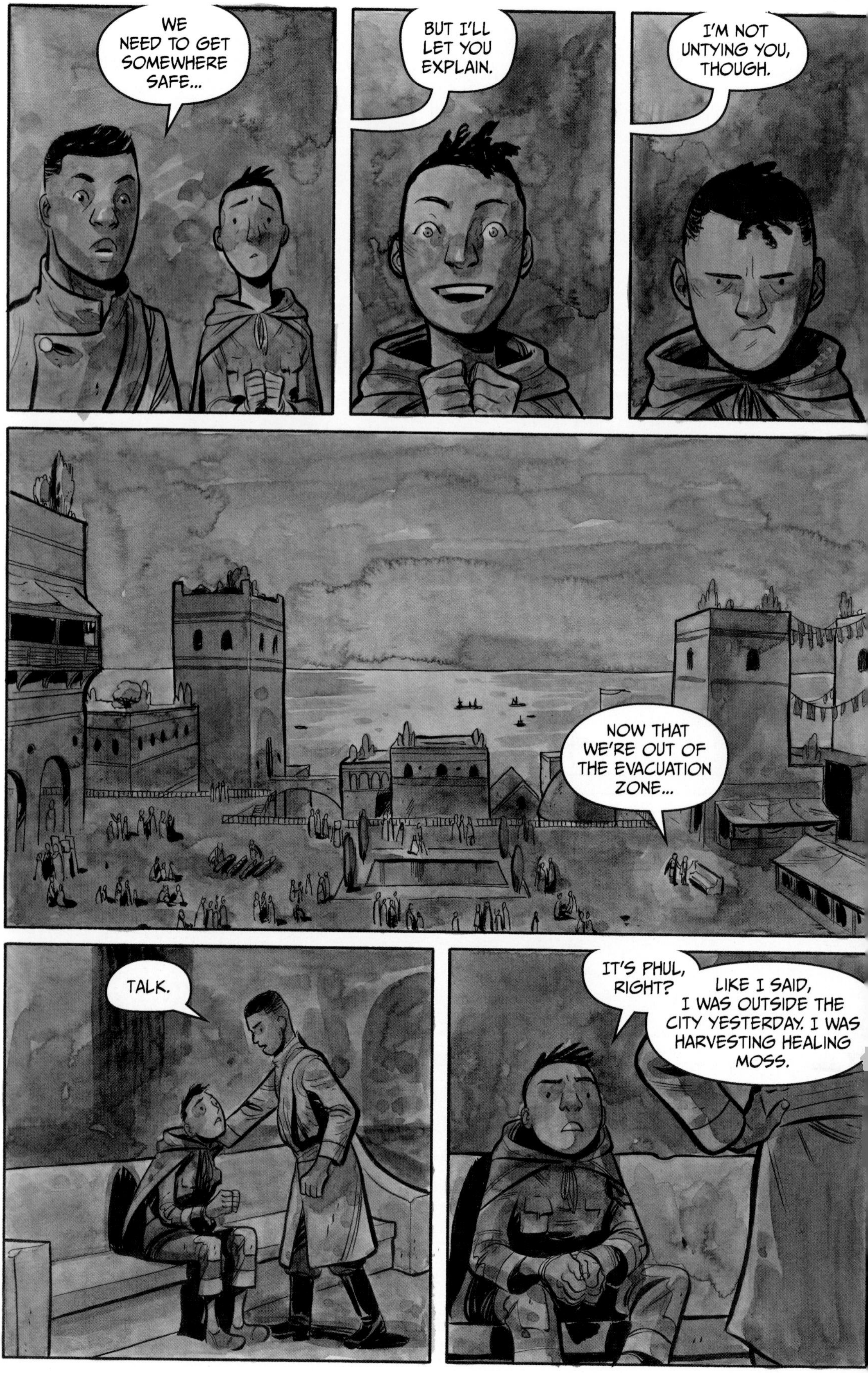
WE NEED TO GET SOMEWHERE SAFE...
BUT I'LL LET YOU EXPLAIN.
I'M NOT UNTYING YOU, THOUGH.
NOW THAT WE'RE OUT OF THE EVACUATION ZONE...
TALK.
IT'S PHUL, RIGHT?
LIKE I SAID, I WAS OUTSIDE THE CITY YESTERDAY. I WAS HARVESTING HEALING MOSS.

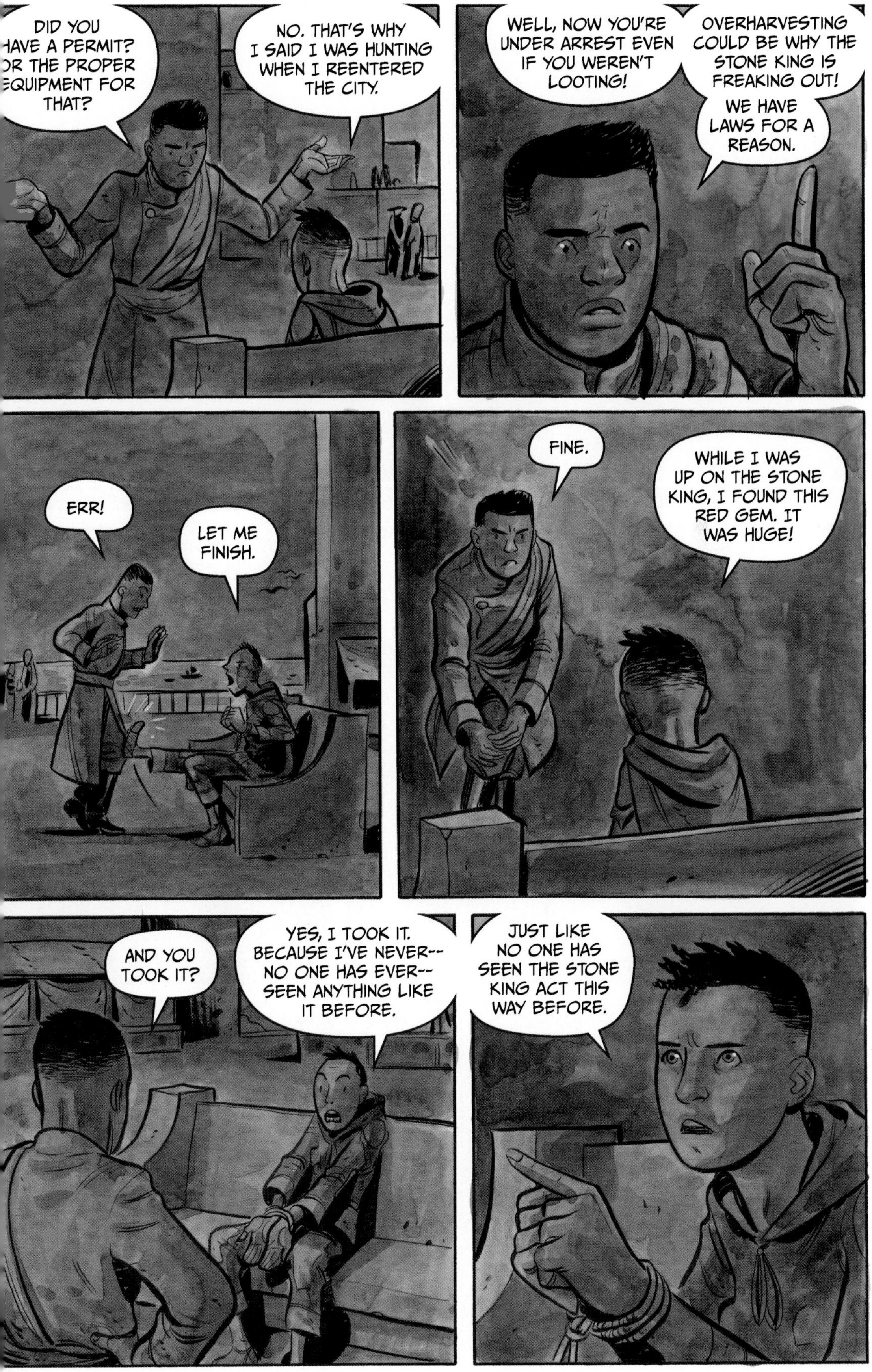
DID YOU HAVE A PERMIT? OR THE PROPER EQUIPMENT FOR THAT?
NO. THAT'S WHY I SAID I WAS HUNTING WHEN I REENTERED THE CITY.
WELL, NOW YOU'RE UNDER ARREST EVEN IF YOU WEREN'T LOOTING!
OVERHARVESTING COULD BE WHY THE STONE KING IS FREAKING OUT!
WE HAVE LAWS FOR A REASON.
ERR!
LET ME FINISH.
FINE.
WHILE I WAS UP ON THE STONE KING, I FOUND THIS RED GEM. IT WAS HUGE!
AND YOU TOOK IT?
YES, I TOOK IT. BECAUSE I'VE NEVER-- NO ONE HAS EVER-- SEEN ANYTHING LIKE IT BEFORE.
JUST LIKE NO ONE HAS SEEN THE STONE KING ACT THIS WAY BEFORE.

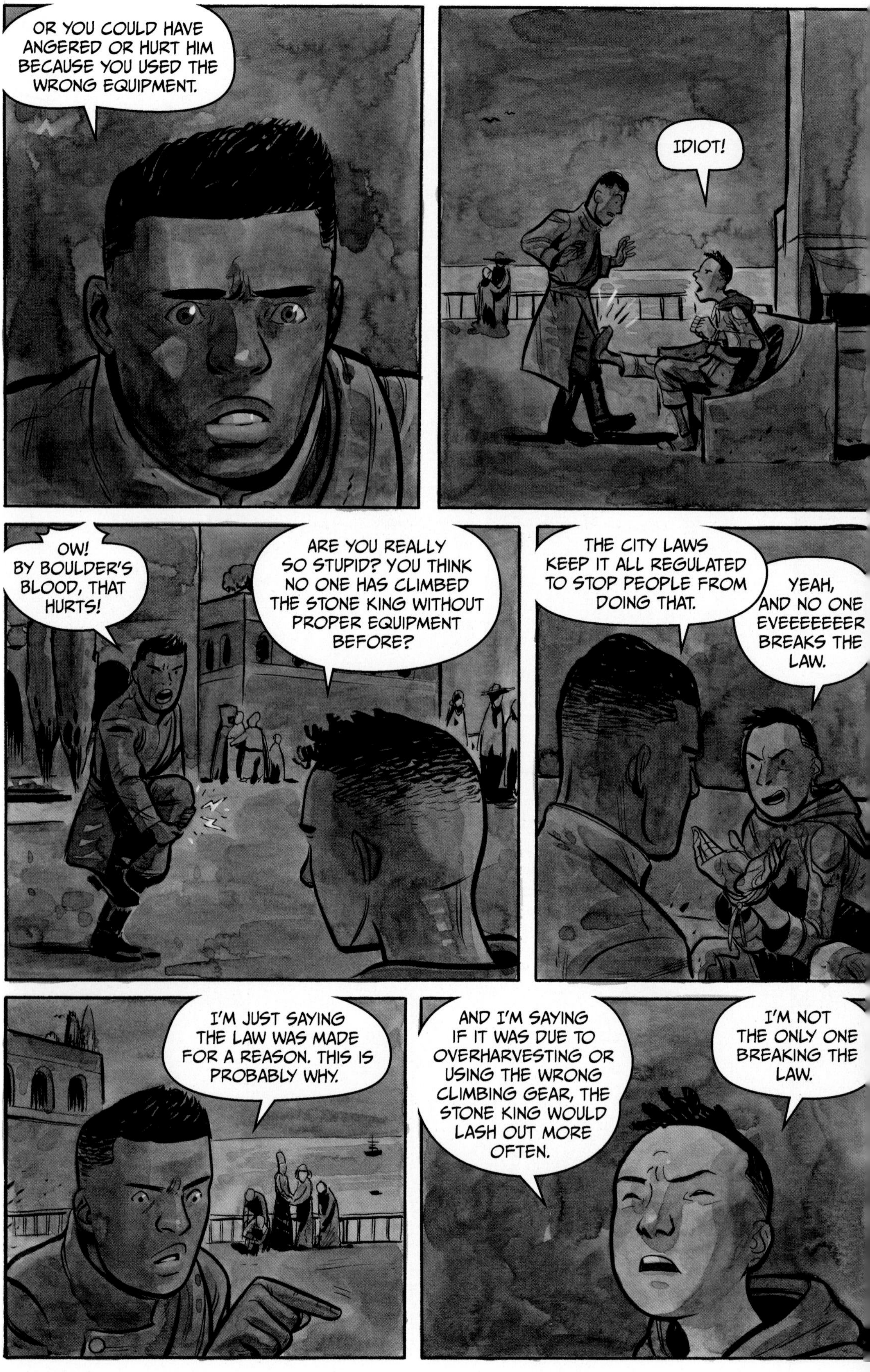
OR YOU COULD HAVE ANGERED OR HURT HIM BECAUSE YOU USED THE WRONG EQUIPMENT.
IDIOT!
OW! BY BOULDER'S BLOOD, THAT HURTS!
ARE YOU REALLY SO STUPID? YOU THINK NO ONE HAS CLIMBED THE STONE KING WITHOUT PROPER EQUIPMENT BEFORE?
THE CITY LAWS KEEP IT ALL REGULATED TO STOP PEOPLE FROM DOING THAT.
YEAH, AND NO ONE EVEEEEEEER BREAKS THE LAW.
I'M JUST SAYING THE LAW WAS MADE FOR A REASON. THIS IS PROBABLY WHY.
AND I'M SAYING IF IT WAS DUE TO OVERHARVESTING OR USING THE WRONG CLIMBING GEAR, THE STONE KING WOULD LASH OUT MORE OFTEN.
I'M NOT THE ONLY ONE BREAKING THE LAW.

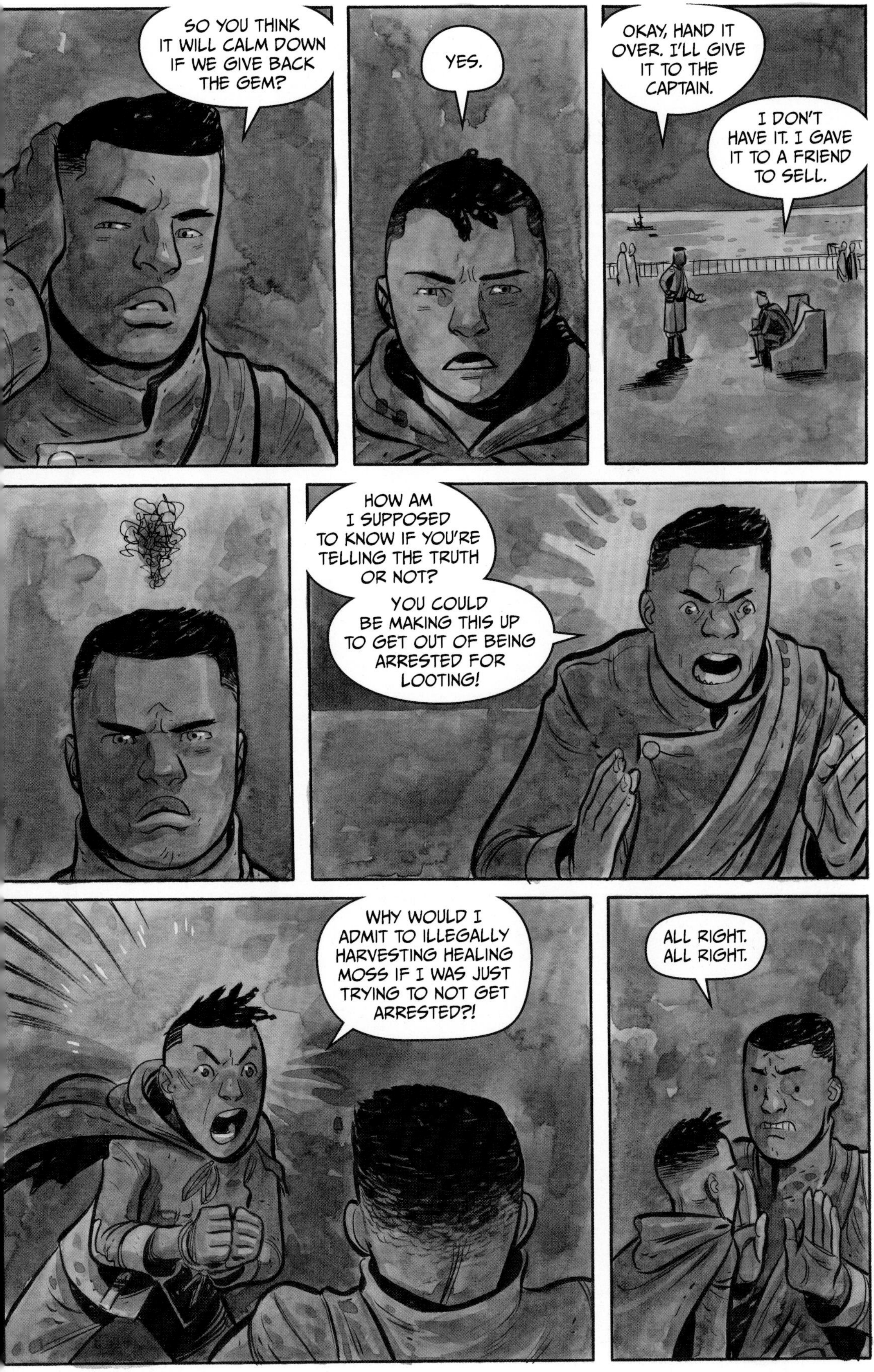
SO YOU THINK IT WILL CALM DOWN IF WE GIVE BACK THE GEM?
YES.
OKAY, HAND IT OVER. I'LL GIVE IT TO THE CAPTAIN.
I DON'T HAVE IT. I GAVE IT TO A FRIEND TO SELL.
HOW AM I SUPPOSED TO KNOW IF YOU'RE TELLING THE TRUTH OR NOT?
YOU COULD BE MAKING THIS UP TO GET OUT OF BEING ARRESTED FOR LOOTING!
WHY WOULD I ADMIT TO ILLEGALLY HARVESTING HEALING MOSS IF I WAS JUST TRYING TO NOT GET ARRESTED?!
ALL RIGHT. ALL RIGHT.

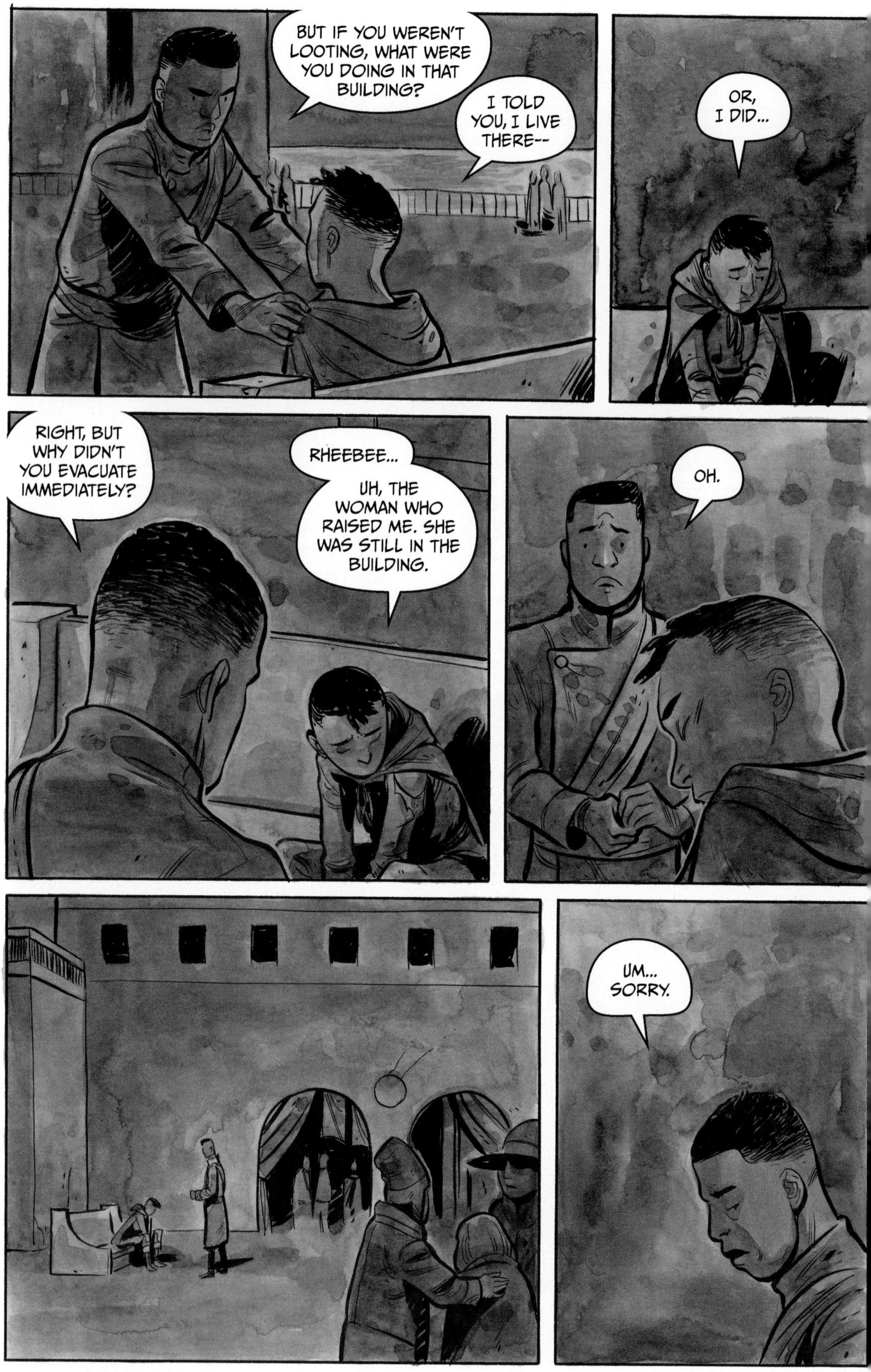
BUT IF YOU WEREN'T LOOTING, WHAT WERE YOU DOING IN THAT BUILDING?
I TOLD YOU, I LIVE THERE--
OR, I DID...
RIGHT, BUT WHY DIDN'T YOU EVACUATE IMMEDIATELY?
RHEEBEE...
UH, THE WOMAN WHO RAISED ME. SHE WAS STILL IN THE BUILDING.
OH.
UM... SORRY.

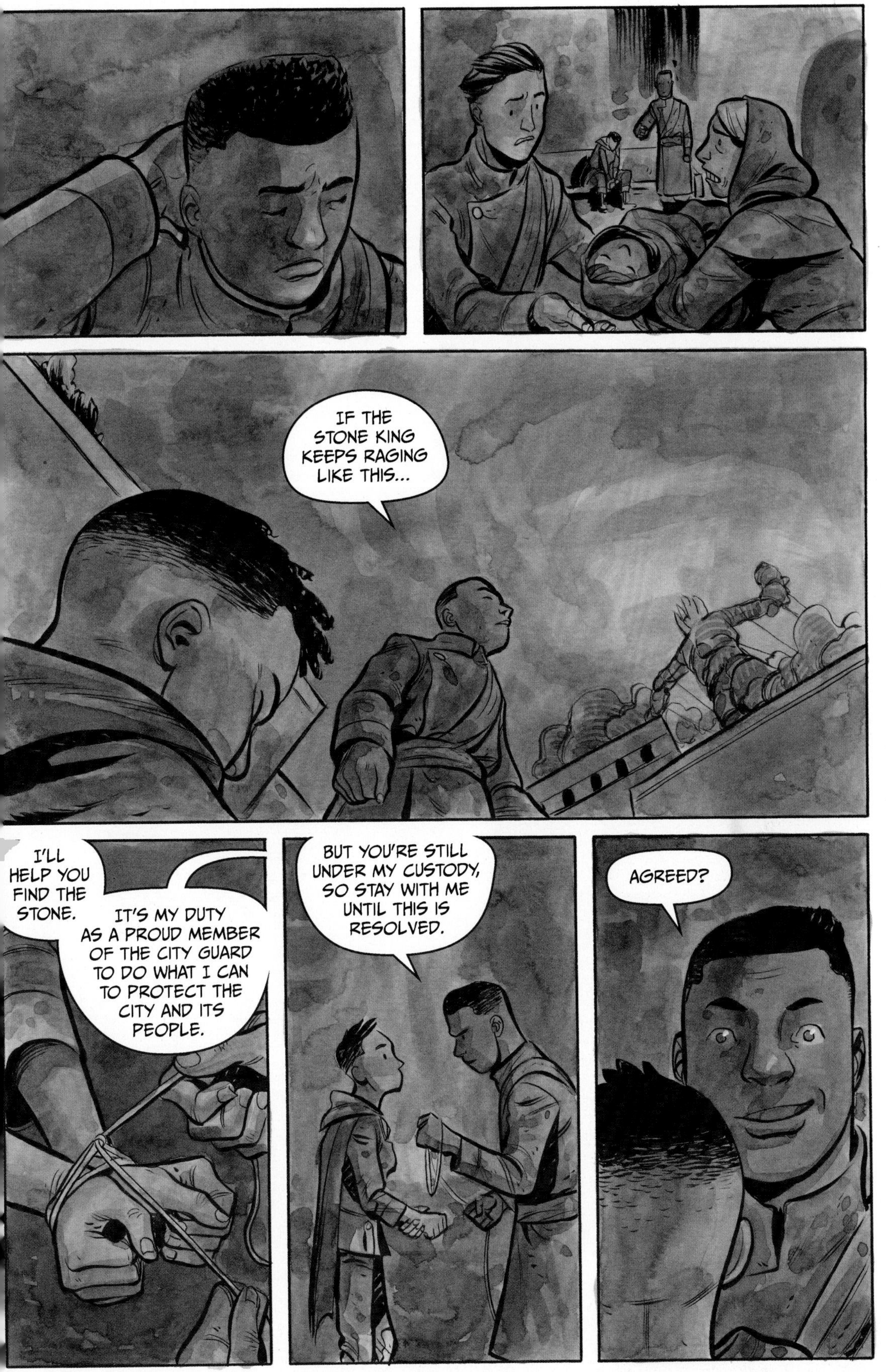

IF THE STONE KING KEEPS RAGING LIKE THIS...
I'LL HELP YOU FIND THE STONE.
IT'S MY DUTY AS A PROUD MEMBER OF THE CITY GUARD TO DO WHAT I CAN TO PROTECT THE CITY AND ITS PEOPLE.
BUT YOU'RE STILL UNDER MY CUSTODY, SO STAY WITH ME UNTIL THIS IS RESOLVED.
AGREED?

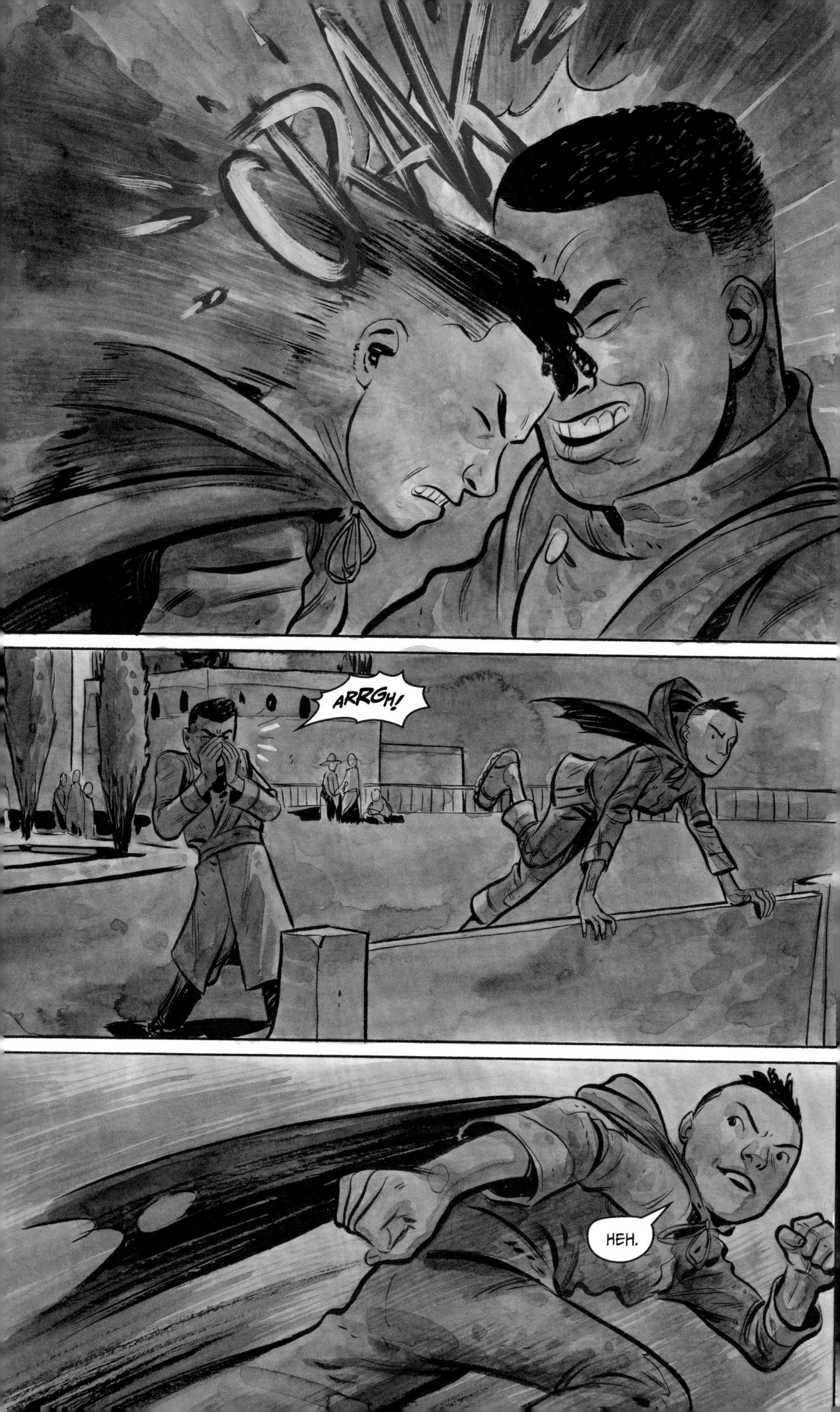
ARRGH!
HEH.

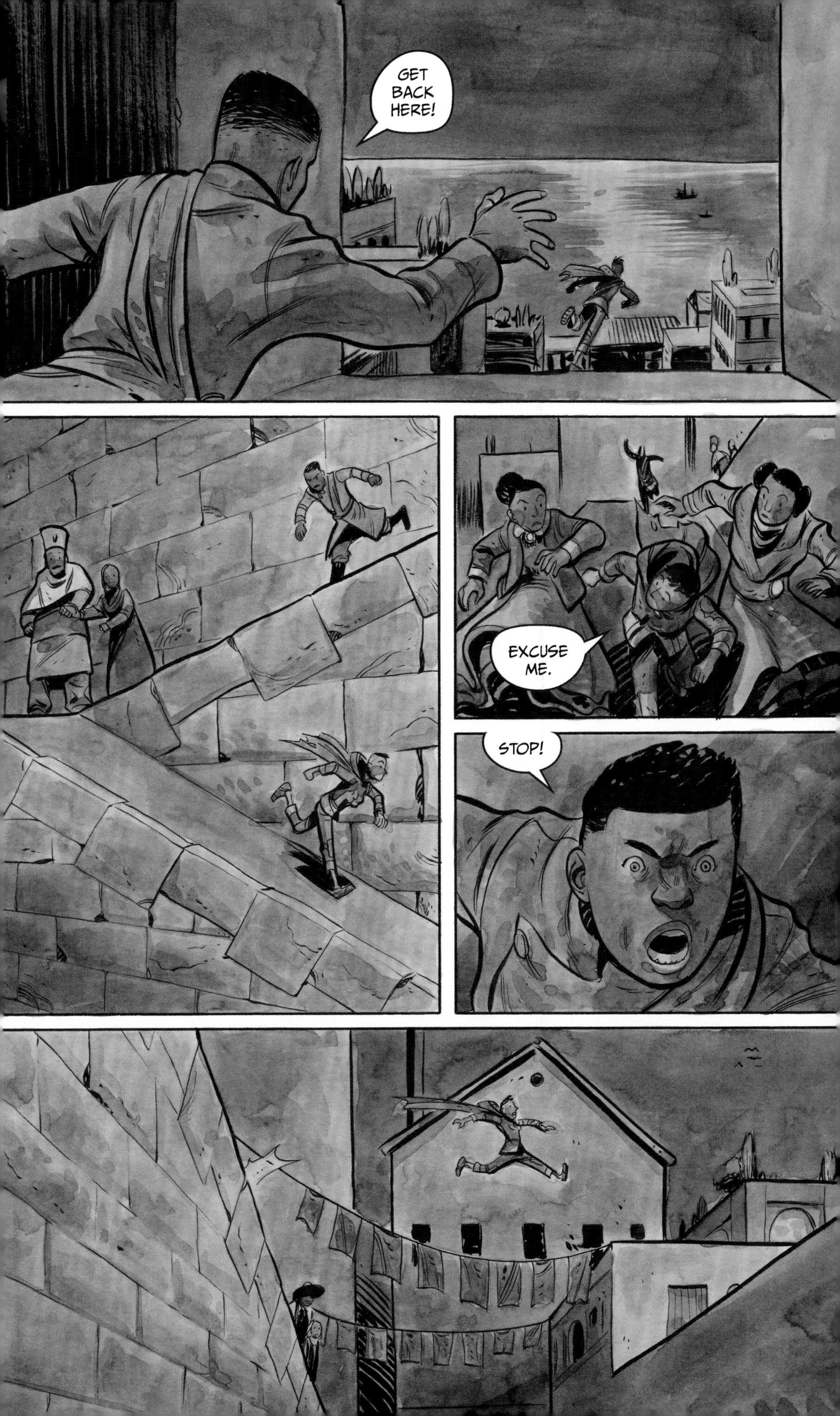
GET BACK HERE!
EXCUSE ME.
STOP!

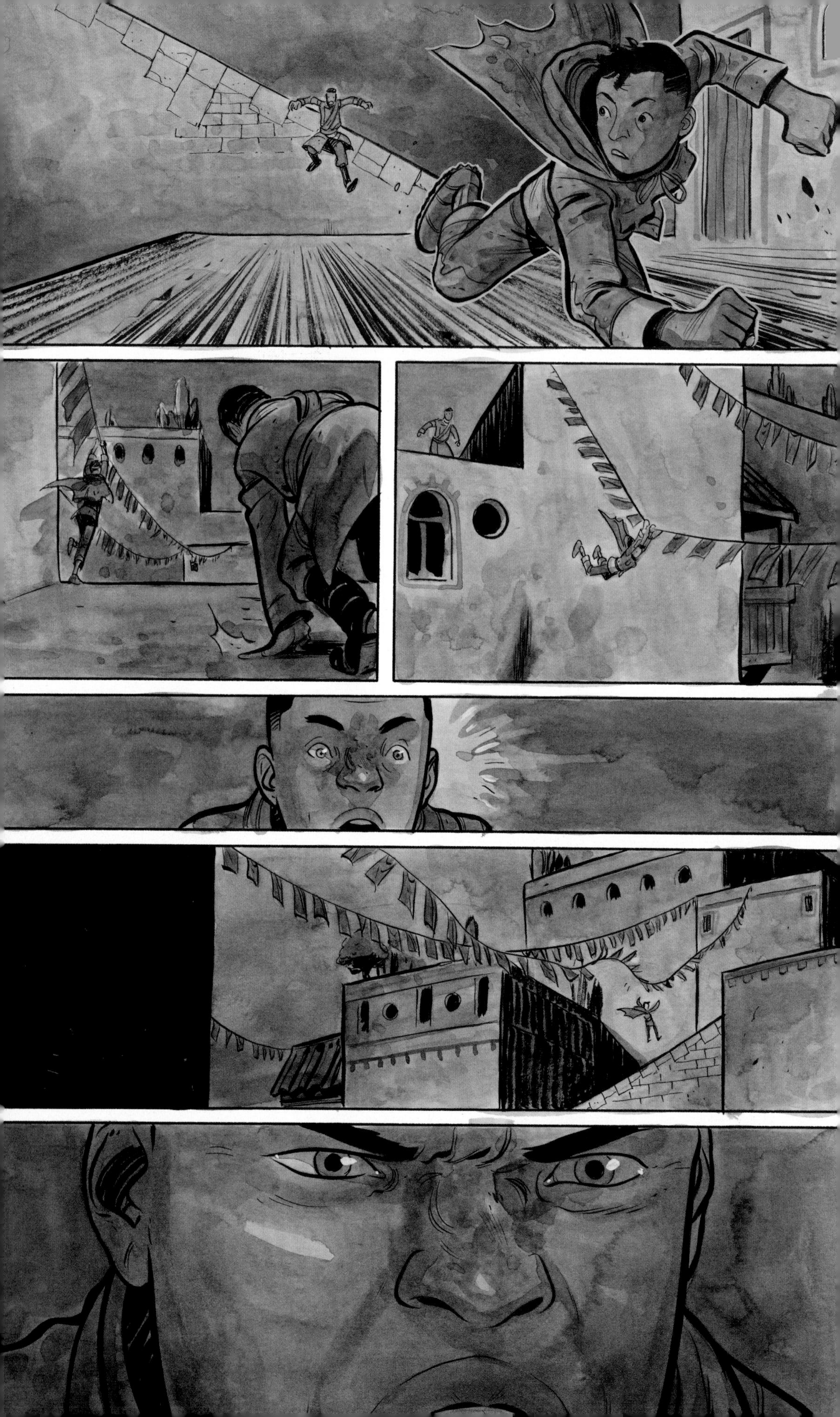

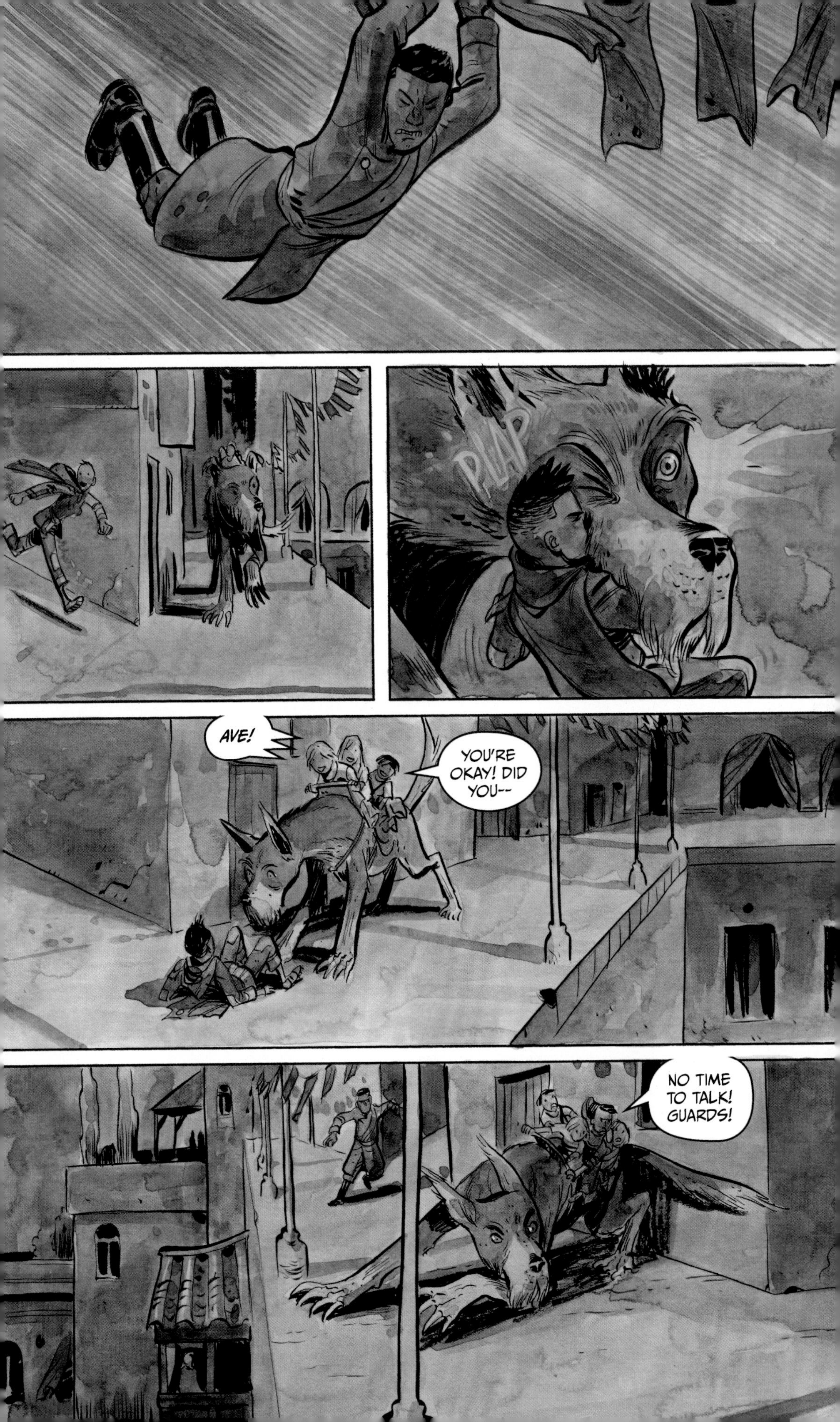
PLAP
AVE!
YOU'RE OKAY! DID YOU--
NO TIME TO TALK! GUARDS!

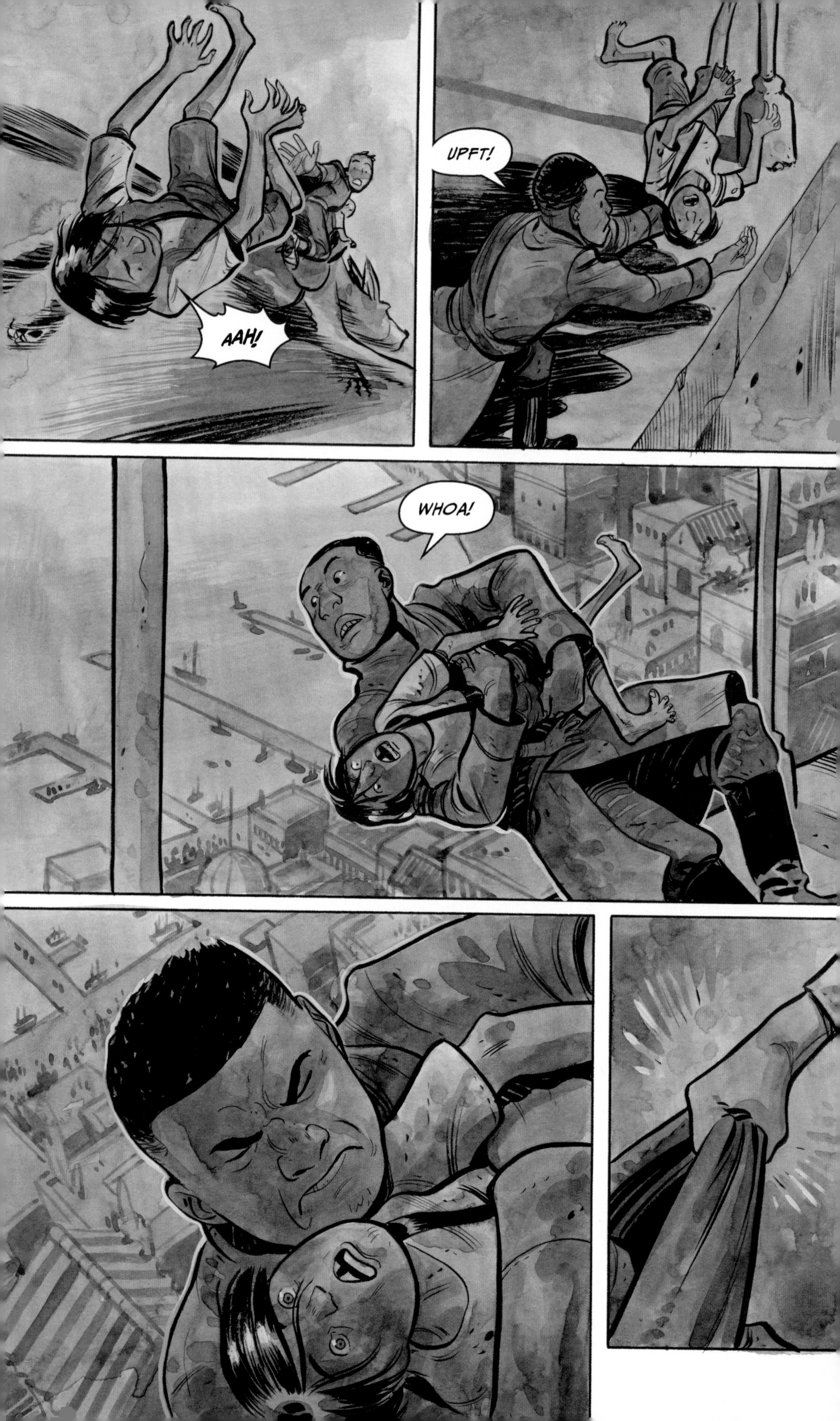
AAH!
UPFT!
WHOA!

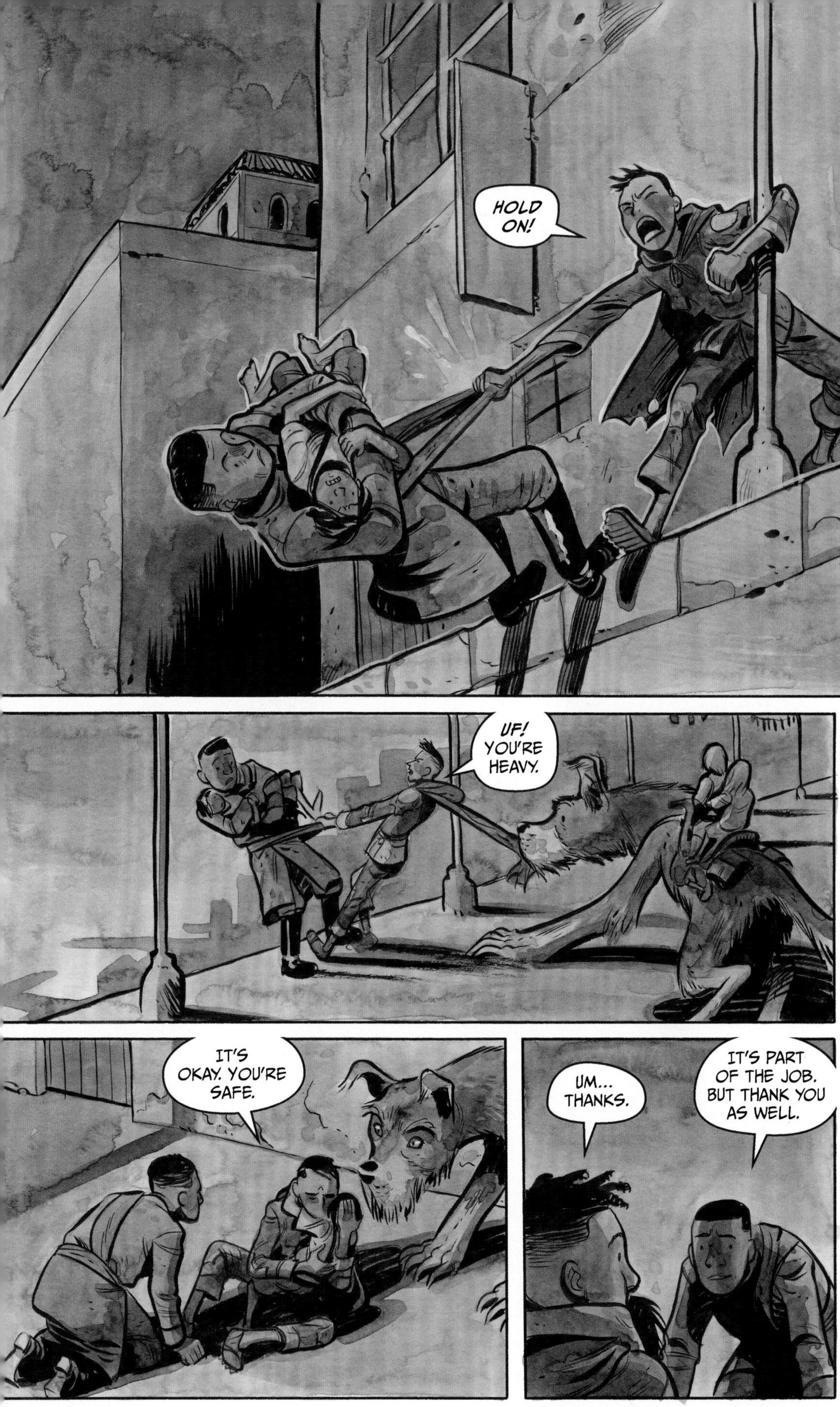
HOLD ON!
UF! YOU'RE HEAVY.
IT'S OKAY. YOU'RE SAFE.
UM... THANKS.
IT'S PART OF THE JOB. BUT THANK YOU AS WELL.

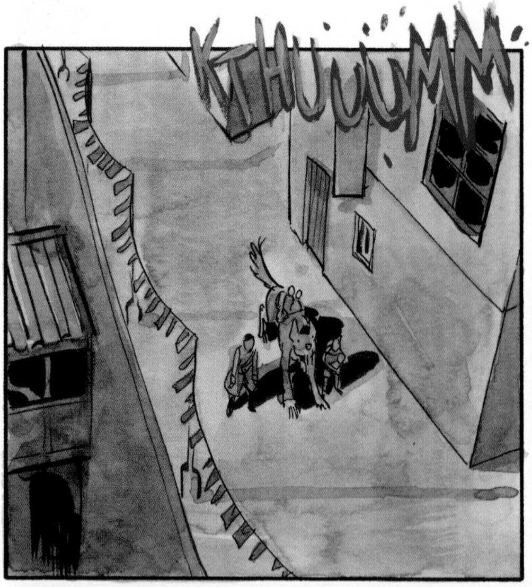
KTHUUUMM

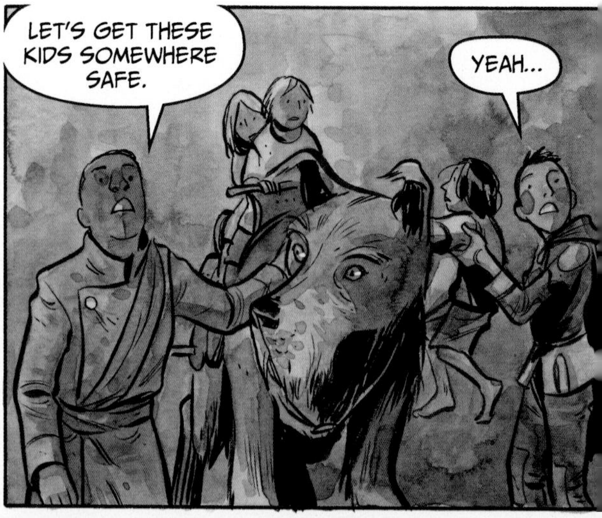
LET'S GET THESE KIDS SOMEWHERE SAFE.
YEAH...

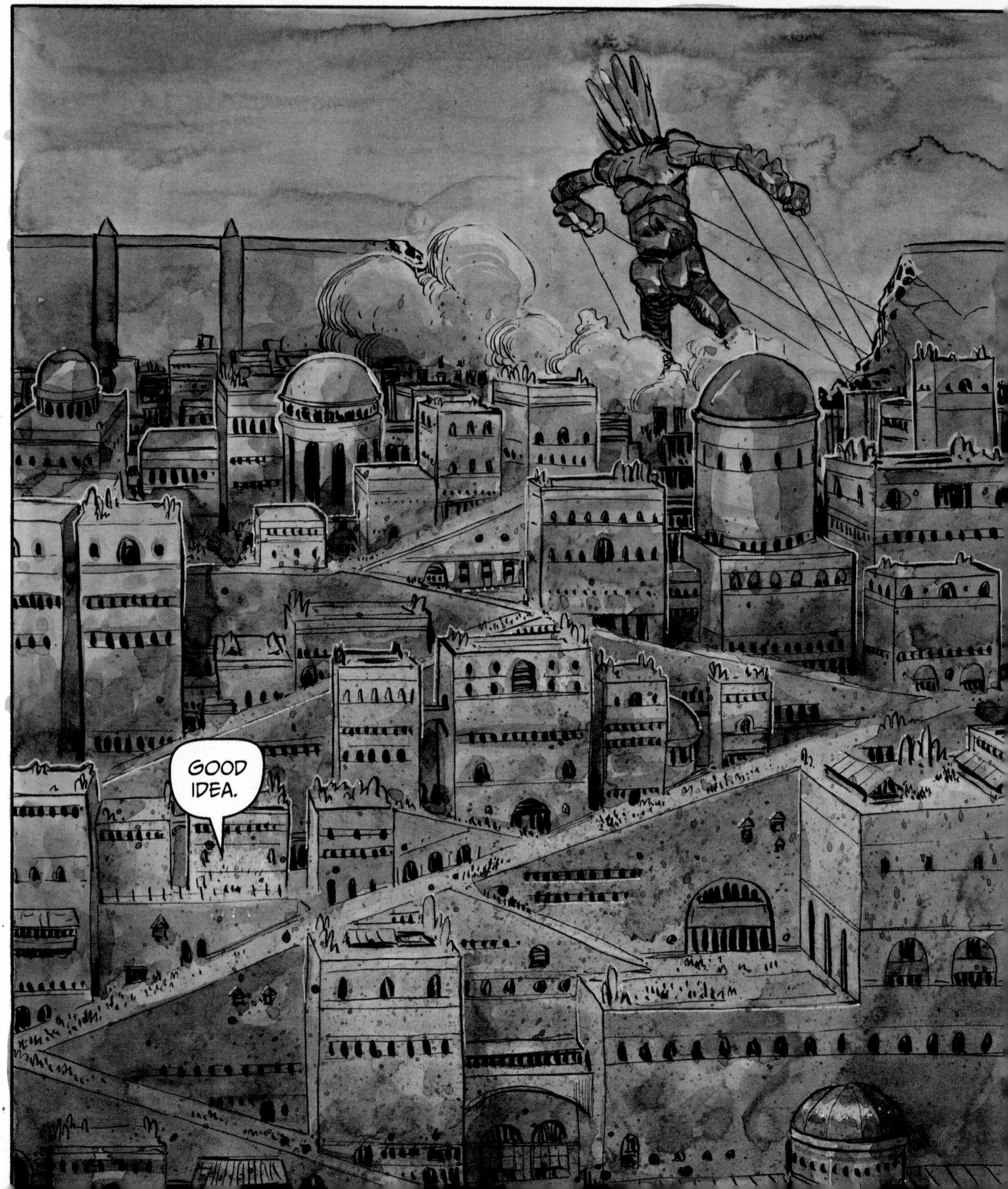
GOOD IDEA.

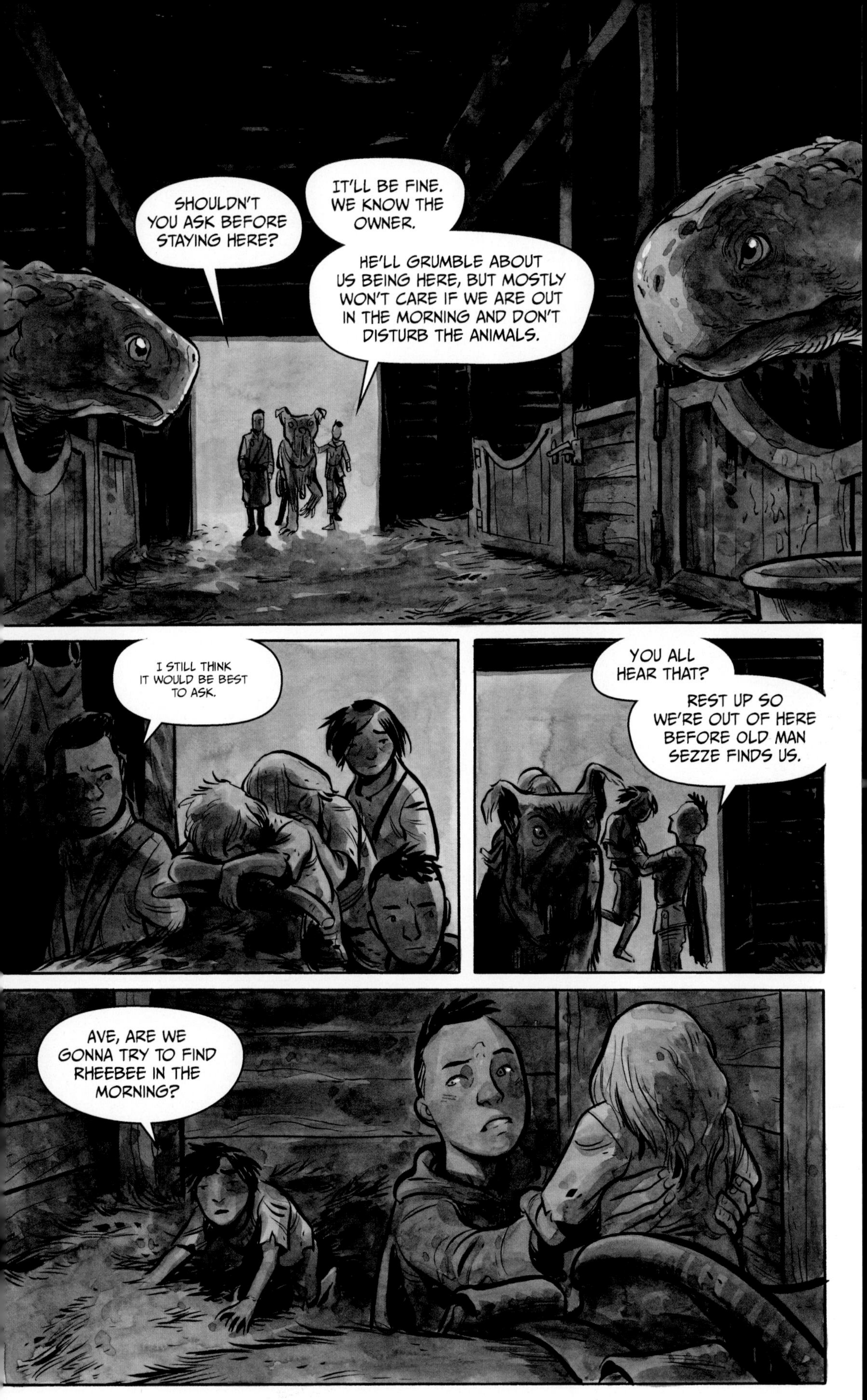
SHOULDN'T YOU ASK BEFORE STAYING HERE?
IT'LL BE FINE. WE KNOW THE OWNER.
HE'LL GRUMBLE ABOUT US BEING HERE, BUT MOSTLY WON'T CARE IF WE ARE OUT IN THE MORNING AND DON'T DISTURB THE ANIMALS.
I STILL THINK IT WOULD BE BEST TO ASK.
YOU ALL HEAR THAT?
REST UP SO WE'RE OUT OF HERE BEFORE OLD MAN SEZZE FINDS US.
AVE, ARE WE GONNA TRY TO FIND RHEEBEE IN THE MORNING?

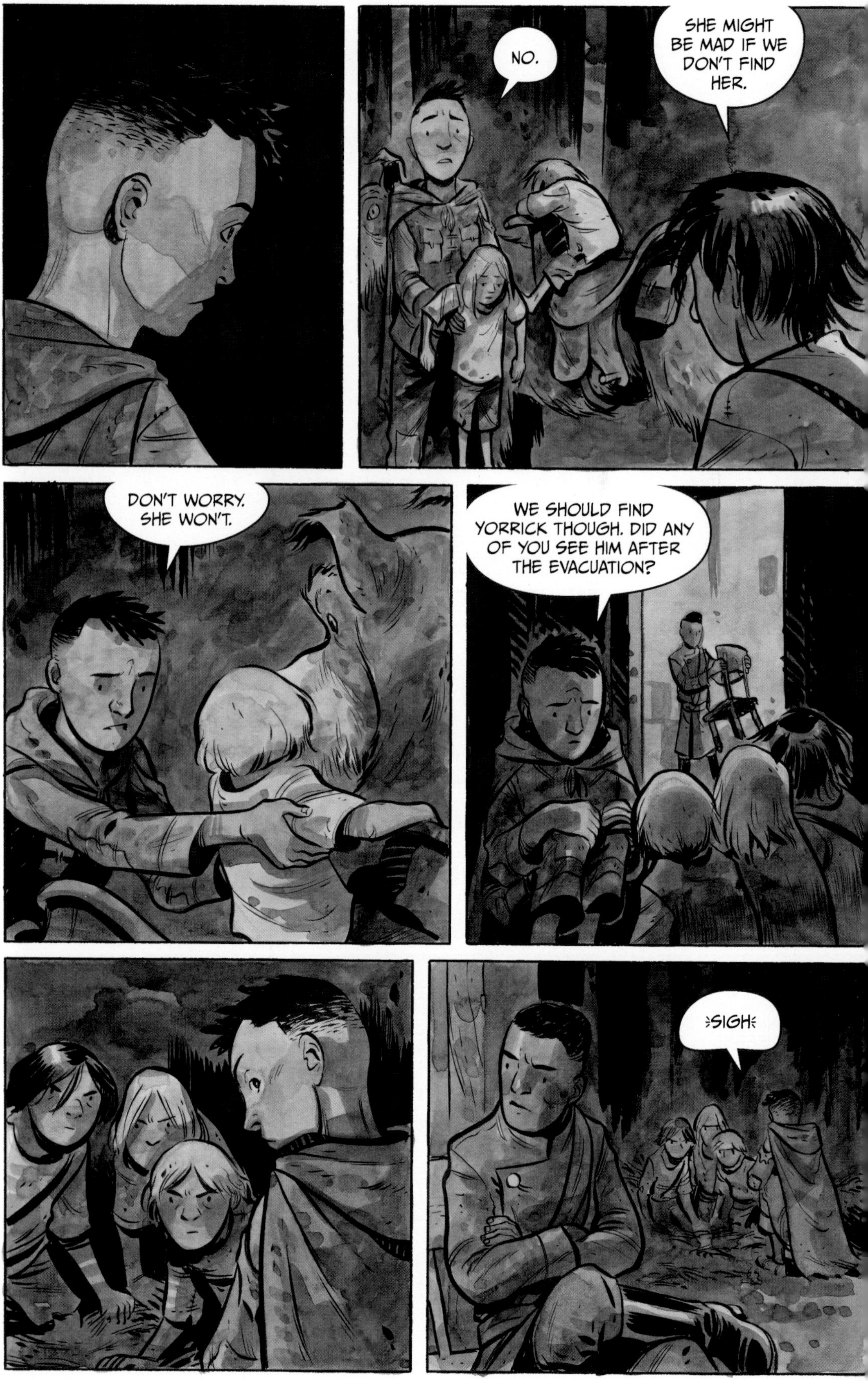
NO.
SHE MIGHT BE MAD IF WE DON'T FIND HER.
DON'T WORRY. SHE WON'T.
WE SHOULD FIND YORRICK THOUGH. DID ANY OF YOU SEE HIM AFTER THE EVACUATION?
SIGH

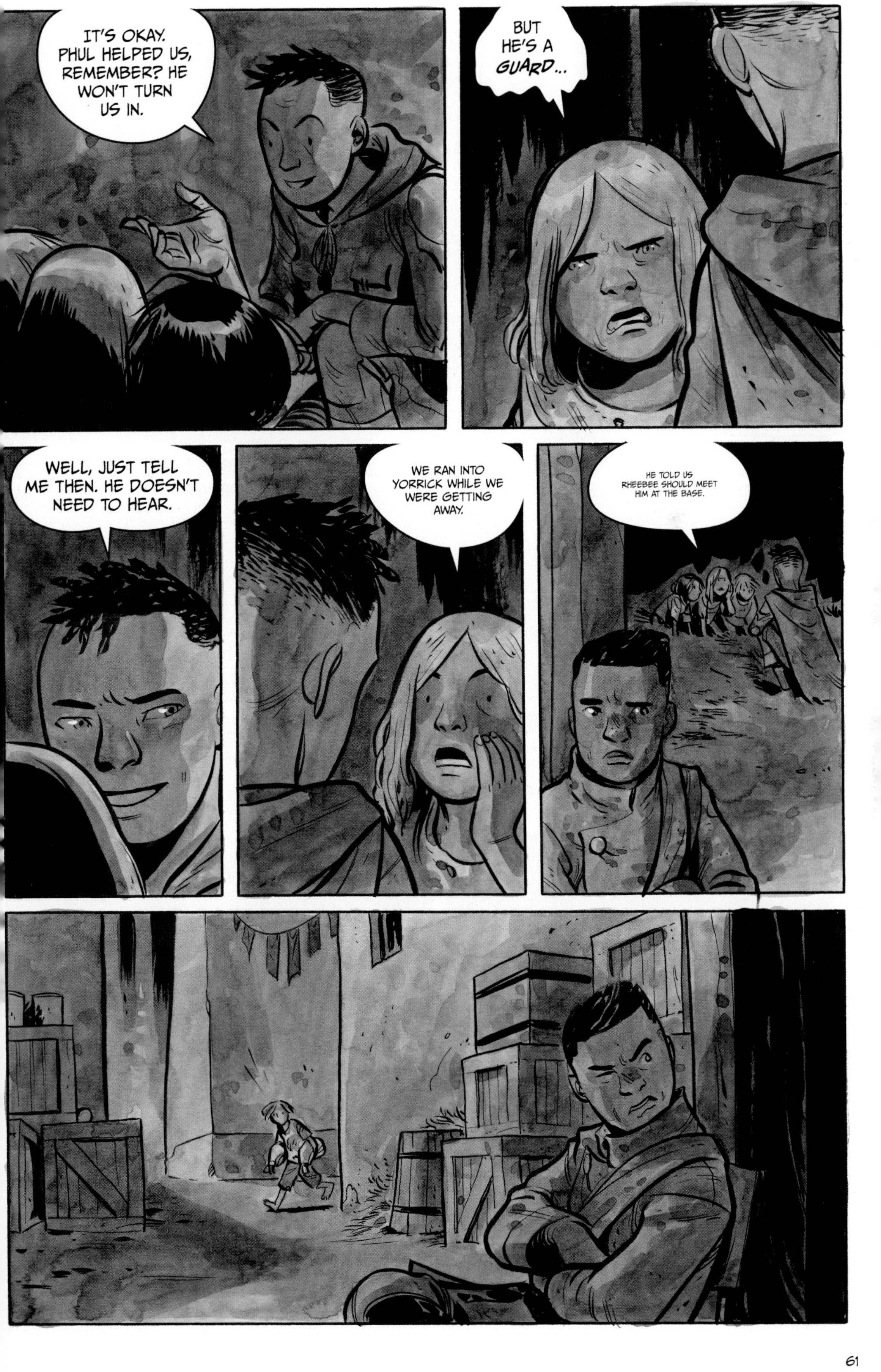
IT'S OKAY. PHUL HELPED US, REMEMBER? HE WON'T TURN US IN.
BUT HE'S A *GUARD*...
WELL, JUST TELL ME THEN. HE DOESN'T NEED TO HEAR.
WE RAN INTO YORRICK WHILE WE WERE GETTING AWAY.
HE TOLD US RHEEBEE SHOULD MEET HIM AT THE BASE.

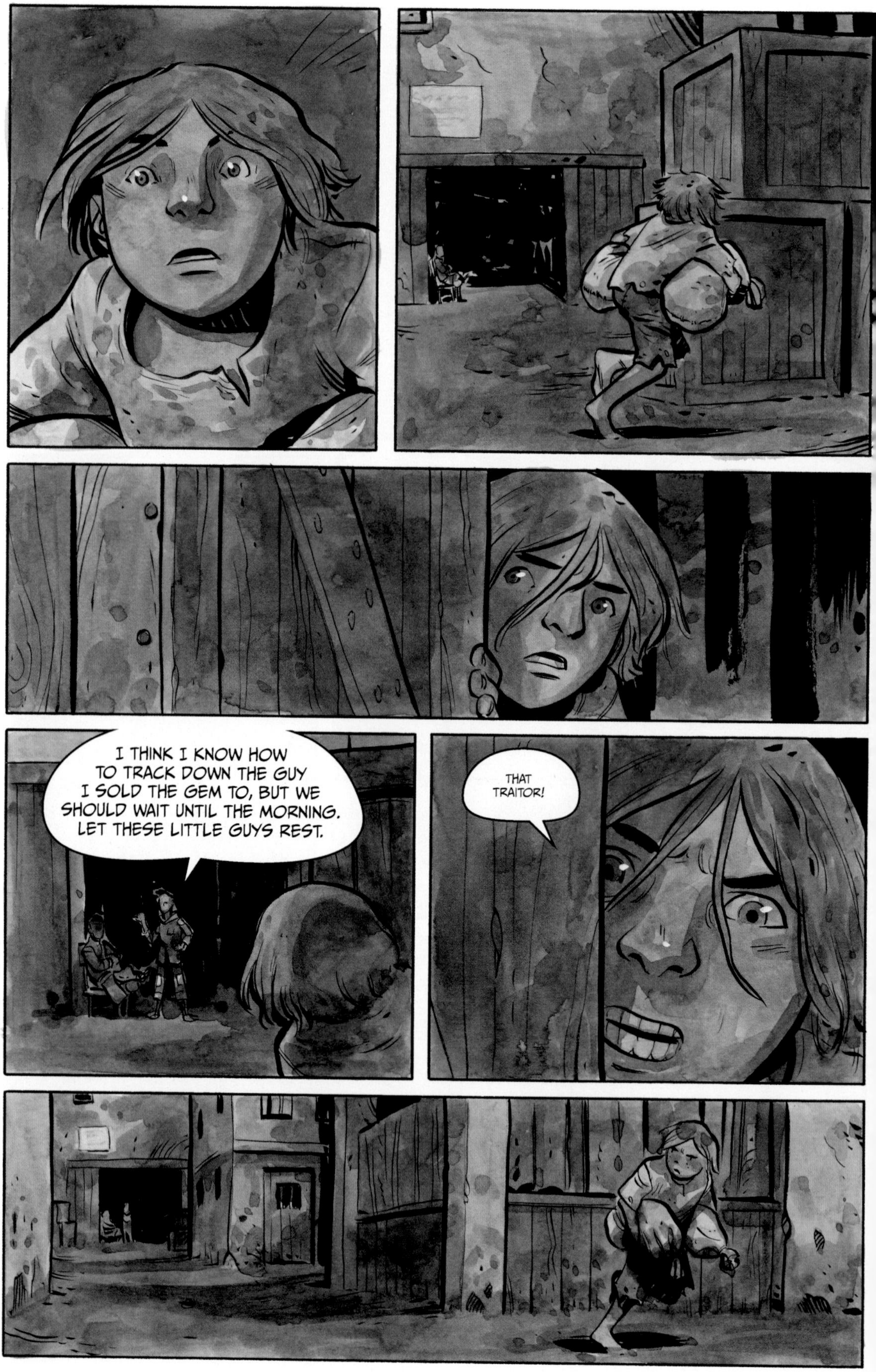
I THINK I KNOW HOW TO TRACK DOWN THE GUY I SOLD THE GEM TO, BUT WE SHOULD WAIT UNTIL THE MORNING. LET THESE LITTLE GUYS REST.
THAT TRAITOR!

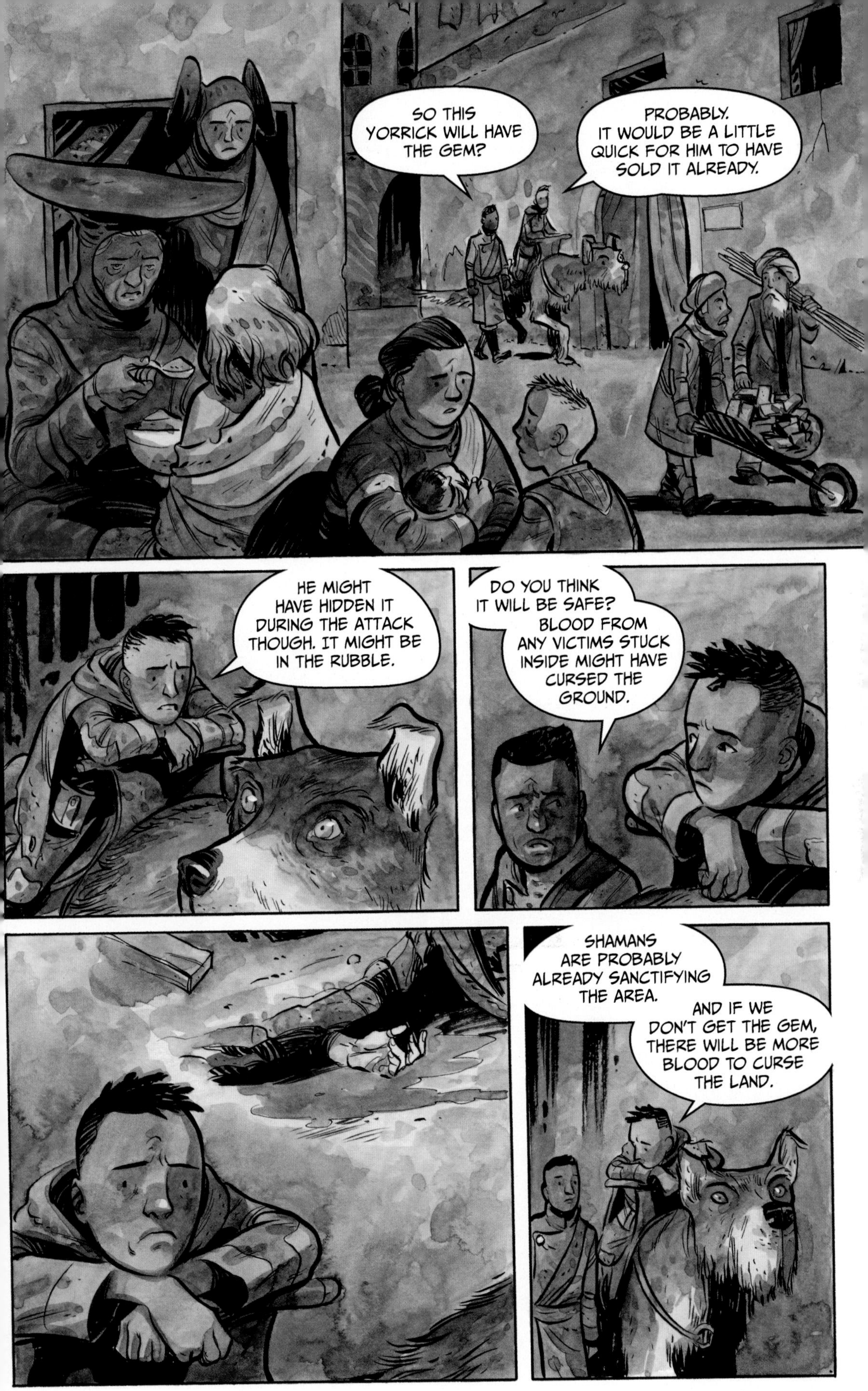
SO THIS YORRICK WILL HAVE THE GEM?
PROBABLY. IT WOULD BE A LITTLE QUICK FOR HIM TO HAVE SOLD IT ALREADY.
HE MIGHT HAVE HIDDEN IT DURING THE ATTACK THOUGH. IT MIGHT BE IN THE RUBBLE.
DO YOU THINK IT WILL BE SAFE?
BLOOD FROM ANY VICTIMS STUCK INSIDE MIGHT HAVE CURSED THE GROUND.
SHAMANS ARE PROBABLY ALREADY SANCTIFYING THE AREA.
AND IF WE DON'T GET THE GEM, THERE WILL BE MORE BLOOD TO CURSE THE LAND.

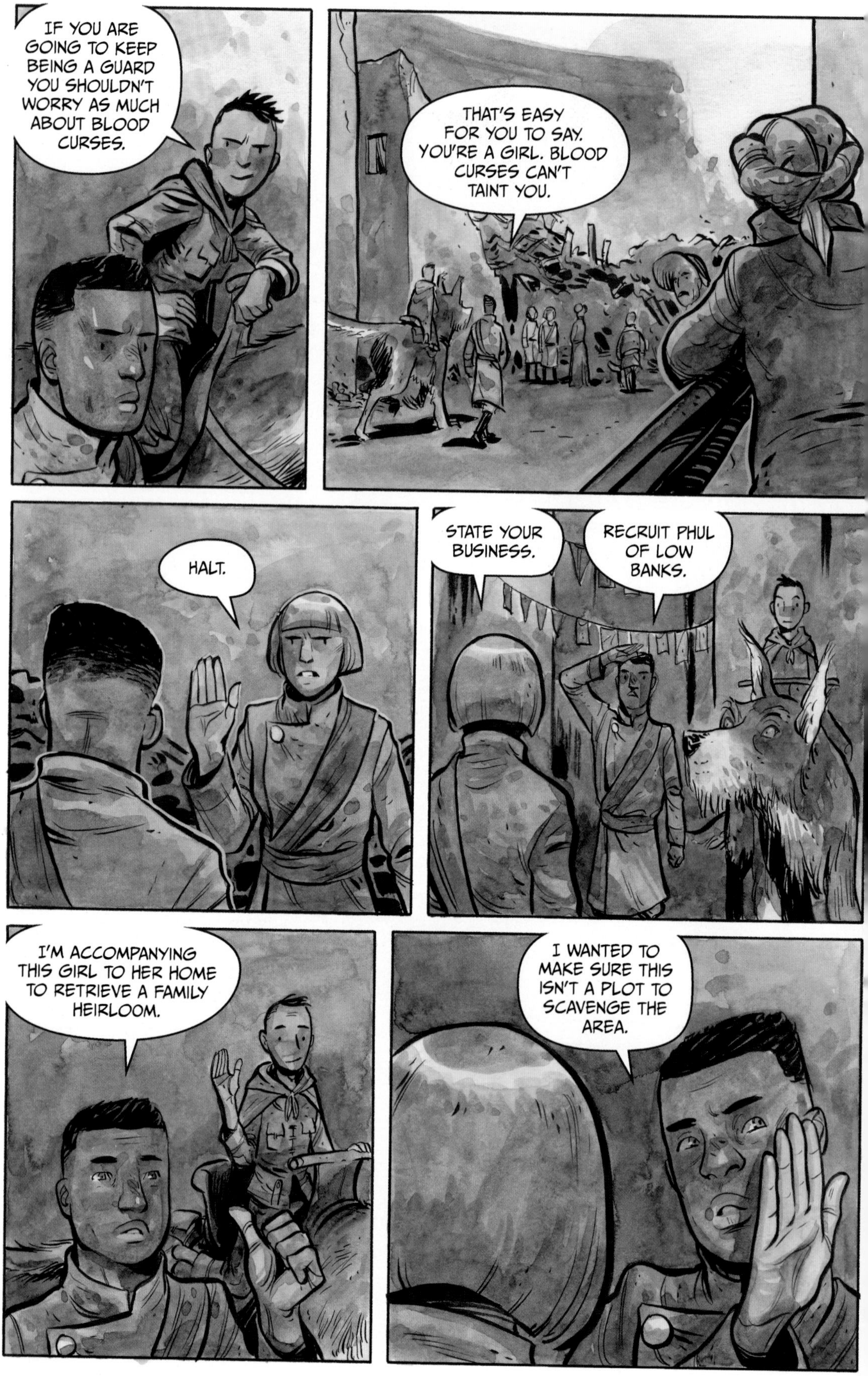
IF YOU ARE GOING TO KEEP BEING A GUARD YOU SHOULDN'T WORRY AS MUCH ABOUT BLOOD CURSES.
THAT'S EASY FOR YOU TO SAY. YOU'RE A GIRL. BLOOD CURSES CAN'T TAINT YOU.
HALT.
STATE YOUR BUSINESS.
RECRUIT PHUL OF LOW BANKS.
I'M ACCOMPANYING THIS GIRL TO HER HOME TO RETRIEVE A FAMILY HEIRLOOM.
I WANTED TO MAKE SURE THIS ISN'T A PLOT TO SCAVENGE THE AREA.

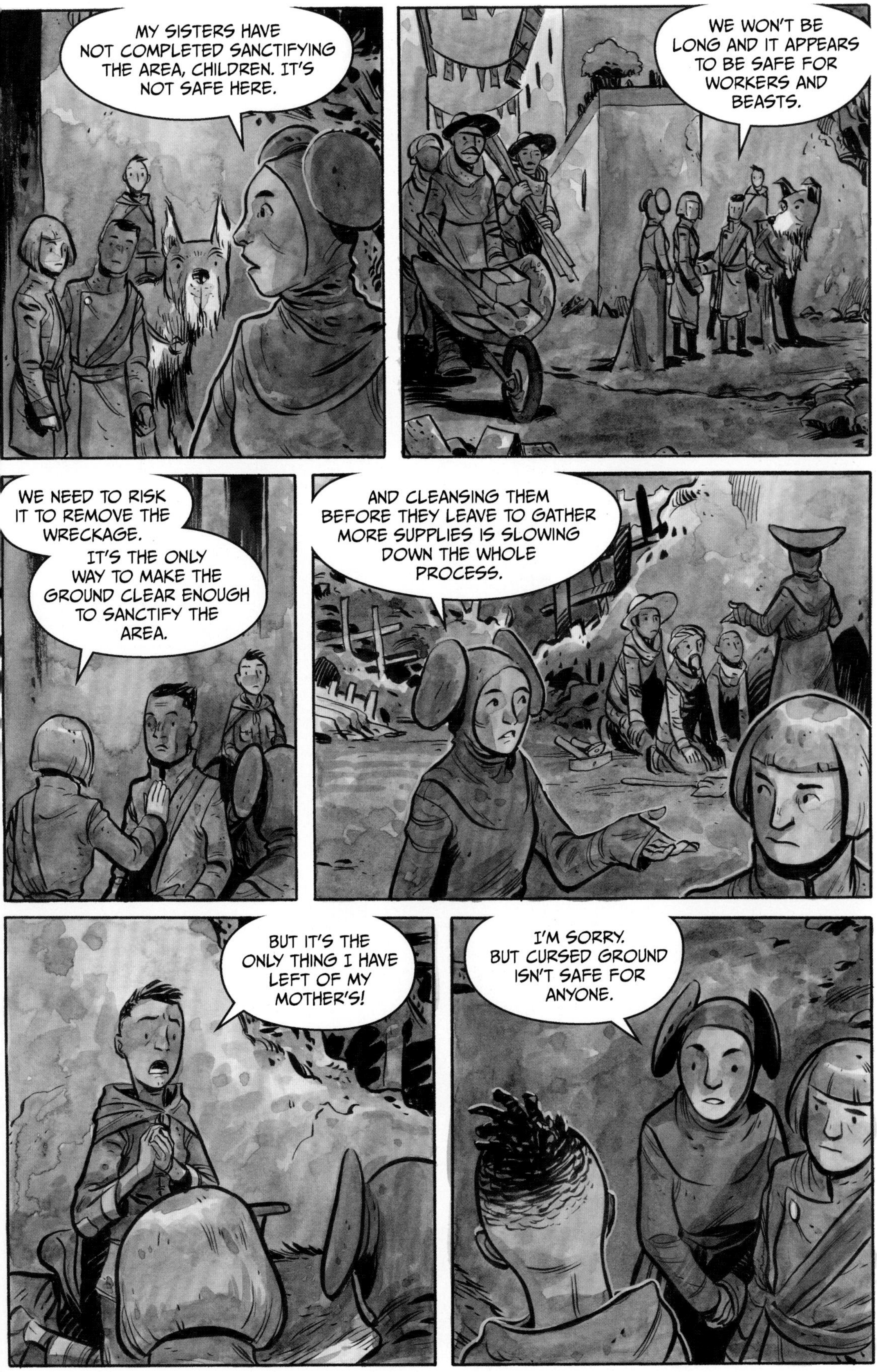
MY SISTERS HAVE NOT COMPLETED SANCTIFYING THE AREA, CHILDREN. IT'S NOT SAFE HERE.
WE WON'T BE LONG AND IT APPEARS TO BE SAFE FOR WORKERS AND BEASTS.
WE NEED TO RISK IT TO REMOVE THE WRECKAGE.
IT'S THE ONLY WAY TO MAKE THE GROUND CLEAR ENOUGH TO SANCTIFY THE AREA.
AND CLEANSING THEM BEFORE THEY LEAVE TO GATHER MORE SUPPLIES IS SLOWING DOWN THE WHOLE PROCESS.
BUT IT'S THE ONLY THING I HAVE LEFT OF MY MOTHER'S!
I'M SORRY. BUT CURSED GROUND ISN'T SAFE FOR ANYONE.

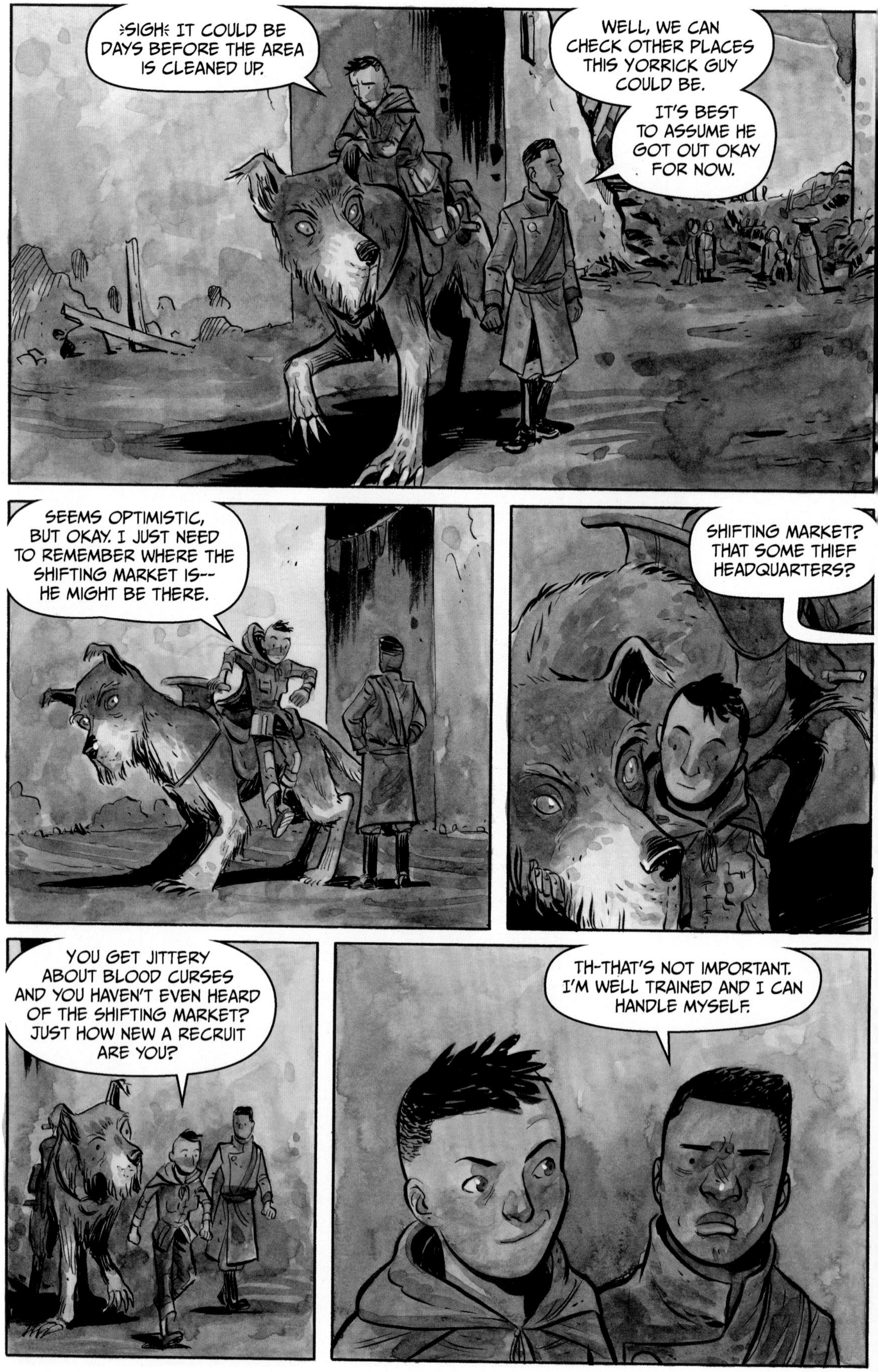

⁑SIGH⁑ IT COULD BE DAYS BEFORE THE AREA IS CLEANED UP.
WELL, WE CAN CHECK OTHER PLACES THIS YORRICK GUY COULD BE.
IT'S BEST TO ASSUME HE GOT OUT OKAY FOR NOW.
SEEMS OPTIMISTIC, BUT OKAY. I JUST NEED TO REMEMBER WHERE THE SHIFTING MARKET IS-- HE MIGHT BE THERE.
SHIFTING MARKET? THAT SOME THIEF HEADQUARTERS?
YOU GET JITTERY ABOUT BLOOD CURSES AND YOU HAVEN'T EVEN HEARD OF THE SHIFTING MARKET? JUST HOW NEW A RECRUIT ARE YOU?
TH-THAT'S NOT IMPORTANT. I'M WELL TRAINED AND I CAN HANDLE MYSELF.

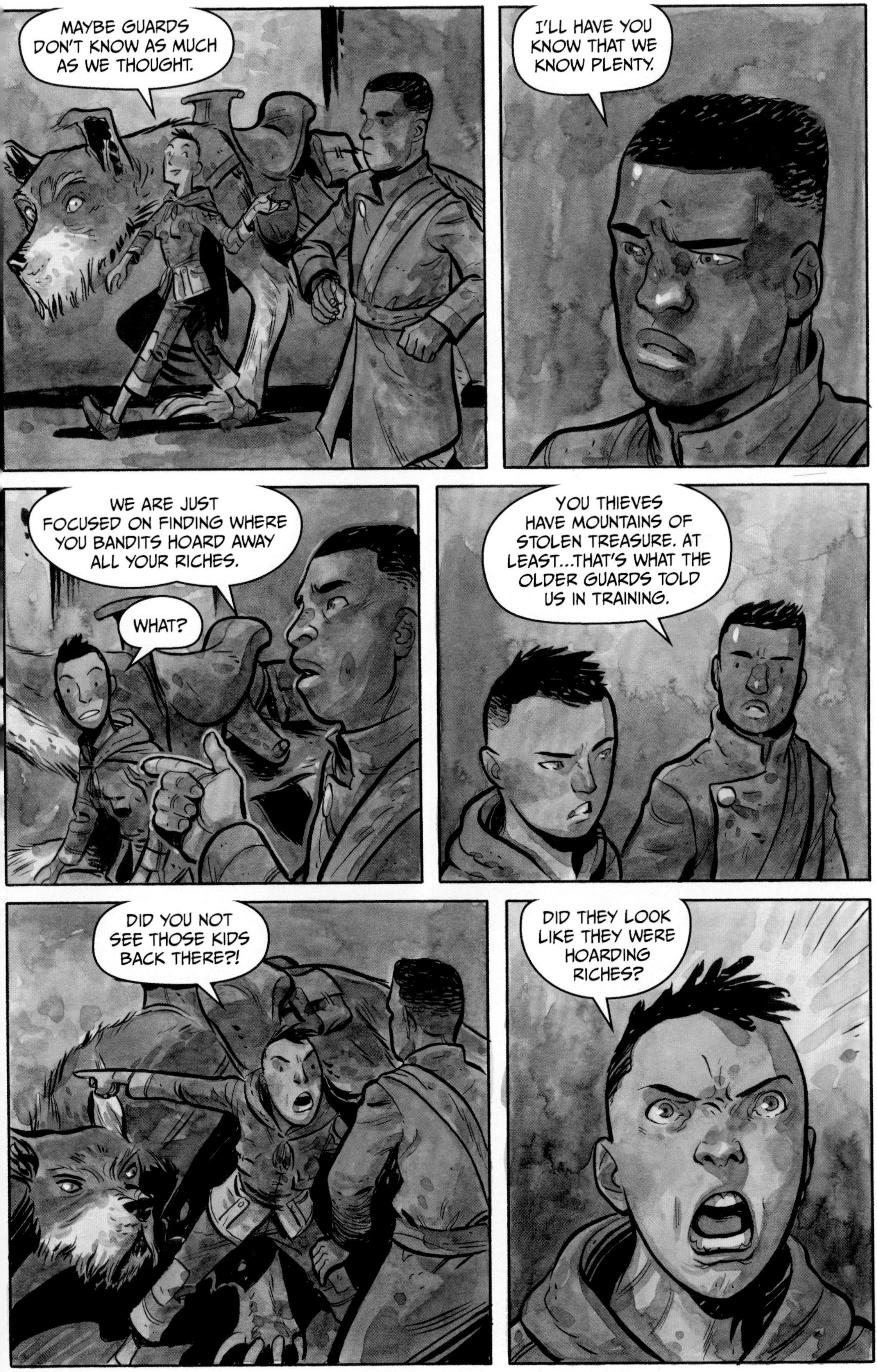
MAYBE GUARDS DON'T KNOW AS MUCH AS WE THOUGHT.
I'LL HAVE YOU KNOW THAT WE KNOW PLENTY.
WE ARE JUST FOCUSED ON FINDING WHERE YOU BANDITS HOARD AWAY ALL YOUR RICHES.
WHAT?
YOU THIEVES HAVE MOUNTAINS OF STOLEN TREASURE. AT LEAST...THAT'S WHAT THE OLDER GUARDS TOLD US IN TRAINING.
DID YOU NOT SEE THOSE KIDS BACK THERE?!
DID THEY LOOK LIKE THEY WERE HOARDING RICHES?

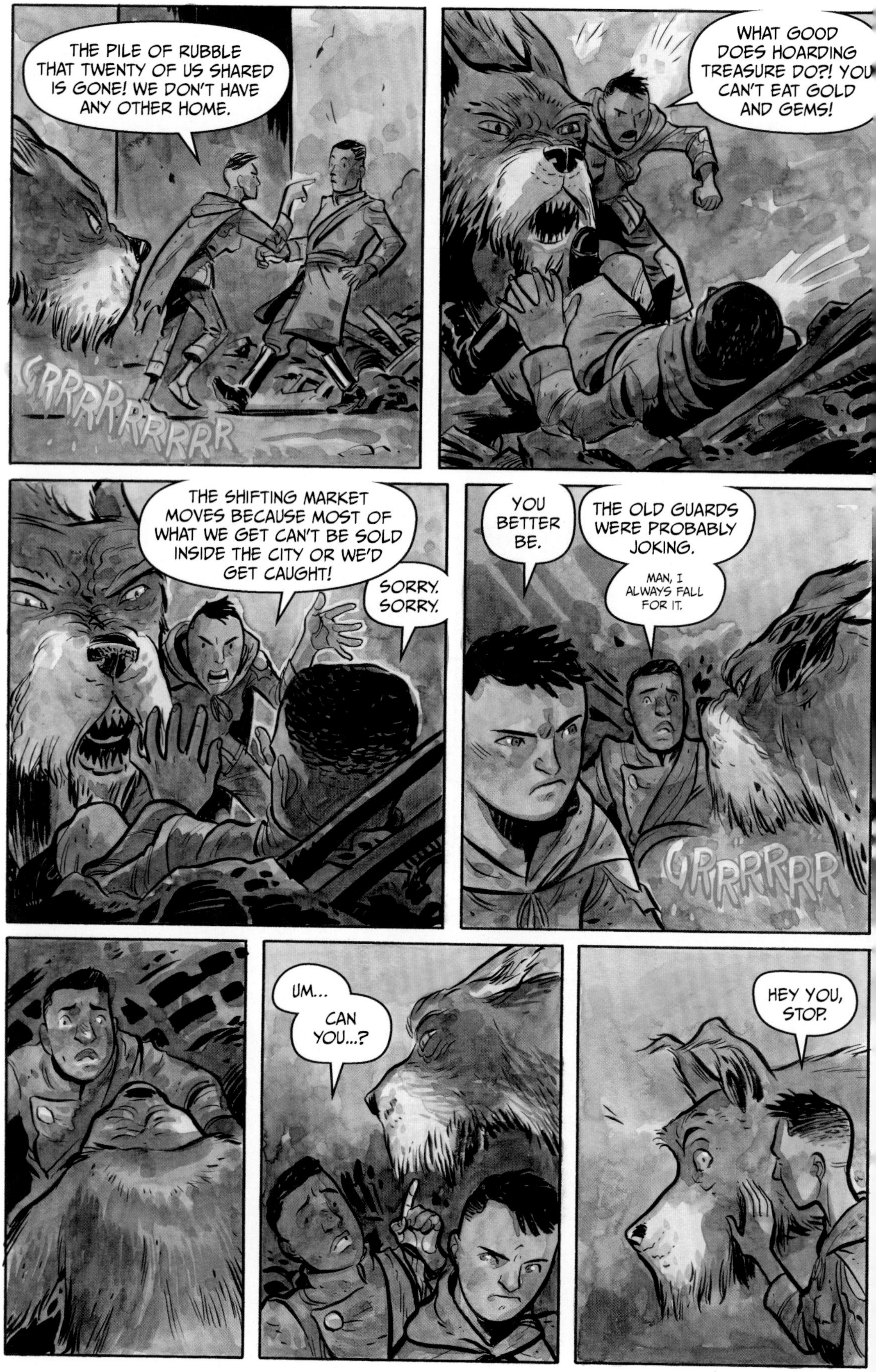
THE PILE OF RUBBLE THAT TWENTY OF US SHARED IS GONE! WE DON'T HAVE ANY OTHER HOME.
GRRRRRRRRRR
WHAT GOOD DOES HOARDING TREASURE DO?! YOU CAN'T EAT GOLD AND GEMS!
THE SHIFTING MARKET MOVES BECAUSE MOST OF WHAT WE GET CAN'T BE SOLD INSIDE THE CITY OR WE'D GET CAUGHT!
SORRY. SORRY.
YOU BETTER BE.
THE OLD GUARDS WERE PROBABLY JOKING.
MAN, I ALWAYS FALL FOR IT.
GRRRRRR
UM...
CAN YOU...?
HEY YOU, STOP.

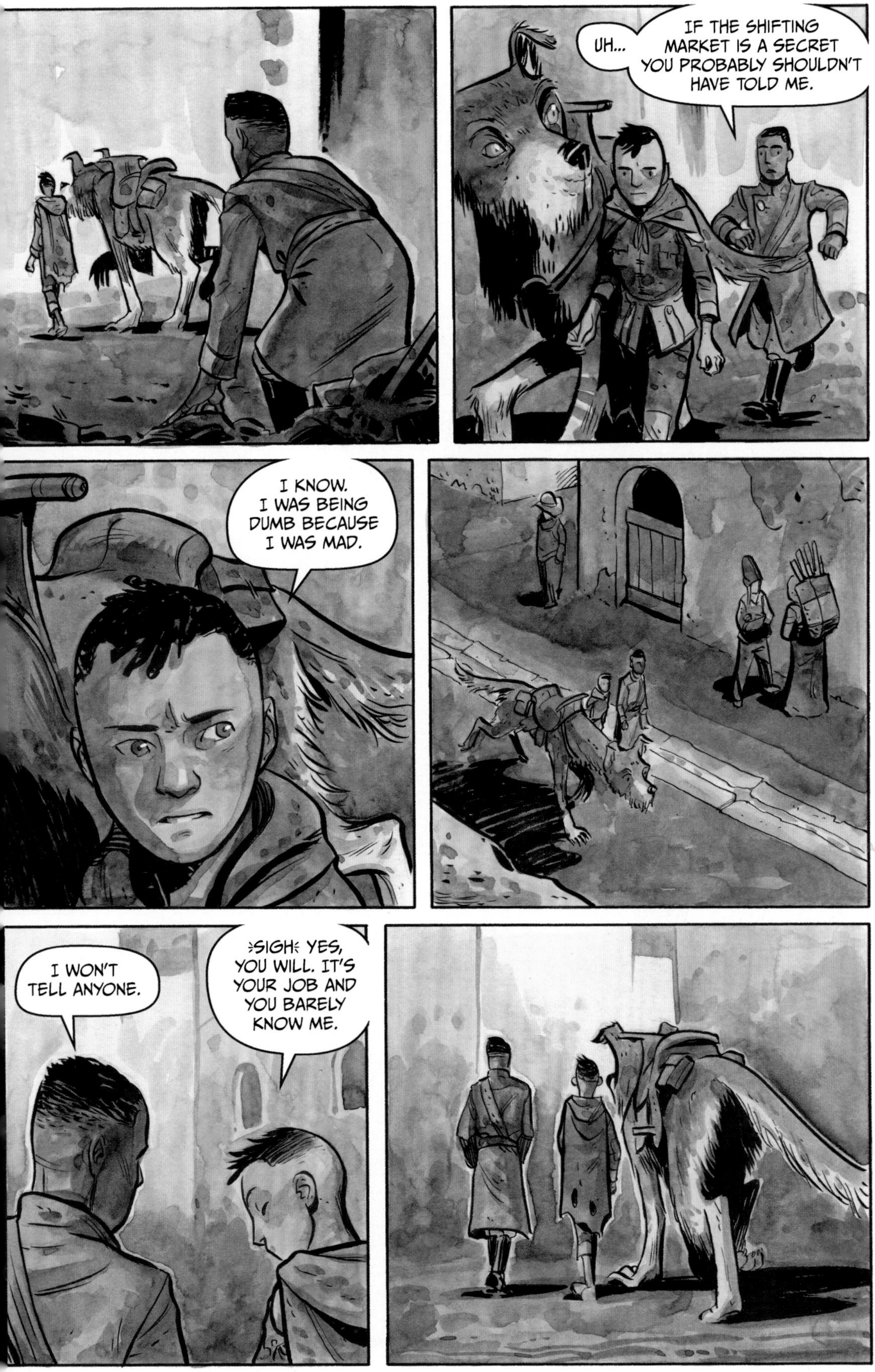
UH...
IF THE SHIFTING MARKET IS A SECRET YOU PROBABLY SHOULDN'T HAVE TOLD ME.
I KNOW. I WAS BEING DUMB BECAUSE I WAS MAD.
I WON'T TELL ANYONE.
⪫SIGH⪪ YES, YOU WILL. IT'S YOUR JOB AND YOU BARELY KNOW ME.

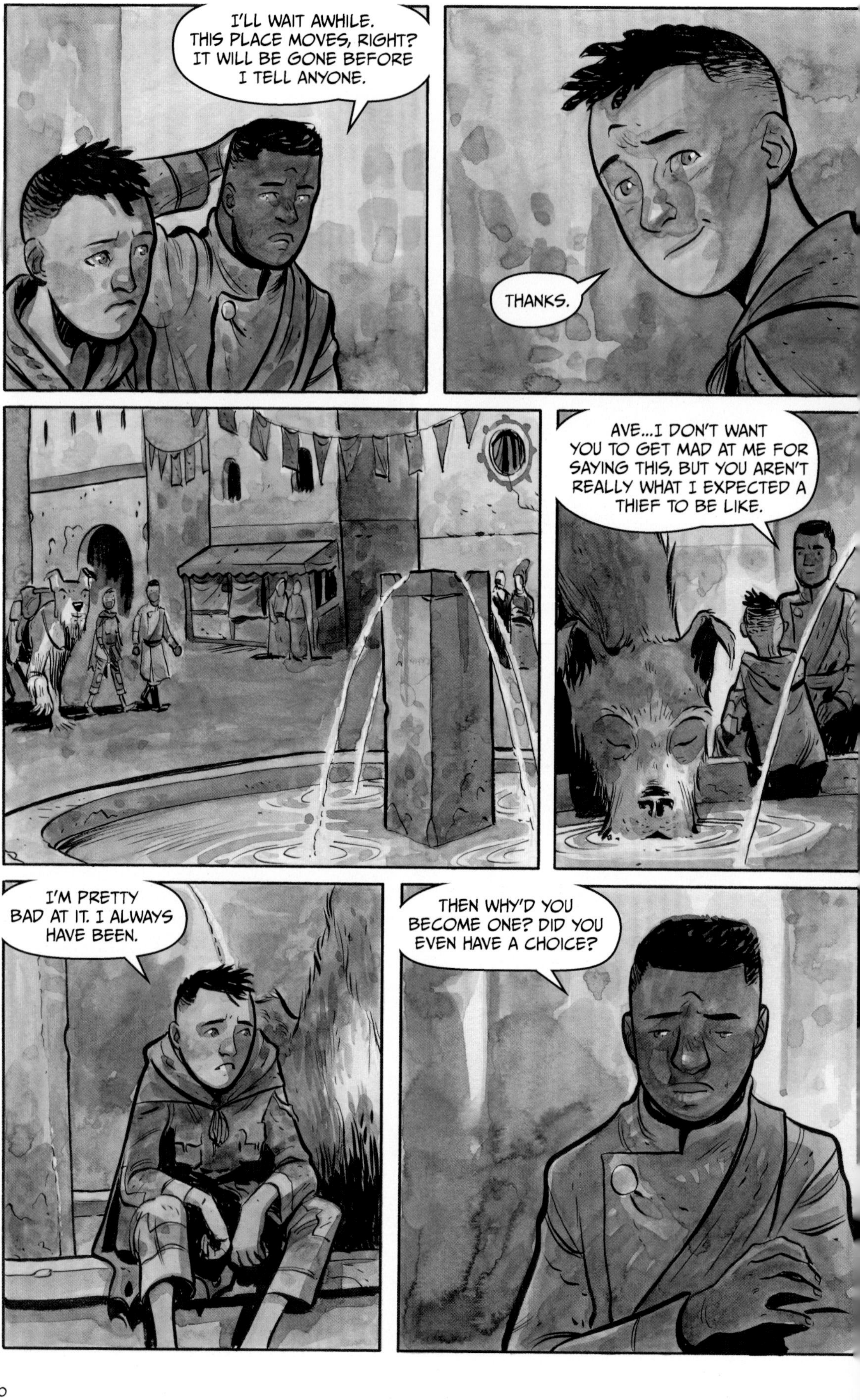

I'LL WAIT AWHILE. THIS PLACE MOVES, RIGHT? IT WILL BE GONE BEFORE I TELL ANYONE.
THANKS.
AVE...I DON'T WANT YOU TO GET MAD AT ME FOR SAYING THIS, BUT YOU AREN'T REALLY WHAT I EXPECTED A THIEF TO BE LIKE.
I'M PRETTY BAD AT IT. I ALWAYS HAVE BEEN.
THEN WHY'D YOU BECOME ONE? DID YOU EVEN HAVE A CHOICE?

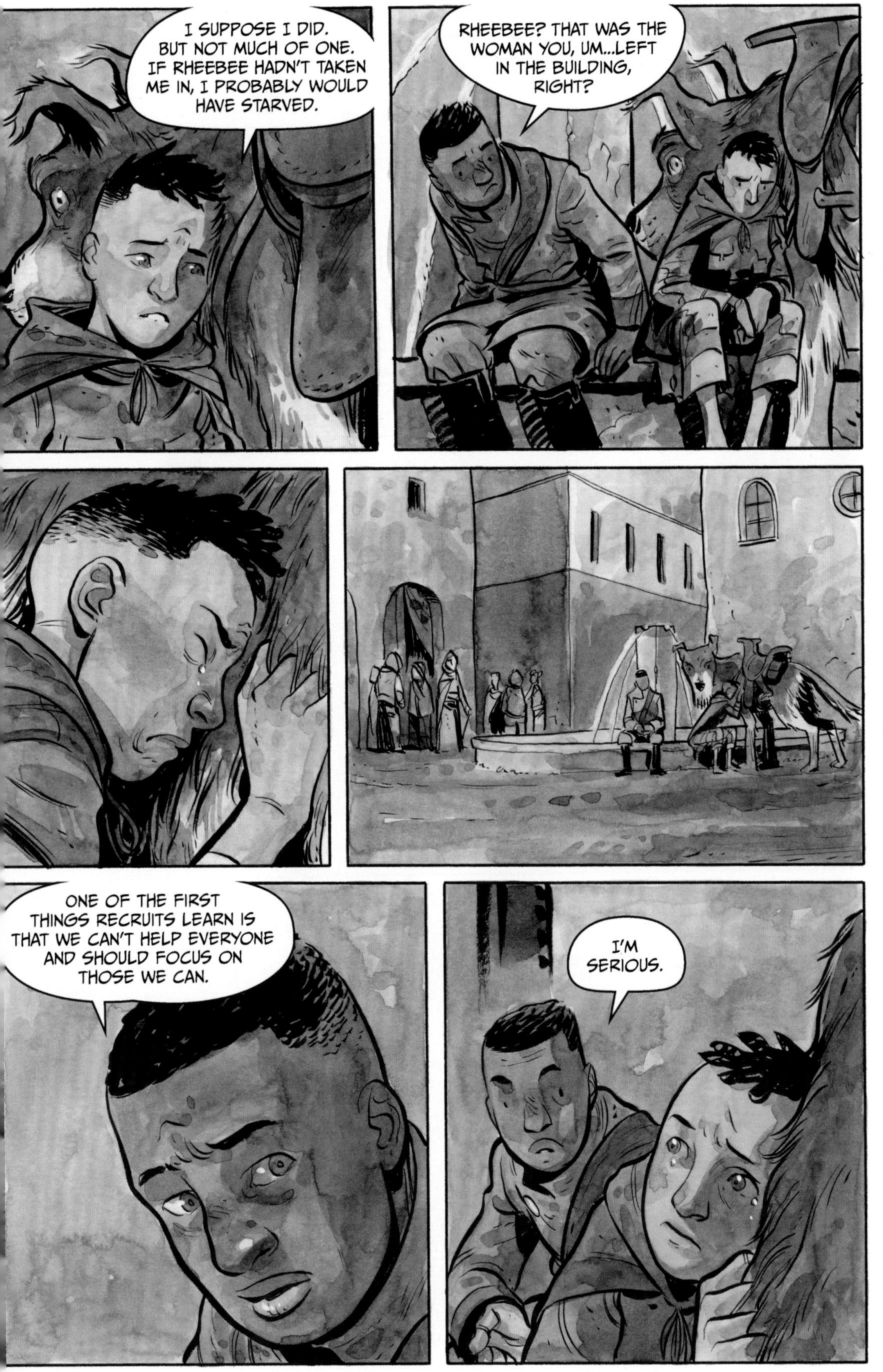
I SUPPOSE I DID. BUT NOT MUCH OF ONE. IF RHEEBEE HADN'T TAKEN ME IN, I PROBABLY WOULD HAVE STARVED.
RHEEBEE? THAT WAS THE WOMAN YOU, UM...LEFT IN THE BUILDING, RIGHT?
ONE OF THE FIRST THINGS RECRUITS LEARN IS THAT WE CAN'T HELP EVERYONE AND SHOULD FOCUS ON THOSE WE CAN.
I'M SERIOUS.

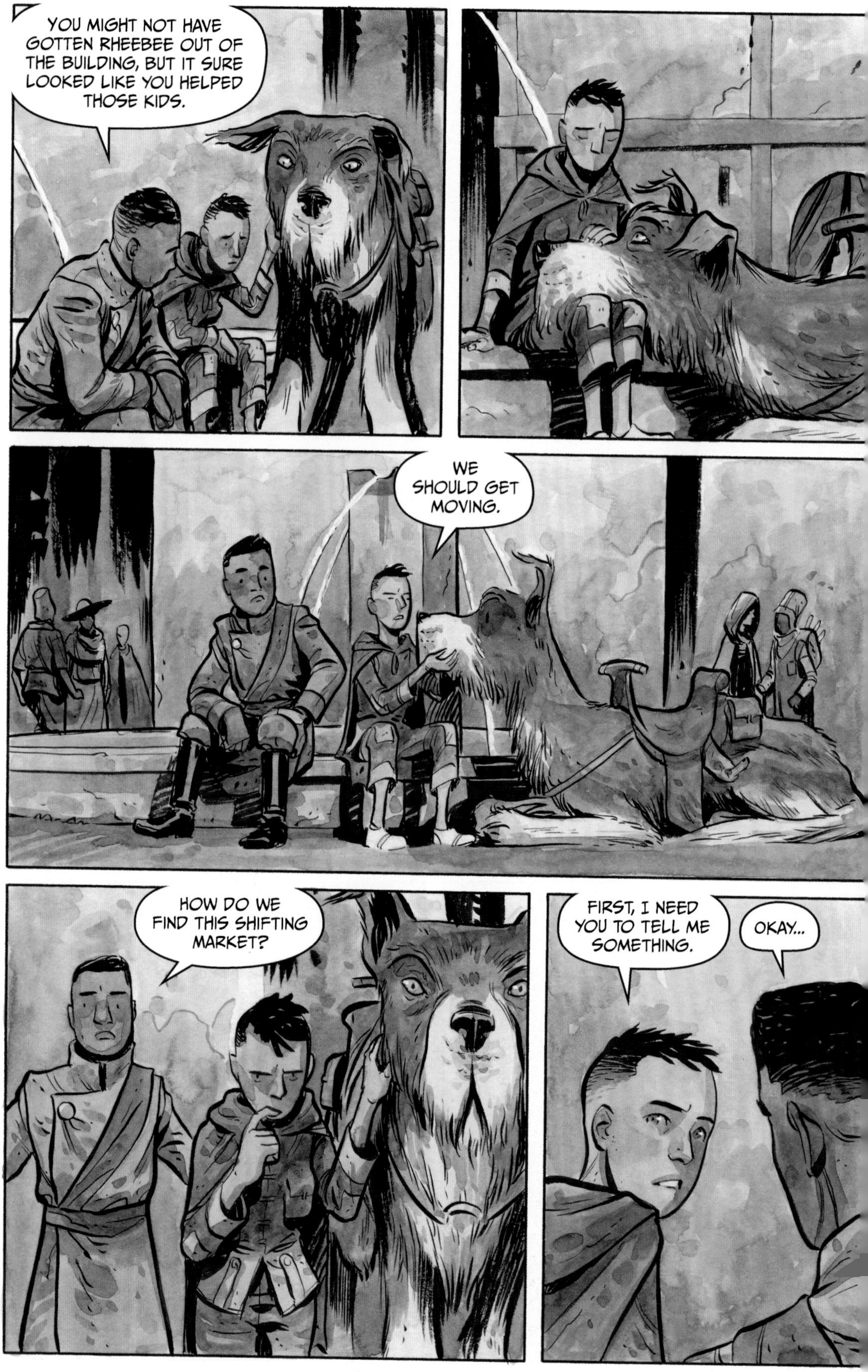
YOU MIGHT NOT HAVE GOTTEN RHEEBEE OUT OF THE BUILDING, BUT IT SURE LOOKED LIKE YOU HELPED THOSE KIDS.
WE SHOULD GET MOVING.
HOW DO WE FIND THIS SHIFTING MARKET?
FIRST, I NEED YOU TO TELL ME SOMETHING.
OKAY...

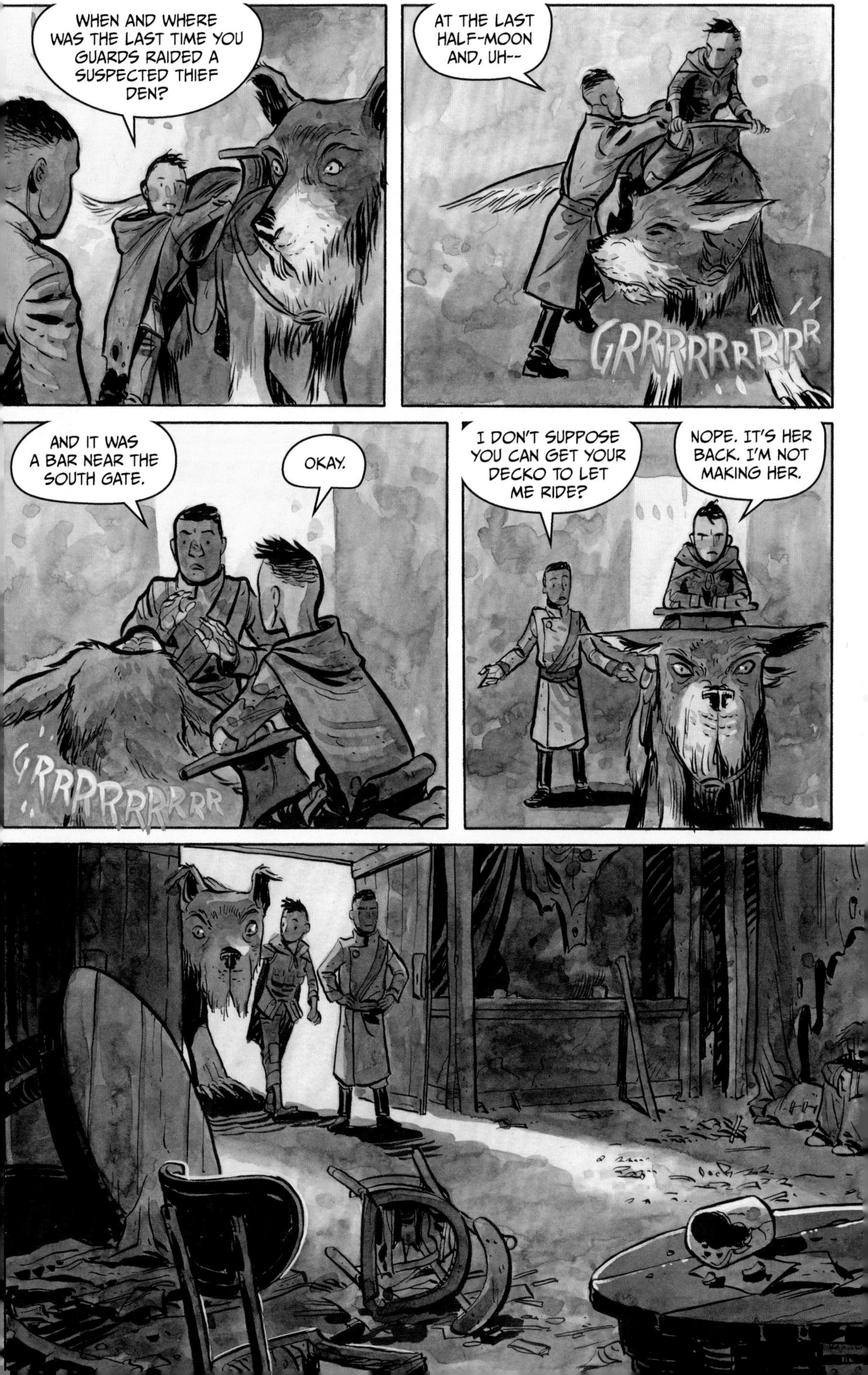
WHEN AND WHERE WAS THE LAST TIME YOU GUARDS RAIDED A SUSPECTED THIEF DEN?
AT THE LAST HALF-MOON AND, UH--
GRRRRRRRRRR
AND IT WAS A BAR NEAR THE SOUTH GATE.
OKAY.
GRRRRRRRRRR
I DON'T SUPPOSE YOU CAN GET YOUR DECKO TO LET ME RIDE?
NOPE. IT'S HER BACK. I'M NOT MAKING HER.

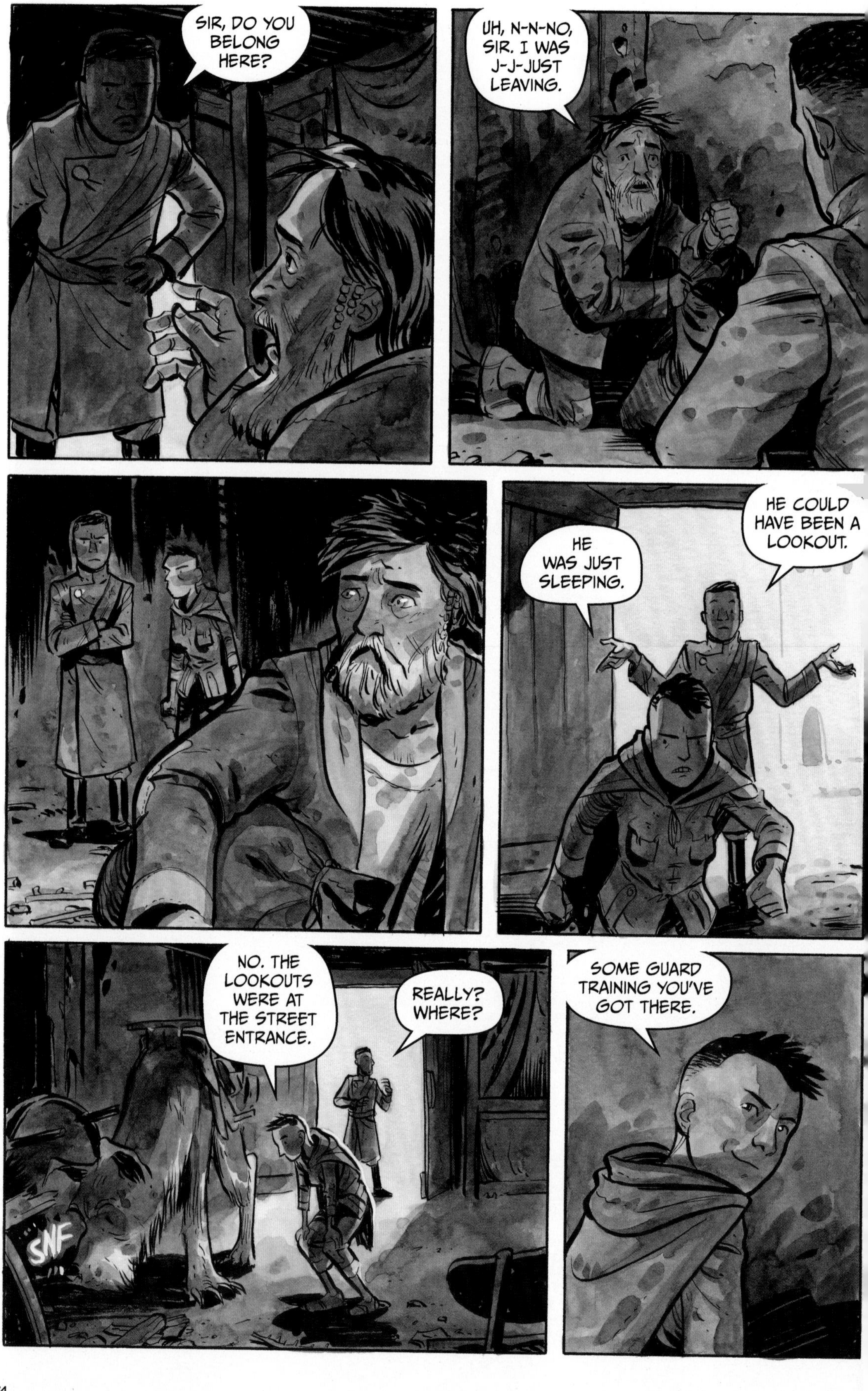
SIR, DO YOU BELONG HERE?
UH, N-N-NO, SIR. I WAS J-J-JUST LEAVING.
HE COULD HAVE BEEN A LOOKOUT.
HE WAS JUST SLEEPING.
NO. THE LOOKOUTS WERE AT THE STREET ENTRANCE.
REALLY? WHERE?
SNF
SOME GUARD TRAINING YOU'VE GOT THERE.

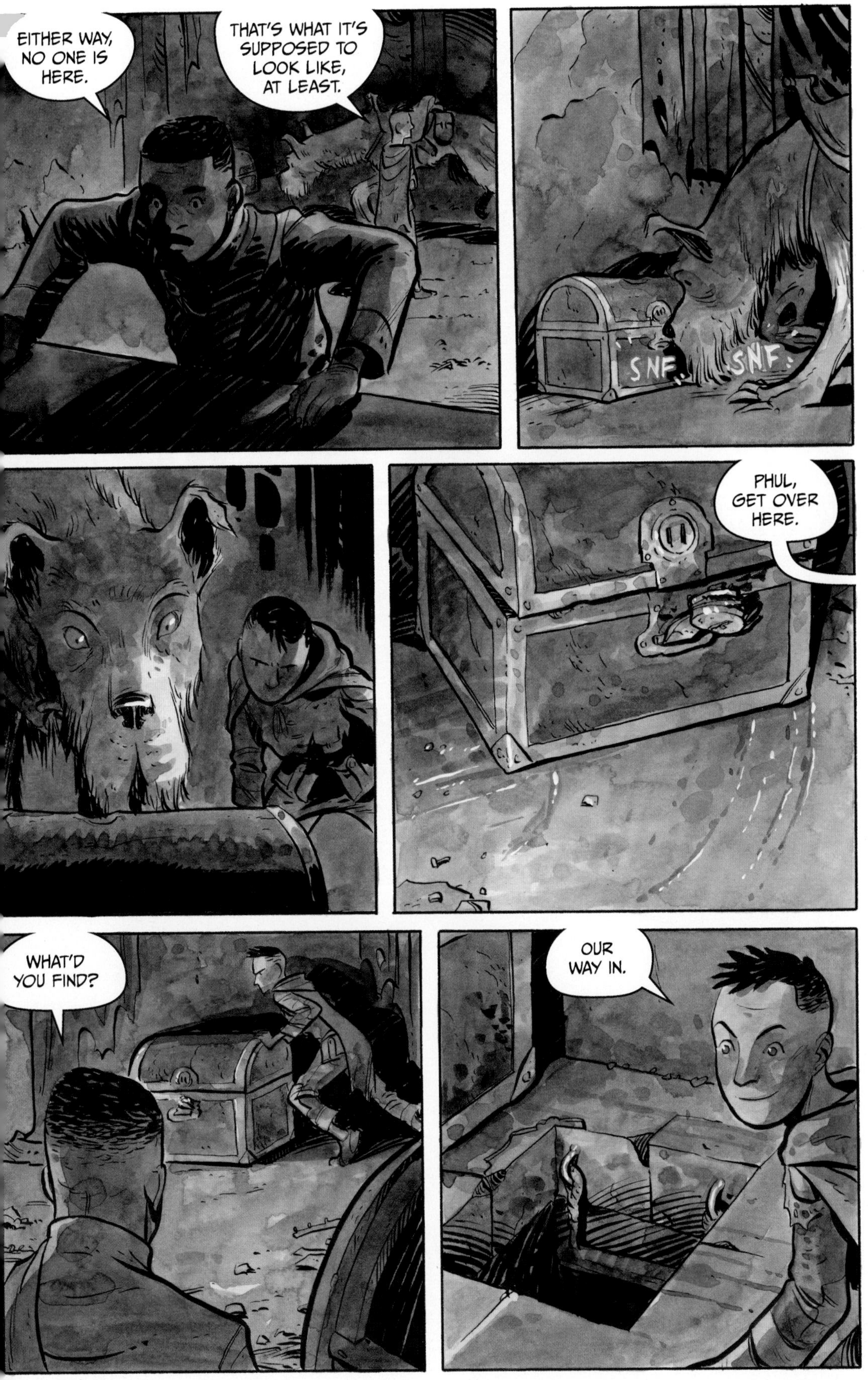
EITHER WAY, NO ONE IS HERE.
THAT'S WHAT IT'S SUPPOSED TO LOOK LIKE, AT LEAST.
SNF
SNF
PHUL, GET OVER HERE.
WHAT'D YOU FIND?
OUR WAY IN.

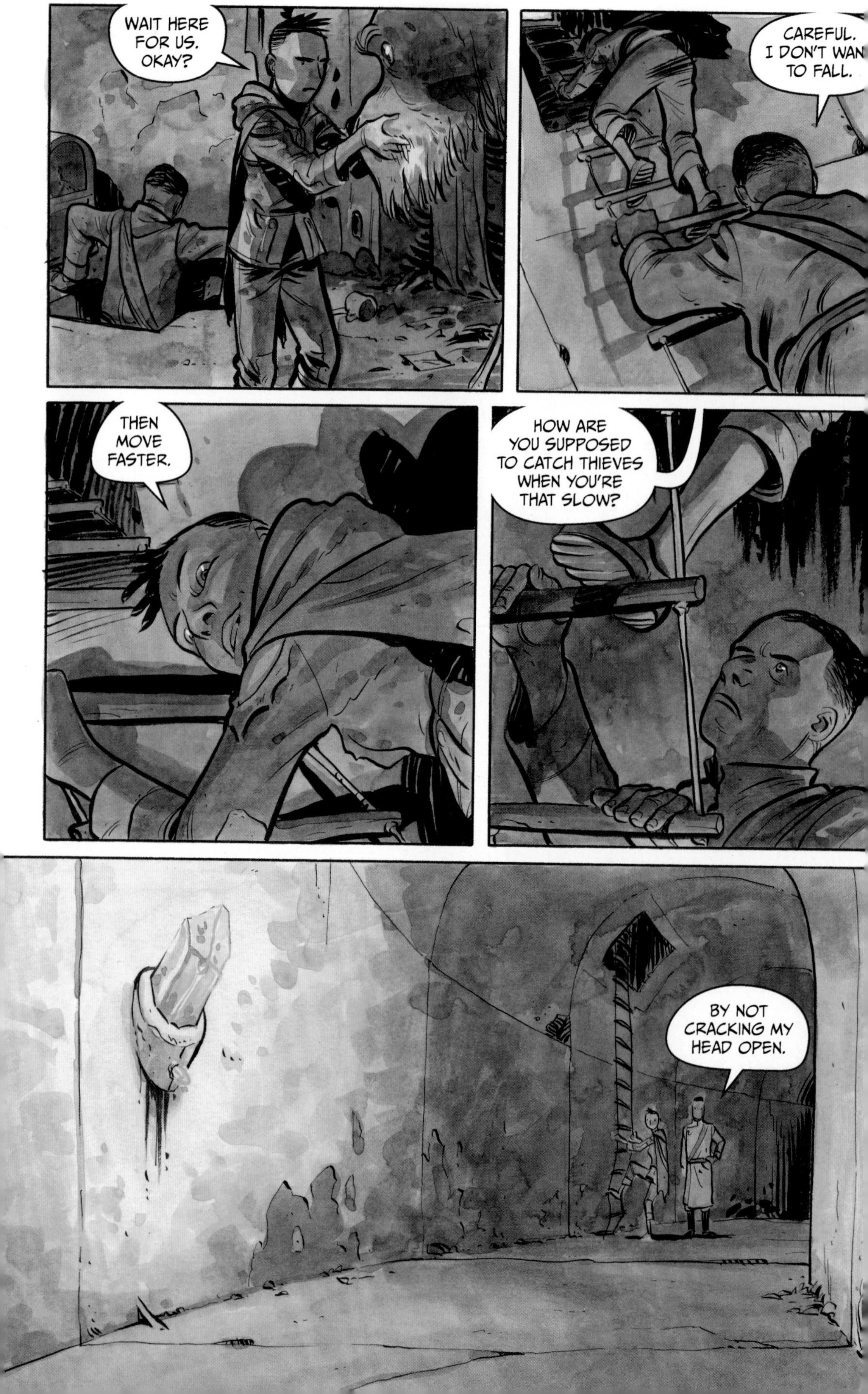
WAIT HERE FOR US. OKAY?
CAREFUL. I DON'T WAN TO FALL.
THEN MOVE FASTER.
HOW ARE YOU SUPPOSED TO CATCH THIEVES WHEN YOU'RE THAT SLOW?
BY NOT CRACKING MY HEAD OPEN.

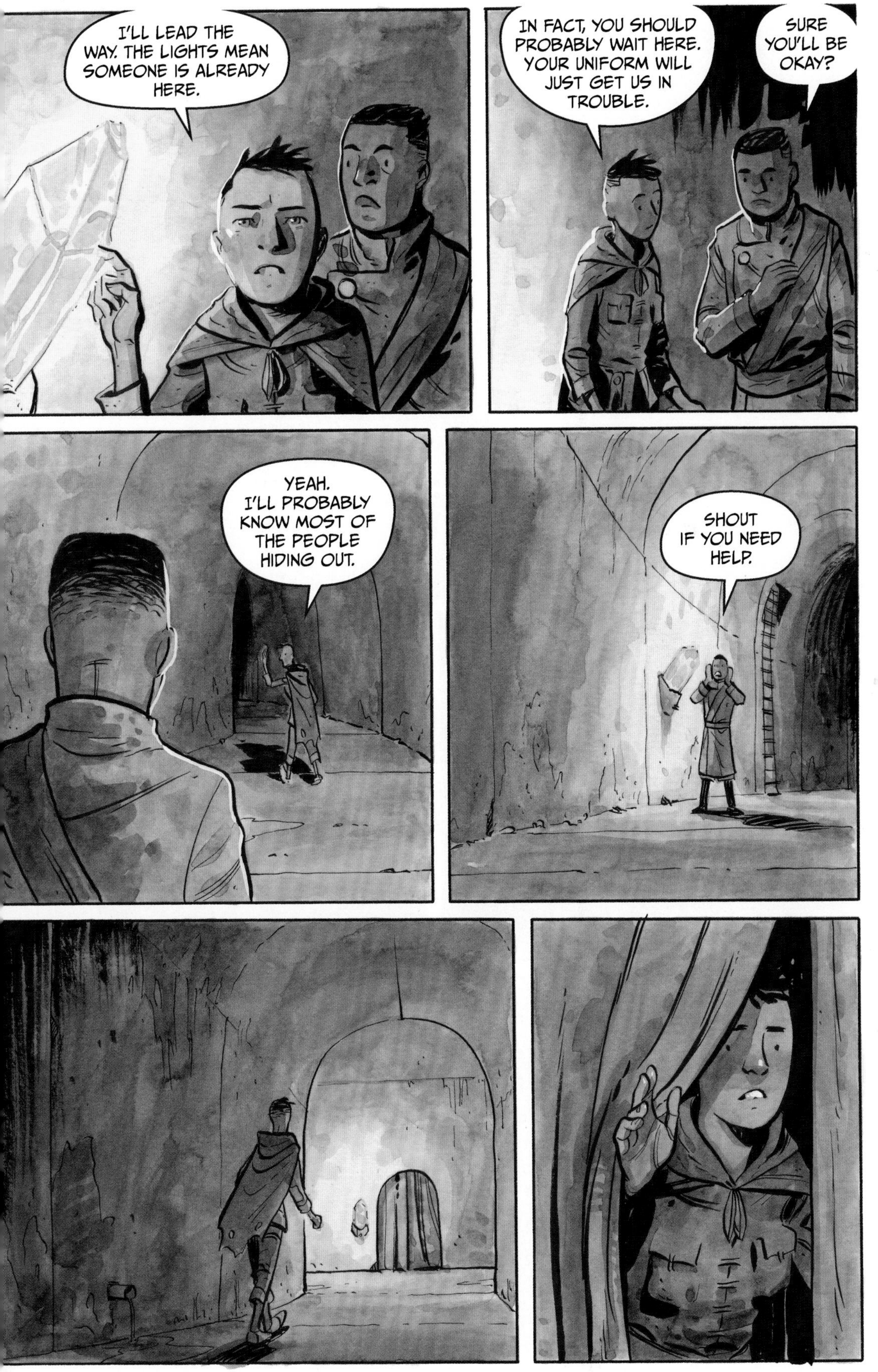
I'LL LEAD THE WAY. THE LIGHTS MEAN SOMEONE IS ALREADY HERE.
IN FACT, YOU SHOULD PROBABLY WAIT HERE. YOUR UNIFORM WILL JUST GET US IN TROUBLE.
SURE YOU'LL BE OKAY?
YEAH. I'LL PROBABLY KNOW MOST OF THE PEOPLE HIDING OUT.
SHOUT IF YOU NEED HELP.

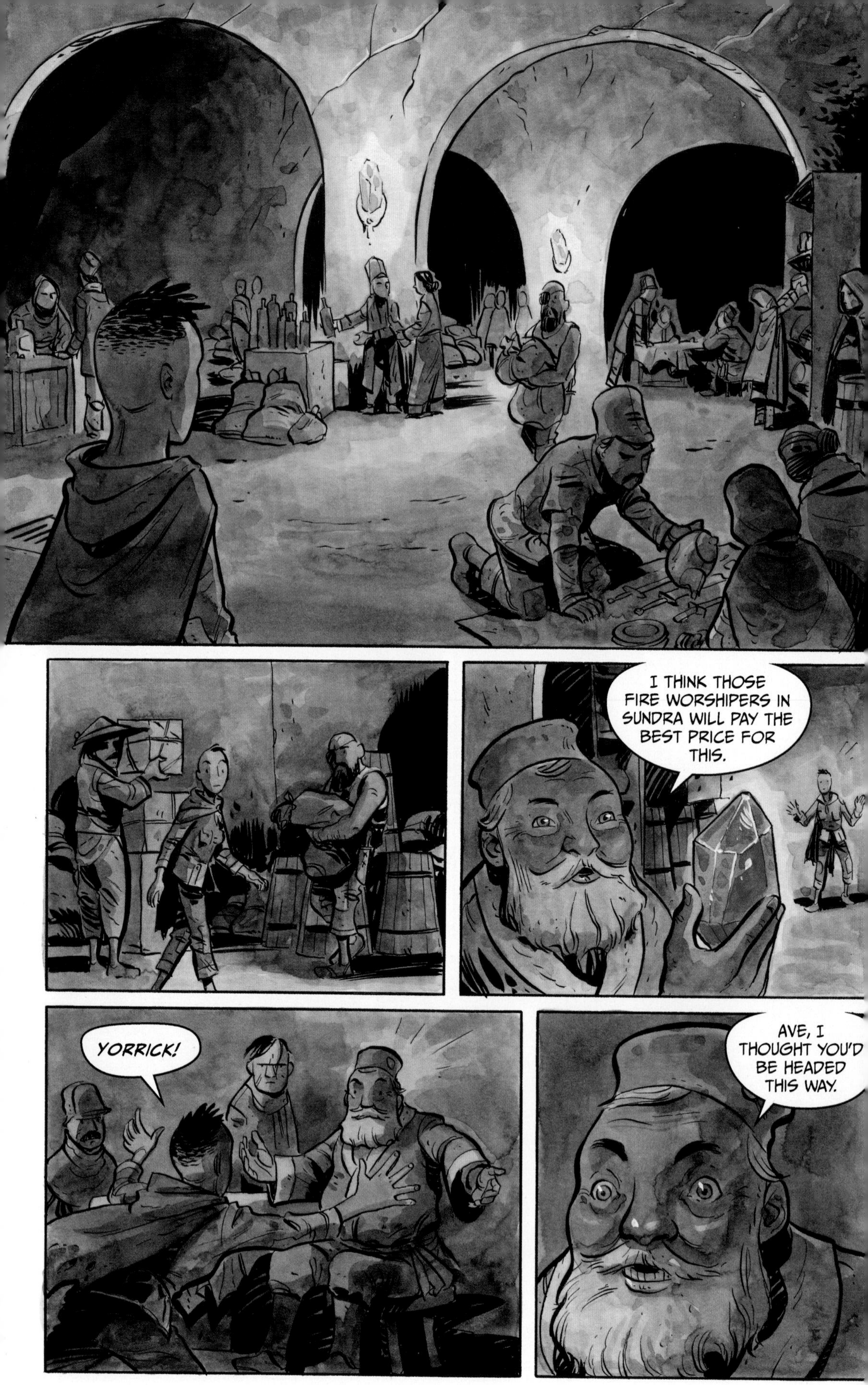
I THINK THOSE FIRE WORSHIPERS IN SUNDRA WILL PAY THE BEST PRICE FOR THIS.
YORRICK!
AYE, I THOUGHT YOU'D BE HEADED THIS WAY.

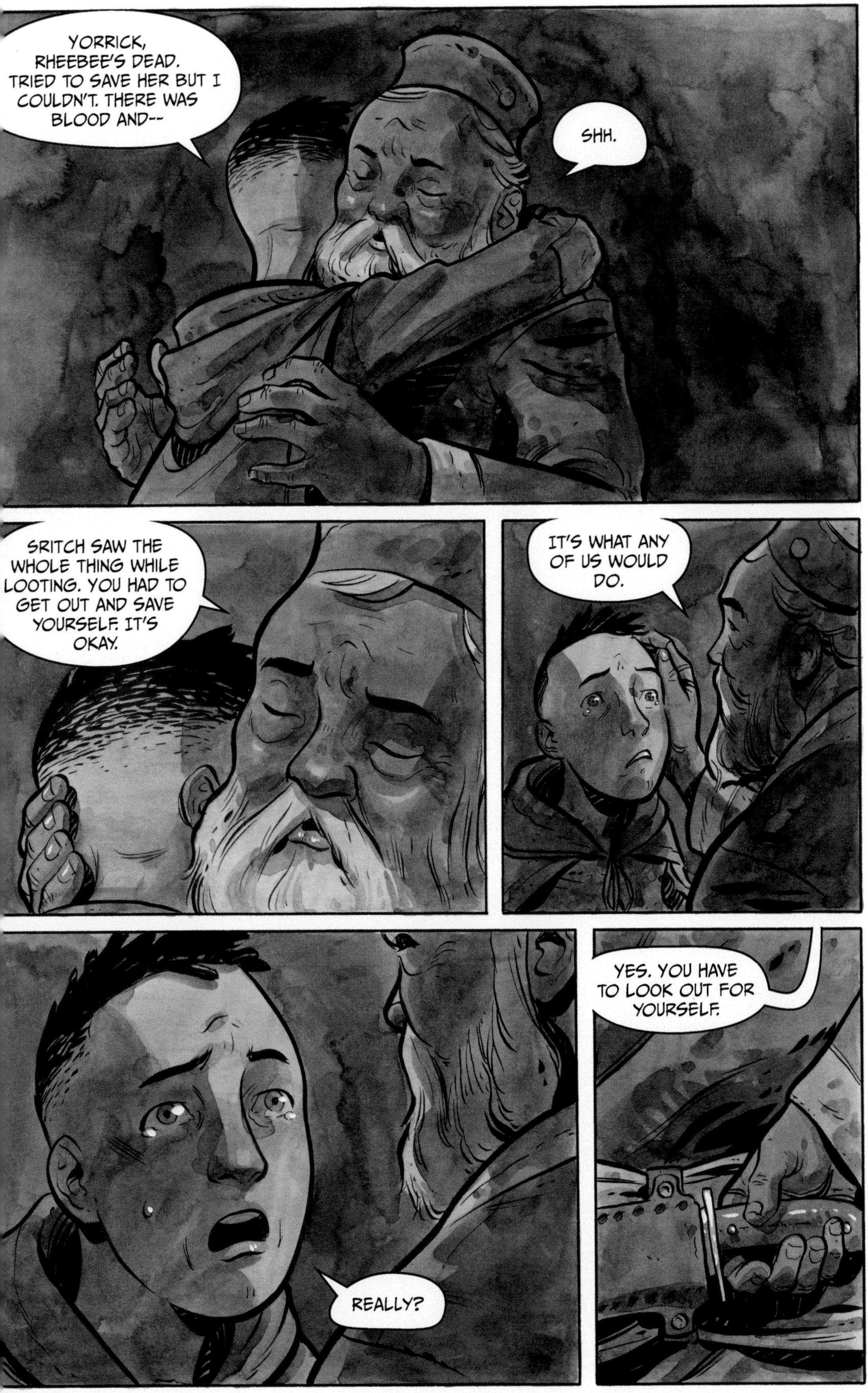
YORRICK, RHEEBEE'S DEAD. TRIED TO SAVE HER BUT I COULDN'T. THERE WAS BLOOD AND--
SHH.
SRITCH SAW THE WHOLE THING WHILE LOOTING. YOU HAD TO GET OUT AND SAVE YOURSELF. IT'S OKAY.
IT'S WHAT ANY OF US WOULD DO.
REALLY?
YES. YOU HAVE TO LOOK OUT FOR YOURSELF.

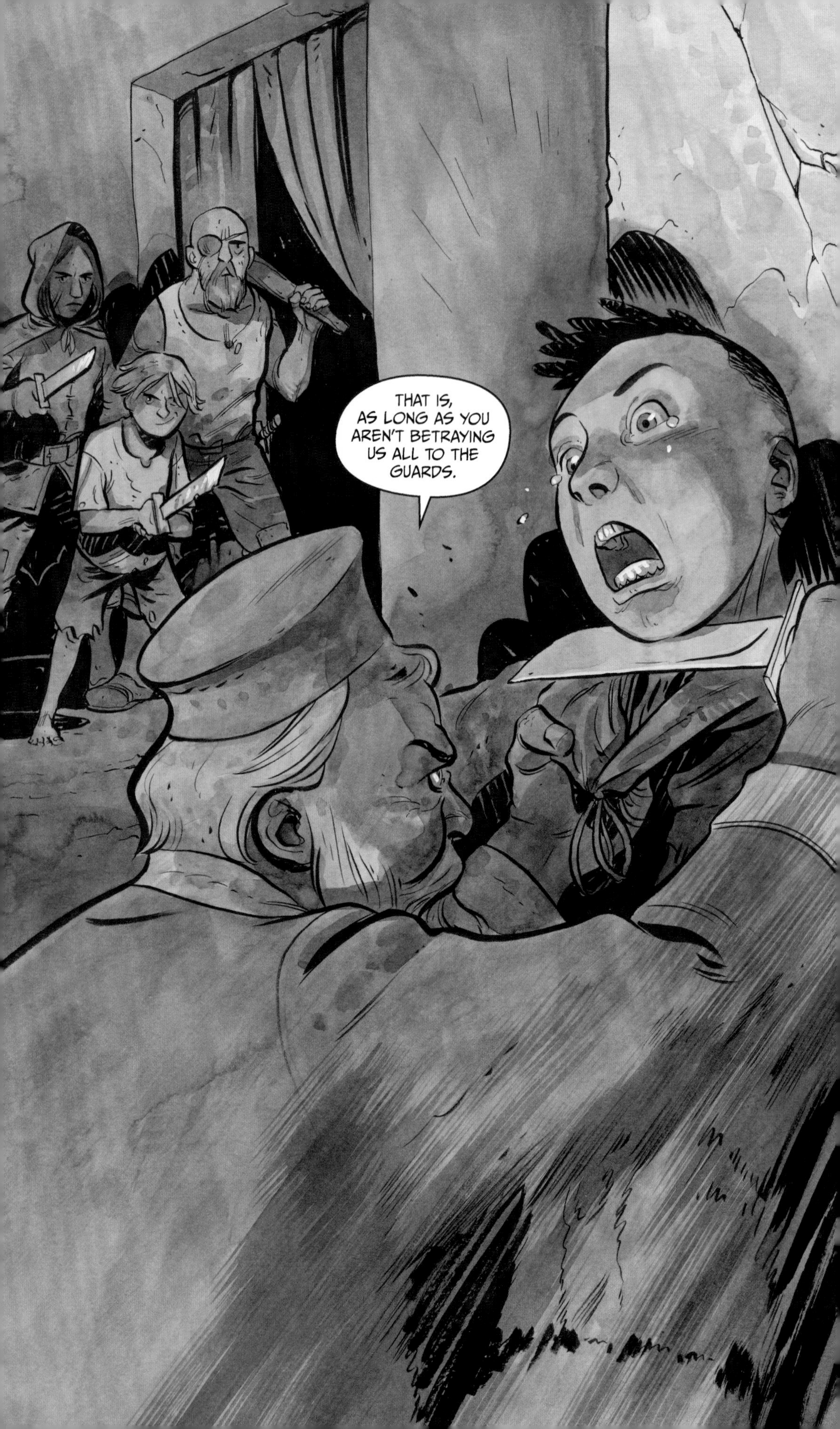
THAT IS, AS LONG AS YOU AREN'T BETRAYING US ALL TO THE GUARDS.

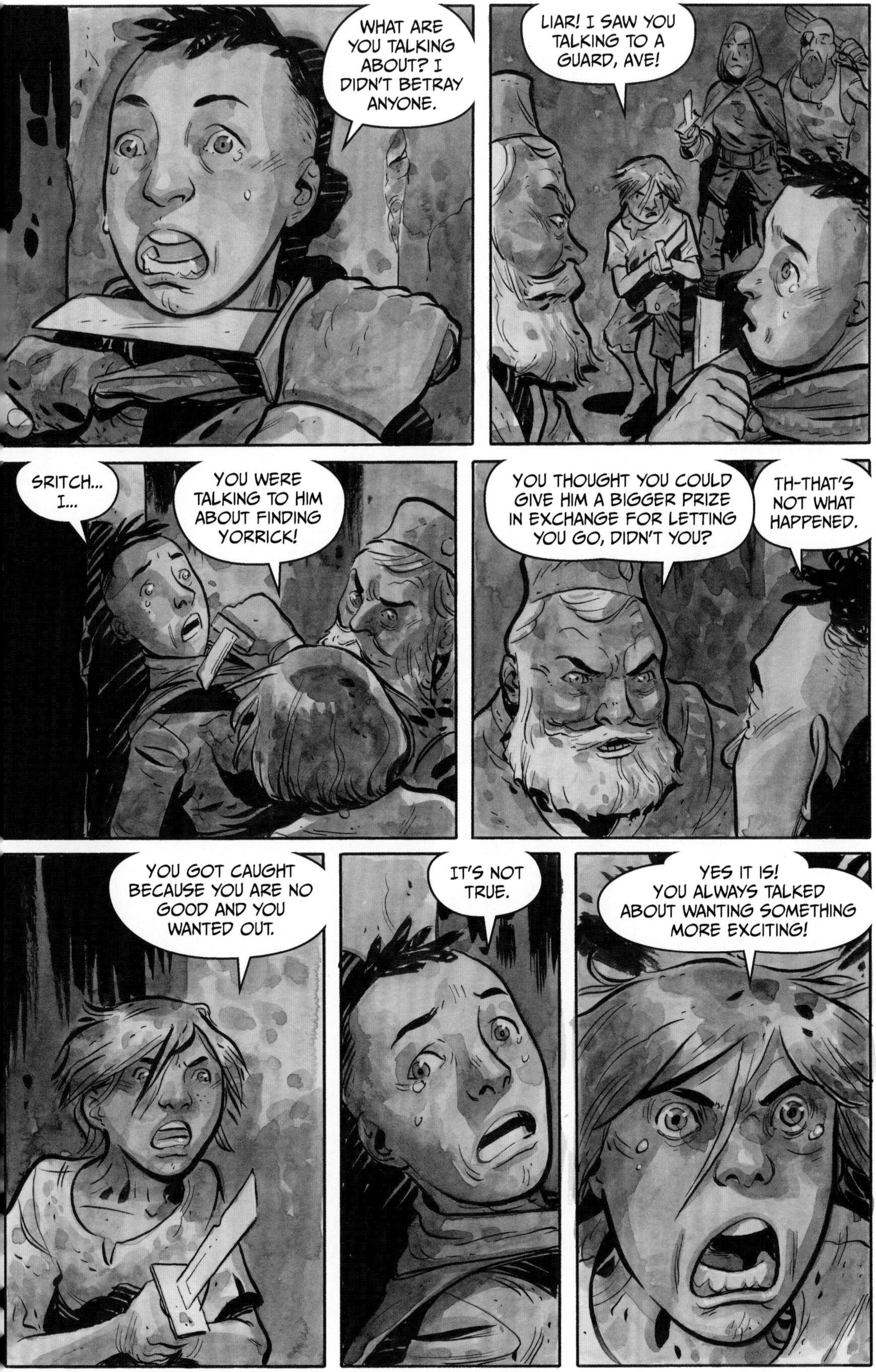

WHAT ARE YOU TALKING ABOUT? I DIDN'T BETRAY ANYONE.
LIAR! I SAW YOU TALKING TO A GUARD, AVE!
SRITCH... I...
YOU WERE TALKING TO HIM ABOUT FINDING YORRICK!
YOU THOUGHT YOU COULD GIVE HIM A BIGGER PRIZE IN EXCHANGE FOR LETTING YOU GO, DIDN'T YOU?
TH-THAT'S NOT WHAT HAPPENED.
YOU GOT CAUGHT BECAUSE YOU ARE NO GOOD AND YOU WANTED OUT.
IT'S NOT TRUE.
YES IT IS! YOU ALWAYS TALKED ABOUT WANTING SOMETHING MORE EXCITING!

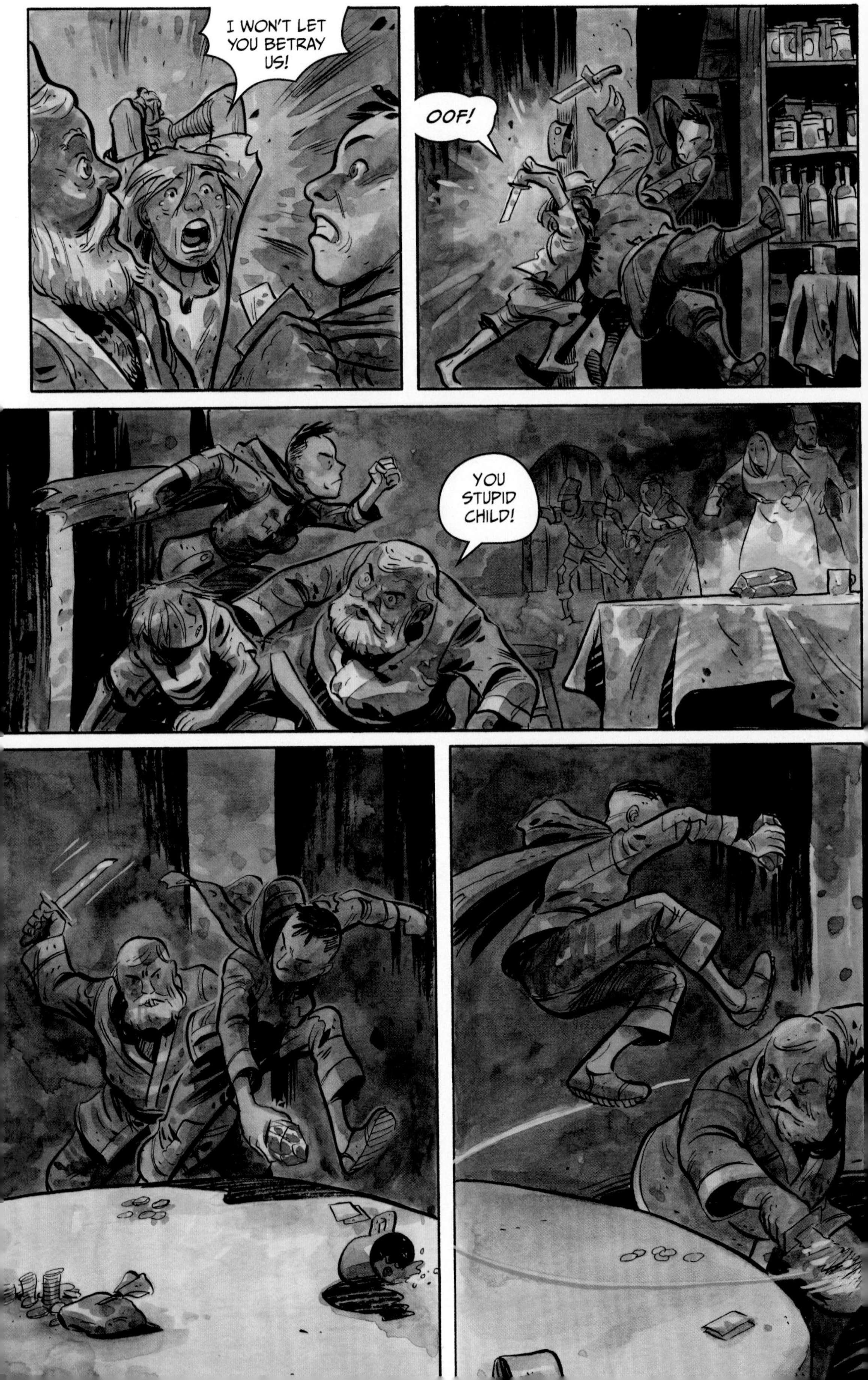
I WON'T LET YOU BETRAY US!
OOF!
YOU STUPID CHILD!

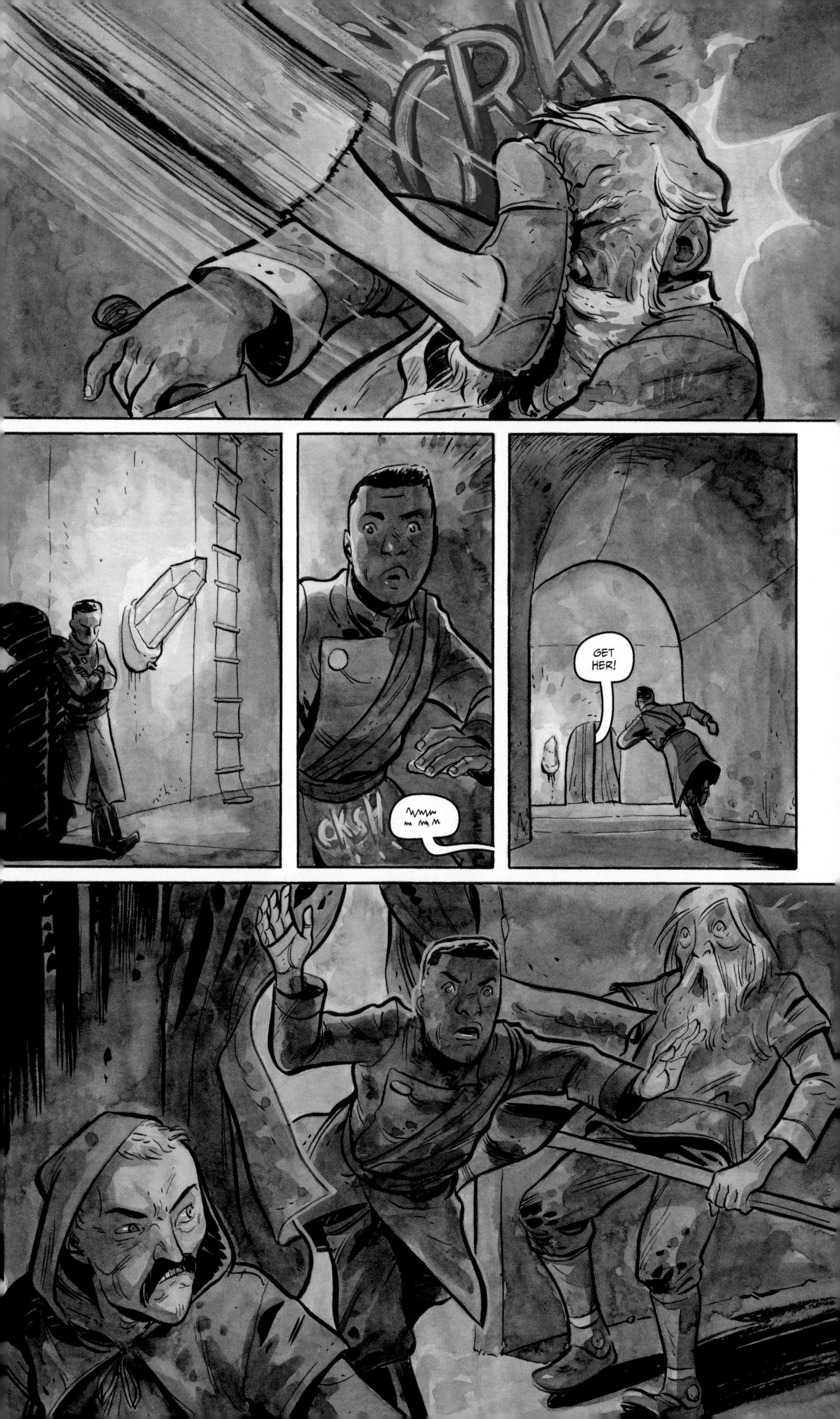
CRK
CKSH
GET HER!

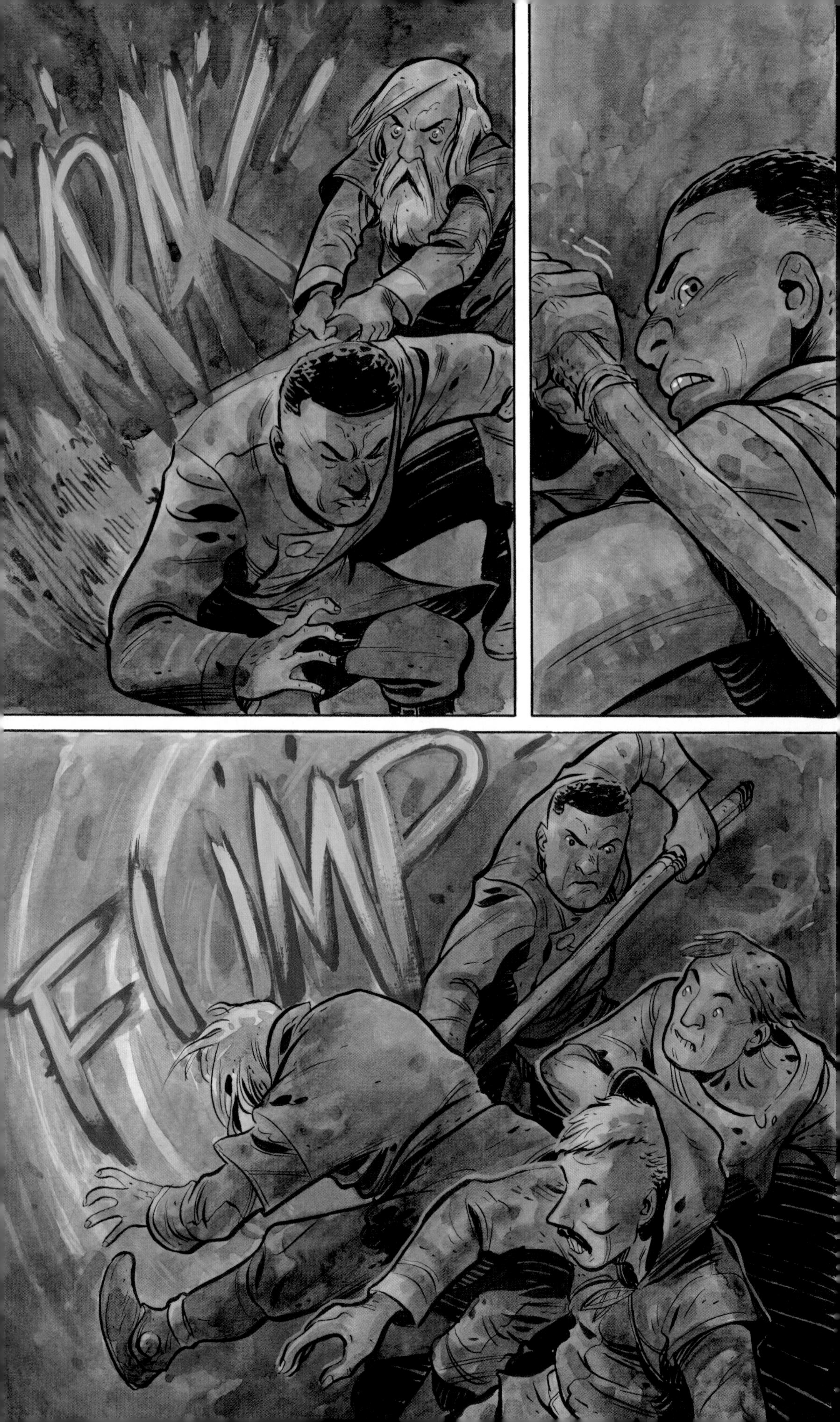
KRAK
FUMP

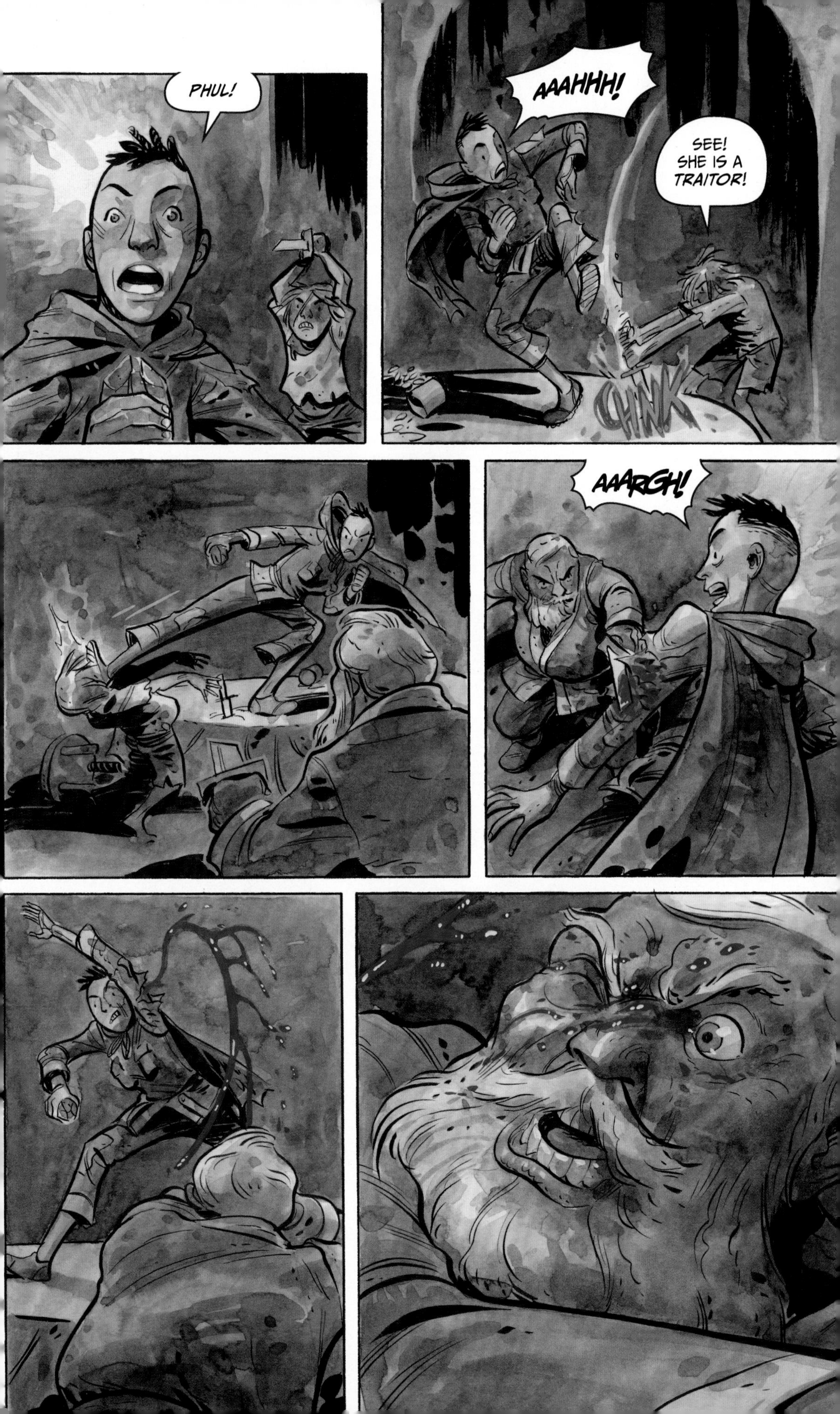
PHUL!
AAAHHH!
SEE! SHE IS A TRAITOR!
CHINK
AAARGH!

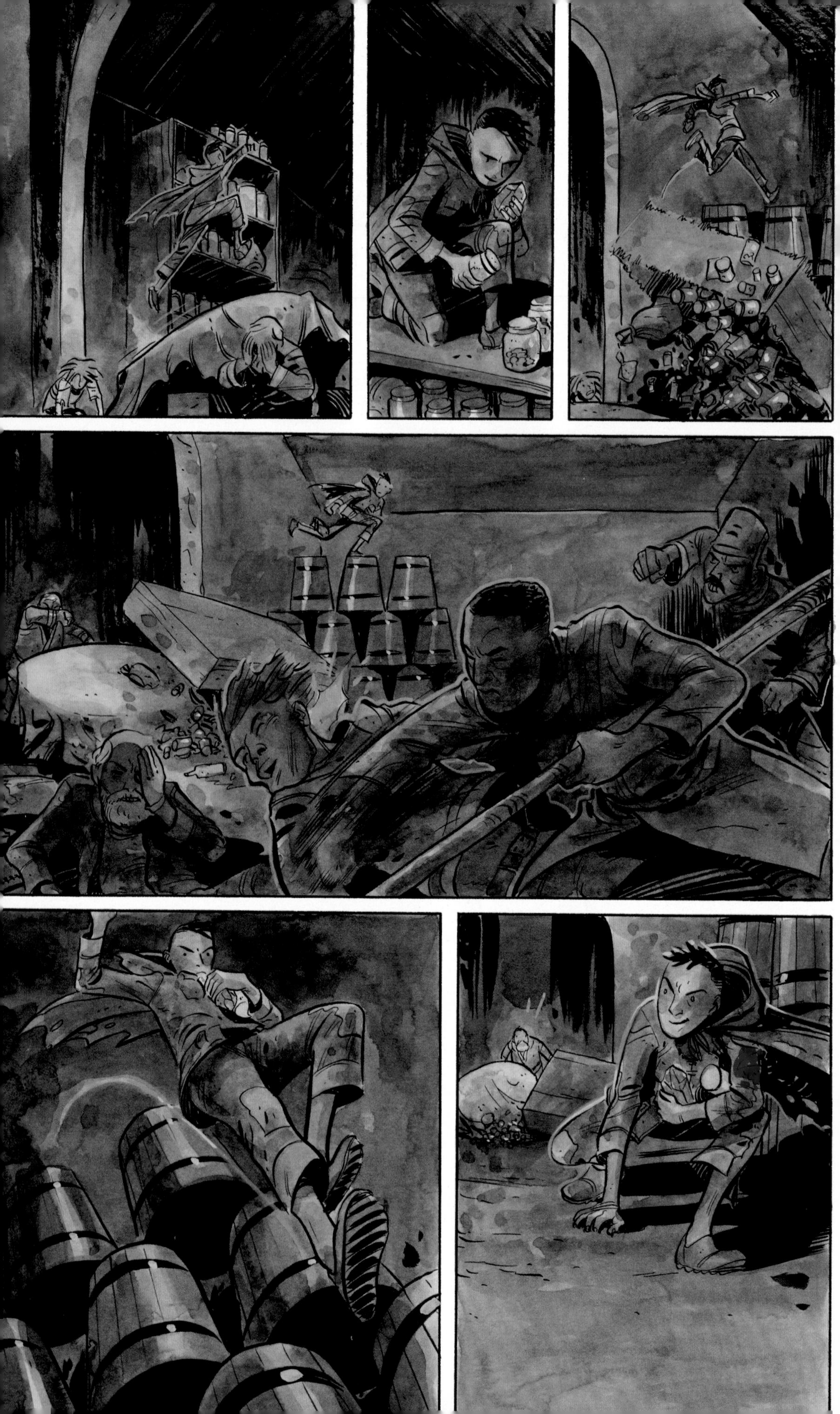

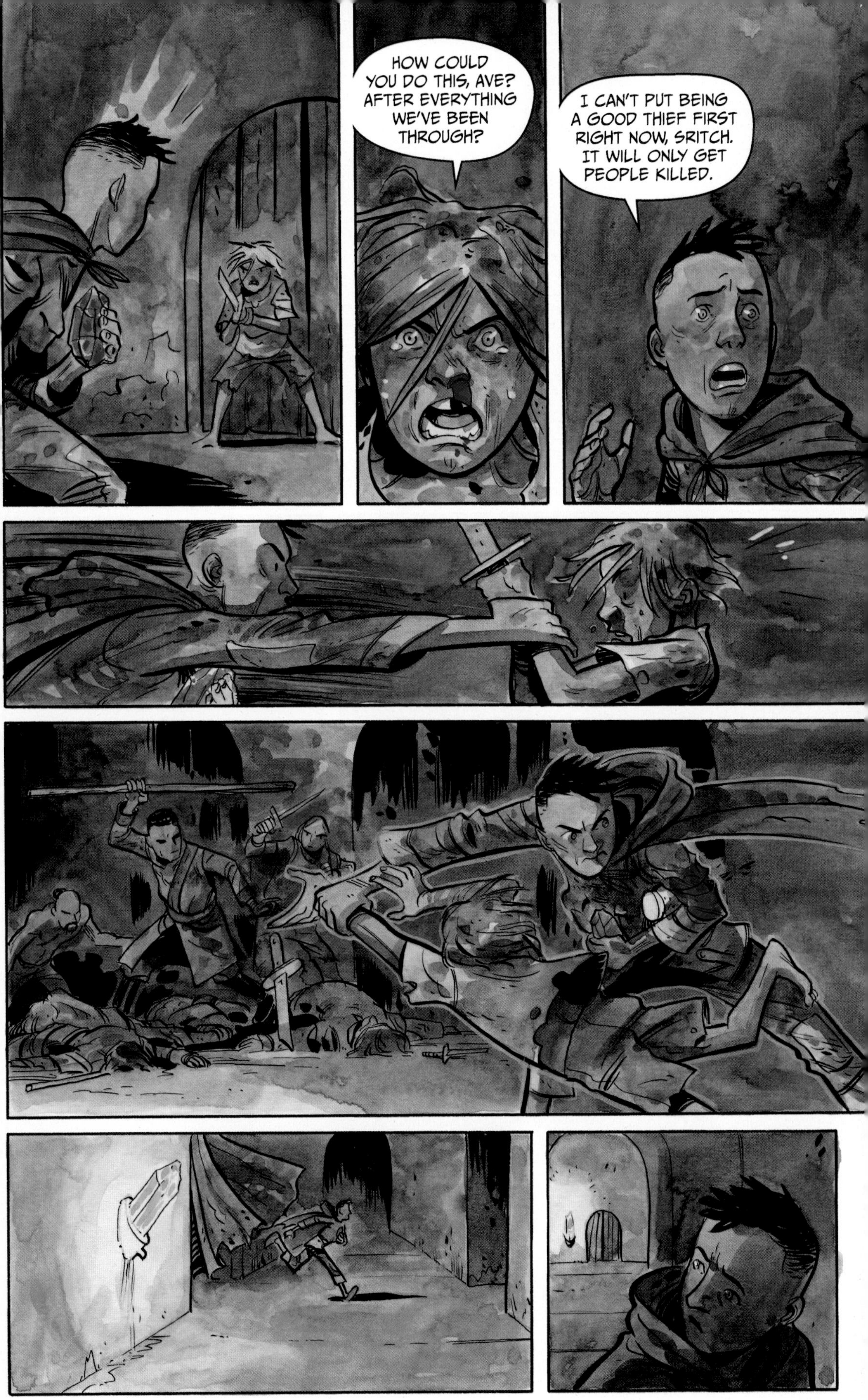
HOW COULD YOU DO THIS, AVE? AFTER EVERYTHING WE'VE BEEN THROUGH?
I CAN'T PUT BEING A GOOD THIEF FIRST RIGHT NOW, SRITCH. IT WILL ONLY GET PEOPLE KILLED.

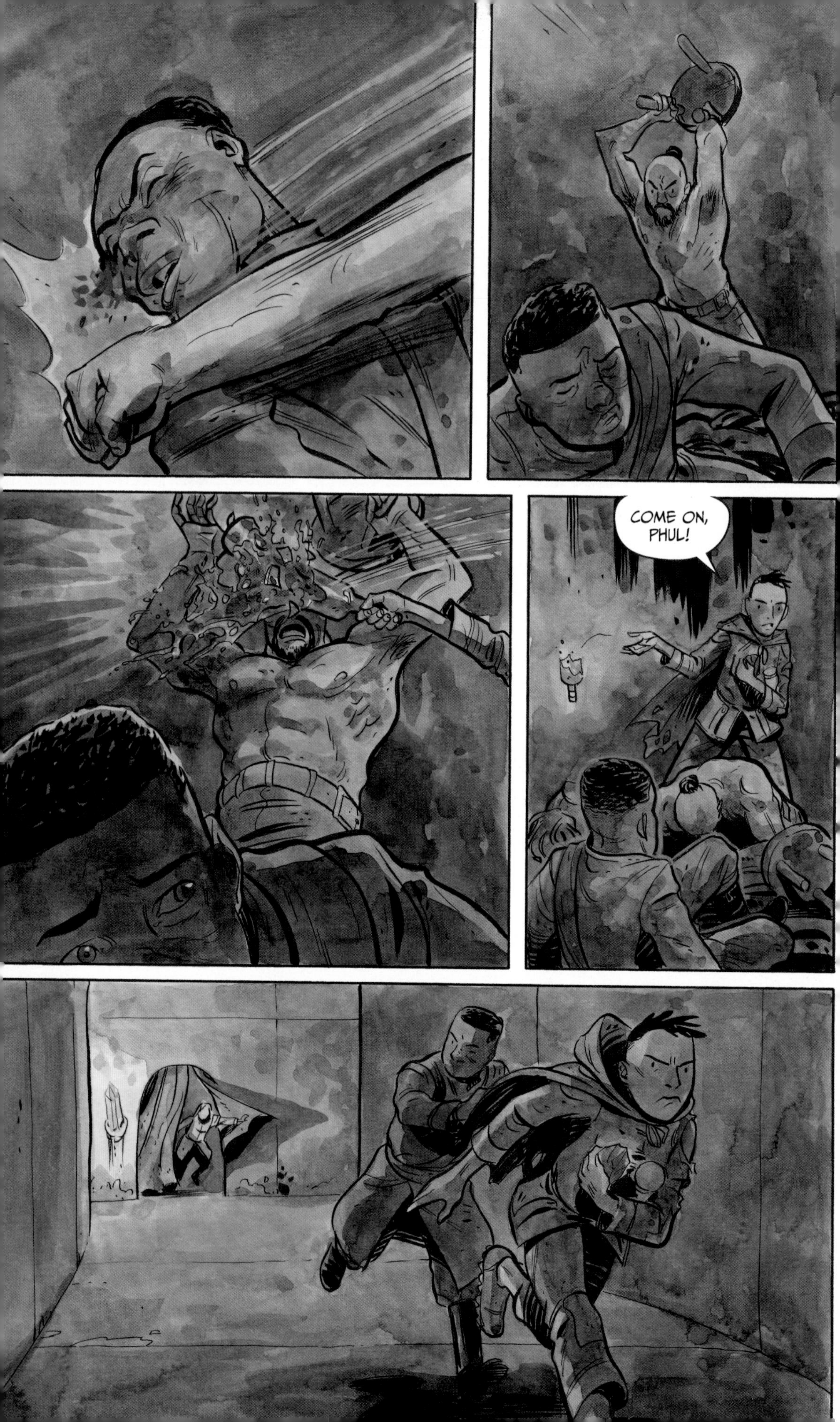
COME ON,
PHUL!

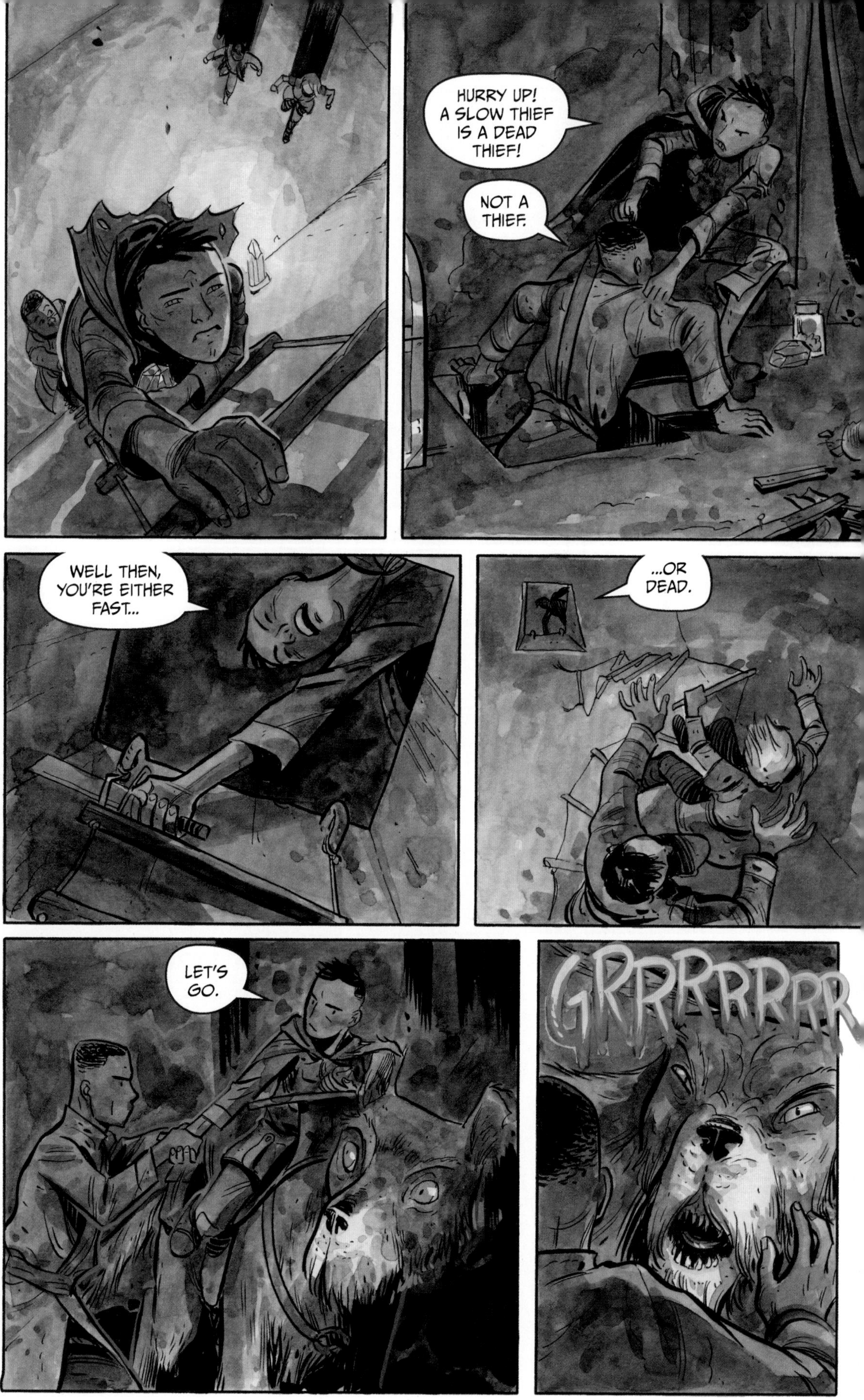
HURRY UP! A SLOW THIEF IS A DEAD THIEF!
NOT A THIEF.
WELL THEN, YOU'RE EITHER FAST...
...OR DEAD.
LET'S GO.
GRRRRRRR

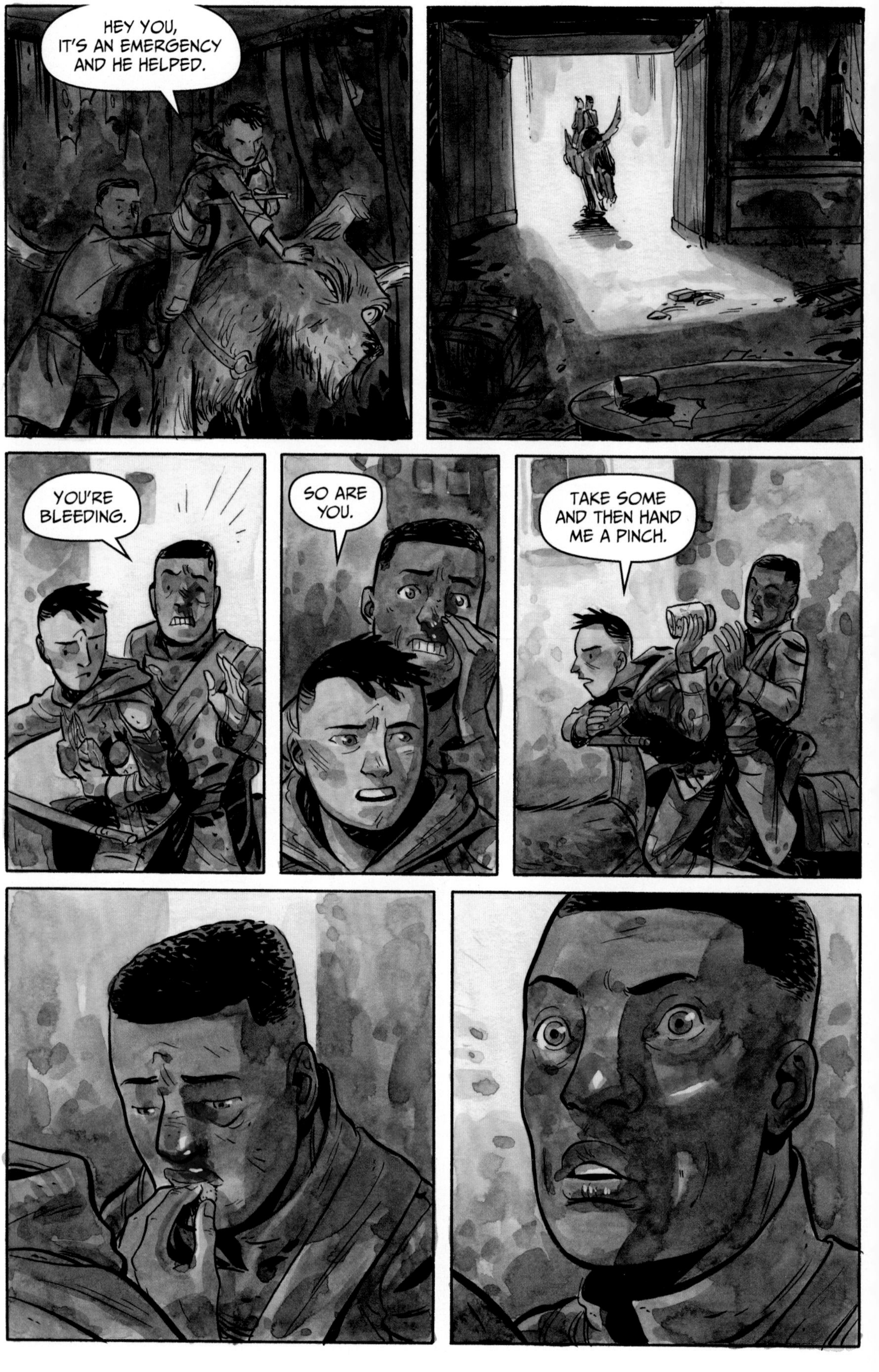
HEY YOU,
IT'S AN EMERGENCY
AND HE HELPED.
YOU'RE BLEEDING.
SO ARE YOU.
TAKE SOME AND THEN HAND ME A PINCH.

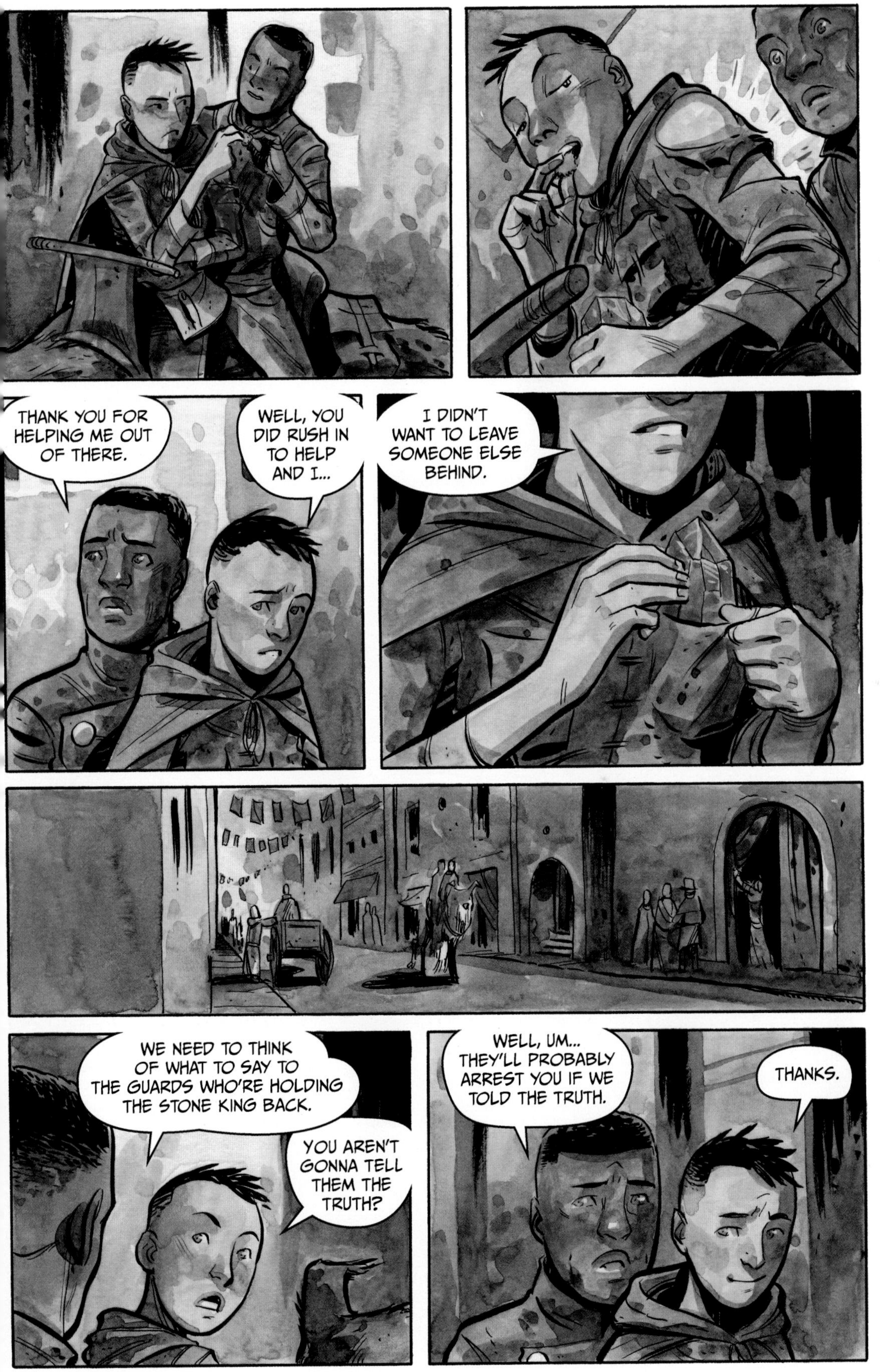
THANK YOU FOR HELPING ME OUT OF THERE.
WELL, YOU DID RUSH IN TO HELP AND I...
I DIDN'T WANT TO LEAVE SOMEONE ELSE BEHIND.
WE NEED TO THINK OF WHAT TO SAY TO THE GUARDS WHO'RE HOLDING THE STONE KING BACK.
YOU AREN'T GONNA TELL THEM THE TRUTH?
WELL, UM... THEY'LL PROBABLY ARREST YOU IF WE TOLD THE TRUTH.
THANKS.

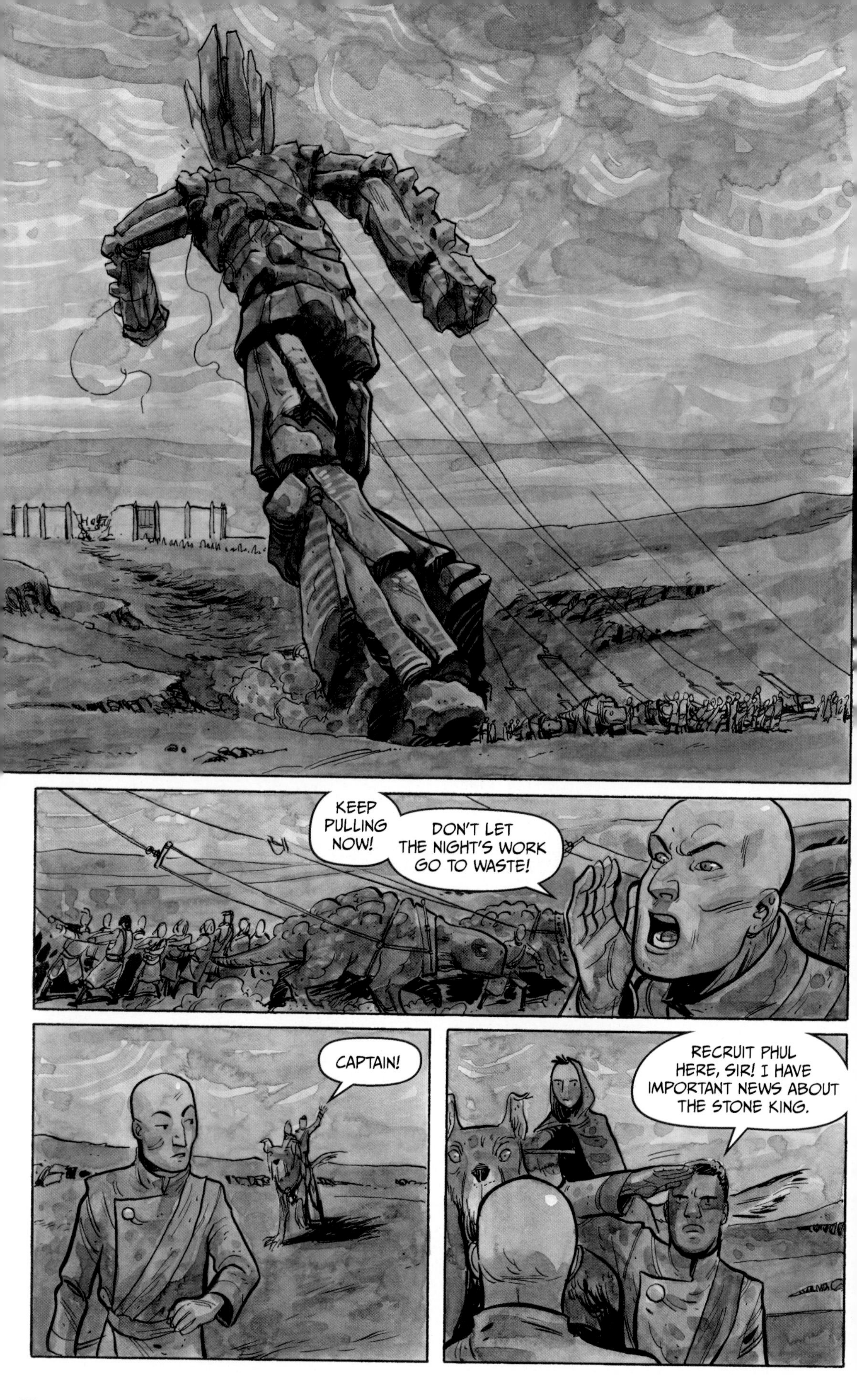
KEEP PULLING NOW!
DON'T LET THE NIGHT'S WORK GO TO WASTE!
CAPTAIN!
RECRUIT PHUL HERE, SIR! I HAVE IMPORTANT NEWS ABOUT THE STONE KING.

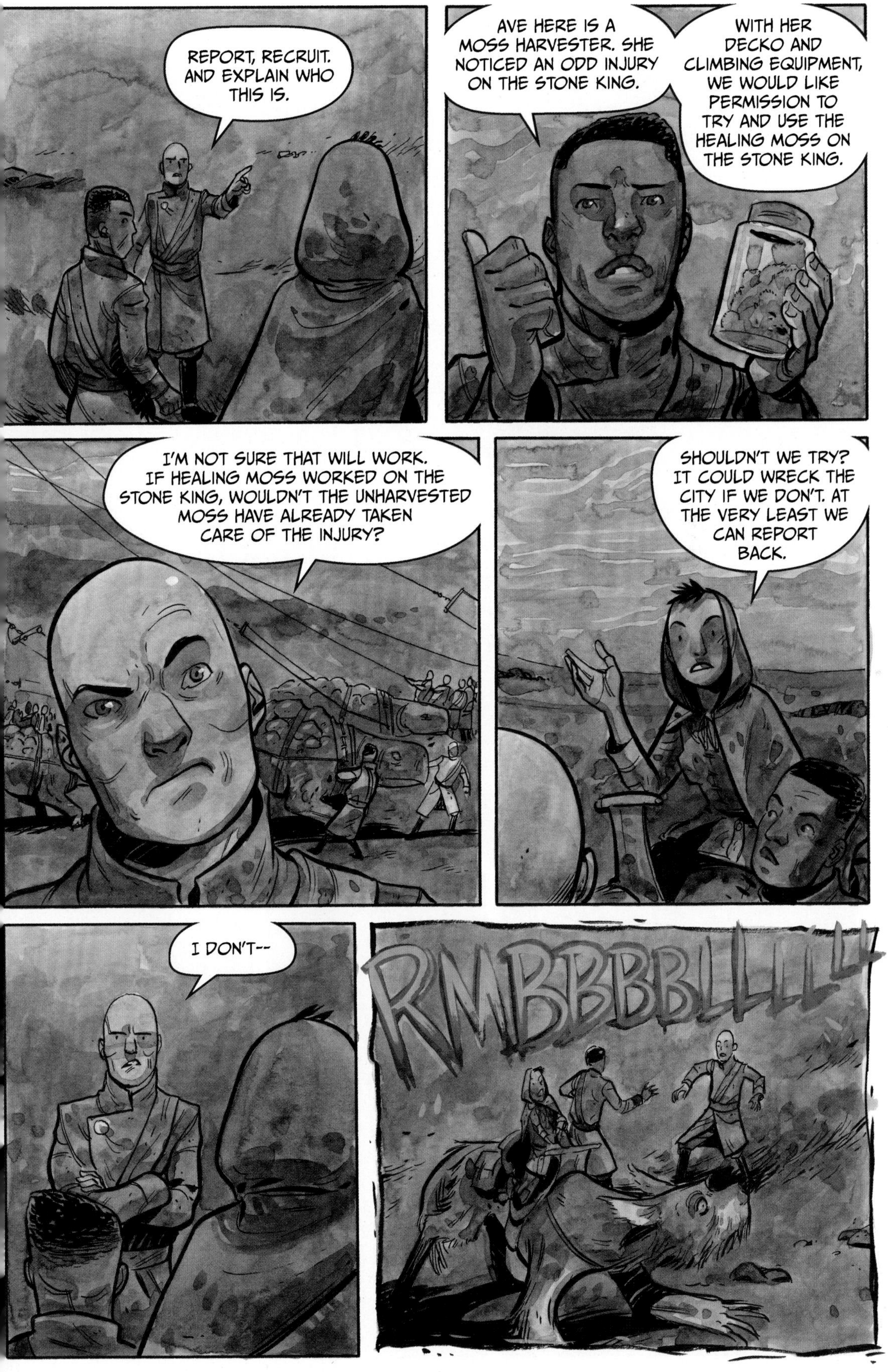
REPORT, RECRUIT. AND EXPLAIN WHO THIS IS.
AVE HERE IS A MOSS HARVESTER. SHE NOTICED AN ODD INJURY ON THE STONE KING.
WITH HER DECKO AND CLIMBING EQUIPMENT, WE WOULD LIKE PERMISSION TO TRY AND USE THE HEALING MOSS ON THE STONE KING.
I'M NOT SURE THAT WILL WORK. IF HEALING MOSS WORKED ON THE STONE KING, WOULDN'T THE UNHARVESTED MOSS HAVE ALREADY TAKEN CARE OF THE INJURY?
SHOULDN'T WE TRY? IT COULD WRECK THE CITY IF WE DON'T. AT THE VERY LEAST WE CAN REPORT BACK.
I DON'T--
RMBBBLLLL

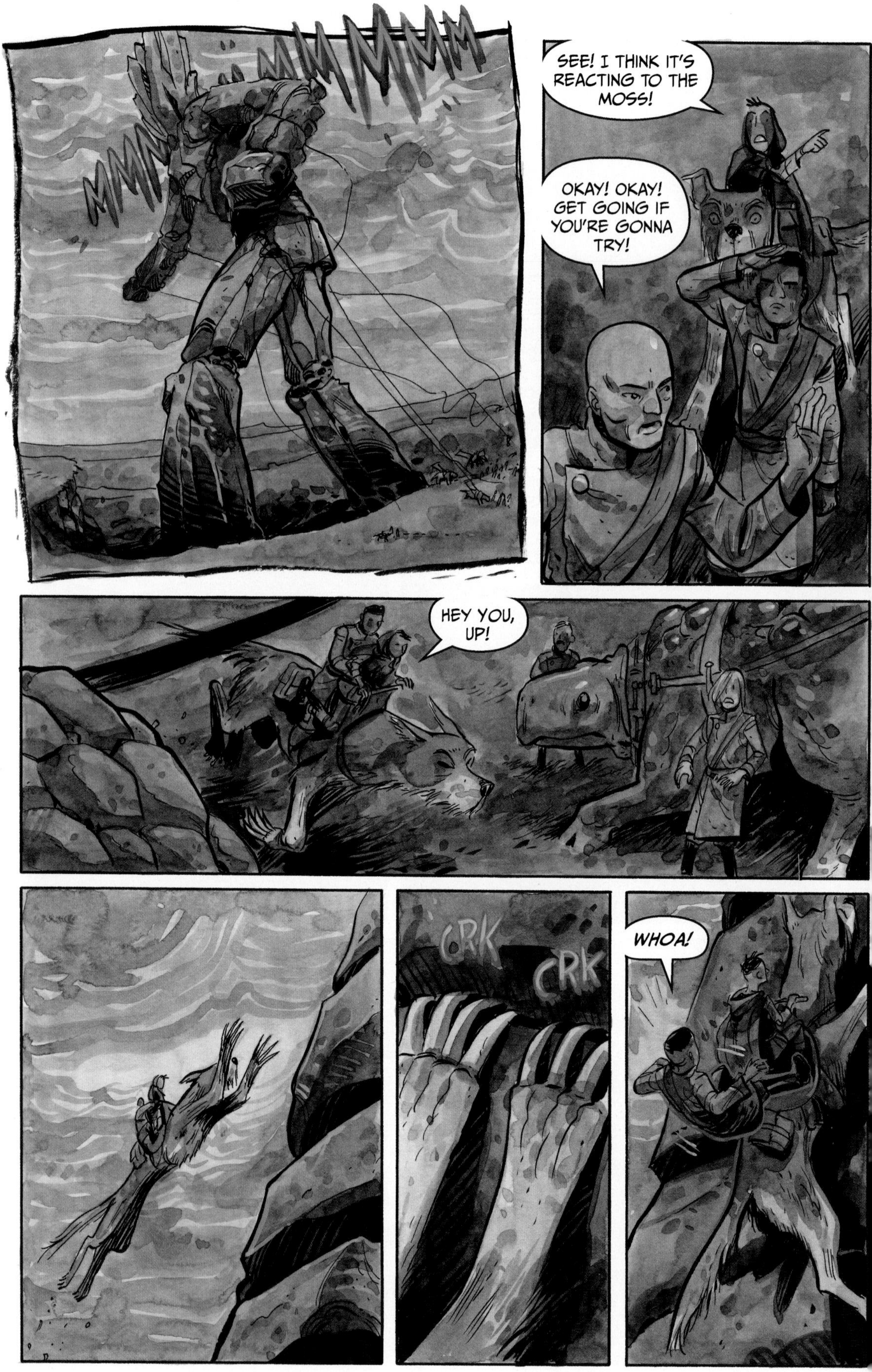
MMMMMMMMMMM
SEE! I THINK IT'S REACTING TO THE MOSS!
OKAY! OKAY! GET GOING IF YOU'RE GONNA TRY!
HEY YOU, UP!
CRK
CRK
WHOA!

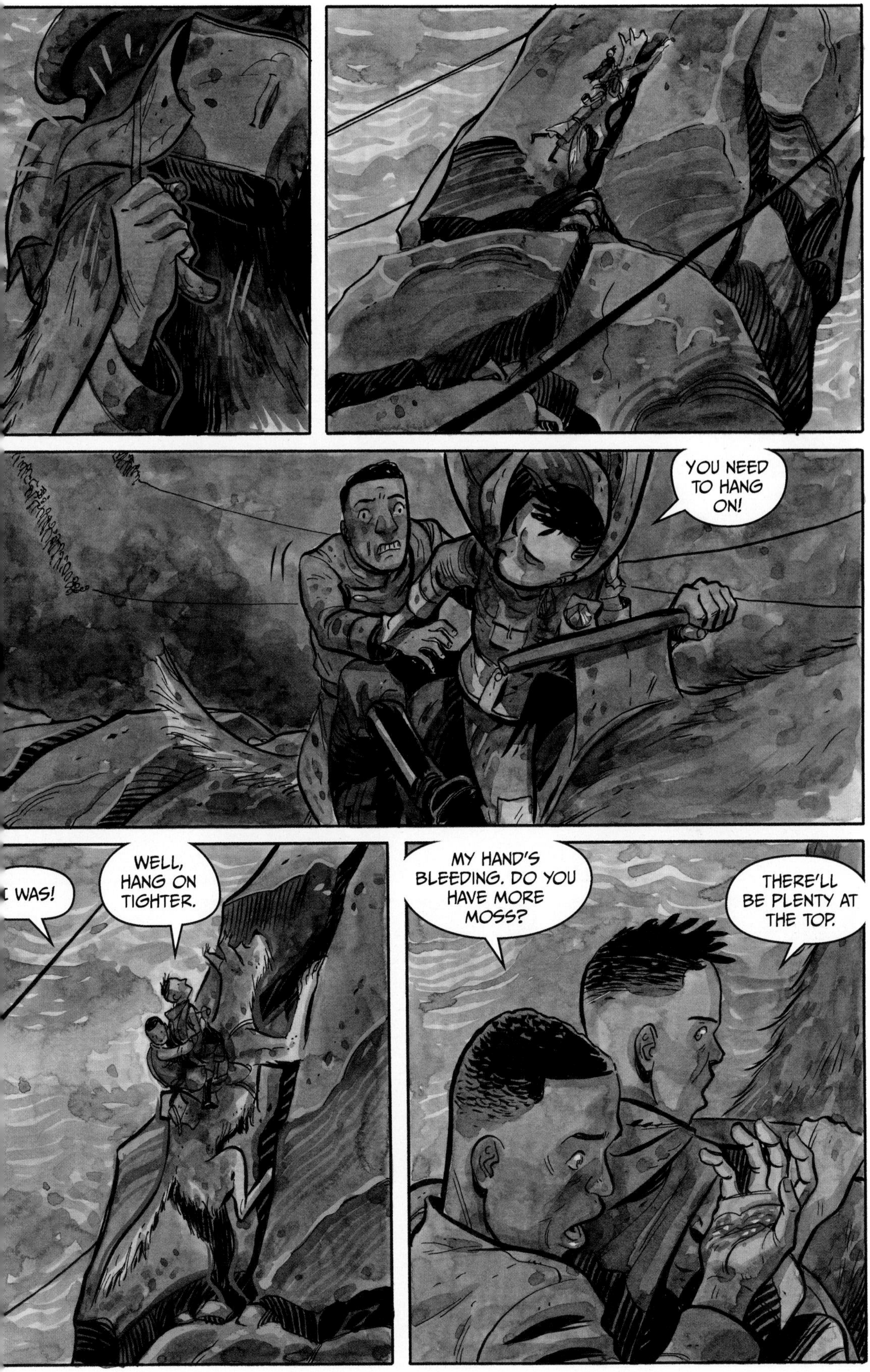
YOU NEED TO HANG ON!
I WAS!
WELL, HANG ON TIGHTER.
MY HAND'S BLEEDING. DO YOU HAVE MORE MOSS?
THERE'LL BE PLENTY AT THE TOP.

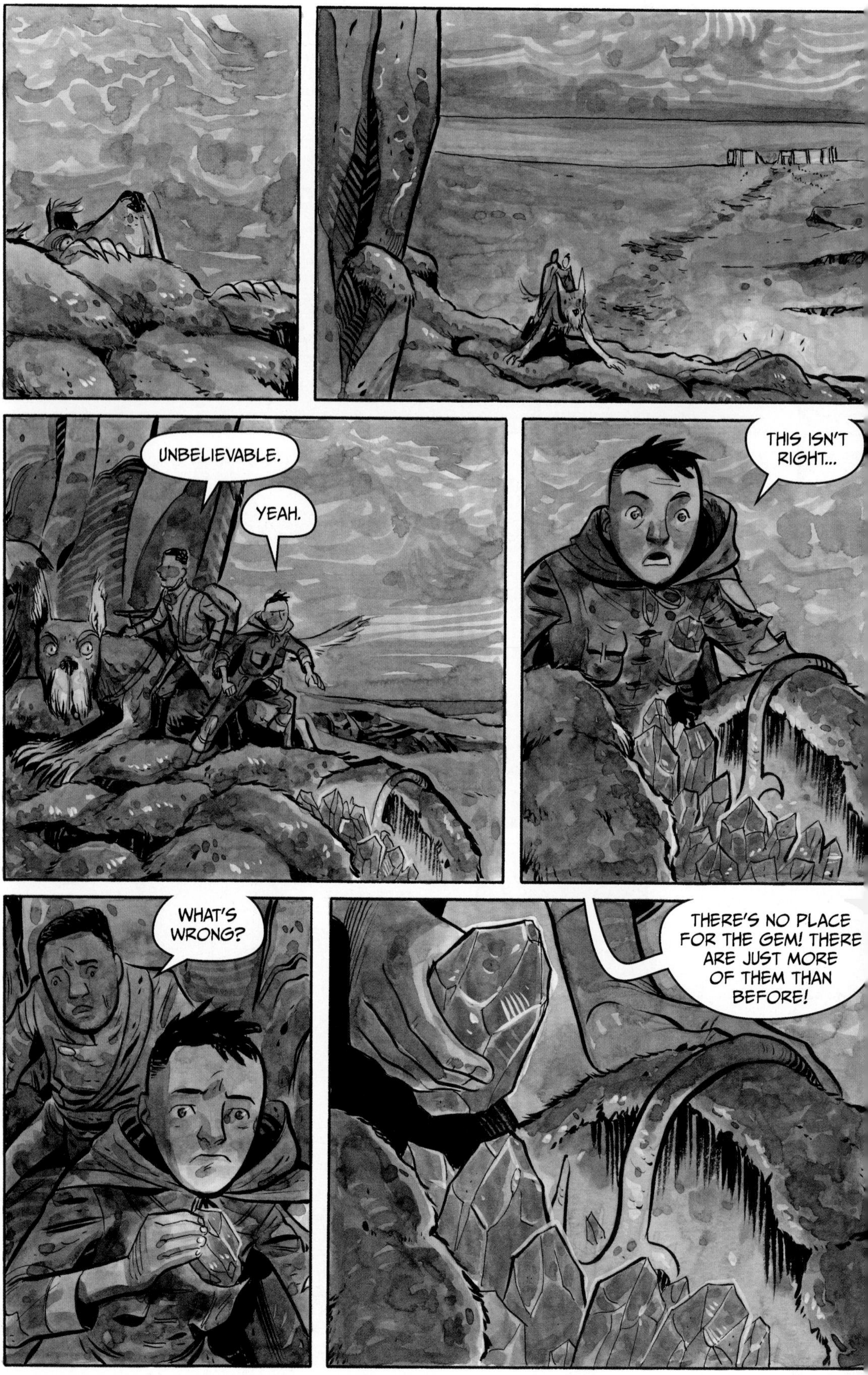
UNBELIEVABLE.
YEAH.
THIS ISN'T RIGHT...
WHAT'S WRONG?
THERE'S NO PLACE FOR THE GEM! THERE ARE JUST MORE OF THEM THAN BEFORE!

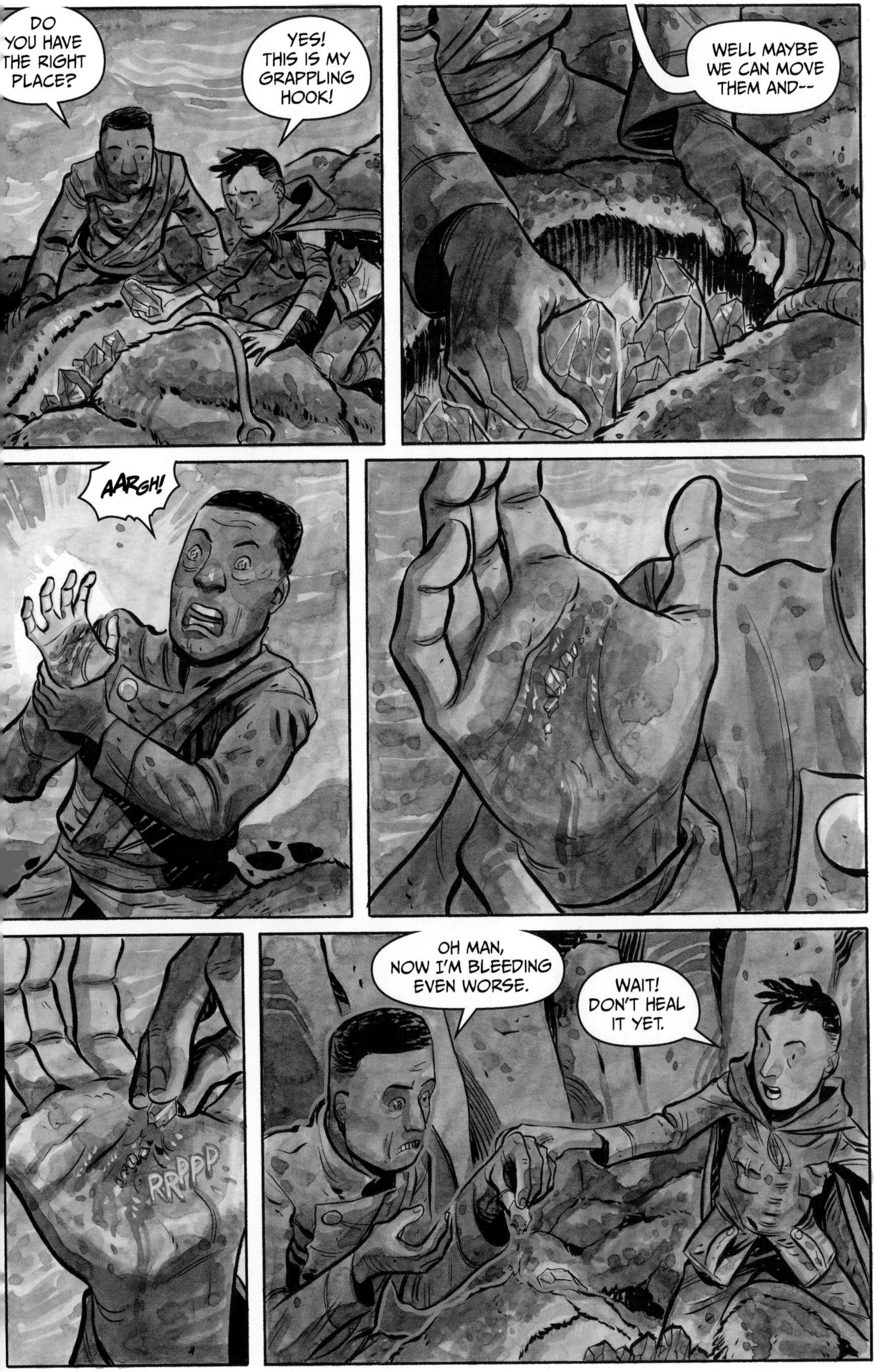
DO YOU HAVE THE RIGHT PLACE?
YES! THIS IS MY GRAPPLING HOOK!
WELL MAYBE WE CAN MOVE THEM AND--
AARGH!
RRPPP
OH MAN, NOW I'M BLEEDING EVEN WORSE.
WAIT! DON'T HEAL IT YET.

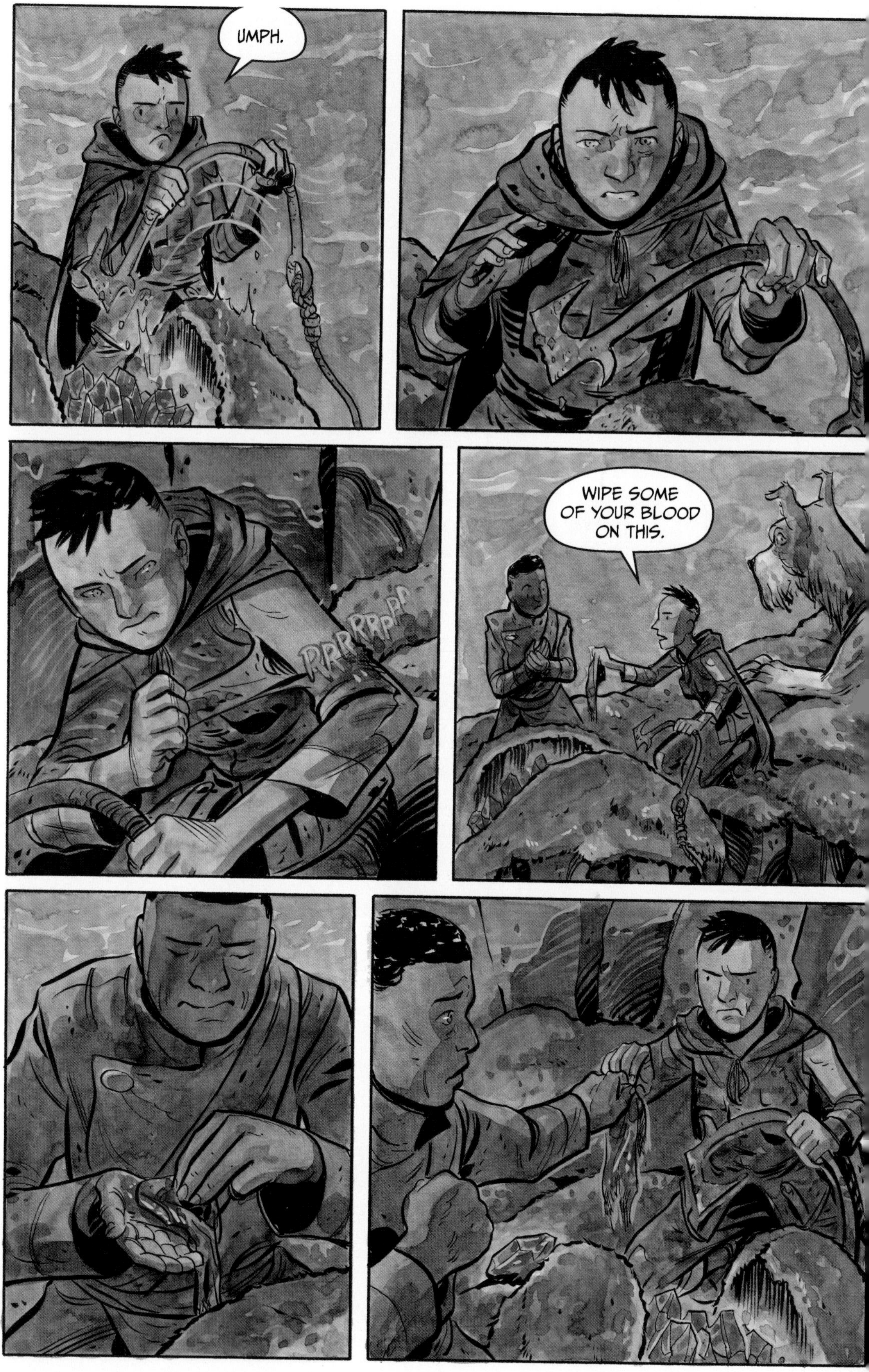
UMPH.
PRRRRRPPP
WIPE SOME OF YOUR BLOOD ON THIS.

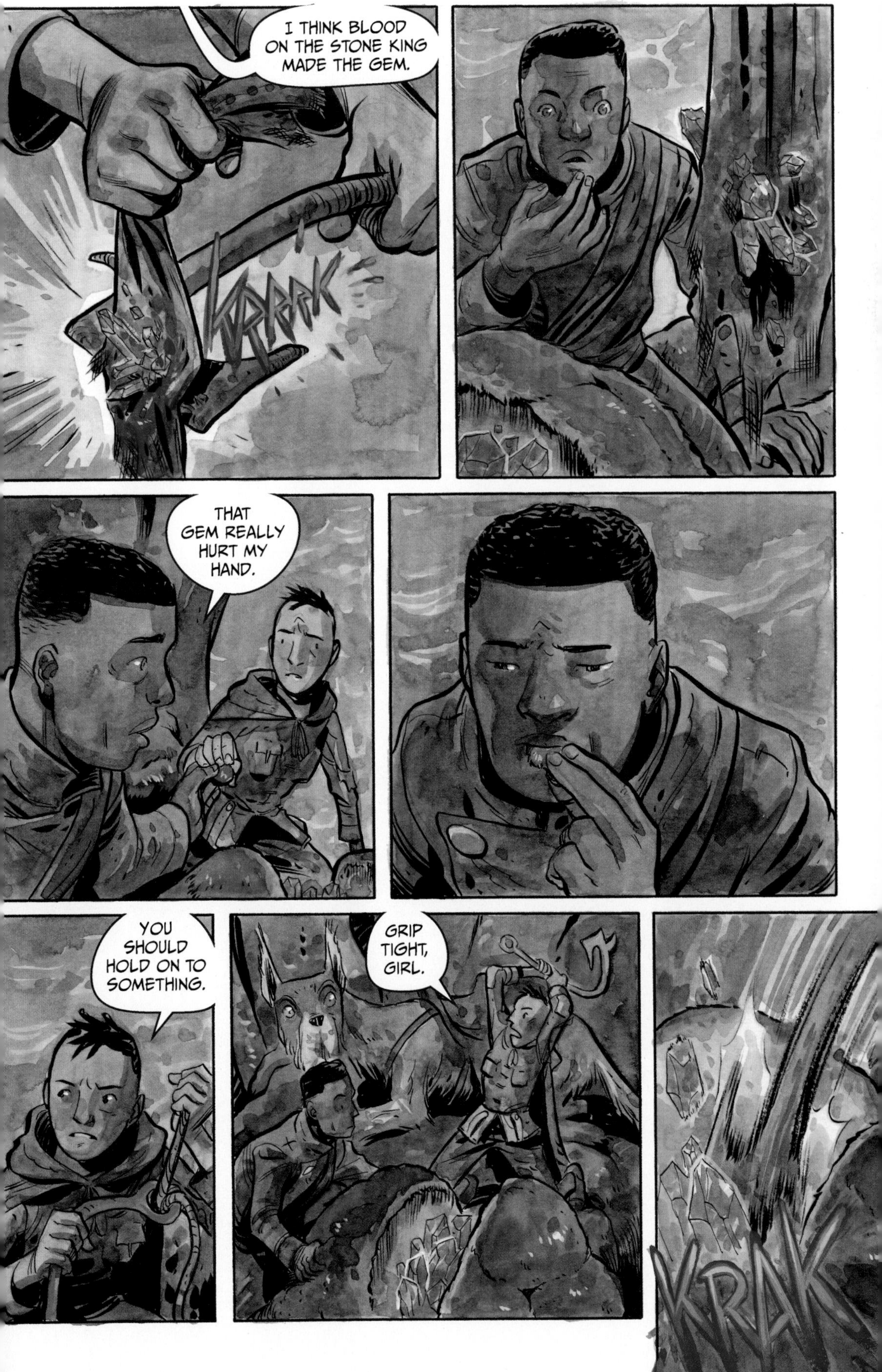
I THINK BLOOD ON THE STONE KING MADE THE GEM.
KRRRK
THAT GEM REALLY HURT MY HAND.
YOU SHOULD HOLD ON TO SOMETHING.
GRIP TIGHT, GIRL.
KRAK

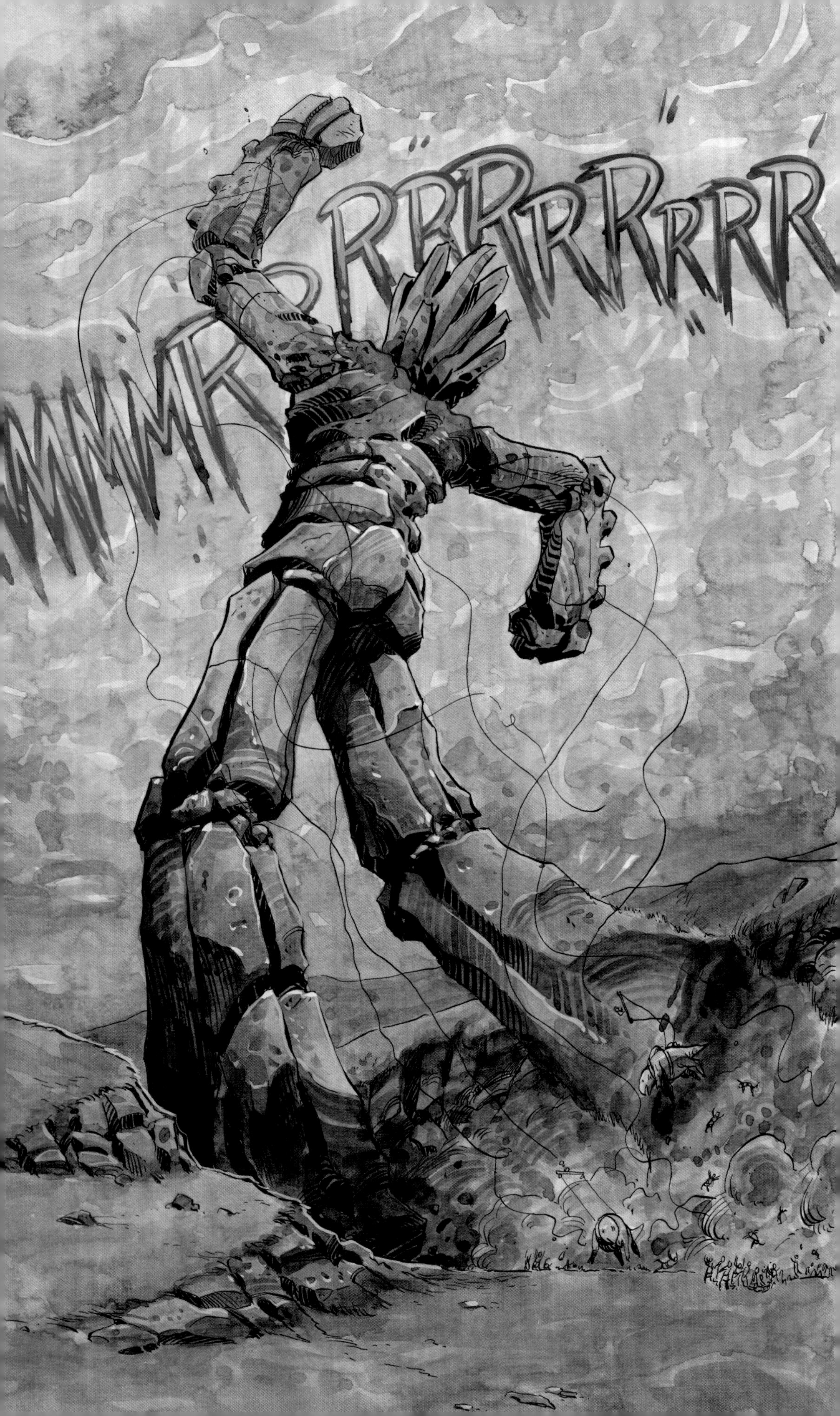
MMMMRRRRRRRrrrR

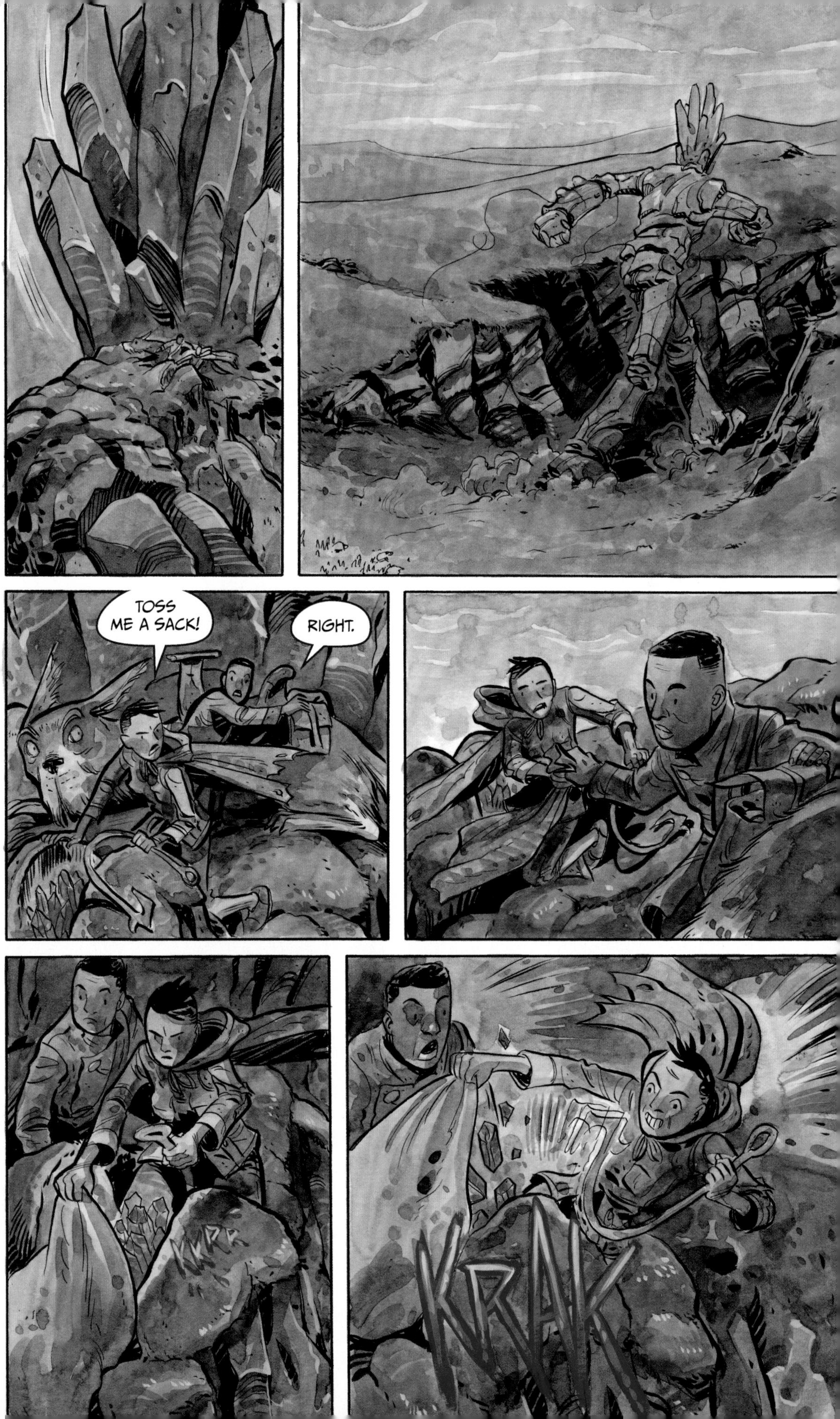
TOSS ME A SACK!
RIGHT.
KRAK

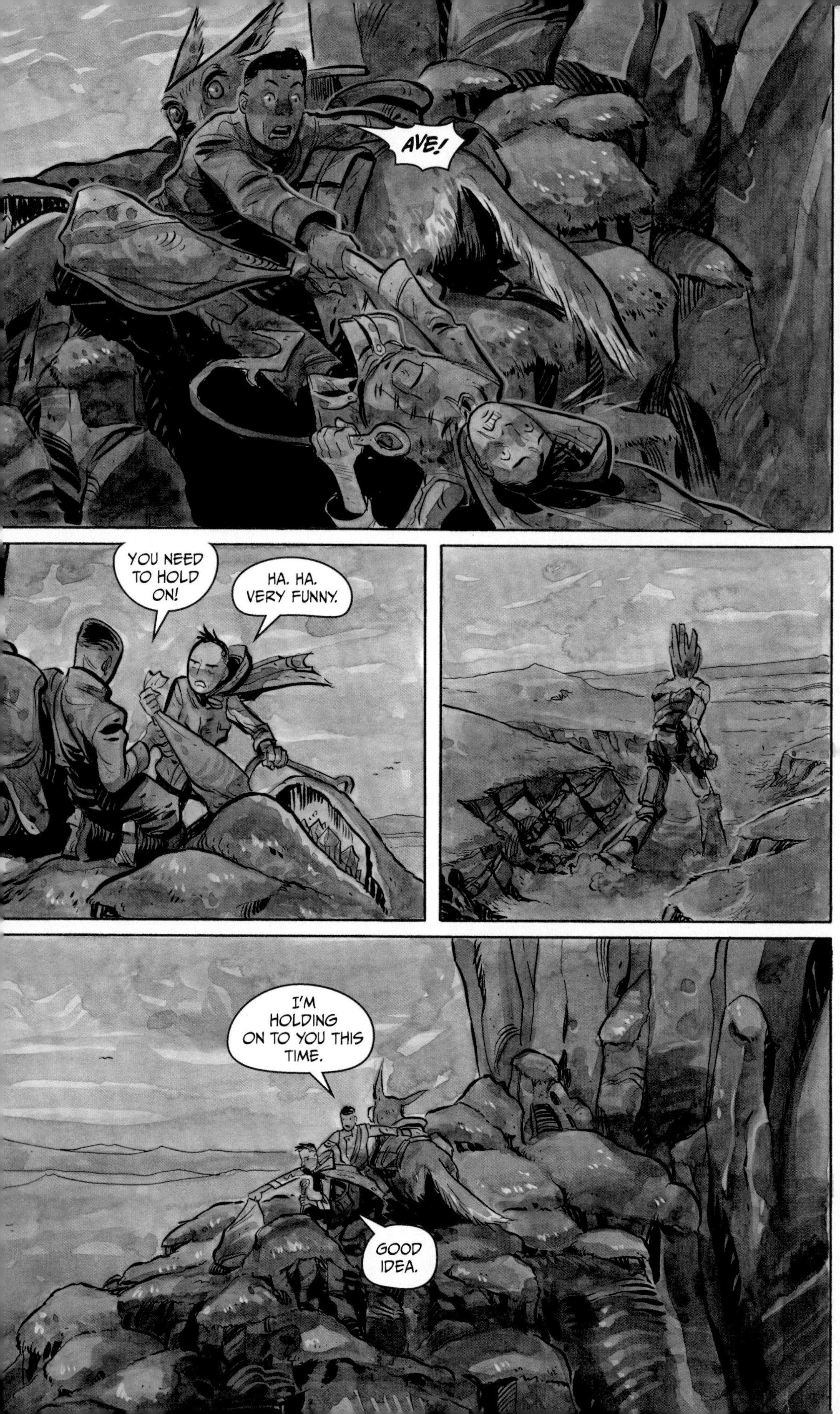
AVE!
YOU NEED TO HOLD ON!
HA. HA. VERY FUNNY.
I'M HOLDING ON TO YOU THIS TIME.
GOOD IDEA.

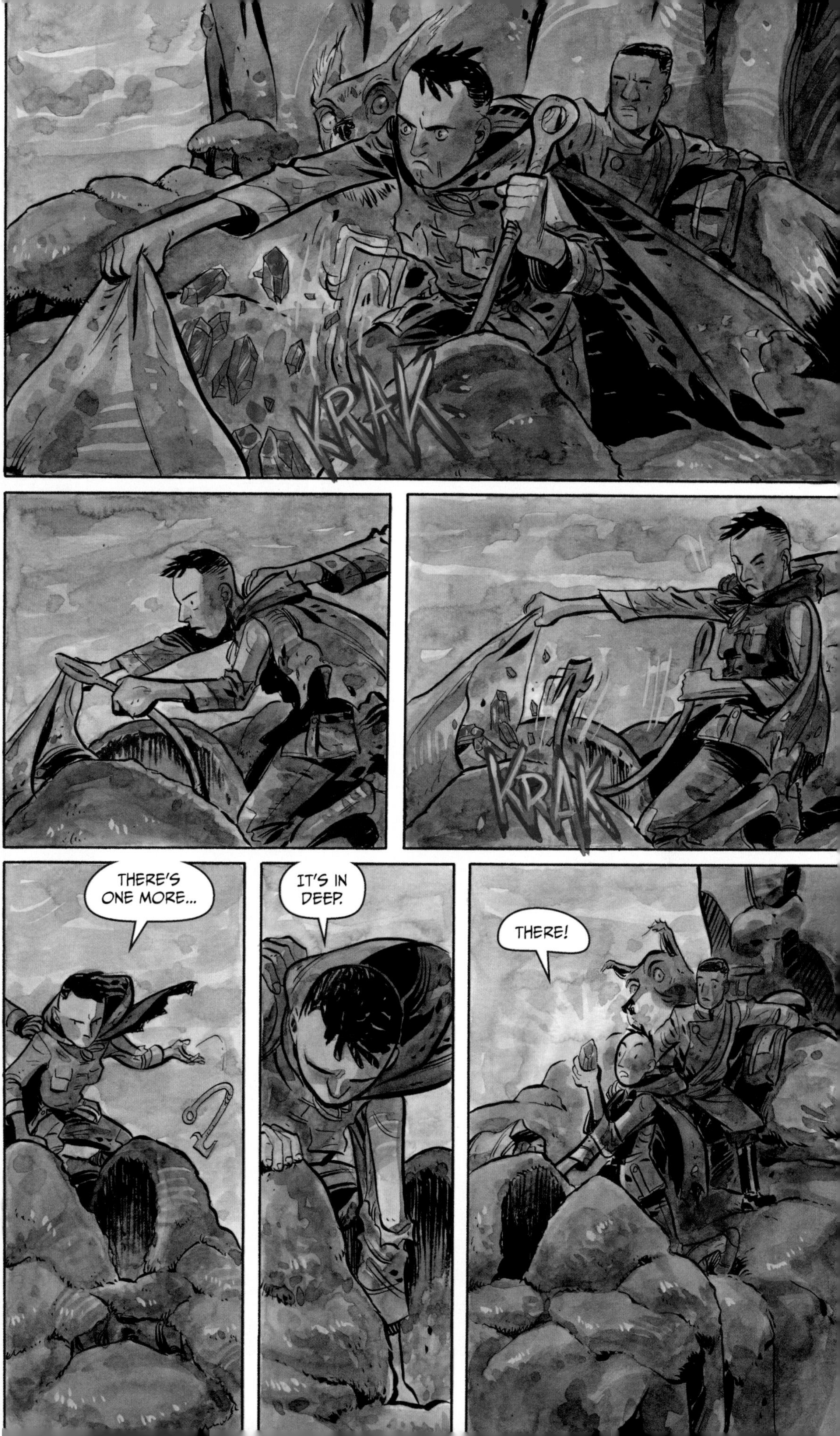
KRAK
KRAK
THERE'S ONE MORE...
IT'S IN DEEP.
THERE!

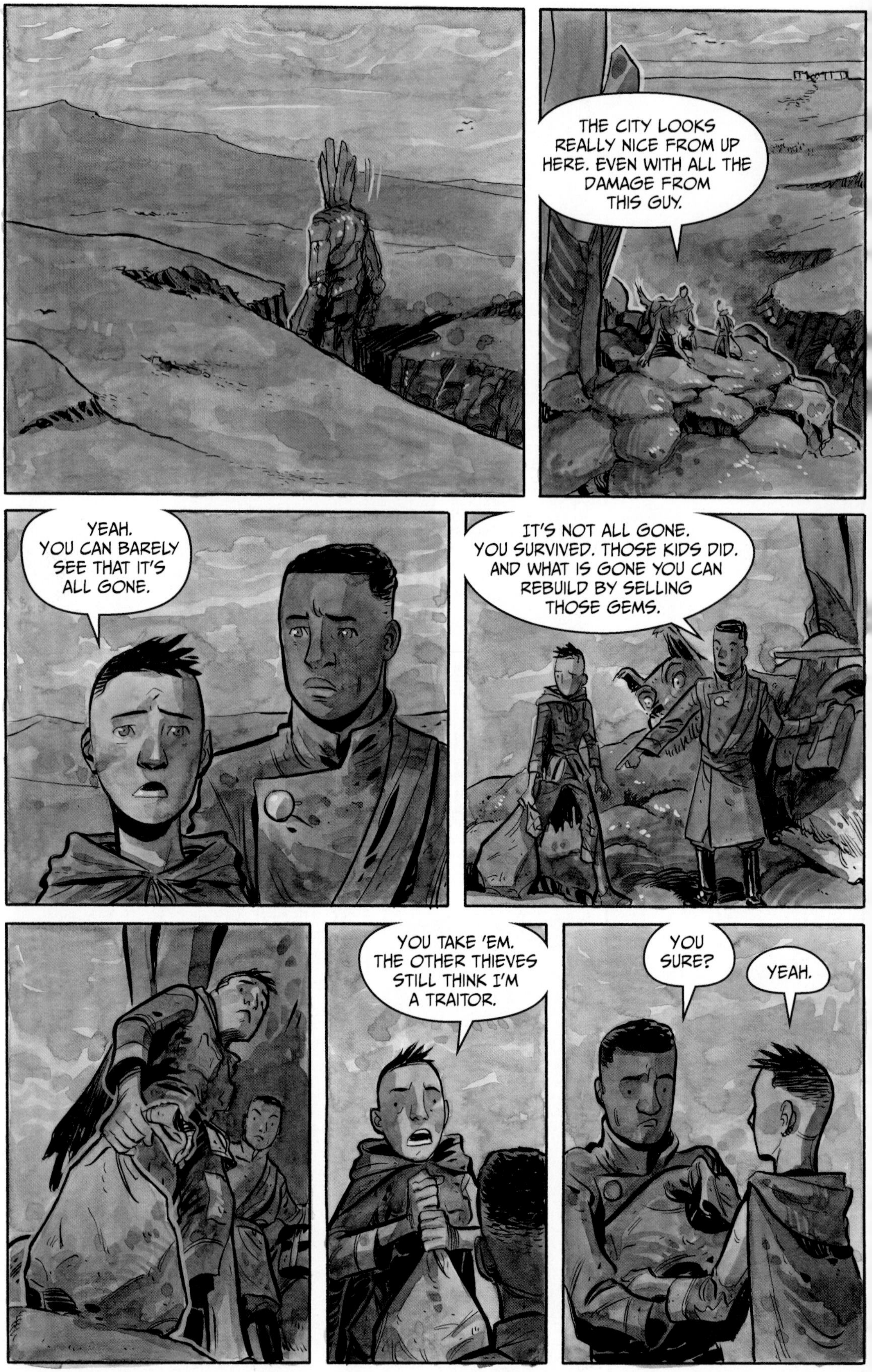
THE CITY LOOKS REALLY NICE FROM UP HERE. EVEN WITH ALL THE DAMAGE FROM THIS GUY.
YEAH. YOU CAN BARELY SEE THAT IT'S ALL GONE.
IT'S NOT ALL GONE. YOU SURVIVED. THOSE KIDS DID. AND WHAT IS GONE YOU CAN REBUILD BY SELLING THOSE GEMS.
YOU TAKE 'EM. THE OTHER THIEVES STILL THINK I'M A TRAITOR.
YOU SURE?
YEAH.

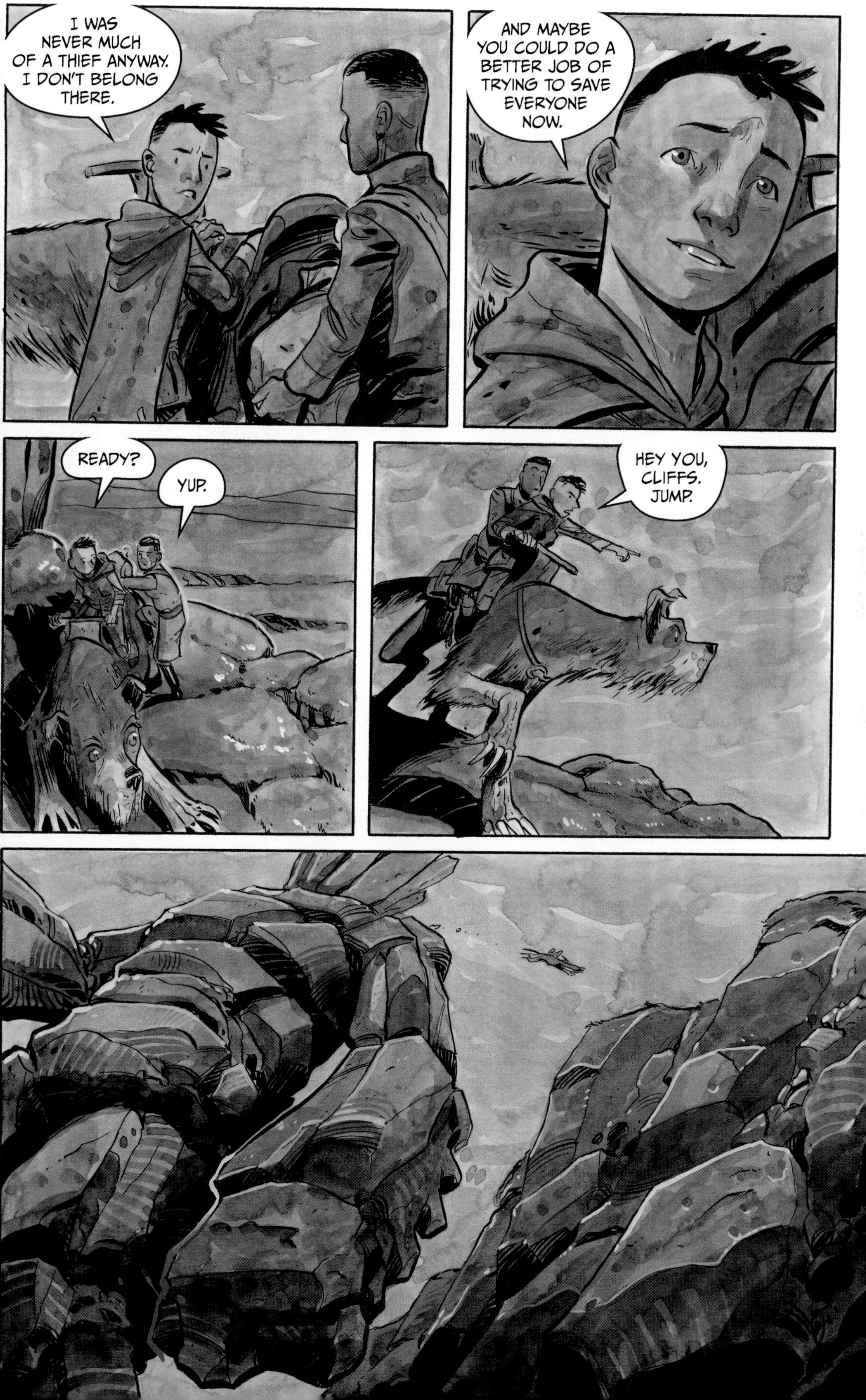
I WAS NEVER MUCH OF A THIEF ANYWAY. I DON'T BELONG THERE.
AND MAYBE YOU COULD DO A BETTER JOB OF TRYING TO SAVE EVERYONE NOW.
READY?
YUP.
HEY YOU, CLIFFS. JUMP.

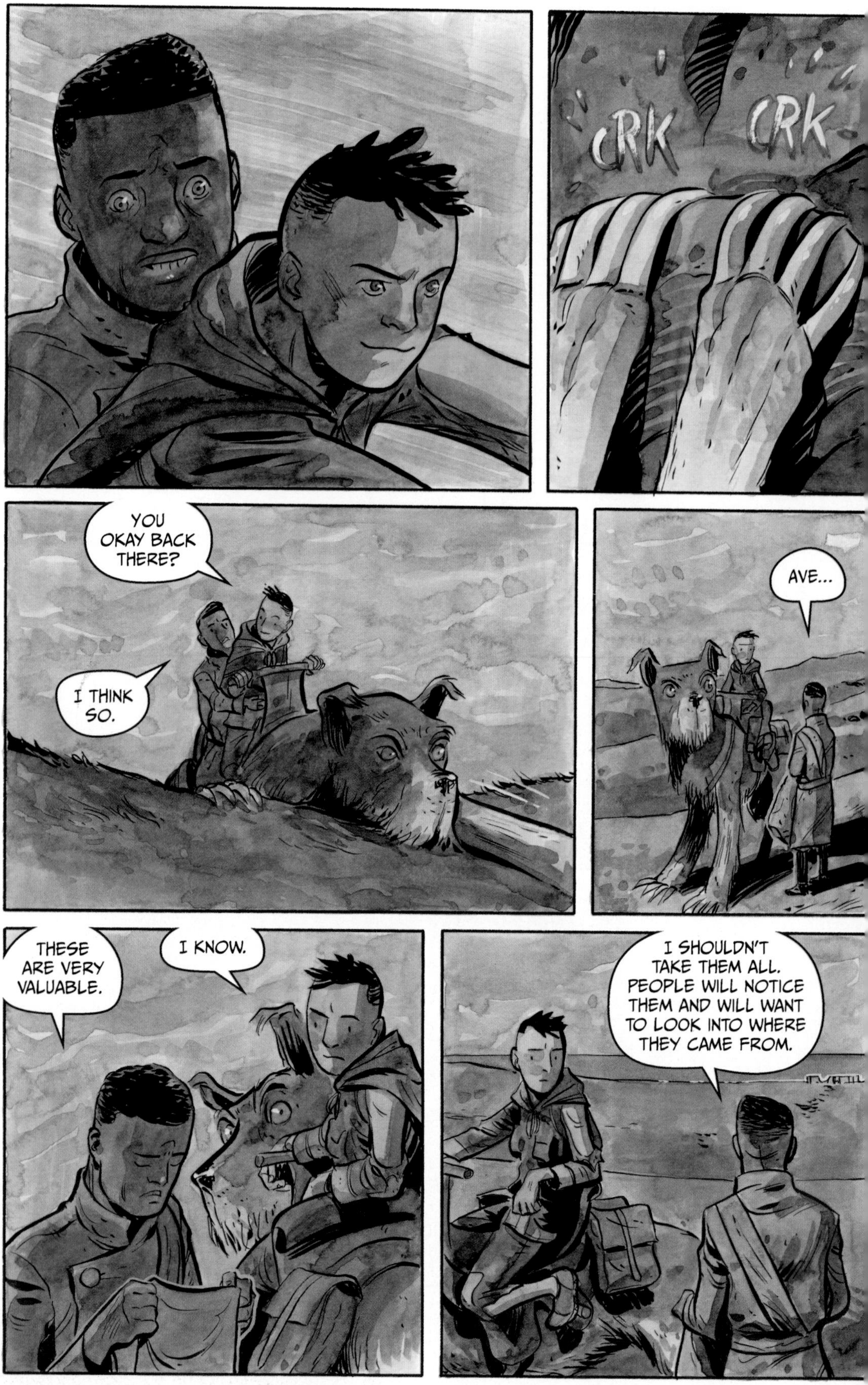
CRK CRK
YOU OKAY BACK THERE?
I THINK SO.
AVE...
THESE ARE VERY VALUABLE.
I KNOW.
I SHOULDN'T TAKE THEM ALL. PEOPLE WILL NOTICE THEM AND WILL WANT TO LOOK INTO WHERE THEY CAME FROM.

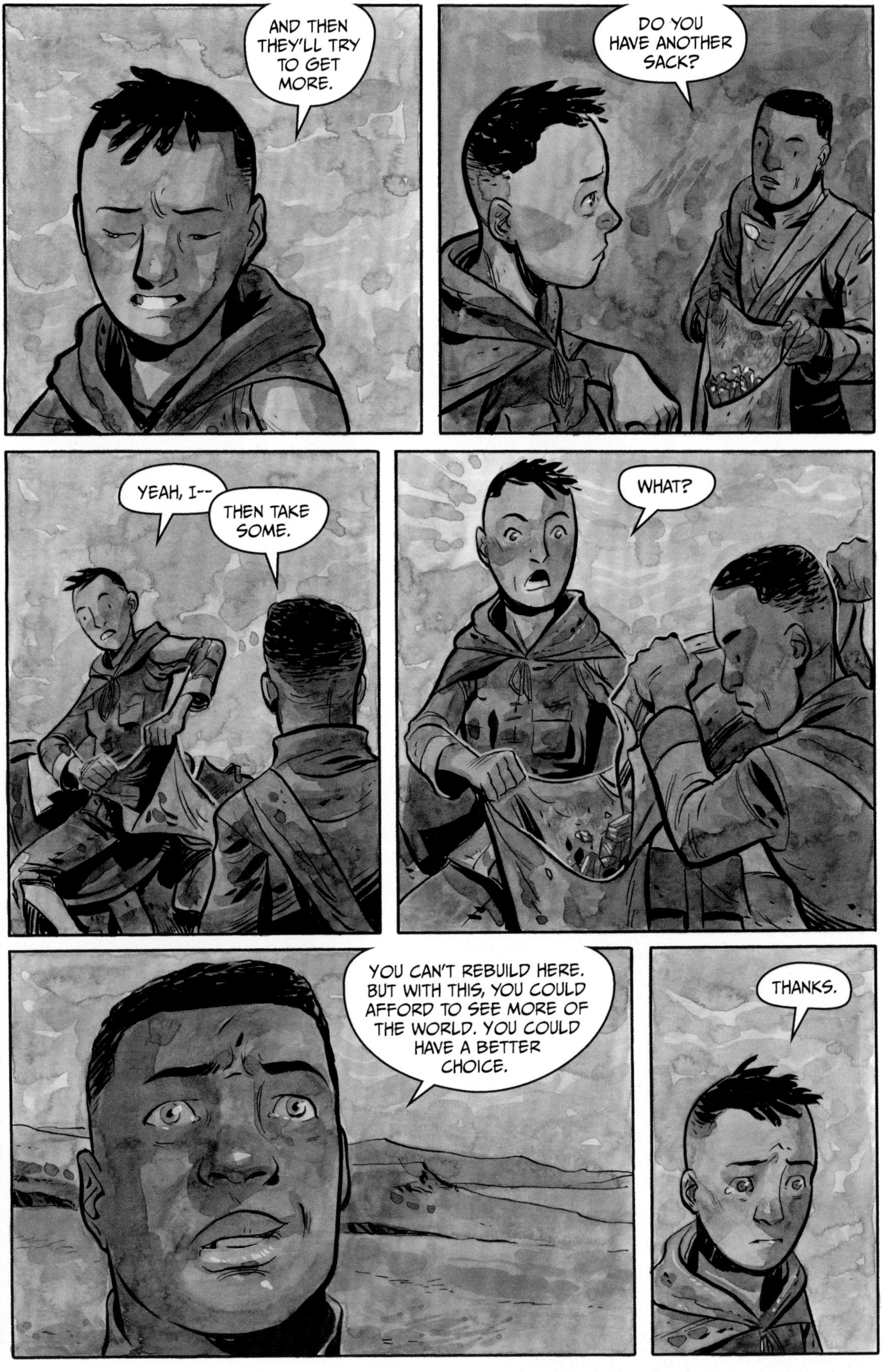
AND THEN THEY'LL TRY TO GET MORE.
DO YOU HAVE ANOTHER SACK?
YEAH, I--
THEN TAKE SOME.
WHAT?
YOU CAN'T REBUILD HERE. BUT WITH THIS, YOU COULD AFFORD TO SEE MORE OF THE WORLD. YOU COULD HAVE A BETTER CHOICE.
THANKS.

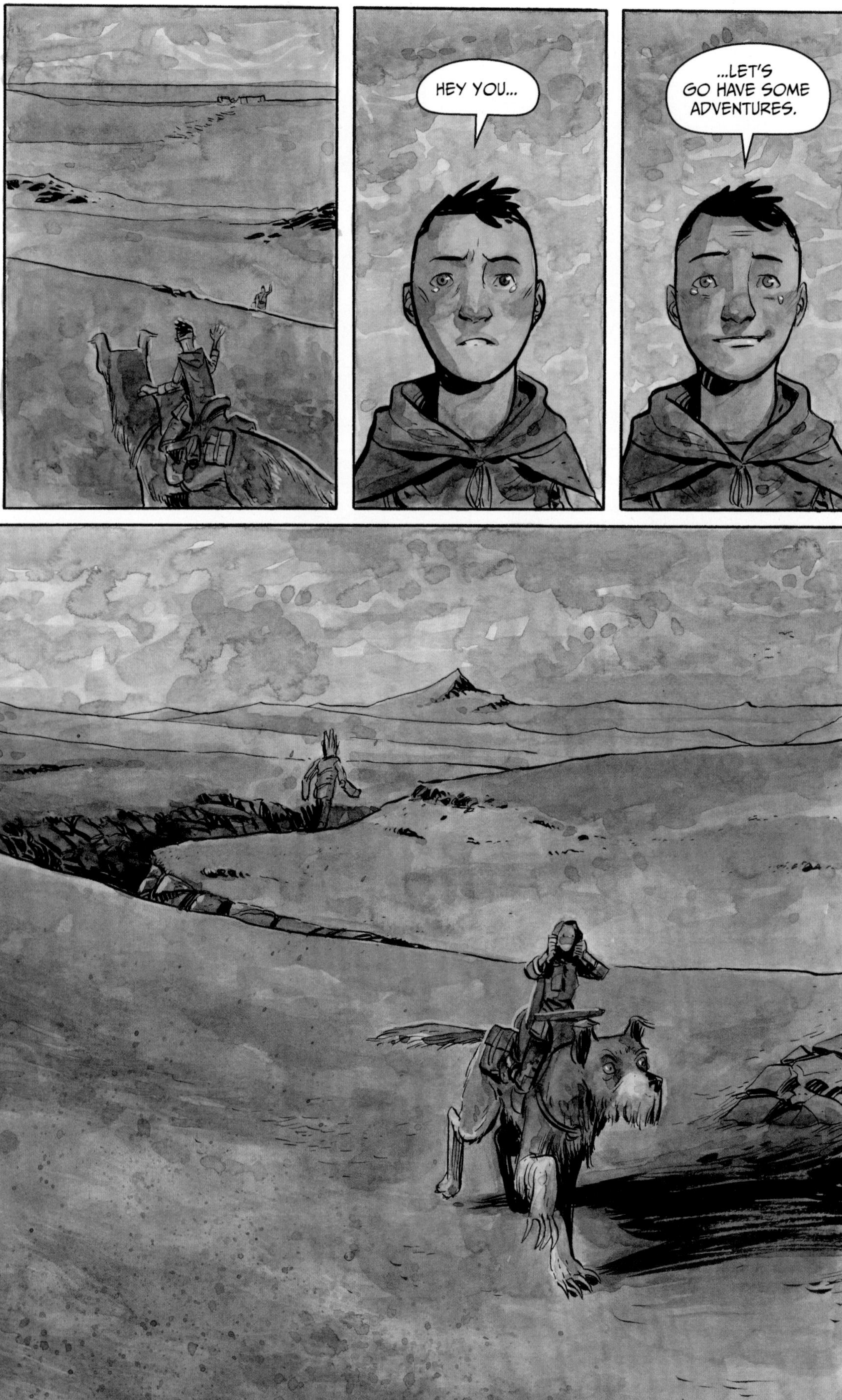
HEY YOU...
...LET'S GO HAVE SOME ADVENTURES.

THE WORLD OF THE STONE KING

NONE CAN REMEMBER HOW LONG THE STONE KING HAS ROAMED THE LAND. THE GIANT IS OLDER THAN ANY OF THE VILLAGES OR THE CITY THAT DEPEND ON IT.

THE MOSS GROWING ON ITS SHOULDERS HAS FANTASTICAL HEALING PROPERTIES. THERE'S A GREAT NEED FOR THE MOSS AND MANY OF THE ELITE HAVE PROFITED GREATLY FROM ITS SALE.

BUT THE STONE KING CARES NOT FOR HUMAN NEED. MANY HAVE FALLEN TRYING TO CLIMB ITS MIGHTY SHOULDERS. THE CITY NOW REQUIRES PROPER TRAINING AND PERMITS. THIS IS TO KEEP THE FOOLISH FROM HARM AND KEEP THE MOSS UNDER THE ELITES' CONTROL.

THOUGH IT IS DISTANT AND SILENT, SCHOLARS AND HOLY WOMEN HAVE TRIED TO COMMUNICATE WITH IT. THE OLDEST SCROLLS SPEAK OF THE STONE KING AND A RED CURSE, WITHOUT A CLEAR CONNECTION.

ONE THING IS CLEAR ABOUT THIS GIANT. THE CITY WOULDN'T BE THE SHINING SPOT OF WEALTH IT IS IF NOT FOR ITS RELATIONSHIP WITH THE STONE KING.

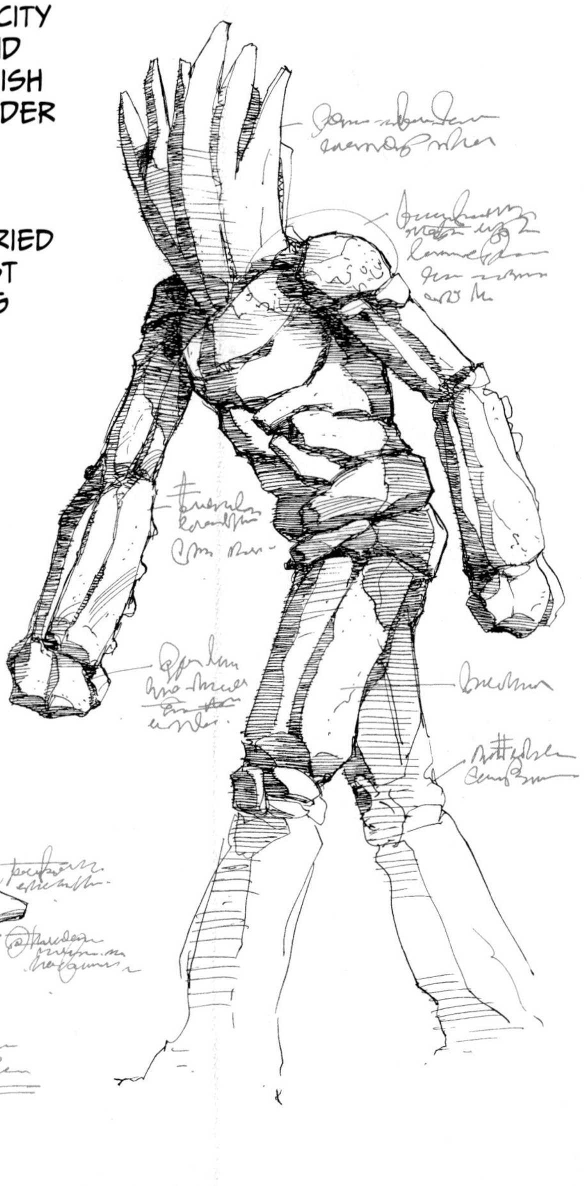

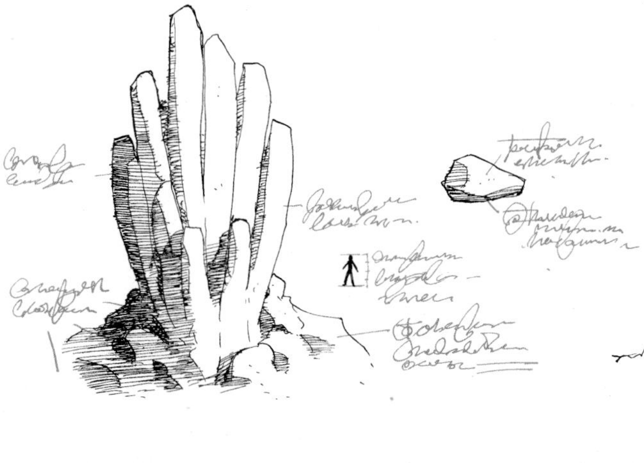

THE WORLD OF THE STONE KING

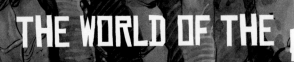

DECKOS

DECKOS ARE A SOLID COMPANION FOR ANY HUNTER OR TRAVELER. WHILE THEY CAN'T CARRY LARGER PASSENGERS FOR LONG DURATIONS, THEIR SPEED AND ABILITY TO CLIMB SHEER CLIFFS MAKE THEM EXCELLENT FOR HARSH MOUNTAIN TERRAIN. THEIR FRIENDLY NATURE ALSO MAKES THEM GREAT COMPANIONS AND PROTECTORS FOR SMALL CHILDREN, WHILE THEIR SIZE IS A DETERRENT TO MOST BANDITS AND WILD ANIMALS.

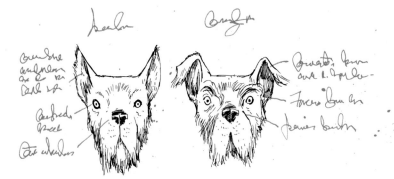

STONEBACKS

TO BUILD A GREAT CITY REQUIRES THE ABILITY TO MOVE A GREAT DEAL OF STONE AND BRICK. SO IT'S UNDERSTANDABLE THAT THE STONEBACKS WOULD BE QUITE COMMON AROUND STONEPORT. THESE LARGE BEASTS ARE SLOW, BUT THEY CAN WORK FOR DAYS WITHOUT REST. AS LONG AS THEY ARE WELL FED, THEY WILL KEEP THEIR STEADY, STRONG PACE.

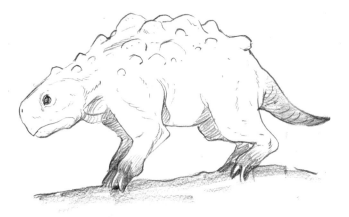

THE WORLD OF THE STONE KING

WOCK

WOCK ARE THE DECKO'S WILD COUSIN. DESPITE THEIR LARGER BUILD, THE MOSS GROWING IN THEIR FUR MAKES THEM HARD TO SPOT ON THE MOUNTAINSIDE. THEIR CLAWS CAN CRUSH HUMAN SKULLS JUST AS EASILY AS THEY CAN DIG INTO ROCKY CLIFFS. MYTHS ABOUT THESE BEASTS CLAIM THE DECKOS WERE A GIFT FROM THE KING OF THE WOCK AFTER HE WAS DEFEATED IN BATTLE BY A GREAT WARRIOR. THIS TALE HAS LED TO MANY YOUNG WARRIORS TESTING THEIR METTLE BY HUNTING A WOCK.

THE WORLD OF THE STONE KING

THANKS TO THE PROXIMITY OF THE STONE KING, THIS SMALL FISHING
TOWN QUICKLY GREW INTO A MIGHTY TRADING FORCE. TALES OF THE
MAGICAL HEALING MOSS SPREAD AND IT BECAME A NECESSITY IN EVERY
PHYSICIAN'S COLLECTION FAR AND WIDE. THE PRECIOUS RESOURCE FROM
THE STONE KING'S SHOULDERS BROUGHT WEALTH TO STONEPORT, BUT
ALSO MADE IT A TARGET.

PROTECTED BY A CLIFF FACE THAT HIDES THE CITY FROM LAND INVADERS
AND A ROCKY CAPE THAT PROTECTS IT FROM PIRATES, THE WALLS AND
LANDSCAPE OF STONEPORT WORK TOGETHER TO HIDE THE CITY—UNLESS
YOU LOOK HARD
FOR IT. THE
GEOGRAPHY AND
ARCHITECTURE
SAVE STONEPORT'S
WONDERS FOR
THE CITIZENS AND
TRADERS ALREADY
WITHIN ITS WALLS.

WITH A
WORKFORCE AND
MILITARY THAT
DON'T NEED TIME
OFF TO HEAL
FROM INJURIES,
STONEPORT
HAS BECOME
PRODUCTIVE AND
STURDY LIKE ITS
NEIGHBOR, THE
STONE KING.

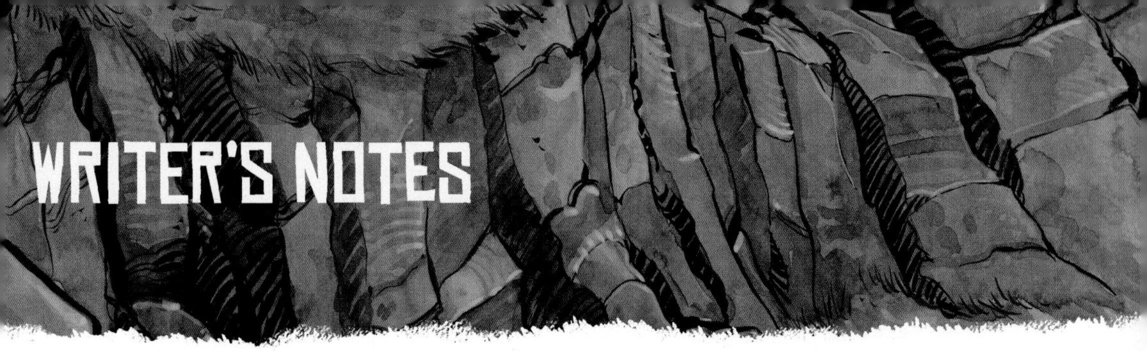

WRITER'S NOTES

PAGES 5–8

I WANTED *THE STONE KING* TO OPEN UP WITH A SILENT ACTION SCENE. IT WOULD BUILD ATMOSPHERE AND MOOD. IT'S KINDA A RISKY APPROACH 'CAUSE IT'S EASY FOR A READER TO SEE THIS SILENT BIT AND THINK, "WHY SHOULD I CARE ABOUT THIS PERSON?" BUT THE STONE KING IS HUGE AND THIS QUIETER OPENING IS A GOOD WAY TO SHOW THE READER RATHER THAN TELL.

IT WAS ORIGINALLY TWO PAGES BUT TYLER SUGGESTED WE ADD MORE TO HELP SHOW OFF THE LANDSCAPE.

THAT FIRST SPLASH PAGE IS KEY TO INTRODUCING THE SILENT GIANT THOUGH.

PAGES 9–13

AVE'S CLIMB UP DOES A LOT OF WORK TO ESTABLISH THINGS VISUALLY.

TYLER'S ART DOES SUCH A GREAT JOB SHOWING THAT ALL OFF THAT THE SCENE DOESN'T NEED DIALOGUE. WHICH IS GOOD, BECAUSE I USUALLY HATE IT WHEN CHARACTERS TALK TO THEMSELVES.

A TINY DETAIL THAT IS EASY TO MISS IS THE BLOOD AROUND THE STONE KING'S CUT. IT'S NOT THERE UNTIL AVE CLIMBS PAST IT TO GET TO THE HEALING MOSS. THE IDEA IS SOME OF HER BLOOD GOT NEAR THE STONE KING'S CUT. IT'S EASY TO FORGET ABOUT IT, BECAUSE AVE FORGETS ABOUT IT TOO. SHE'S TOO DISTRACTED BY HER NEW RUBY—A GLOW IN THE CUT THAT WASN'T THERE UNTIL AFTER HER BLOOD GOT SMEARED THERE.

PAGES 14–18

THE RUBY IS OUR STORY MACGUFFIN. AVE'S EXCITEMENT ABOUT IT, RATHER THAN THE MOSS HEALING HER, IS TO MAKE IT CLEAR THAT THE MOSS IS A KNOWN THING TO HER. THIS GEM IS SOMETHING NEW AND EXCITING.

TYLER AND I BRAINSTORMED A REPLACEMENT FOR "HOLY CRAP!" WE ARE AIMING FOR A MIDDLE-GRADE AGE RANGE, SO THIS HAS THE ADDED BIT OF BOTH WORLD BUILDING AND KEEPING OUT REAL-WORLD CURSES. OUR IDEA WAS THAT THEIR CULTURE AND SUCCESS IS BUILT AROUND THE STONE KING, SO THEIR CURSES SHOULD REFLECT THAT.

AVE SHOWING IT OFF TO HEY YOU AND HAVING HER ATTEMPT TO EAT IT WAS SOMETHING I THOUGHT WOULD BE CUTE. TYLER ADDED THE LINE OF DROOL WHEN AVE TAKES IT FROM HER MOUTH.

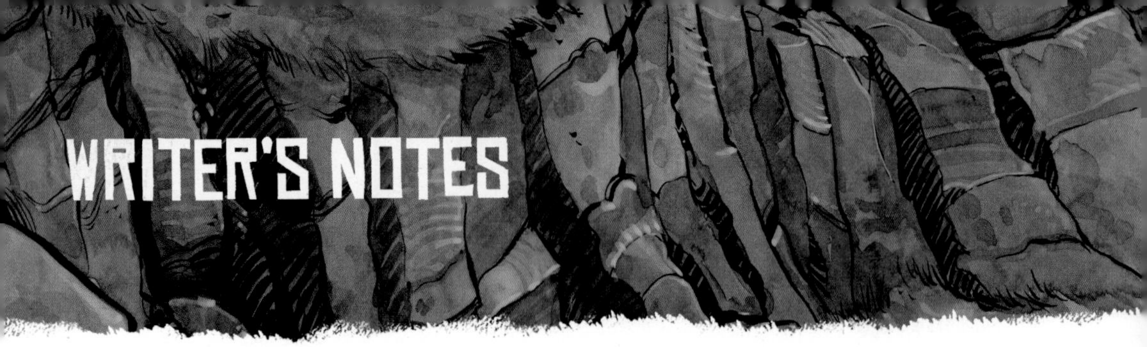

WRITER'S NOTES

AND WITH AVE'S FIRST REAL BATCH OF DIALOGUE (RATHER THAN JUST CURSES AND "OH NO"S) WE GIVE YOU SOME CONTEXT FOR HER CLIMB AND IMMEDIATELY START THE THREAD OF HER NOT ENTIRELY LIKING HER ROLE IN LIFE.

PAGES 19–20

THE FIRST DRAFT DIDN'T HAVE THIS SCENE. IT WENT STRAIGHT TO HER IN THE CITY. BUT TYLER WANTED TO ESTABLISH MORE OF THE LANDSCAPE AND WHAT THE CITY WAS LIKE FROM THE OUTSIDE. I ALSO REALIZED WE SHOULD INTRODUCE PHUL SOONER. HE IS OUR SECOND MAIN CHARACTER BUT WASN'T APPEARING IN THE FIRST CHAPTER.

I THOUGHT THIS LITTLE GATE-GUARDING SCENE WOULD WORK TO SHOW PHUL IS STILL LEARNING HOW TO BE A GUARD. IT ALSO GIVES AVE SOMETHING TO GIVE CREDIT TO HER STORY WHEN SHE ASKS PHUL FOR HELP.

PAGES 21–22

I ALWAYS LIKE ESTABLISHING SETTINGS LIKE THIS. I THOUGHT OF THE OPENING INTRO OF THE *COWBOY BEBOP* MOVIE AND HOW THAT MAKES THE CITY FEEL LIVED IN AND SHOWS SHOTS OF THE DAILY LIFE.

HERE IS WHERE HAVING A GREAT COLLABORATOR HELPS. I TOLD TYLER THE HIGH POINTS OF WHAT'S GOING ON IN THE CITY. LIKE, THIS IS THE MAIN STREET AND ON IT ARE THESE TYPES OF THINGS, THEN AVE TURNS TO THIS STREET THAT IS LESS POPULATED AND HAS THIS, THEN SHE FINALLY TURNS DOWN ON HER STREET, WHICH IS RUNDOWN AND MORE EMPTY. I ALSO GAVE TYLER THE DIALOGUE THAT RANDOM PEOPLE ARE SAYING. HE COULD THEN BREAK IT UP AND ZOOM IN ON WHAT HE DID AND DIDN'T WANT.

THE ONE THING THAT NEEDS TO BE SEEN CLEARLY, THOUGH, IS THE SHAMAN SAYING A PRAYER OVER THE INJURED PERSON. THAT PRAYER POPS UP AGAIN. IT'S SOMETHING THAT WOULD BE KNOWN TO ANY RESIDENT OF STONEPORT.

PAGES 23–25

RHEEBEE'S INTRO TO THE READER WAS IMPORTANT 'CAUSE SHE IS GONNA INFORM A LOT OF WHO AVE IS AND ADD EMOTIONAL CONFLICT TO AVE'S LIFE. IN THIS SCENE NOTICE THAT RHEEBEE DOESN'T EVER PRAISE AVE. SHE ACCUSES AVE OF LYING AND TRIES TO CHEAT HER OUT OF HER SHARE OF THE PRIZE. ALL SHE GIVES AVE IS HER NEW ASSIGNMENT AND A CYNICAL STATEMENT ABOUT LIFE. IT GIVES YOU A GLIMPSE OF WHAT AVE WANTS TO ESCAPE.

WRITER'S NOTES

PAGES 26-29

I WANTED TO BUILD ON MORE OF AVE'S DISCONTENTMENT WITH THE CITY AND HER LIFE BEFORE EVERYTHING FALLS APART. THERE IS A LITTLE BIT OF "BE CAREFUL WHAT YOU WISH FOR." SHE'S GOT A LONGING FOR MORE, AND ALL SHE HAS IN HER LIFE IS FOLKS WHO TELL HER IT WILL NEVER HAPPEN. I ALSO REALLY LIKE SILENT, CONTEMPLATIVE PANELS.

PAGES 30-33

WHEN THE STONE KING ATTACKS YOU GET TO SEE THE DIFFERENCE BETWEEN SRITCH AND AVE. WHEREAS AVE DOESN'T GET ANY JOY FROM THEIR CIRCUMSTANCES, SRITCH IS THE IDEAL OF WHAT RHEEBEE WANTED OUT OF THE KIDS. DISASTER MAKES AVE THINK OF GETTING EVERYONE OUT, WHEREAS SRITCH THINKS OF GETTING EVERYONE'S STUFF OUT.

THIS LAST DOUBLE-PAGE SPREAD MARKS THE BIGGEST DIFFERENCE BETWEEN THE COMIXOLOGY VERSION AND THE PRINT VERSION. WE WROTE THE SCRIPT BUT THEN GOT SOME GUIDELINES FROM COMIXOLOGY THAT TOLD US NO DOUBLE-PAGE SPREADS. IT MAKES SENSE 'CAUSE THEY DON'T WORK SUPER WELL IN COMIXOLOGY'S GUIDED VIEW. BUT IT'S A GREAT PAGE TURN IN THE BOOK, SO WE KEPT IT THERE. THE DIGITAL VERSION JUST HAS HALF THE SPREAD AND AVE'S INSERT MOVED OVER.

PAGES 34-35

WHEN I WROTE *THE STONE KING*, I DID IT ALL AT ONCE. IN THE COLLECTION, THESE PAGES COME RIGHT AFTER THE BIG DOUBLE-PAGE SPREAD. SO TYLER AND I REUSED THAT SPLASH TO ACT AS THE TITLE PAGE.

THIS IS ALSO THE LAST WE SEE OF SRITCH FOR A WHILE. WHILE AVE IS BUSY GETTING EVERYONE OUT, SRITCH IS LOOTING.

PAGES 36-41

THIS IS THE BIG EMOTIONAL BEAT OF THIS CHAPTER. IT WAS IMPORTANT TO STICK THE LANDING.

ORIGINALLY THIS SCENE PLAYED OUT A LITTLE DIFFERENTLY. IT WAS MOSTLY THE SAME UNTIL AVE NOTICES HOW MUCH RHEEBEE IS BLEEDING, THEN REALIZES RHEEBEE WOULD BLEED OUT IF AVE LIFTED THE RUBBLE AND GET CRUSHED IF AVE DIDN'T. BUT THEN LATER AVE IS BEATING HERSELF UP OVER RHEEBEE'S DEATH WHEN SHE COULDN'T DO ANYTHING EITHER WAY.

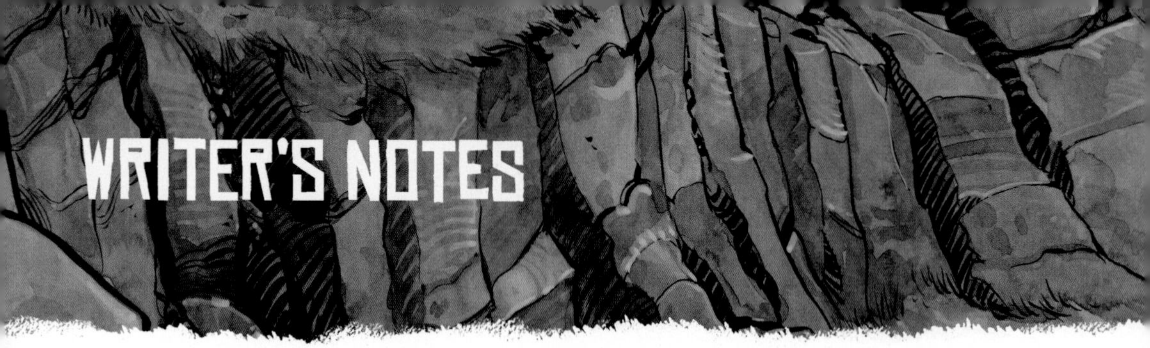

WRITER'S NOTES

THE CHANGE TO AVE LEAVING AND THEN PAUSING TO THINK ABOUT THE MONEY ADDED MORE EMOTIONAL CONFLICT. THE DECISION CAN REPRESENT THE CONFLICT BETWEEN WHAT SHE THINKS IS THE RIGHT THING, WHAT RHEEBEE WANTS HER TO VALUE, AND WHAT CAN GET AVE TO A BETTER LIFE. BAM! SYMBOLISM! RHEEBEE TEACHING ALL THE KIDS TO VALUE SELFISHNESS PARTLY LEADS TO HER OWN DEATH, WHILE RHEEBEE'S MANTRA, "A SLOW THIEF IS A DEAD THIEF," PROVES TO BE TRUE.

RHEEBEE STARTS WITH BERATING AVE BUT THEN YOU KNOW IT'S REAL BAD WHEN SHE IS PLEADING. THAT NEEDS TO BE CONVEYED WITH DIALOGUE SINCE AVE AND THE READER CAN'T SEE HER. SO THERE'S THE "PLEASE" THAT GETS AVE TO STOP THINKING ABOUT THE MONEY.

I LOVE NONTALKING SCENES THAT CONVEY EMOTIONS. THEN THE SOUND OF THE STONE KING LETS AVE KNOW SHE DOESN'T HAVE TIME TO PROPERLY GRIEVE. SHE DOES KEEP THE MONEY THOUGH. BECAUSE SHE'S NOT ENTIRELY LEAVING RHEEBEE BEHIND.

PAGES 42–44

HEY, THAT GLOWY SPOT WASN'T THERE BEFORE!

WE GET PHUL'S SECOND INTRODUCTION AND HIS NAME. HIS EAGERNESS TO HELP IS BIGGER THAN THE RESPONSIBILITIES HE'S BEING GIVEN. IT GIVES AVE ROOM TO WIGGLE IN AND GET THEM TO TEAM UP.

PAGES 45–49

THIS IS MOSTLY SOME EXPOSITION TO GET TO WHAT THE GOAL IN THE STORY WILL BE. IT DOES A LOT OF THE HEAVY LIFTING FOR EXPLAINING STUFF. THE EXPRESSIONS ARE REALLY IMPORTANT BECAUSE THESE LONG SCENES OF JUST TALKING CAN GET VERY VISUALLY BORING.

PAGES 50–51

WHILE AVE'S MOTIVE IS CLEAR AT THIS POINT, WE NEEDED PHUL TO HAVE A CLEAR REASON FOR GOING AGAINST ORDERS. GIVING HIM A MOMENT TO SEE ALL THE PEOPLE WHO ARE AFFECTED HELPS PUSH HIM INTO HELPING.

PAGES 52–58

THIS WHOLE CHASE SCENE IS ALL TYLER. I TOLD HIM I WOULD LIKE THE CHASE SCENE TO BE MORE BUILT INTO THE CITY BUT HE HADN'T COMPLETELY DESIGNED THE CITY. SO I TOLD HIM, "IT'S A CHASE SCENE. AT ONE POINT AVE RUNS INTO HEY YOU AND THE KIDS. ONE OF THE KIDS FALLS OFF.

WRITER'S NOTES

PHUL SAVES THE KID BUT PUTS HIMSELF IN DANGER. AVE SAVES PHUL." THE DETAILS BEYOND THAT WERE UP TO TYLER. THEN WHEN HE SENT ME THE PAGES, I WENT IN AND ADDED THE DIALOGUE.

PAGES 59-62

THE CREATURES IN THE STABLE ARE CALLED STONEBACKS. I ASKED TYLER FOR SOMETHING BIG AND STURDY LIKE A RHINO. HERE THE TWO IMPORTANT REACTIONS FROM THE KIDS ARE WHEN THEY ASK ABOUT RHEEBEE AND HOW THEY FEEL ABOUT PHUL. THE KIDS DON'T THINK SHE WILL BE WORRIED, JUST MAD. I STILL WANTED TO PUSH THIS POINT ABOUT RHEEBEE BEING A BAD PARENTAL FIGURE, EVEN THOUGH AVE STILL FEELS BAD ABOUT HER DEATH.

THEIR REACTION TO PHUL IS JUST TO SHOW HOW EARLIER THE KIDS ARE TAUGHT NOT TO TRUST OR TALK TO GUARDS. SRITCH, BEING EVERYTHING RHEEBEE WAS TRYING TO MAKE THEM, IMMEDIATELY THINKS YOU WOULD ONLY TALK TO A GUARD TO SNITCH.

PAGES 63-65

I WANTED TO GIVE A LITTLE MORE CONTEXT TO THE BLOOD TABOO IN THIS CULTURE. IT'S A HINT OF THE REVEAL AT THE END SO I WANTED TO KEEP BRINGING IT UP. SO YOU GET A LITTLE MORE DETAIL ABOUT IT. IT'S BLOOD TOUCHING THE GROUND THAT IS THE BIGGEST PROBLEM. I ALSO WANTED TO SHOW THAT RHEEBEE IS WEIGHING ON HER, EVEN IF SHE ISN'T SHOWING IT.

PAGES 66-68

WHILE AVE IS MORE OF A KNOWN QUANTITY AT THIS POINT, I NEEDED TO GIVE THE AUDIENCE MORE ABOUT PHUL. HE WANTS TO HELP BUT IS MORE NAIVE ABOUT THE WORLD THAN AVE. THEY ARE BOTH KIDS BUT PHUL IS BIGGER, SO SOMEONE MIGHT MISTAKE HIM AS OLDER.

PAGES 69-72

AVE'S OUTBURST IS WHAT MAKES PHUL REALIZE SHE'S GOT MORE GOING ON THAN HER GOAL-FOCUSED EXTERIOR. UNTIL NOW HE COULD DISMISS IT AS A DISTRACTION. AFTER ALL, THE LAST TIME IT CAME UP WAS RIGHT BEFORE SHE BROKE HIS NOSE. IT TAKES THEM A MOMENT OF QUIET TO LET THINGS PASS.

I ALSO THINK PHUL'S "I WON'T TELL ANYONE" VERSUS AVE'S "YES, YOU WILL. IT'S YOUR JOB" IS THE IDEALIST VERSUS THE REALIST.

AVE HASN'T HAD MUCH TIME TO DEAL WITH HER FEELINGS. AND THIS SPACE IS IMPORTANT.

WRITER'S NOTES

PAGES 73-75

THIS SHOWS THAT IN GENERAL, PHUL AND THE REST OF THE GUARDS AREN'T AS ON TOP OF THE LOCAL THIEVES AS THEY'D LIKE. IT'S MOSTLY AVE THAT SHOWS HOW TO FIND THE THIEF HIDEOUT.

PAGES 76-80

THE GREEN LIGHTS IN THE THIEF TUNNEL LOOK GREAT. TYLER IS AWESOME.

WHEN AVE SEES YORRICK IS WHEN SHE FEELS LIKE SHE CAN FINALLY LET HER GUARD DOWN. HE WAS SORTA THE ONLY ONE WHO WOULD GIVE HER COMFORT WHEN RHEEBEE WAS HARSH WITH HER. WHICH LEADS TO MORE OF HER SHOCK WHEN YORRICK PULLS A KNIFE ON HER.

PAGES 81-86

BIG FIGHT SCENE. I ALWAYS HAVE TROUBLE WRITING THESE. I TRIED TO USE THE SURROUNDINGS A LOT SO IT WASN'T A FIGHT THAT COULD BE RANDOMLY PLACED ANYWHERE. ONE IDEA THAT TYLER AND I HAD FOR PHUL IS THAT WHILE HE IS A NEW RECRUIT, ONE THING HE DOES THAT GIVES HIM AN ADVANTAGE IS HE CAN TAKE A HIT REALLY WELL. SO WHILE AVE IS JUMPING AROUND AND MOSTLY DODGING FOLKS, HE IS TAKING PEOPLE MORE HEAD ON.

PAGES 87-89

I REALLY LIKE SRITCH'S BEAT-UP FACE.

I WANTED TO HAVE AVE START TO LEAVE AND THEN COME BACK FOR PHUL AS A REVERSE OF HER DELAYING SAVING RHEEBEE. THIS TIME SHE STARTS BY BEING SELFISH BUT THEN LISTENS TO HER OWN MORAL INSTINCTS. THEN AS THEY LEAVE SHE CHANGES RHEEBEE'S MOTTO.

PAGES 90-91

I REALLY LIKE THE FACE TYLER GAVE PHUL WHEN HE REALIZES HOW MUCH BLOOD THERE IS.

MUCH LIKE AVE IS STARTING TO LEAVE HER UPBRINGING BEHIND, PHUL IS LEARNING TOO. SO HE NEEDED TO BE THE ONE TO SUGGEST THEY LIE TO HIS SUPERIOR OFFICER.

WRITER'S NOTES

PAGES 92-93

IN CASE ANYONE WAS WONDERING WHERE THE STONE KING HAS BEEN ALL THROUGH THE LAST HALF OF THE STORY, HE'S LITERALLY GETTING PULLED AWAY. I LIKE THE GROOVE TYLER PUT IN THE LANDSCAPE TO SHOW THAT. THEY HAVE A GENERAL PLAN FOR SOMETHING LIKE THIS, BUT THIS HASN'T HAPPENED IN RECENT MEMORY AND THE PLAN ISN'T QUITE WORKING. THAT GIVES AVE AND PHUL THEIR OPENING.

PAGES 94-99

THESE PAGES ARE IMPORTANT BECAUSE THEY HAVE TO ESTABLISH WHAT THE SOLUTION IS. BASICALLY STONE KING "BLOOD" AND HUMAN BLOOD MIXING MAKES THE GEMS. SO THE STONE KING DOESN'T WANT THE GEM BACK. THIS IS MORE A THORN IN THE LION'S PAW SITUATION. THEIR PRAYER ABOUT BLOOD IS ACTUALLY A WARNING ABOUT THIS. BUT THIS HASN'T HAPPENED IN SO LONG THAT THE WARNING HAS EVOLVED INTO A BLOOD TABOO OVER TIME. SO BRINGING THAT UP AT THE BEGINNING WAS KINDA TO PUT THE IDEA OF BLOOD ON STONE BEING BAD IN PEOPLE'S MINDS. THEN THIS SOLUTION ISN'T COMING OUT OF NOWHERE.

PAGES 100-103

THE GEMS HAVE BEEN GROWING ALL NIGHT SO THEY ARE IN PRETTY DEEP AND THERE ARE A LOT OF THEM.

PAGES 104-108

I LIKE QUIET MOMENTS IN COMICS. AVE AND PHUL APPRECIATING THE VIEW WOULD BE SOMETHING NEITHER OF THEM HAVE HAD TIME TO DO DURING THE REST OF THE STORY. IT ALL TAKES PLACE IN ROUGHLY A DAY.

IT ALSO GIVES AVE A MOMENT TO LET IT SINK IN THAT SHE SAVED THE CITY BUT CAN'T RETURN TO IT. AS THEY SAY GOODBYE TO EACH OTHER I WANTED THEM TO BRING UP THINGS THEY SAID TO EACH OTHER THROUGHOUT THE DAY. SHOWING THAT THEY UNDERSTOOD EACH OTHER. WHEN AVE TELLS PHUL HE CAN DO A BETTER JOB SAVING EVERYONE, I ASKED FOR A SAD SMILE. THAT'S AN EXPRESSION WHICH IS HARD TO NAIL. TYLER KNOCKED IT OUT OF THE PARK.

I REALLY WANTED TO END ON THAT LAST VIEW OF AVE RIDING HEY YOU AWAY FROM THE CITY, HAVING SORTA GOTTEN WHAT SHE WANTED.

THANKS FOR READING, EVERYONE!

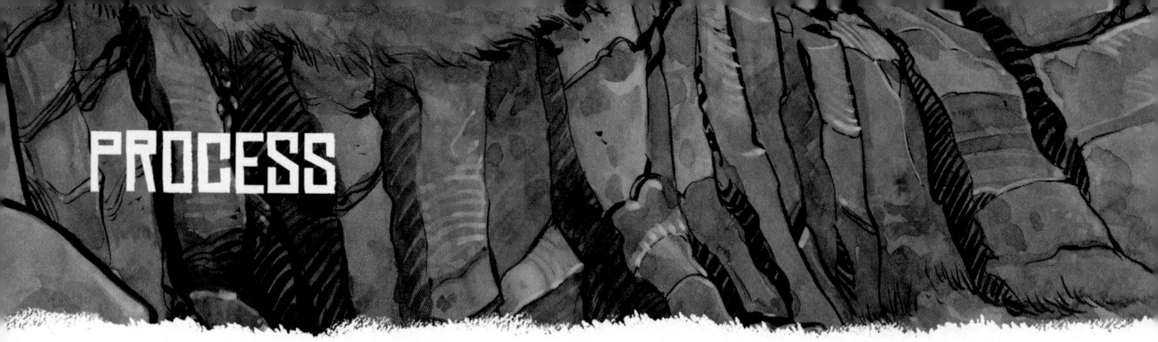

PROCESS

SO HERE'S A BREAKDOWN OF HOW *THE STONE KING* IS MADE.

FIRST KEL WRITES THE SCRIPT.

TYLER MAKES THE LAYOUTS AND LETTERS ON TOP OF THAT.

AFTER KEL AND TYLER GO OVER IT TOGETHER, TYLER STARTS THE PENCILS.

THEN IT'S PAINTING TIME!

PAGE 15

PANEL 1 – AVE RIDES UP TO THE HIGH WALLS OF THE CITY, WHERE SOME GUARDS WAIT AT THE ENTRANCE. BIGGEST PANEL ON THE PAGE.

PANEL 2 – A YOUNG GUARD BLOCKS HER WAY. IT'S PHUL, BUT WE AREN'T GONNA GET HIS NAME HERE. THE OTHER SIDE OF THE ENTRANCE HAS AN OLDER GUARD WHO LOOKS BORED.

PHUL: HALT!

PANEL 3 – HEY YOU STOPS WALKING AND AVE LEANS FORWARD, ANNOYED.

PHUL: WHO ARE YOU? WHAT IS YOUR BUSINESS HERE?

AVE: MY NAME'S AVE. I LIVE HERE.

PANEL 4 – PHUL IS TRYING HARD TO THINK OF THE NEXT STEP. OLDER GUARD GIVES HIM HIS LINE WITH A BORED EXPRESSION, NOT EVEN GLANCING AT PHUL.

PHUL: OKAY THEN...

PHUL: UH...

OLDER GUARD: ASK HER WHAT SHE WAS DOING OUTSIDE THE WALLS.

PROCESS

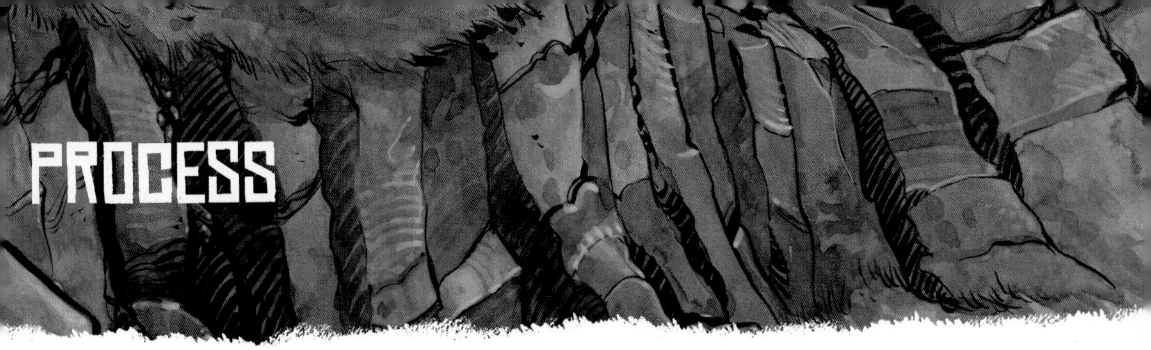

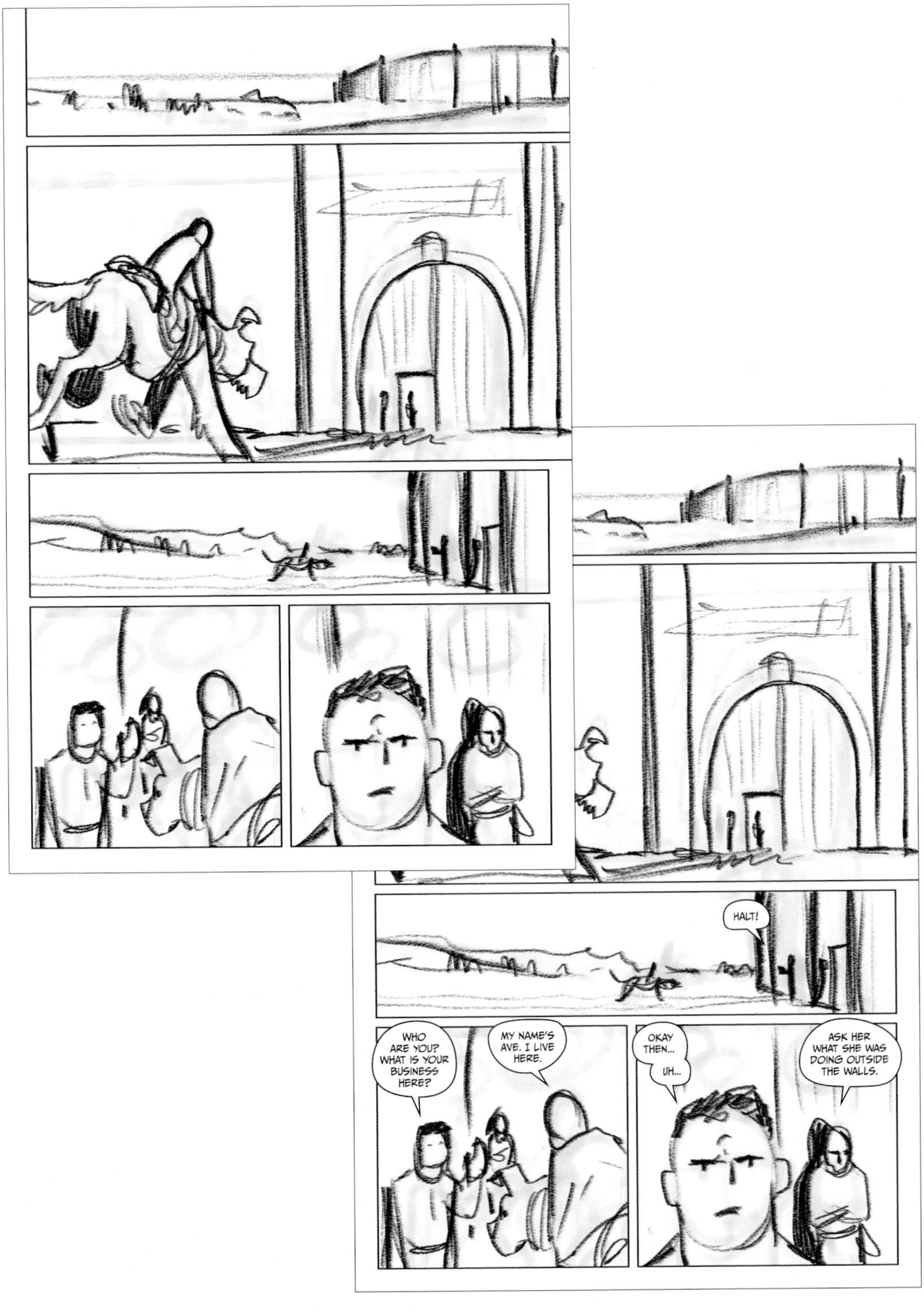
HALT!
WHO ARE YOU? WHAT IS YOUR BUSINESS HERE?
MY NAME'S AVE. I LIVE HERE.
OKAY THEN...
UH...
ASK HER WHAT SHE WAS DOING OUTSIDE THE WALLS.

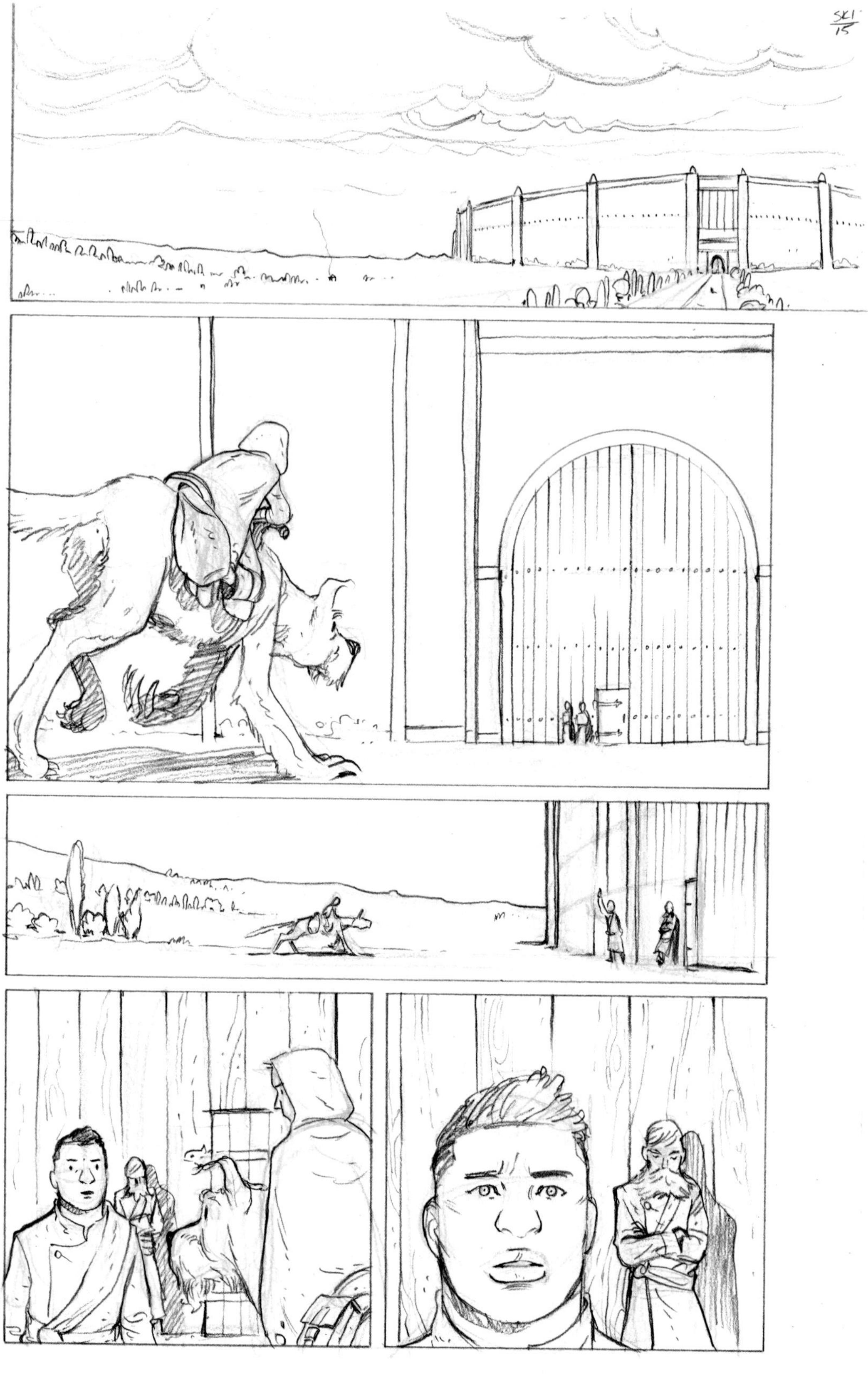
SK1
15

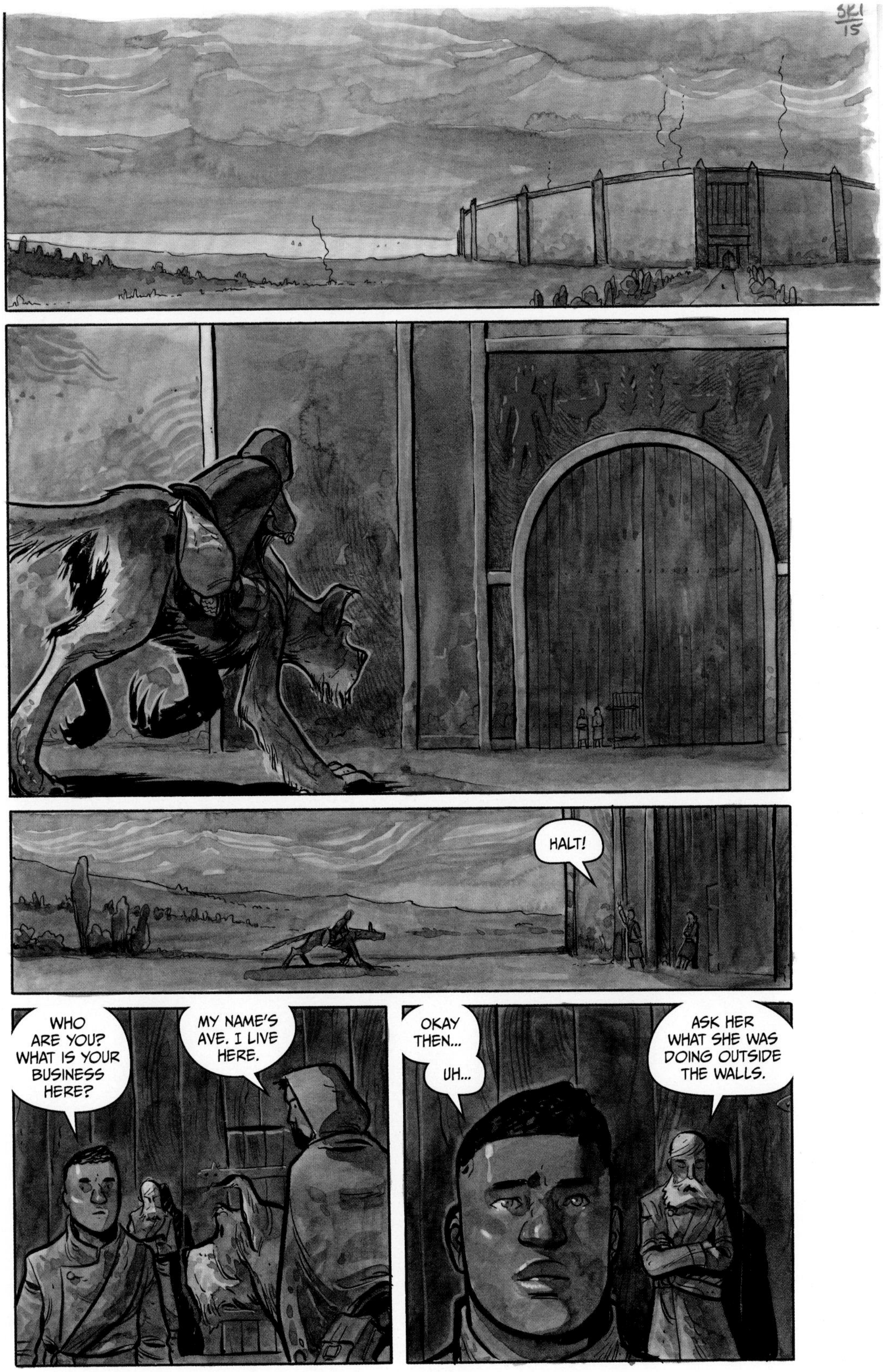
SKI 15
HALT!
WHO ARE YOU? WHAT IS YOUR BUSINESS HERE?
MY NAME'S AVE. I LIVE HERE.
OKAY THEN...
UH...
ASK HER WHAT SHE WAS DOING OUTSIDE THE WALLS.

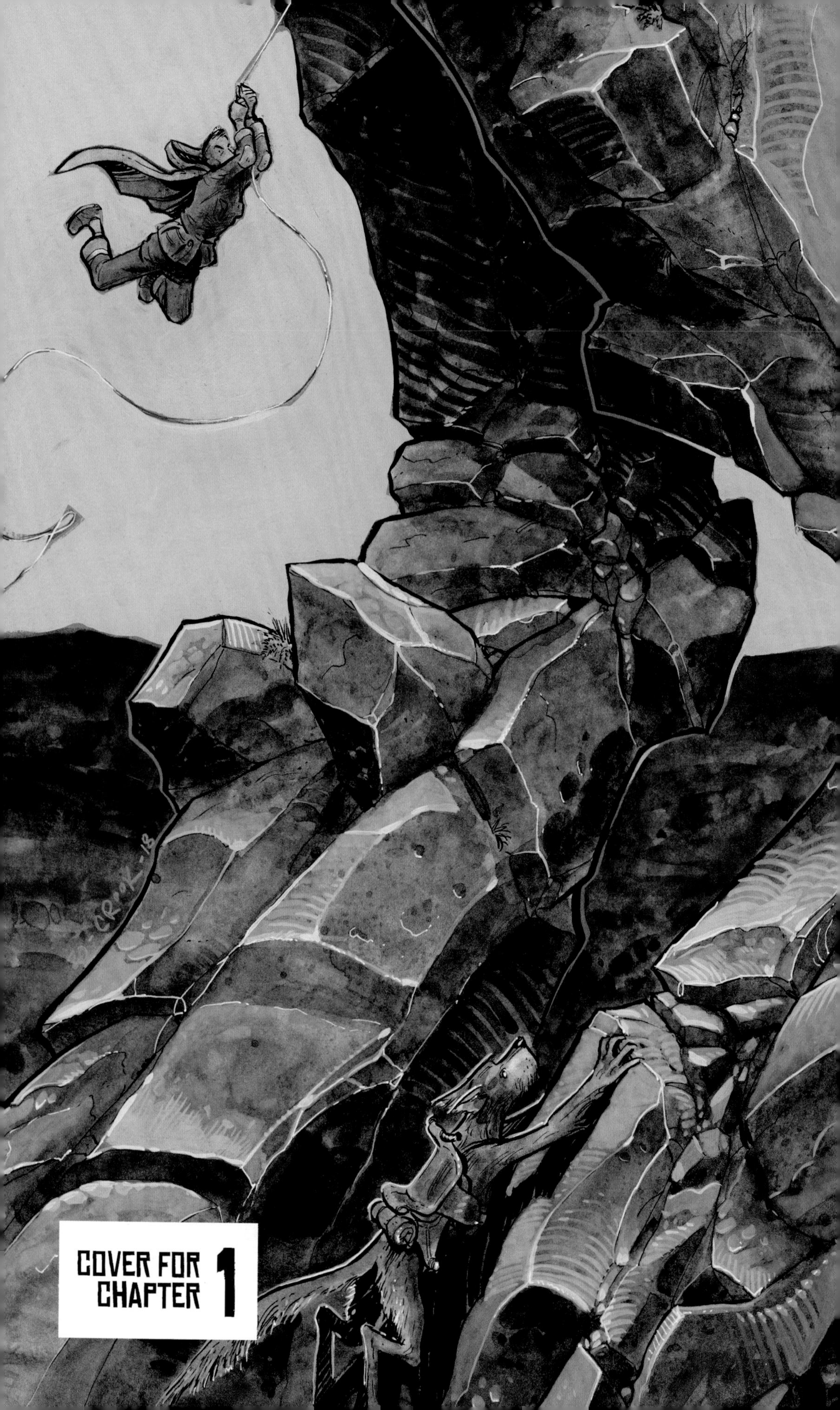
COVER FOR CHAPTER 1

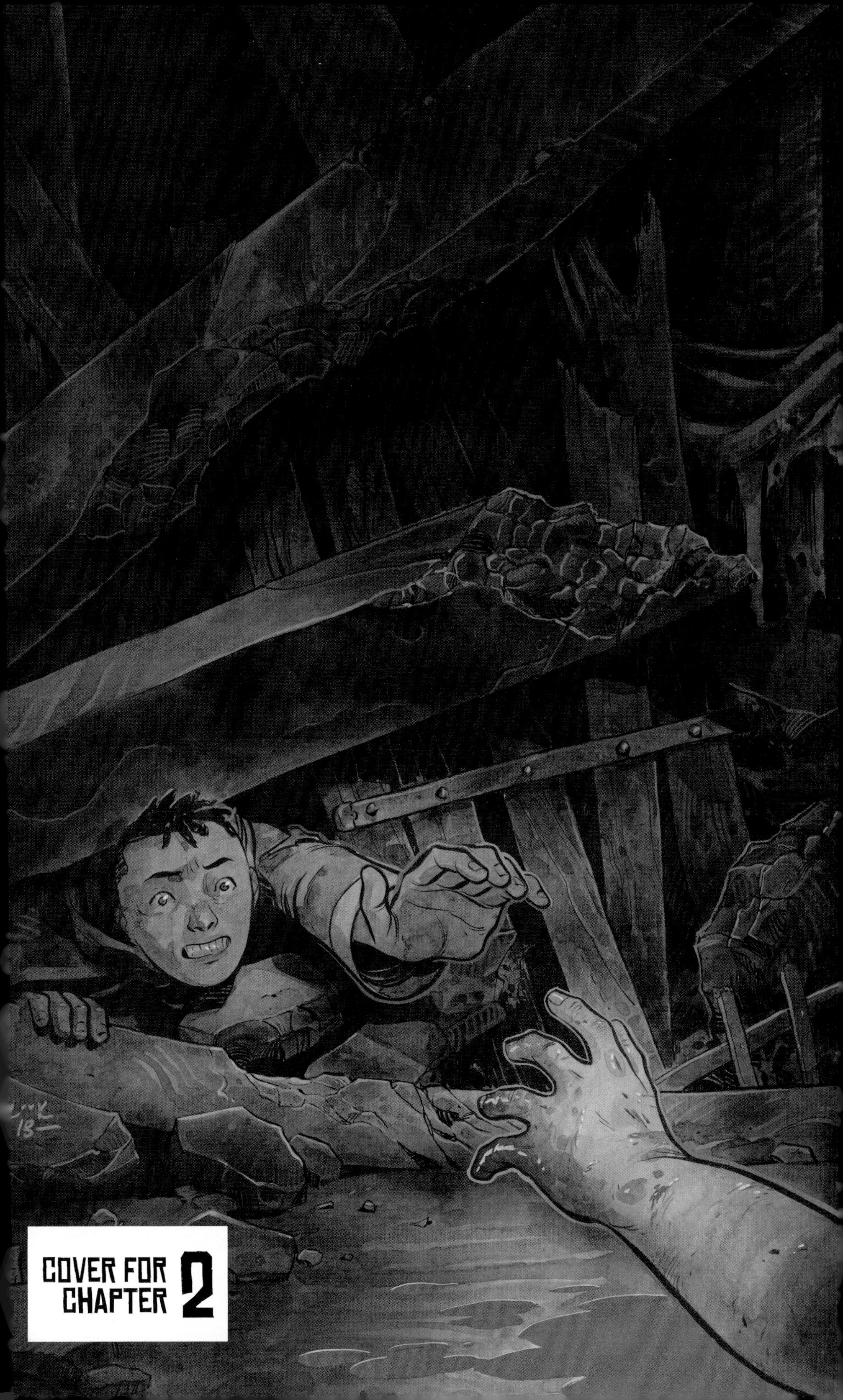

COVER FOR CHAPTER 2

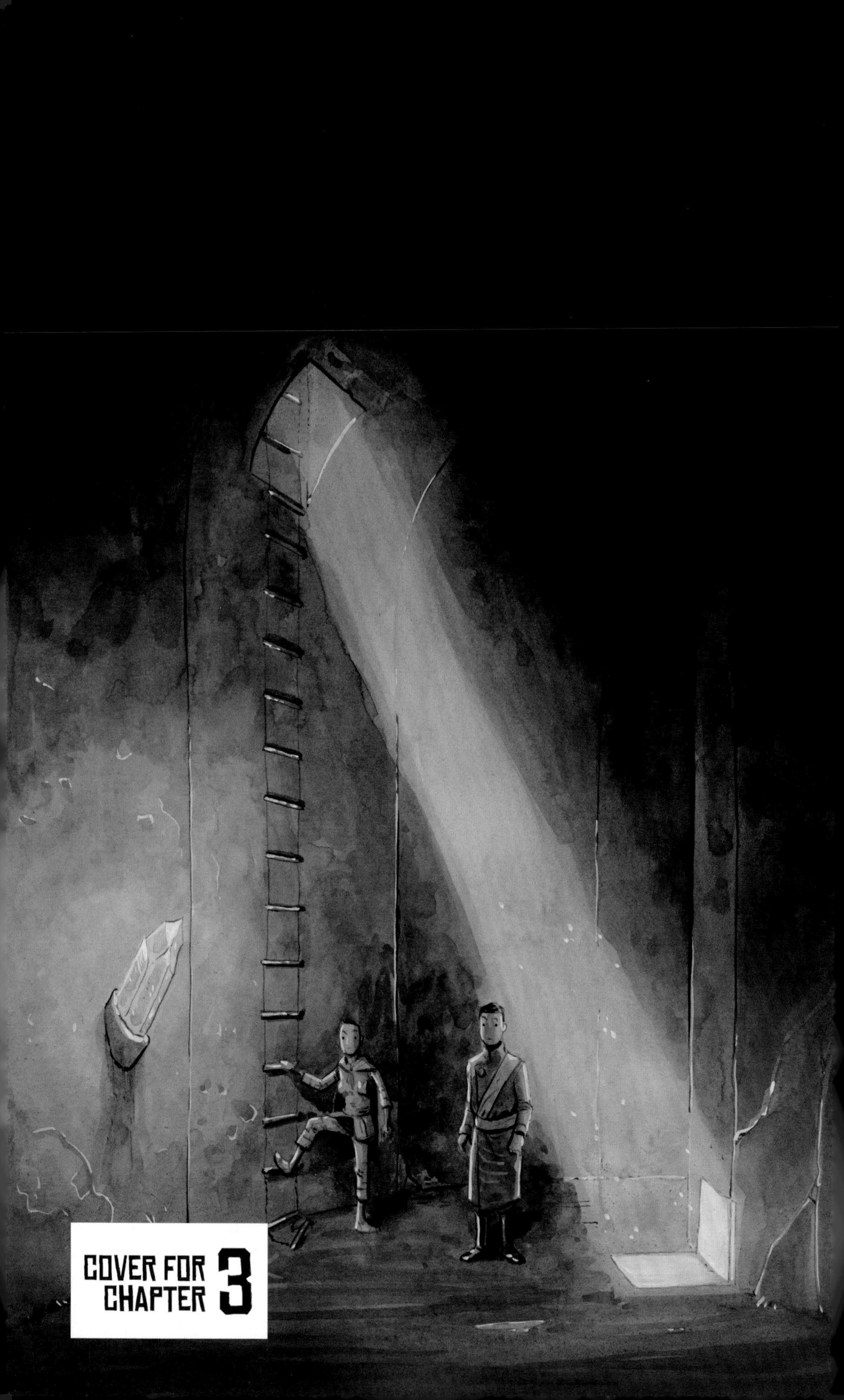
COVER FOR CHAPTER 3

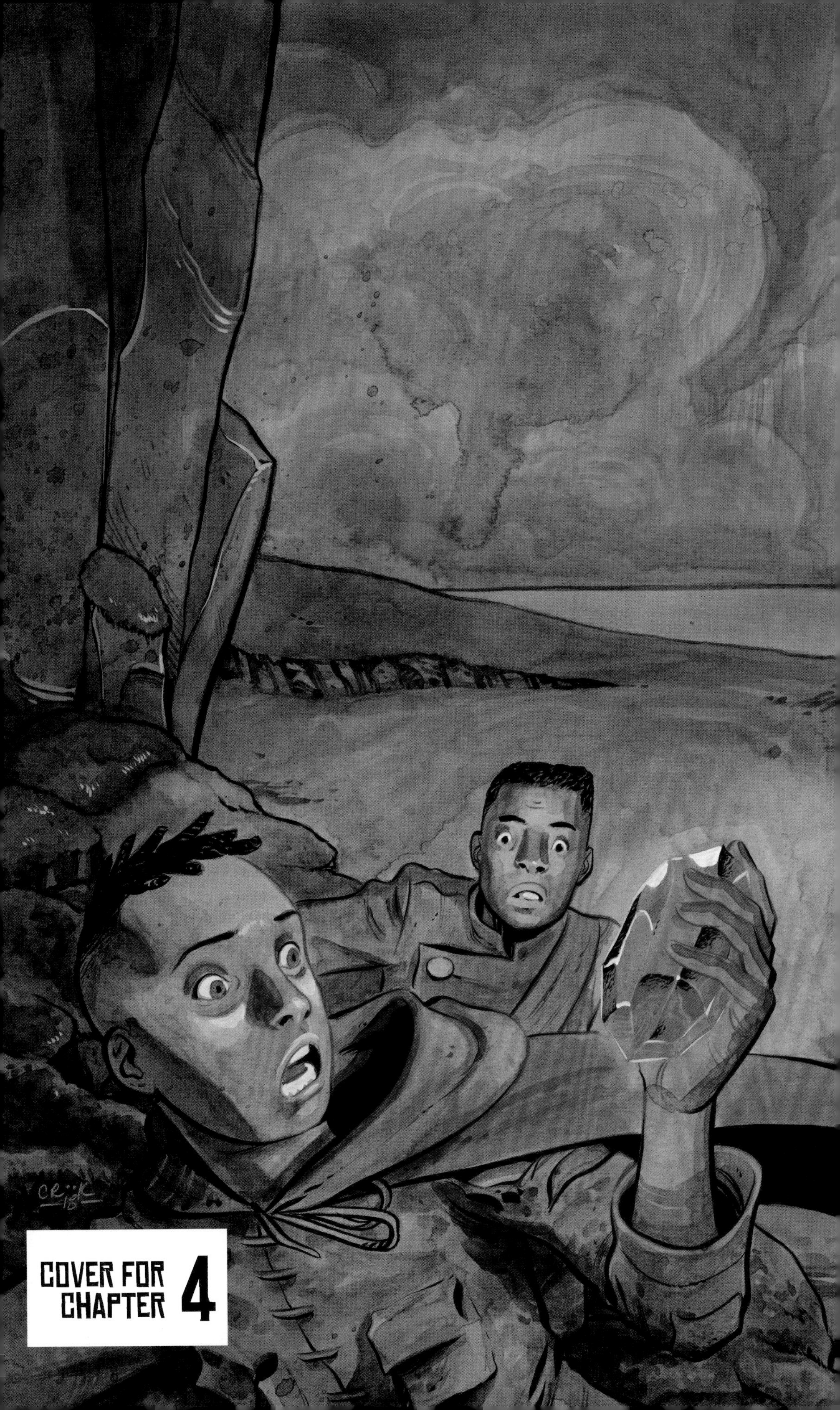

COVER FOR CHAPTER 4

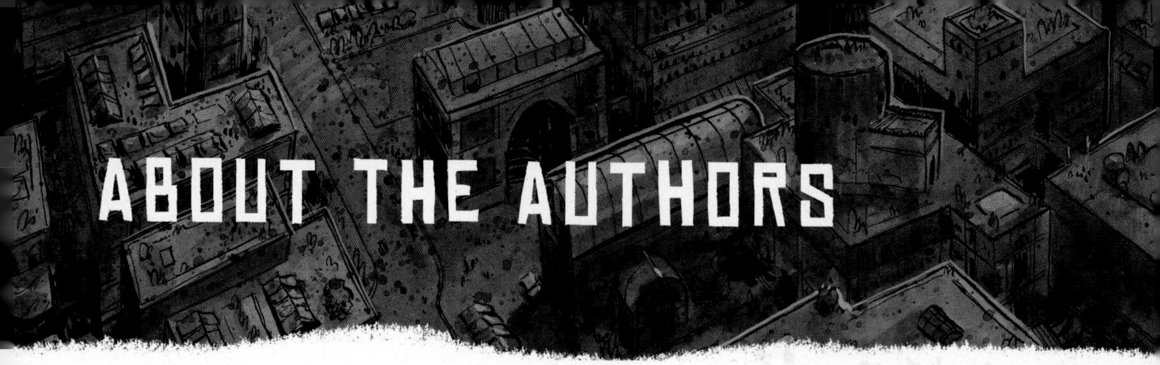

ABOUT THE AUTHORS

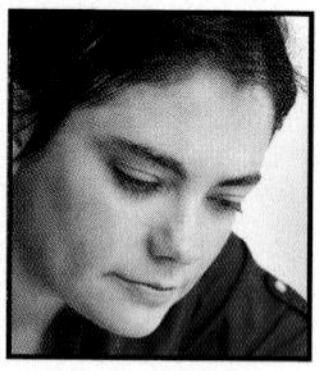

Written by Kel McDonald
Kel McDonald has worked in comics since 2005. Most of that time has been spent on her webcomic *Sorcery 101*. More recently, she has organized the *Cautionary Fables and Fairytales* anthology series and wrote *Buffy: The High School Years*. She recently finished her creator-owned series *Misfits of Avalon* for Dark Horse Comics. She is currently working on her self-published series *The City Between* and *The Stone King* for ComiXology Originals. Find all her work at KelMcDonald.com.

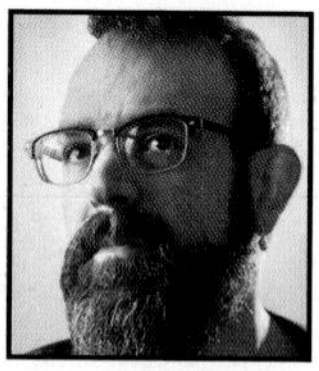

Art by Tyler Crook
Tyler Crook is an American artist and illustrator. He began his art career as a graphic designer and 3D modeler. After twelve years of making art for sports video games, he made the switch to illustrating comic books. His first book, *Petrograd* (Oni Press), came out in 2011 and earned him a Russ Manning Promising Newcomer Award at the age of thirty-seven. That same year, Tyler became a regular artist on Mike Mignola's *B.P.R.D. Hell on Earth* (Dark Horse Comics). He also contributed regularly to *The Sixth Gun* (Oni Press) by Cullen Bunn and Brian Hurtt. In 2014, Tyler worked with award-winning author Jonathan Maberry on the *Bad Blood* limited series (Dark Horse Comics)—his first fully painted comic series. Not long afterward, Tyler teamed up with Cullen Bunn again to create *Harrow County* (Dark Horse Comics). In 2016, *Harrow County* was nominated for an Eisner Award for Best New Series and won Ghastly Awards in 2015 and 2016 for Best Ongoing Series. *Harrow County* ended in 2018 with thirty-two issues and eight collected volumes.